ANN -

ENJOY THE GAME!

Matty

ROCK PAPER SCISSORS

Matty Dalrymple

WILLIAM KINGSFIELD
—PUBLISHERS—

Publisher's Note: This is a work of fiction. Names, characters, places, and incidents are products of the author's imagination. Locales, events, and public names are sometimes used for atmospheric purposes. Any resemblance to actual people, living or dead, or to businesses, companies, or institutions is completely coincidental.

All rights reserved
ISBN-10: 0-9862675-2-X
ISBN-13: 978-0-9862675-2-9

For my husband, Wade Walton,
and my sister, Mary Dalrymple,
for their tireless support and encouragement.

CHAPTER ONE

Lizzy Ballard started down the street toward the rendezvous point, but after half a block she knew she wouldn't make it. The trip down the stairs had started the flow of blood from her arm again. When she glanced down, she saw that a stain was spreading on the fine wool of the suit jacket she had taken, a vivid red in the sodium-vapor glare of the streetlights. She leaned against a building, trying to summon the strength to cover the next few yards. Through the haze of pain, she counted herself lucky that at this time of night the Center City street was deserted.

Just then, two couples rounded the corner and began walking toward her. She tipped her head forward so that her shaggy purple-black bangs hung over her face. She looked around frantically for somewhere to hide, and realized that her view was limited not only by the bangs, but also by the encroaching blackness at the borders of her vision.

A few steps away, a narrow alley separated two of the skyscrapers, and she staggered into it. She pressed her back against the wall and tried to slow her breathing, then almost screamed when she heard a voice coming from the other side of the alley.

"You okay, girl?"

As her eyes adjusted to the darkness, she saw that what she had thought was a carelessly discarded garbage bag was actually a person sitting against the wall.

"Somebody after you?" asked the voice. It was soft, almost dreamy—she couldn't even tell if it was a man or a woman.

She nodded.

"Well you sit right down here and wait till they go by. Nobody's going to come in here looking for you," said the voice. "You runnin' away? You can hide in here."

"Run away and hit a pillow," she mumbled.

"What's that, girl?" asked the voice.

The alley tilted as a wave of dizziness washed over her, and she slid down the wall until she was seated opposite her advisor.

"Run away and hide," she rasped out in a hoarse whisper.

"That's right, girl," the voice soothed. "Run away and hide."

The cold seeped into her from the frozen pavement. The rancid stink of the dumpster, which even the frigid temperatures couldn't conquer, enveloped her. The raised voices and drunken laughter of the couples approached the alley, and she cowered into the shadows until they receded down the street. Trying to ignore the sizzling throb in her arm and fighting the narrowing circle of her sight, she worked her phone out of her pocket and painfully pressed out a text message.

cant get to mtg place, come get me. She added her best approximation of her location.

She leaned her head back against the wall and felt the sobs she had held back bubbling up, beyond her control.

In a moment a response came back.

i'll be there as soon as i can are you ok?

She tried to type a response, but her fingers loosened their grip and the phone fell to the ground. She slid to the side until she was resting against the filthy dumpster, and finally succumbed to the encroaching blackness.

CHAPTER TWO

Eighteen Years Earlier

Patrick Ballard pushed open the door to the Sleeping Owl Saloon and was greeted by a wash of happy noise from the post-work crowd, many of them faculty or, like him, staff of William Penn University. He spotted Owen at their regular four-top at the back of the dining area and, giving a wave, made his way through the gathering throng at the bar.

Patrick pulled off the jacket he was wearing against the chill of the autumn evening, draped it over the back of one of the chairs, and sat down. Owen already had a pint of Guinness.

"Hey, man," said Patrick, clapping Owen on the shoulder.

"Careful, I'm delicate," said Owen, waving to the waitress.

Patrick snorted. Although Owen's coloring might be called delicate—pale blue eyes in a pale pink face framed by a patchy reddish beard and mustache—his overall appearance was anything but. He was grossly overweight, with a height that almost, but not quite, matched his girth. Patrick had always wondered how anyone in the healthcare profession could look as unhealthy as Owen did. But he had always looked like that, as far back as freshman year at Penn, when Patrick and Owen would go out for pizza to commiserate about the vagaries of college life and college girls.

Their regular waitress, Susie, came by the table. "Hey, Pat, what'll it be tonight?"

Patrick glanced at the chalkboard listing the beers on tap. "How's the porter?"

"A little dark for me, but the guys who like porter say it's good."

"I'll try that." He turned to Owen. "Okay if we order now? I'm starving."

"I'm never one to postpone a meal," said Owen agreeably.

Susie ran through the specials and Patrick chose meatloaf. She jotted down the order and turned to Owen. "Cheesesteak?"

"Yup. Light on the onions—"

"I know, light on the onions, heavy on the cheese."

"You got it," he said, handing her his menu.

She shook her head. "Creature of habit."

As she made her way toward the kitchen, Patrick said, "She's right, you are a creature of habit. You should shock her someday. Order a salad."

Owen shuddered. "Shock to my system, more like."

"I remember at Penn you had scrambled eggs, bacon, toast, and coffee for breakfast every day for four years."

"Well that's just not true. Sometimes I had a bagel instead of toast. With cream cheese."

"Right. You were a paragon of unpredictability." Patrick looked around the bar. "We should try some other place for dinner. We've been coming to the Owl for—what—ten years? There are lots of other places around Penn we could try."

"Longer than that if you count when we were students. What's wrong with the Sleeping Owl?"

"Nothing, I'm just saying—there are other bars out there, you know."

The waitress appeared at his elbow with his beer. "I heard that, Pat."

"Susie, tell him he needs to branch out," said Patrick.

"I'm not telling anyone who tips as good as Owen McNally to try other bars," she said tartly.

Owen smiled at him beatifically and Patrick shook his head.

They worked through their dinners, although Patrick's

attention was not really on the topics—his job in the IT department at Penn, Owen's in its Department of Neurobiology, the latest trials and tribulations of the Eagles.

When they were sitting with cups of coffee, plus pumpkin pie for Owen, Owen broached the topic that was on Patrick's mind. "So, how's Charlotte doing?"

Patrick set aside his napkin. "Actually, I wanted to talk with you about Charlotte."

"Is everything all right?" Owen asked, his brows knitted.

"Yes, generally … the thing is, we've been trying to get pregnant."

"Since you're saying 'trying,' I take it congratulations are not yet in order?"

Patrick sat back and slowly turned his empty glass on the table. "We've been trying for a while." He shook his head and smiled. "Charlotte's just born to be a mother. Her parents tell this story about taking her to see Santa when she was little and he asked her what she wanted for Christmas and she said, 'A baby.' And she didn't mean a doll, either." He glanced at Owen. "Charlotte had some tests done. It looks like her body isn't quite as enthusiastic about a baby as she is. We're thinking about trying some kind of fertility treatment."

Owen nodded. "Sure. But I wouldn't think you'd need to be in a huge hurry. She's younger than us—not even thirty, right? There's plenty of time."

"I'd be willing to wait and see, but not Charlotte. She's watching the days without a baby slip by, and it's making her kind of crazy. When we got married, we figured we'd have two by now."

"Well, I can't argue with that, I guess," said Owen.

"Do you have any suggestions for where we should go?"

Owen thought for a moment, then said, "I was at a conference a year or so ago and heard a talk by this guy named Gerard Bonnay who heads up a company called Vivantem, based in Philly. He's not a medical guy—as I recall, his wife runs that side of things—but he was very knowledgeable, and

Vivantem has an impressive success rate. And Bonnay himself is a pretty impressive guy. He's on the board of a couple of charitable organizations. Rumor has it that he's laying the groundwork for a run for political office."

"Vivantem? I don't think I've heard of them," said Patrick.

"It's a boutique operation—not much publicity, most of their advertising is word of mouth."

"I'm not sure we can afford 'boutique.'"

"I understand they do sometimes make concessions in terms of cost in specific cases, especially if it's a referral. I could give him a call."

"That would be fantastic, Owen, I'd really appreciate it."

"Sure, no problem, I'll see what Bonnay says." Owen took a sip of coffee. "Charlotte *would* be a wonderful mother. And you'd be a wonderful father."

"And you'll be a wonderful godfather," said Patrick with a grin.

"Ah, now you're just bribing me," said Owen, finishing up his last bite of pie.

CHAPTER THREE

Two weeks later, Owen stepped out of the elevator into the Vivantem offices in Center City. The floor was marble and at the far end of the lobby was a wall of ocean-blue tile, over which slipped a stream of water. In front of the water, the company's name was spelled out in brushed-nickel letters.

Two doorways opened off the elevator lobby, each marked with a brushed-nickel sign—the one to the right reading *Clients*, the one to the left *Offices*. Owen turned left and stepped through a door set in a glass wall and into a waiting area guarded by a reception desk. Here the atmosphere was tailored corporate, the waiting area furnished with Lucite tables and some low, mid-century-style couches covered in black leather. Owen hoped that he wouldn't be required to sit on one of them—or, worse, to get out of one of them. Behind the seating area, floor-to-ceiling windows looked out over Center City. A young woman with sleek, shoulder-length brown hair and a generic but well-tailored blue suit and white blouse sat behind the desk.

"Dr. McNally?"

"Yes."

She stood. "Thank you for coming by—Mr. Bonnay will just be a few minutes, but he asked me to show you to the conference room when you arrived." She circled the reception desk. "May I take your coat?"

Owen shrugged out of his gigantic overcoat and handed it over.

She draped it over her arm. "Right this way."

He followed her down another marble-floored hallway.

Owen heard the murmur of voices as he passed by a few offices, and caught a glimpse of a tastefully decorated break room, in which a man in a suit sat reading a magazine.

When they reached a glass-walled conference room, the receptionist pulled open the door and stood aside to let him enter. "Would you like some water or coffee?"

"No thank you, I'm fine," said Owen.

"Mr. Bonnay shouldn't be long," she said, and left the room.

Owen crossed to the window and looked out on the dizzying view. Here on the fourteenth floor, he was looking down at the roofs of most of the surrounding buildings—historic brick structures squeezed between twentieth-century office buildings. He could see tiny pedestrians walking the ribbons of sidewalks, had an aerial view of gridlock forming and dissolving.

True to the receptionist's word, Gerard Bonnay arrived just a few minutes later.

If the rumors about his political ambitions were true, then life's casting director couldn't have done a better job than Gerard Bonnay. He was tall but not towering, with shoulders that were just broad enough to allow for the perfect drape of his bespoke suit. The precise cut of his hair tamed its slight wave, but it was easy to picture the waves springing free at the helm of a sailboat off the Cape.

He crossed to Owen and shook his hand. "Dr. McNally, good of you to come." He waved Owen toward one of the conference room chairs and took the one next to it himself, placing a manila folder on the table in front of him. He crossed his legs and knit his fingers loosely in his lap.

"It's been quite a few months since the conference where we met," said Gerard. "Where was that, Atlanta?"

"San Diego," said Owen.

"Ah, yes, San Diego. Unless you have a chance to venture outside, you could be in any city in the world in those conference hotels."

"I enjoyed your talk very much," said Owen. "You have a very sophisticated grasp of the scientific side of fertility treatment, considering, as I understand it, that you're more involved in the business side."

"Yes, my wife is the scientist," replied Gerard. "She doesn't enjoy those conferences much, so she's been happy to train me up to speak at those types of events—to be the public face of Vivantem." He recrossed his legs. "And how about you? You're at William Penn, correct?"

"Yes, the Department of Neurobiology."

"And focused primarily on research, as I recall."

"Yes, I teach occasionally, but not this year."

"Which do you enjoy more—the teaching or the research?"

Owen shrugged. "I love the students, but teaching is exhausting. Given the choice, I'd almost always pick holing up on my own with a paper." He smiled. "I'm with your wife—the idea of being the public face of anything gives me the willies."

Gerard laughed. "The idea of holing up with a scientific paper gives *me* the willies." He picked up the folder he had brought with him and flipped it open. "I'm very pleased that you considered sending the Ballards to Vivantem. Based on Mrs. Ballard's medical records and questionnaire responses, they seem like excellent candidates."

Owen nodded. "Yes, I think they're just what Vivantem would be looking for. Healthy. Intelligent. Well educated. Emotionally stable. Financially comfortable."

Gerard nodded. "Yes, of course. You know them well? Not just a professional involvement, correct?"

Owen nodded. "I was an undergrad at Penn with Patrick Ballard, and I got to know Charlotte quite well when they were dating. I was the best man at their wedding."

"Did Mrs. Ballard ever speak with you about her ability to get pregnant? With you being a doctor, she might have asked you for advice. Or speculated about her ability to get pregnant."

Owen shook his head. "No, she never spoke to me about it. The first I knew about it was when Patrick mentioned to me that they were looking into fertility treatments. He asked me for some advice about finding a reputable clinic."

"And I appreciate you thinking of Vivantem," said Gerard. After a moment he continued, "I'm considering doing a study of how a woman's belief about her ability to get pregnant correlates to her success in doing so. Mrs. Ballard's answers to some of the questions relating to emotional intelligence suggest that she's sensitive to such things." He raised his eyebrows questioningly.

"I'm not sure what you mean," said Owen. "What things?"

Gerard shrugged. "Oh, you know, aware of her own condition—physically and emotionally."

Owen thought for a moment. "I'm not sure she's any more or less self-aware of her physical state than anyone else, but from an emotional self-awareness point of view … yes, I'd say Charlotte Ballard is perhaps more emotionally self-aware than most."

"And aware of others' thoughts or feelings? Do you feel she is more sensitive in that way?"

Owen knit his brow. "I'm sorry, I really don't understand what you're getting at."

Gerard sat back in his chair. "In addition to possibly studying women's belief in their own ability to get pregnant, I believe a valuable companion study could be done on the ability of certain women to sense that in other women. You know how there are sometimes women who can predict which of their friends will and won't get pregnant. Or can even guess the gender of the child with a higher rate of accuracy than luck would explain."

"Uh, yes …" said Owen uncertainly.

"Or," continued Gerard, "who can guess the gender of the child when only the parents know but haven't told anyone else."

Owen laughed. "Are you asking me if Charlotte Ballard is telepathic?"

Gerard also laughed, and waved his hand. "No, of course not. I'm still honing the questions I'd like to address in this potential study, but I believe that some people have a special talent for this type of thing, a special talent for perceiving what others are thinking. The answers Mrs. Ballard gave on the questionnaire suggested she might be one of those people."

Owen considered. Eventually he said, "I do recall a few situations where Charlotte might have exhibited that kind of talent. When I bought my house, I picked up the Ballards and told them I was taking them somewhere special. Right away, Charlotte said, 'Owen, did you buy a house?' And once when the three of us were at a party, Charlotte said that she thought that two of the guests were having an affair. Sure enough, a year later they were divorced from their original spouses and married to each other. But who's to say what's behind that kind of skill. Maybe it's just a matter of being more sensitive to the clues that people unintentionally give off that telegraph their knowledge or their intentions."

"Yes, of course, that is likely it," said Gerard. He flipped the folder closed. "Well, in any case, the Ballards seem like excellent candidates. I'll contact them to discuss the options. Will you be involved in those discussions as their medical advisor?"

Owen held up his hands. "Oh, no, not directly. I'm sure if they have any questions they think I can help with, they'll contact me, but you can have any further discussions with them directly."

"Very good," said Gerard, and stood.

Owen hoisted himself out of his chair. "I appreciate you being willing to take the Ballards on as patients."

"My pleasure, Dr. McNally, and I appreciate the referral. Thank you for stopping by to answer my questions."

Gerard led Owen down the hallway toward the reception

desk. The receptionist saw them coming and disappeared behind a partition, emerging a moment later with Owen's coat. She appeared ready to help Owen with it, but Owen, anticipating an awkward tussle based on the discrepancy in their heights, smiled and took it from her.

"Thank you." He turned back to Gerard and gestured toward the offices. "Do you have your lab here?"

"Yes, in this building but on a different floor. We have a higher level of security there than for the offices."

"Large staff?"

"No, actually quite small. My wife does most of the research herself, has just a few research assistants. And, of course, the staff who manages the actual fertility treatments."

"Well, you're certainly doing impressive work," said Owen.

They shook hands and Owen stepped through the door to the lobby, disappearing a moment later into one of the elevators.

When the elevator doors had closed behind Owen McNally, Gerard turned to the receptionist.

"Is Dr. Mortensen in the lab?"

"Yes, I think so," she replied.

Gerard went through the lobby to the service stairway. He went down one flight, then pressed a security code into the keypad by the door and stepped through into a deserted, featureless white hallway. He went to the first door and keyed in another code.

The room was a lab, the white here punctuated by the glint of stainless steel and the glow of computer screens. At one of the tables sat a slender woman in her early forties, auburn hair tucked behind ears decorated with pearl studs, a gray dress of fine wool protected by a spotless white lab coat. She turned from the microscope where she was working, her capable-looking fingers—free of jewelry except for a plain gold wedding band—still resting on the adjustment knob.

"How did it go?" she asked without preamble.

"It seems very promising. I'm to work with Mr. and Mrs. Ballard directly."

The woman nodded briskly. "That's good, but if you can stay in touch with McNally, it would be a good way of keeping track of what's happening with the Ballard child."

"Yes, I'm sure I can arrange that," said Gerard.

The woman gestured toward a computer next to her. "I think I've figured out what went wrong with the last one."

Gerard crossed to the computer and glanced at the screen. "We can't have that happen again. The lawyers were able to deal with that as a one-off, but—"

"It won't happen again," she interrupted. "I feel quite confident in this new approach."

"And it's ready to test?"

"Yes, and the Ballard baby will be the perfect subject."

CHAPTER FOUR

"Happy birthday dear Lizzy, Happy birthday to you!"

Patrick and Charlotte Ballard and Charlotte's sister Marilyn, who was visiting from Vermont, wrapped up the chorus, to the wide-eyed surprise of the Ballards' daughter. In front of Lizzy, but out of her inquisitive reach, was a miniature banana muffin with one candle on it.

"You guys help her blow out the candle," said Marilyn, readying the camera.

Charlotte and Patrick moved to flank Lizzy, Charlotte straightening the birthday hat that Lizzy kept knocking askew. Patrick bent toward the muffin and puffed his cheeks out dramatically, prompting a laugh from Lizzy.

Marilyn laughed too. "Perfect." She snapped the picture.

Patrick and Charlotte blew out the candle and Lizzy giggled with delight.

After the birthday muffin and the present opening—a Paddington Bear that Charlotte had cajoled a London-based college friend into obtaining for her from Paddington Station—they retired to the living room. Patrick sat on the floor with Lizzy, entertaining her with a monologue delivered by Paddington in an atrocious British accent: "I'm not a criminal, I'm a bear! Things are always happening to me, I'm that sort of bear!"

Outside the windows of their Paoli home, a light New Year's Day snow fell. A year before, Lizzy had narrowly missed being the subject of the traditional article in the *Daily Local* about the first baby of the year in Chester County. The Christmas tree was still up and lit, the remains of the Ballards'

Christmas celebration still scattered around the living room.

Marilyn flopped onto the couch. Charlotte perched on the edge with a cup of coffee and opened the hefty photo album on the coffee table.

"Should we put her birthday pictures in her first-year album or her second-year album?" she asked, turning the pages idly.

"Well, her birth pictures are in the first-year album," said Patrick, "so I suppose her first birthday pictures should go in the next one." He danced Paddington in front of Lizzy, who was starting to fall asleep.

"That makes sense," said Charlotte. She turned to the first few pages of the album. "Look, I even have pictures from when I was pregnant in this one."

Marilyn looked over. "I can't believe you started wearing maternity clothes when you were still so skinny," she said. "It looks like you're wearing a tent."

"But look how cute that dress was," said Charlotte. "That was my favorite."

"Very cute," said Patrick agreeably.

"Here's one from the baby shower," said Charlotte. "How did we get all that stuff home?"

"I think I took some in my car," said Marilyn.

"That was sweet that you came down for the shower," said Charlotte.

She continued to page through the album.

There was the first picture in which Charlotte had caught Lizzy smiling. Charlotte had started playing the piano again after Lizzy was born, something she hadn't done regularly for years. She would prop Lizzy on the couch and play Brahms or some of the lighter Beethoven pieces, and she caught the first smile that wasn't likely due to gas when she glanced back in the middle of "Moonlight Sonata." She was able to snap a picture of the tail end of the smile before Lizzy spit up some milk and required a change of clothing.

There was Lizzy on a blanket in the back yard on a

beautiful spring day, the tulips that Charlotte had planted the year before providing a colorful backdrop.

Their backyard again, this time during the neighborhood's yearly "progressive picnic," the two little girls from next door flanking Lizzy in her red, white, and blue dress.

Early fall, when they had spent the week at Patrick's parents' cabin in the Poconos, Lizzy caught in the act of cramming a leaf into her mouth.

And the photo from just a few weeks ago, when Patrick had set up his camera on a tripod in the living room and captured their holiday picture—Patrick self-conscious, Charlotte beaming, Lizzy perplexed by a voluminous red and green plaid dress with red velvet trim and an enormous poof of petticoated skirt.

"Oh, look at this one!" Charlotte exclaimed periodically, turning the album toward Patrick or Marilyn.

They spent most of the day lazing around the house, with the exception of an hour when Marilyn took Lizzy out for a drive. "So your parents can have some grown-up time together," she said, rolling her eyes.

For dinner, Charlotte made pork, sauerkraut, and mashed potatoes. After Lizzy was tucked in, they opened the bottle of champagne that Patrick had bought for New Year's Eve, but that had remained unopened when Patrick and Charlotte had said sheepishly that they couldn't stay awake until midnight. Marilyn went out to one of the Paoli bars to celebrate the ball drop.

As Patrick handed around the glasses, Charlotte asked, "Do I get to make a wish?"

"I thought New Year's was for resolutions," said Marilyn.

"Okay," said Charlotte, "then I'm going to make a resolution." She raised her glass. "I resolve to do everything I can to make the coming year just as wonderful as the last year has been, thanks to you guys. And to Lizzy."

"Hear hear," said Patrick.

"Sounds good to me," said Marilyn.

Charlotte Ballard's resolution held for a time—for four years, in fact. But then Lizzy's accident happened, and Charlotte's headaches began.

CHAPTER FIVE

Charlotte was wrestling with a cake recipe one of the neighbors had given her, five-year-old Lizzy playing in the corner of the kitchen. Lizzy was hosting a picnic for her stuffed animals, a picnic for which Charlotte had provided a bowl of applesauce at Lizzy's request. Eventually Charlotte realized that Lizzy's hummed version of "Beyond the Sea"— which Charlotte had heard so much that it had eventually receded into white noise—had quieted.

"Whatcha up to, chicken?" Charlotte asked.

"Giving facials."

Charlotte turned. "What?"

"Facials."

Charlotte put down the spoon and crossed to the play area.

Lizzy had lined up her animals on their backs, and was applying applesauce to their faces with a spoon. A fair amount of applesauce had made its way onto the floor.

"What in the world—"

"They're having facials."

"How do you know about facials?"

"TV."

"Lizzy," said Charlotte, exasperated, "you're making a mess." She went to the cupboard under the sink to get a rag. "Why don't you go sit in the den and wait for dad to come home while I clean that up." Lizzy picked up a fuzzy stuffed airplane and began making buzzing noises, wending her way circuitously from the kitchen to the living room.

The cupboard under the sink had become a jumbled mess. Charlotte sighed. She should really do a major straightening of all the kitchen cupboards. She'd put it on her list. She knew she had put a stack of rags in there after doing laundry that weekend. She moved aside some disinfectant wipes, a spray can of Lysol, and a tangle of loose plastic grocery bags and had just spied the rags when she heard a shriek behind her.

She whirled around on her knees to see Lizzy lying by the refrigerator, her hands over her mouth, blood smeared down her chin.

Charlotte scrambled to her feet and rushed to her side. Lizzy reached her arms up to Charlotte, revealing a split in her lip. With her hands no longer covering the wound, the smear of blood turned into a stream.

"Oh my God," gasped Charlotte. She snatched up Lizzy and ran to the powder room. She grabbed a hand towel off a stack of clean ones and tried to press it to Lizzy's mouth. Lizzy screamed, and Charlotte felt a stab of pain behind her eyes—a sensation she had first begun to experience a few months before, and had been experiencing more and more frequently.

She ran back to the kitchen, to the chair where her purse was. She propped the screaming Lizzy on her hip, and wrapped her arm around her in an attempt to hold her in place and keep the towel on her mouth. She dumped the contents of the purse onto the kitchen table, snatched up her cell phone, and pressed 911, her thumb leaving bloody prints on the buttons.

"911. What's your emergency?"

"My daughter hurt herself. I think she fell. She cut her mouth. It's bleeding a lot."

"What is your name and address?"

Charlotte was giving the dispatcher the information when she heard the muffled rumble of the garage door, and a moment later Patrick burst into the kitchen. Alerted to the emergency by Lizzy's screams, his face was white and his eyes wide.

"What happened?"

The dispatcher said, "An ambulance should be there in just a few minutes, ma'am. I'll stay on the line with you until they get there."

"Okay," said Charlotte. She held the phone away from her mouth. "I don't know what happened," she quavered. "She was lying over there." She gestured toward the refrigerator.

Patrick glanced over and noticed a smear of blood on the corner of the refrigerator door. "Did she run into the fridge?"

"She must have."

Patrick tried to convince Charlotte to let him drive them to the hospital, and she had almost capitulated when they heard the siren. Patrick ran to the front door to let in the EMTs—an older man and a younger woman, who introduced themselves as Ken and Janel.

"I'm Patrick Ballard. My daughter Lizzy fell and hit her mouth on the refrigerator. At least we think that's what happened." He led them to the kitchen.

Charlotte sat on one of the kitchen chairs with Lizzy in her lap, the bloody towel in her other hand, her face pale and drawn. Lizzy's shrieks had tapered off into whimpers and the bleeding had almost stopped, but the sight of the two strangers in uniforms set her off again, and the bleeding started afresh.

Ken went to kneel by Lizzy. "Lizzy, what happened? Did the fridge get in your way?" He opened his bag and took out a few squares of gauze. "Could I put this on you, Lizzy? It will make the bleeding stop."

"No!" wailed Lizzy, sending a fresh stream of blood down her chin and onto her shirt, lending a gory aspect to the scene of dancing turtles that decorated it.

Ken winced and shook his head, then turned back to Lizzy. "It would make you look like Santa Claus," he said. "Here, I'll show you." He put two squares of gauze over his own upper lip and taped them in place. "What do you think?"

Lizzy's crying trailed off. She pointed to Ken's chin.

"Beard too."

"Ah, you're right!" said Ken, and taped a few squares of

gauze to his chin. "Better?"

Lizzy sniffled and nodded.

"Can I put a beard and mustache on you?" asked Ken.

After a long moment, Lizzy said uncertainly, "Okay."

Ken took a bottle of saline out of his bag. "Can I squirt a little of this on your mouth to clean it off?"

Lizzy looked doubtful. "You first."

Ken squirted some of the water onto the gauze patches on his face, then raised his eyebrows. "Okay?"

Lizzy nodded. She let Ken clean the cut with only a small whimper, and let him tape the gauze to her upper lip.

"Beard too," she mumbled through the gauze.

"Right," said Ken, and lightly taped a gauze square to Lizzy's chin.

Ken stood up. "Now we're on a mission, Lizzy. We're going to take you to let an expert check you out and make sure everything's okay, all right?"

Lizzy was patting the gauze on her chin. "Can I see?"

Charlotte stood, holding Lizzy. "Yes, chicken, we'll go to the bathroom to look in the mirror, and then we'll go on our mission, okay?"

"Okay."

Charlotte turned to Patrick. "Pat, would you put my stuff back into my purse? I dumped it out when I called 911."

"Sure." Patrick started sweeping the contents, including a jumbo container of aspirin, off the table and back into the purse. Charlotte went into the powder room with Lizzy so she could see her new beard and mustache, while Ken removed the gauze squares from his own face and packed up his bag.

"Wow, you handled that great," said Patrick. "Thanks so much."

"She seems like a brave little girl," said Janel.

"Where do you want to go—Chester County?" asked Ken.

"Yes, that's fine," said Patrick.

Charlotte and Lizzy emerged from the powder room, Lizzy still patting the gauze on her chin. Charlotte maneuvered so that Patrick could hook the purse over her shoulder.

"Why don't I ride in back with Mrs. Ballard and Lizzy," said Ken. "Mr. Ballard, if you're feeling okay, you can follow in your car so that you have a way to get home afterwards. How does that sound?"

"That sounds fine," said Patrick.

"Everything's under control, so slow and steady wins the race, right, Lizzy?" Ken asked Lizzy, who nodded.

When they stepped outside, Lizzy's attention transferred from the gauze on her chin to the ambulance parked at the curb. Their neighbors on both sides were standing on the sidewalk, looking concerned. Patrick hurriedly assured them that everything was all right, and declined their offers of a ride to the hospital.

Ken and Charlotte got Lizzy settled in the back of the ambulance while Patrick got his car from the garage, then Janel began a sedate drive to Chester County Hospital.

Charlotte opened her bag and got out the aspirin bottle. "I don't suppose you have any water back here?" she asked Ken.

Ken reached into his bag and pulled out a bottle and passed it to Charlotte.

"Thanks." Charlotte shook four tablets into her hand and swallowed them down with the water.

"Are you okay?" asked Ken.

"Just a headache."

Ken nodded toward the bottle. "You go through a lot of those?"

"Yeah, I do," said Charlotte with a weak smile.

Ken rubbed his forehead. "I think I'm going to be hitting my own supply once we get you guys situated."

Lizzy, who had returned her attention to her gauze beard, began humming a wobbly rendition of "Here Comes Santa Claus."

CHAPTER SIX

Lizzy came home with four stitches in her lip. Rather than being traumatized by her temporary disfigurement, as Charlotte feared she would be, Lizzy took a gleeful delight in sneaking up behind her playmates and scaring them with her "Frankenstein face."

"You know that little boy, Dylan, at school?" Patrick asked Charlotte over martinis one evening a few days after the accident. "Lizzy evidently *literally* scared the crap out of him."

Charlotte's jaw dropped. "No!"

"Yup!" Patrick chuckled.

Charlotte swatted his arm. "It's not funny, Pat!" But she was doing a bad job of hiding her own smile. "I'll talk to her."

In the weeks after the accident, Charlotte tried to resist the urge to hover protectively over her daughter, but it was hard not to succumb to the desire to snatch her immediately out of any situation that posed the least threat. Lizzy might reach for a gardening tool that a month ago she had been allowed to play with, but that Charlotte now removed from her curious hands. Lizzy would protest, and Charlotte would get that now-familiar stab of pain behind her eye, as if her daughter's unhappiness was being poured, like some caustic liquid, into her brain.

One day, when the stab had been replaced with the more usual dull throb that no amount of aspirin seemed to lessen, Charlotte decided that if she was going to feel bad anyway, she might as well feel bad doing something pleasant rather than hanging around the house. She took Lizzy to the market where they bought some groceries for dinner, and picked up some cut flowers.

When they returned home, she got Lizzy settled at the kitchen table.

"I'm just going downstairs to get a vase for the flowers, can you sit right there until I get back?"

"Uh huh," said Lizzy, examining the plastic-swathed bouquet.

Charlotte flipped the basement light switch and stepped onto the first step. She felt a twinge of pain just behind her forehead, and closed her eyes for a moment, gripping the handrail. When she opened her eyes, the stairway was a dark tunnel, with just a glimmer of light at the bottom. She reached around the door and flipped the switch again, but rather than illuminating the stairway, the result was total darkness. She flipped the switch back on.

"What, Mom?" asked Lizzy.

Charlotte laughed unsteadily. "I thought I had forgotten to turn on the light. It's on now." But the stairway still looked unusually dark.

She took another step, and again the darkness at the edges of her vision crept toward the center. She shook her head, but the only result was a throb of pain.

She continued down, one hand on the railing, the other on the stairway wall, when suddenly her foot found air instead of stair and she was flailing for balance. The momentum of her fall wrenched her hand off the railing. She banged to a rude stop on the concrete floor.

"Mommy?" called Lizzy, her voice squeaky with panic.

"I'm okay, baby," Charlotte called back. She got shakily to her feet.

Lizzy appeared at the top of the stairs. "What happened?" she asked, her eyes wide.

"I just tripped on the stairs."

"You okay?"

"Yes, I'm okay." Charlotte checked herself for damage. It

was true that there didn't seem to be anything seriously wrong.

"You fell?"

"Yes, just a little ways."

"Why, Mom? Headache?"

Charlotte was embarrassed that she complained enough to her daughter about her headaches that it was the first explanation Lizzy went to as to why her mother would have tripped on the stairs.

"Maybe. But I should have been paying more attention. That's why it's important always to hold the handrail, chicken."

"Did you hold the handrail, Mom?"

"Yes, but evidently not as tight as I should have," she said.

Charlotte retrieved the vase and made her way carefully back up the stairs.

As she and Lizzy arranged the flowers in the vase, a pack of frozen peas rubber-banded to a wrenched wrist that had only made itself known once the adrenaline of the fall had worn off, she realized that the fall hadn't been caused by the distraction of a headache—she had just lost track of where her left foot was. And she began to realize with a growing unease that the fall, although the most dramatic, was just one of a number of incidents she had experienced lately. She sometimes got a tingling in her left hand, and one day when she was driving, she had almost run into another car when switching lanes, the car lost in a blankness that had replaced her peripheral vision. After a steady improvement in her piano-playing skills over the previous years, she suddenly fumbled fingerings she could have played effortlessly a month before.

She made an appointment with Dr. Pitts, convincing herself that it would be a relief to find out what the real, benign cause of her symptoms was, and asked a neighbor to babysit Lizzy. She came home with a prescription for a CT scan, and spent a miserable few days debating whether or not to tell Patrick. She longed to hear him echo her position that it couldn't be serious—everyone got headaches—but if it really was nothing, then she would have worried him for no reason.

But the day of the scan, she could tell from the grim look on the technician's face that it wasn't nothing. She told Patrick that evening, in a flood of tears, about the continuing headaches, the fall, the loss of range of vision. Patrick went with her for her return visit to see Dr. Pitts and find out the results of the CT scan, while Lizzy went to a neighbor's house for a play date.

Dr. Pitts ushered them into his office and gestured them to a table with three chairs. He took the one in front of which lay a thin manila folder with Charlotte's name on it.

He sat, then took off his glasses and put them to one side. "I'm afraid I have bad news for you. It appears that you have been having some strokes, Mrs. Ballard," he said. "Many small strokes … and a couple not so small." He leaned back in his chair and flipped on the light of a wall-mounted view box.

"This is Mrs. Ballard's scan. The areas where bleeds have occurred appear white." He pointed with a pen to a scattering of kernel-sized spots. "These are lacunar infarctions, or lacunar strokes, occurring in the right side of the brain. The positioning explains the motor impairment and other symptoms you describe experiencing on your left side." He pointed to a larger white area. "This indicates a hemorrhagic stroke. This is more likely the cause of your headaches and the reduction in your field of vision." He put down the pen and turned to them. "It's extremely unusual to see both of these kinds of strokes in one person, especially when, as with you, Mrs. Ballard, there's no family history or other causes that would lead to a predisposition for stroke."

Charlotte raised her right hand to cover her eyes. Patrick tried to speak and failed. He cleared his throat. "Is there anything we can do?"

Dr. Pitts shook his head. "I'm afraid not. You'll need to make some arrangements as time goes on. This condition is not going to get better, and I can't tell you how quickly it will get worse. I'm afraid I can't tell you how long you have, Mrs. Ballard."

CHAPTER SEVEN

Gerard Bonnay and Owen McNally sat over the remains of their lunches in a restaurant near the Vivantem offices. Gerard had suggested the get-togethers, which his assistant arranged quarterly, and he suspected that Owen McNally was a bit flattered by the attention; he always came well prepared with information about some topic related to Vivantem and its services. Gerard usually had the lunches scheduled at a sushi restaurant, since he liked sushi but had few other opportunities to eat it since it was not a favorite of his wife. He suspected sushi would not have been Owen's first choice, either—the modest portions could hardly fill that enormous stomach.

Gerard leaned back and patted his lips with his napkin as the server cleared away the delicate plates and bowls. "And how about the Ballards? How is little Lizzy doing?"

"Lizzy's doing fine," replied Owen.

"And her parents?" asked Gerard.

"Patrick Ballard is fine," said Owen. "Charlotte Ballard is having some health issues."

"I'm sorry to hear that," said Gerard, setting aside his napkin. "What seems to be the problem?"

"She's been having headaches and then began having some restriction of her field of vision, some motor impairment."

"Any idea what the cause is?"

Owen hesitated.

"I have great respect for discretion in medical matters," said Gerard, "but Mrs. Ballard was a patient of Vivantem. Perhaps there's something we can do to help."

"I don't think there's anything Vivantem can do," said Owen, "but at this point we're grasping at straws. Any help is appreciated." He set his own napkin aside. "She got a CT scan and it showed a number of strokes, which is surprising considering her age. I did wonder if there was any possibility of a connection with the fertility treatments, but as far as I can see, none of the medications she was given has any history of causing those sorts of symptoms."

Gerard nodded gravely and waved off the server's offer of dessert, catching a shadow of disappointment as it crossed Owen's face. "No, certainly not. No family history of strokes?"

"No."

"If Mrs. Ballard feels she would like to consult with Dr. Mortensen about her symptoms, or about any treatments her doctors might suggest, I'm sure that my wife would be happy to provide additional information," said Gerard. "Is Mrs. Ballard getting to the point where her activities are curtailed?

"Well, she's stopped driving. I understand that during the week a neighbor sometimes takes her to the grocery store and to run errands, and on the weekends and evenings her husband is with her. Otherwise, she's generally able to manage, but obviously the concern is what happens if her condition deteriorates. I'm afraid they may need to get some help dealing with Lizzy."

Gerard nodded gravely. "If I might make a suggestion?"

"Of course."

"Unless Mrs. Ballard becomes physically incapacitated. Or mentally impaired ..." He raised his eyebrows and Owen shook his head. "... it may be best to allow her to continue caring for the child, and look for someone who can help with other things—housework, grocery shopping, that kind of thing."

"That would certainly be helpful," said Owen. He sighed. "I know they have some concerns about being able to afford help."

"From a practical point of view," replied Gerard, "someone who's providing housekeeping services is going to be less expensive than someone who's providing child care. But more importantly, it's beneficial for Mrs. Ballard to maintain a relationship with her daughter throughout this formative period of Lizzy's life. Especially if her condition continues to deteriorate."

Owen nodded dejectedly.

Gerard sat back. "I think I may have a lead for you. Before I get your hopes up, let me make a couple of calls to make sure the person I have in mind is still available."

"That would be great," said Owen, surprised. "I appreciate it."

They settled up the tab and stepped out of the restaurant onto the bustling Center City sidewalk. A black sedan idled at the curb.

"Can I give you a ride to your car?" asked Gerard.

"Oh, no, thank you." Owen patted his stomach. "It will hardly make a difference, but I might as well get a little bit of exercise."

"Very well. I'll be in touch."

As the car glided away, Gerard turned to look out the back window just in time to see Owen disappear into a hoagie shop next to the sushi restaurant. He shook his head with a chuckle.

He pulled out his phone and dialed his wife's number.

"Yes?" came her usual brusque greeting.

"I had an interesting lunch with Owen McNally," he said.

"I find that hard to believe," said Louise.

"There are developments with the Ballards," said Gerard.

"Oh?"

"Mrs. Ballard has evidently been suffering strokes. Many strokes."

"Strokes?"

"Yes."

"Damn it." After a moment, she asked hopefully, "Family history?"

"No."

"Damn it," she repeated.

"It's not what we were aiming for, but that doesn't mean it might not be useful."

There was a long pause. He could almost see the considerations ticking through her brain, like a calculating machine.

"Yes," she said eventually. "Not as strategically useful as telepathy, but perhaps tactically useful as a weapon."

"An untraceable weapon," added Gerard.

"True," she agreed. "So, what now?"

"I'd say we sit back and see how things develop. And I have an idea for how we can keep an eye on the Ballards." He described his plan to Louise.

"Yes, that sounds good," she said. There was silence on the line for some time. When she spoke again, he could tell from her voice that she was smiling one of her rare smiles. "It had been so long with no sign of the results we were looking for, or even something close, I'd begun to think the experiment was a failure. Even if it's not telepathy, it's still very interesting. Very promising."

"Absolutely," said Gerard. "Well done, sweetheart."

CHAPTER EIGHT

On a Saturday morning a few days later, Gerard Bonnay sat in a conference room at Vivantem with three folders in front of him. Of the candidates who had applied for the job, he had selected three to interview. The first, as he had suspected might be the case, had been too young and flighty. The second, who on paper had appeared more promising than the first, turned out to be sullen and unintelligent. They had both proven unsuited to his specific needs, although for the sake of appearance he had run through a standard set of housekeeping-related questions with them. He was most interested in the final candidate.

He flipped open the third folder in the stack. Ruby DiMano.

"George, please bring in the third candidate," he said to the man who stood by the door. George nodded and slipped out of the room. He returned a moment later, holding the door for a middle-aged woman.

"Miss DiMano? Please come in," said Gerard.

She stepped into the room and George closed the door behind her. Gerard gestured her to one of the chairs, then took the seat across the table from her. He sat back and examined her over steepled fingers.

She had wary eyes in a narrow face. Her form was hidden beneath a shapeless dress that must have been new a decade ago, but he could tell she was thin from her corded neck and skinny wrists. She held her purse in front of her like a shield, her fingers gripping its top, the bones raised ridges on the backs of her hands.

"So, you're interested in a housekeeper position?" he asked.

"Yes sir."

Gerard flipped open a manila folder on the table in front of him. "I appreciate you sending over your letters of references. Very impressive."

"Thank you."

"And why are you looking for a new job?"

"I need to be making more money than my current employers are able to pay."

"And why are you looking for more money?"

Ruby DiMano hesitated. "Personal reasons."

Gerard nodded. "Well, there's certainly nothing wrong with wanting to earn more if you have the qualifications to do so. And it certainly looks like you do."

"Thank you."

"I see that you've helped care for your brother-in-law, who is paralyzed."

"Yes. My sister—his wife—does most of it, but I've helped out."

"And have acted as a companion for an elderly woman."

"Yes sir."

"You helped her with daily tasks? Helped her dress and so on?"

"Yes sir."

Gerard turned over a few pages in the folder.

"Your experience with your elderly employer and your brother-in-law would come in handy in this job. The lady of the house isn't elderly, but has some disability as a result of a few minor strokes she's suffered."

"Yes sir."

"And you've worked in households with small children, which would also be a plus."

"Yes sir."

A woman of few words. Gerard was liking her better and better.

"I have to tell you that this family is of somewhat modest circumstances, so the housekeeper salary would be paid partially by them and partially by me."

"If that's the arrangement you have with the family, that's no business of mine," she said.

"Ah, but they are proud people and I'd prefer that they not know that I am supplementing your pay."

"Oh." She hesitated. "Well, I suppose that's your business, sir."

"Quite," said Gerard agreeably. He flipped to another page in the folder.

"So, Miss DiMano, you live alone?"

"Yes sir."

"But are close to your nephew, am I correct?"

Ruby DiMano's eyebrows raised fractionally. "Yes."

"Angelo Celucci."

Ruby leaned forward slightly, trying to see what was on the paper in Gerard's folder. Gerard let the first sheets fall back in place. She sat back.

"What do you know about Angelo?" she asked, her eyes narrowing.

Gerard flipped the folder closed. "I know he has encountered some financial difficulties."

"What kind of job are you interviewing for, anyway? I came here to interview for a housekeeper job."

"Yes, and I would like you to have that job."

"And this somehow involves Angelo?"

Gerard nodded. "I understand that he owes money to some unpleasant people."

"How do you know about that?" she asked sharply.

"I have my sources. I also understand that he has experienced some unpleasantness as a result of this debt."

After a long pause, during which her eyes never left his face, she said, "They broke his thumbs. He's a mechanic— *was* a mechanic—and now he can't do the one thing he could have done to earn back the money they want."

Gerard shuddered. "A horrible situation. And one I'm sure you would want to resolve if possible."

After another long pause, Ruby said, "Only thirty-five thousand dollars is going to resolve that situation."

"Good heavens," said Gerard mildly. "That much?"

"He gambles. He knows he shouldn't, but he can't help himself. But he's a good boy other than the gambling."

Gerard leaned forward. "Miss DiMano, I think that you and I can help each other out."

After a moment, she said, "How do you figure that?"

He sat back. "I could give you the thirty-five thousand dollars your nephew needs to stop having his bones broken."

Her eyebrows rose slightly but, Gerard was gratified to see, there was no other change in her expression. Yes, this was promising.

When he didn't say more, she asked, "And why would you do that?"

"I have reason to want to know what's going on with the family's little girl. And with her mother. That's it, just information. Nothing illegal."

"I'm pretty sure there's a law against spying on people."

"'Spying' sounds so unpleasant. This would just be an arrangement between the two of us. I will secure you the position with this family and give you thirty-five thousand dollars. And then you can collect the wages they will pay you, plus I'll pay you an additional amount each month on top of that." He jotted numbers on a sheet of paper and slid it across the table to her.

She leaned forward to read it, then sat back. After a moment she asked, "What would I need to tell you?"

Gerard shrugged. "Basically, just what the little girl does all day. And how the mother's condition is progressing. Or deteriorating."

"And why do you want to know that?"

"That's not something you need concern yourself with."

She looked at him appraisingly, then said, "Let's say I

took the job and you gave me the thirty-five thousand. How long would I have to keep the job until you would feel you'd gotten your money's worth?"

"I would expect you to work for them, and report back to me, for a year. At the end of that year, I would pay you another bonus, on top of your monthly payments, to continue for another year. Assuming, of course, that I am satisfied with your performance."

"I guess I can report on what a little girl and her mother do," she grumbled.

"But if you didn't last the full year, or if you felt it was necessary to tell anyone about our arrangement, I would not be happy about that."

She shifted. "How unhappy would you be?"

"Quite unhappy. And your nephew might feel the brunt of my unhappiness. I think he's suffered enough for his own folly. I'm sure you wouldn't want him to suffer for yours."

A fine sheen of sweat had broken out on Ruby DiMano's upper lip. "Thirty-five thousand now, then the housekeeper salary for a year to tell you what this little girl and her mother do. And then at the end of a year I can walk if I want to?"

"That's right."

"And how would I get this money?"

Gerard reached under the table and pulled out a briefcase. He placed it on the table, snapped it open, and then turned it to face Ruby.

Her eyes widened. She reached toward the case, then hesitated and glanced at Gerard. He nodded, and she reached into the case and picked up a bundle of cash.

"Used fifties," he said. "And quite a number of them, as you can see."

"Yes, I see," she said, her voice monotone. "How did you know ahead of time how much he owed?"

"Oh, I have my ways," said Gerard.

She nodded silently and put the cash back in the briefcase.

"Do you know the person your nephew owes the money

to?" asked Gerard.

"Yes. And I'm guessing you do too."

Gerard smiled. "And do you know where he can be found?"

She nodded.

"Then to make sure you know I have upheld my side of the bargain, I suggest that you accompany my assistant while he delivers the money to the recipient."

"All right."

"And, assuming Angelo doesn't incur any additional debt, if this person bothers him again, please let me know and my assistant will deal with it."

"All right."

Gerard leaned forward. "But if your nephew gets himself into any more trouble, that's his issue, not mine. Are we in agreement?"

Ruby began to speak and her voice caught. She cleared her throat. "Yes."

"Excellent," said Gerard. He turned the briefcase back and snapped the lid shut. "I believe you and I will have a very successful partnership, Miss DiMano." He stood and extended his hand.

She stood and, after an almost imperceptible pause, released her grip on her purse to shake his hand. Gerard barely contained a wince—it was like shaking hands with a nutcracker.

She was turning to go when Gerard stopped her. "Miss DiMano, if I might make a suggestion …?"

She turned back, her eyes wary. "Yes?"

"If I were you, I'd confine my services to housekeeping only. Let the mother take care of the little girl."

"If you say so, sir."

"Just my recommendation," said Gerard. "Now, if you will just wait outside for a moment while I speak with my assistant …"

Gerard followed her to the door and opened it. George

was leaning against the wall, extracting a mint from a roll. He popped it in his mouth and straightened as Gerard and Ruby came out of the conference room.

"George, may I see you for a moment?" Gerard turned to Ruby. "We won't be long, Miss DiMano. Please make yourself comfortable in the lounge." He gestured across the hall.

Ruby nodded and disappeared into the room.

George followed Gerard into the conference room. Gerard shut the door.

"She'll take you to the person who's owed the money," said Gerard.

George nodded. He crossed to the table and picked up the briefcase.

"She should see you hand the money over, but not be within earshot."

"I can arrange that."

"I want you to let this person know that it's no concern of mine if Angelo Celucci incurs more debt with him."

George raised his eyebrows. "You don't care if he keeps gambling?"

"No. As I said, it's no concern of mine. Make sure the man he owes the money to knows that."

"No problem," said George, and let himself out of the conference room.

Gerard walked to the window and looked out across the skyscrapers of Center City. He was pleased with his hire. And, if he remained pleased with the results, he was quite sure he could keep her on the payroll as long as he liked.

CHAPTER NINE

The Ballards interviewed Ruby DiMano the next day and hired her on the spot, pleasantly surprised at the modest salary she was willing to accept.

Patrick had hoped that having Ruby around might take some pressure off Charlotte, maybe even help reverse her condition, but over the following months, Charlotte's impairment increased and her field of vision became more restricted.

And the headaches grew worse. During one particularly bad week, when Ruby was off to help her sister care for her brother-in-law after a hernia operation, Charlotte's sister Marilyn had driven down from her home in Vermont to help out with the house and with Lizzy.

Marilyn was five years younger than Charlotte, and it was always a source of wonder to Patrick that the sisters' parents could have raised two daughters who were so totally different. Charlotte dressed in carefully coordinated slacks and blouses, while Marilyn dressed in airy cotton tops and worn jeans. Charlotte enjoyed chatting with almost anyone, while Marilyn was more reserved. Charlotte spent her outdoor hours tending the flower garden surrounding their deck, while Marilyn weeded a vegetable garden at a community plot. But despite, or perhaps because of, their differences, Patrick had never seen them argue, or even exchange a cross word. He recalled a time, before Lizzy was born, when Marilyn had shown up for a visit with a baggie of pot, and after trying unsuccessfully to talk Charlotte into joining them, he and Marilyn had shared a joint while Charlotte waved the smoke away from her face and shook her head good-naturedly at their increasing silliness. She even baked them chocolate chip cookies when they got the munchies.

For this visit, almost a decade later, Charlotte was not in a baking frame of mind. She had spent the two days since Marilyn had arrived in bed, the curtains drawn, a cold washcloth over her eyes. Despite Marilyn trying to tempt her with her favorite food, she had eaten little, since the headaches made her nauseated.

Six-year-old Lizzy was also out of sorts, but in her case the response was hyperactivity and the evident intent to make as much noise as possible. After several unsuccessful attempts to distract her with a snack or a game of Go Fish, Marilyn popped her head into Charlotte's darkened bedroom.

"Char, I'm sorry, I can't keep her quiet. I'm going to take her to the Playland to let her burn off some energy, okay?"

"Sure, thanks," came the weary response from the bed.

Marilyn eased the door shut, grabbed her car keys, and returned to the den, where Lizzy was racing two Matchbox cars back and forth on the couch, with accompanying vrooming noises.

"Come on, Lizzy, want to go to McDonald's?"

"No," said Lizzy, climbing onto the couch so she could run the cars along the back.

"We can have fries."

"No." One of the cars plummeted off the back of the couch, accompanied by dramatic sound effects of its crash.

"Lizzy, if you want to stay home, you're going to have to play quieter. Your mom doesn't feel well."

"No." Lizzy sent the second car careening after the first.

"Lizzy, you can either play at home quietly or be noisy at Donald's, but you can't be noisy at home. You decide."

"No!" said Lizzy, "I'm playing cars!"

"Okay, kiddo, we're going for a drive," Marilyn said, and bent down to pick up Lizzy.

"No!" yelled Lizzy, and a jolt of pain shot through

Marilyn's head and stars danced in front of her eyes.

She dropped the car keys and staggered back.

Lizzy stared at her, her eyes wide, and burst into tears. "Sorry!"

Marilyn backed away from her. She grabbed a chair and lowered herself onto it. When the pain receded, she looked toward Lizzy.

"Did you do that, Lizzy?" she whispered.

"Sorry!" sobbed Lizzy. "Sorry! I didn't mean it!"

When Patrick got home from work that evening, he found Marilyn at the kitchen table with a bottle of beer. Lizzy sat at the table next to her, apparently absorbed in her coloring book.

"Hi, girls," said Patrick, crossing to the table and kissing Lizzy on top of the head.

"Hi, Dad," she mumbled, not looking up from her work.

"How's Charlotte?" he asked Marilyn.

"She's okay. She was up for a while but she went back to bed."

Patrick started to open the fridge for a beer, but then did a double take as he glanced toward Marilyn. "What happened to your eye?"

Marilyn herself had noticed it shortly after Lizzy's outburst—the outside half of her left eye was a blood-bright red.

"Let's go in the den," said Marilyn, nodding her head meaningfully at Lizzy.

Patrick glanced over at Lizzy, then back to Marilyn. "Okay."

"Lizzy, you stay right here, your daddy and I are just going to be in the next room."

Lizzy nodded.

Patrick followed Marilyn into the den, where she took up a position from which she could monitor Lizzy.

"Lizzy was getting fussy and noisy and I wanted to take her to McDonald's," she said. "She didn't want to go, but I tried to take her anyway, and she got really upset. And then this happened." She gestured toward her eye.

"What do you mean?" asked Patrick.

"I mean," said Marilyn, her voice dropping to a whisper, "that she started to have a tantrum, and suddenly I got this pain in my head and couldn't see clearly, and then later I see that there's a burst blood vessel in my eye."

"Marilyn, I don't know what you're saying," said Patrick uncertainly.

"I think you do, Pat," said Marilyn, a tremor in her voice. "The effect was at exactly the moment Lizzy started pitching a fit—she got angry with me, and suddenly I get these symptoms. Like a stroke."

"But that doesn't make any sense—" started Patrick.

"Think about it. Every time Charlotte had an episode, it was right when Lizzy was angry with her. She was taking away a toy, or trying to put a towel on Lizzy's lip when she ran into the refrigerator."

"How do you know it was at the same time?" asked Patrick.

"I asked Charlotte."

Patrick ran his fingers through his hair and glanced into the kitchen. Lizzy sat at the table staring at the book, but no longer coloring.

"And that's not all," continued Marilyn. "When it happened, Lizzy started crying and said that she was sorry, that she didn't mean it."

"She might have been talking about something else."

Marilyn crossed her arms and glared at Patrick.

After a moment, he asked, "Did you tell Charlotte your idea?"

Marilyn sighed. "I did. She didn't believe it."

"It does seem kind of … unbelievable," said Patrick.

"I thought you'd say that," said Marilyn tightly. "So I made an appointment to see my doctor. I'm going to tell him I think I need a CT scan, and I'm betting it shows the symptoms of a stroke."

A week later, Marilyn had the results of her CT scan back. It showed one tiny white spot. One tiny stroke.

CHAPTER TEN

Charlotte wouldn't let Marilyn come back to visit them after they learned of her diagnosis. "Pat, if Lizzy's really doing this, we can't let her hurt other people," said Charlotte. "I remember going to pick her up at school one day a few weeks ago and Mary Ann told me that Lizzy and another little girl had gotten in an argument and then the little girl had to go home because she didn't feel well." Her voice hitched with tears. "What if Lizzy hurt her?"

"Sweetheart, I feel like there are lots of explanations for what's happening—"

"Like what?" Charlotte shot back.

"I don't know. But I think we need some help here."

"What kind of help?"

"Expert advice, someone who knows more—"

"No! What if Lizzy really is doing these things? They might take her away from us, lock her away, do experiments on her—like a lab rat!"

There was a long silence, during which they both sat looking vacantly into space, listening to the clock ticking on the mantel and the sounds of Lizzy playing upstairs in her room.

"What are we going to do about Ruby?" asked Charlotte eventually.

Patrick sighed. "I've thought about that. I don't recall her ever complaining about having a headache—"

"She doesn't strike me as the complaining type," said Charlotte.

"True. But I also don't recall seeing her showing any

symptoms like you've been having. But I don't spend that much time with her. Do you recall ever seeing anything like that?"

Charlotte shook her head. "No, I don't. So doesn't that mean Lizzy can't be doing what Marilyn thinks she's doing? Wouldn't Ruby be having the same symptoms?"

"I don't know," said Patrick. "The whole point of getting Ruby was to let you spend your energy on Lizzy. How much time does Ruby really spend with her?"

Charlotte sighed. "Not much, I guess. And until we know what's going on, we need to make sure that it stays that way."

Patrick took her hand—her left hand—and was shocked at how limp and lifeless it felt. "I think we should ask Owen for his opinion."

"Owen?" said Charlotte. "I don't know …"

Patrick leaned forward. "Lottie, we need to ask someone for advice. He's got the medical background, he can help us understand if this theory is even feasible. But more importantly, he's her godfather. We're the only people who love Lizzy more than Owen does. I would trust him with any secret. I think you would, too."

Charlotte nodded slowly. "Yes. Maybe Owen."

Patrick patted her hand. "I'll call him in the morning."

CHAPTER ELEVEN

Owen had bought his house ten years earlier, a dilapidated but authentic Craftsman with the characteristic gabled roof and overhanging eaves, and a deep, shady porch supported by enormous pillars that tapered slightly at the top. Owen had brought it all back to its original glory, meaning that it was worth about twice what the other houses on the modest block were.

Owen opened the door to Patrick and Charlotte's knock, and Lizzy said, as she always did, "Mr. Big!"

Patrick laughed and Charlotte rolled her eyes and said, "Lizzy, really!"

Owen bent toward Lizzy. "As big as a house?"

Lizzy giggled and shook her head.

"As big as a mouse?"

Lizzy laughed. "No!"

They settled this time on "as big as a raccoon," and Owen waved them in.

The restoration of the house was complete, but the furnishing of it was an ongoing project, and it was Craftsman throughout. Owen claimed it was because the furniture was designed to stand up to his bulk, but in truth he liked its clean lines, its honest simplicity, and, in the case of the pieces he bought, its quality. Owen McNally was well known to antique dealers in Philadelphia and New York, and had developed a reputation as something of an expert himself. He only bought a piece if he loved it, but he always bought a piece if he loved it. The result was that the dining room, even after ten years, was still unfurnished, but his living room was crammed with museum-quality chairs, tables, and an antique Stickley grandfather clock.

Lizzy headed for the dining room which, although not furnished in the traditional sense, did contain a basket of toys, games, and books for her visits.

The adults passed through to the living room, Charlotte leaning on a cane she had recently begun to use to counteract the weakness in her left leg. Owen retrieved coffee and homemade coffee cake from the kitchen.

When they were settled, he asked, "Am I right in assuming this isn't a completely social call?"

"We think we might know what's causing Charlotte's strokes," said Patrick.

They had brought copies of Marilyn's CT scan and Charlotte's medical records, and described Marilyn's theory about the connection between Lizzy's outbursts and the symptoms she and Charlotte were experiencing. Owen listened to the story with nods but no comments.

"Have you ever heard of such a thing?" asked Charlotte when they were done. "Of someone having that effect on other people?"

Owen leaned back in his chair. "There's a story out there for about any phenomenon you care to imagine," he said, "but I can't say I recall reading about such an effect in any reputable source, and as you can imagine, I've done quite a bit of reading about strokes since I found out about Charlotte's situation. But," he said with a shrug, "there is still a lot we don't know about the human body, and even more we don't know about the human mind."

"Do you think it's possible Lizzy's responsible for what's happened to Lottie and Marilyn?" asked Patrick.

Owen considered. "Well, the brain's nerve cells generate an electrical field, and certainly electrical fields can have an impact on the physical world. People even talk about being able to send those electrical signals over a network, the same way you'd send an email message. But to create the kind of physical effect you're suggesting—it would require an enormous amount of power." He considered in silence for a few moments. "Not impossible, I suppose."

"Could we come up with a way to test it?" asked Charlotte.

"The trick would be to figure out how to do it without risking harm to someone in the process."

"How about monkeys?" asked Patrick.

Owen gave a small smile. "What would you suggest, that we create a situation where Lizzy gets really angry with a monkey? Even if we could lay our hands on a subject, it seems like a bad idea for both your daughter and the monkey."

"True," sighed Patrick.

Owen tapped his fingers together over the mound of his stomach. "I'm having a little trouble getting my brain around the idea that Lizzy is causing this problem," he said. "However, if it turns out that she *is* the cause, then the first priority is controlling the situation so she doesn't do any further damage."

"How do you suggest we do that?" asked Charlotte.

"Let's assume for the moment that she does have this ability," said Owen. "She's approaching an age when I think you could start talking about the situation with her, explain to her what effect she's having on people, or may be having. But she's not quite old enough to fully understand yet, and even once she understands, it will be a bit longer before she can reliably control her emotions. Hell, sometimes even into adulthood people never gain that kind of control." He took a contemplative sip of coffee. "The safest course of action for *you* would be to never allow a situation to develop that's going to make her angry, which means acceding to her every demand. That might prevent further damage to you, but it would create obvious behavioral issues, and not only when she's a child. A person who never has boundaries set for them as a child grows up to be an adult who can't deal with the boundaries that society naturally sets, and once she's an adult and out of your control, then the danger to other people increases if they don't realize the consequences of saying 'no' to her."

He glanced again at the medical documents spread out on the coffee table. "Let me do some research and some thinking about how we might be able to figure out if Marilyn's theory is correct. In the meantime, I think it's best to limit her interactions with other people. She's in school now, correct?"

Charlotte nodded. "The Montessori school."

"You should withdraw her for now. Keep her home as much as possible—no play dates. And for the time being, don't let her get mad at either of you."

Just then, Lizzy called from the dining room, "Uncle Owen, come look what I made!"

He pushed himself out of his seat. Charlotte stood too, and staggered a bit. Patrick caught her elbow.

Owen shook his head. "We have to come up with a plan quickly," he said.

CHAPTER TWELVE

A Toyota SUV pulled up in front of a large stone house in Paoli and Owen hoisted himself out. He adjusted his tweed touring cap, pulled an old-fashioned leather briefcase from the back seat, and made his ponderous way up the walk to the entrance. Next to the door was a wooden sign: Happy Hours Montessori Academy.

He knocked, and in a moment a middle-aged woman with a slightly harried expression opened the door. "Yes?"

"Ms. Totnam?"

"Yes. Are you Dr. McNally?"

"Yes."

"Come in," she said, pushing the door open. "And please call me Mary Ann." She turned toward the back of the house. "Jenna," she called, "I'm going to be in my office for a few minutes."

"Okay!" called Jenna then, at a slightly lower volume, "Dylan, you put that down!"

Mary Ann led Owen to a small room off the central hallway that was crammed with an odd jumble of office supplies, bales of paper towels, and plastic totes of toys. She waved him toward a flimsy-looking chair.

"Please have a seat."

"I'm afraid that chair might not be up to the challenge," he said with a smile.

She blushed. "I'm sorry—there's a couch in the den."

"Yes, that might be best." He sometimes had difficulty extracting himself from low furniture like couches, but he'd cross that bridge when he came to it. He followed Mary Ann down a short hallway to an equally cluttered living room. She pushed a few toys to one side of the couch to clear a space for him. He lowered himself onto the couch carefully. Yes, this one was going to be a challenge.

He took off his cap, put his briefcase in his lap, and snapped it open.

"I appreciate you taking the time to talk with me. As we discussed on the phone, William Penn University is doing a study of the impacts on children's physical development of various environments—home, daycare, private or public schools." He pulled some forms from his briefcase, pushed himself forward, and handed them to Mary Ann.

"Physical development?" she asked. "I can imagine psychological development, but physical?"

"It's a highly under-researched area," said Owen. "But very important. For example, one might assume that children in a more social environment get more exercise through more vigorous physical play, and that might translate into faster physical development."

She nodded. "Yes, I can see that."

"So we're asking the supervising adults in each environment to answer some questions related to their charges' physical characteristics. For example, heights and weights over time, and physical well-being such as incidents of illness, or patterns of headache." He pushed himself forward again and handed several official-looking postage-paid envelopes to Mary Ann. It was amazing what those office service centers could produce on short notice. "The results are completely confidential—there will be no way of tracing the responses back to any particular facility or home." Except that in the case of this survey, only one facility would be submitting a response.

She took the form and looked at it uncertainly. "I don't know. I'm a firm believer in the benefits of the social environment that schools like mine provide—otherwise I wouldn't be in this business. But sometimes people interpret the results of these studies in weird ways. People are always looking for a way to pin blame on someone else."

"All the results will be presented cumulatively, and over eighty facilities are already signed up to participate," said Owen, wincing inwardly.

She nodded. "Okay, I guess I can do that."

"I would be much obliged," said Owen. "The more specific you can be, the better." He extracted himself from the couch on his second attempt, with a grunt. "Obviously the forms for gathering the information regarding height and weight progression need to be completed over time, but if you could provide the information related to the physical condition of the children by the end of the week, it will be extremely helpful."

Mary Ann glanced over the form. "Yes, I should be able to do that."

She led Owen to the front door. "You said you were asking about headaches?"

Owen covered his start by placing his cap on his head. "Yes, among other things. Why do you ask?"

"We have had one little boy who's been complaining of headaches. It's not something you normally hear children complain about, so it struck me as unusual."

"Yes, that is unusual," said Owen. "How long has this being going on?"

She thought for a moment. "At least several months."

Owen did a quick calculation. It was about the same amount of time that Lizzy had been attending the school.

There was a crash at the back of the house, and Jenna's irritated voice. "Dylan!"

Mary Ann gave a tired smile. "Speak of the devil."

"Dylan is the boy who has been having headaches?"

"Yes." She dropped her voice. "He's quite the terror. I'm actually thinking of asking his parents to keep him home for a few more months until he's a little better socialized."

"That would certainly be understandable," said Owen.

"We had a little girl here for a while, and Dylan was particularly unpleasant to her. Her parents recently withdrew her from school. I hope it wasn't because of Dylan."

"Ah, too bad," said Owen. "What was the little girl's name?"

"Lizzy."

When he left the school, Owen drove to the Ballards' house. Patrick opened the door to his knock.

"How did it go?" Patrick asked.

"Very productive, I think. Where's Lizzy?"

"She's in the den watching *Monsters, Inc.* She's sulking because she misses school. I'll get Charlotte."

Owen took his usual seat, a roomy armchair in the living room, then levered himself up when Charlotte and Patrick arrived. Charlotte was leaning more heavily than usual on her cane, and her face was pale, her eyes bright with anxiety.

"What did you find out?" she asked.

When they were seated, Owen repeated the conversation he had had at the school, including the story of the troublesome Dylan's headaches. "I'd still like to see what the owner has to report if she returns the survey, but we already know of three people—Charlotte, Marilyn, and now Dylan—who have suffered similar symptoms after Lizzy got angry with them. I think it's safest to proceed under the assumption that Lizzy does have the power to cause strokes."

Charlotte, sitting on the couch next to Patrick, raised her right hand to her face and covered her eyes. Her left lay motionless in her lap. "Oh my God. Dylan Jorgensen? I know his mother. Is he going to be all right?"

"I don't know. Let's hope he didn't pester Lizzy too much. I'll see if I can find out who his pediatrician is, and maybe I can suggest a CT scan."

"But how?" asked Charlotte, her voice thick with tears. "How can you convince him to order a CT scan?"

Owen rubbed his beard. "We may have to tell his doctor

what we suspect about Lizzy—"

"No!" Charlotte tried to rise from the couch, but fell back.

Patrick reached out to her. "Lottie, sweetheart—"

"No!" she said again, and struggled to the edge of the couch. "No one can know! What would they do to her if they knew? They would take her away from us!" The tears that up until now she had held at bay spilled down her cheeks. "I won't let them do that. You can't tell anyone."

"Who's 'they'?" asked Owen.

"I don't know," said Charlotte. "The government, some giant corporation. To us she's just our little girl, but to them … if she *is* doing what we think, they would want to use her for their own ends."

"Lottie, what choice do we have?" asked Patrick, putting his hand on her arm. "She's hurting people. She's hurt you, and we can't let that happen to anyone else."

Charlotte shook Patrick's hand off. "I'm not going to let anyone else get hurt, and I'm not going to let them take our baby."

Patrick turned to Owen. "Owen, tell her it won't be like that. Tell her we can find someone who can help us deal with this."

Owen shook his head. "I hate to say it, Pat, but Charlotte's concerns aren't outlandish. There are plenty of people in business and in the government who would be very interested in understanding what Lizzy seems to be capable of, and might not keep her best interests at heart."

"But what can we do?" said Patrick, his voice breaking. "How can we make sure nobody else gets hurt—not Lizzy, and not anyone else?"

They sat in morose silence for a minute, the sounds of *Monsters, Inc.* drifting in from the den, then the panic abated a bit in Charlotte's eyes. "I know. I'll take her to the cabin," she said.

CHAPTER THIRTEEN

Patrick's family had a place in the Pocono Mountains, about eighty miles north of Philadelphia and two hours from Paoli on a good day, three and a half on a bad one. Patrick's father had bought it when Patrick was young as a refuge for the family, and then held onto it as an investment. When it became clear the investment would never quite pay off, he held onto it mainly out of habit—even after he and Patrick's mother moved to Santa Fe—and the place was used only a few times a year.

Charlotte was convinced that it could become Lizzy's refuge.

While the Ballards got ready to relocate Charlotte and Lizzy to the Poconos, Owen arranged to do some tests on Lizzy.

He stopped by the Ballards' house on a sunny Sunday morning. Lizzy clambered into his SUV and waved enthusiastically to Patrick and Charlotte as they pulled away, off on her first "big girl adventure."

Their first stop was the Main Line Diner for breakfast, Lizzy holding Owen's hand while they waited for a table and gawking at the other patrons. When they were seated, Owen ordered pancakes and scrapple and a cup of coffee for himself.

"What would you like, Lizzy?" he asked.

"I'll have that, too."

The waitress said with a smile, "Aren't you a little young for coffee? How about some milk?"

"Nope. I'll have what Uncle Owen is having," replied Lizzy.

The waitress glanced at Owen.

"Coffee for two," he said. "I'd like mine with extra sugar. And *lots* of extra milk," he added, arching his eyebrows meaningfully at the waitress. He turned to Lizzy. "Is that how you'd like yours?"

"Yes, please," she said, watching a waitress pass with an enormous tray loaded with steaming plates of food.

"You got it," said the waitress. She tucked her pencil behind her ear and headed off toward the counter.

"So, did your parents tell you what your adventure was going to be?" Owen asked.

"Nope. It's a surprise."

"But I can tell you now, right?"

She considered for a moment. "Okay."

"We're going to where I work and you're going to help me with an experiment."

"Like what?"

"Well, I study people's brains for a living, and I have a machine that shows me what's going on in their brains."

"Like dreams?" asked Lizzy, excited.

"Well, not the dreams themselves, but what the brain does while the person is dreaming."

Lizzy looked blankly at him.

"Have you ever seen the machine that measures an earthquake?"

"No."

Owen pulled his laptop from the briefcase he had brought in with him and pulled up a video he had downloaded.

"It's called a seismograph, and it measures earthquakes."

Lizzy peered intently at the video.

"See, there's a little pen attached to that moving part that moves if the ground moves. The ground is always moving a little bit, although it's *such* a little bit that people usually can't feel it. But when there's an earthquake—" he fast forwarded the video—"the needle bounces around like crazy and the pen draws those lines on the paper."

"Cool!" exclaimed Lizzy, staring at the video.

"The machine I have—it's called an EEG—does the same thing, except it records what's going on in your brain."

Lizzy sat back. "Weird."

The waitress arrived with two cups of coffee and placed one in front of each of them. The coffee was the color of extremely weak tea. She looked sympathetically at Owen.

"Two coffees, extra sugar, extra extra milk."

Lizzy picked up her cup, took a sip, and smacked her lips. "Hot, too," she said.

Owen and the waitress burst out laughing, and Lizzy looked surprised.

"Where did you hear that?" Owen asked.

"That's what Dad says when he drinks his coffee in the morning," she said.

The waitress, still laughing, shook her head. "I'll be back with your food."

Owen took a sip from his cup and found it not bad, although barely lukewarm.

"So does that sound like something you'd want to help me out with? Help me out with my experiment?"

"Sure," said Lizzy, distracted by another passing tray of food.

"We'll put the machine on my head," he said, "and you can read my brain waves. That's what the machine measures, kind of like waves in an ocean—"

"Or in the ground," said Lizzy.

"Yes, exactly, or in the ground. And then we can put the machine on your head and I can read your brainwaves."

"Okay," she said agreeably, and took another slurp of her coffee.

After they finished their breakfasts—Lizzy liked the pancakes once she had added a pool of syrup to the plate, but declared the scrapple to be gross—they drove to Owen's office at William Penn University. Owen began to realize that, with Patrick working long hours and Charlotte limited by the effects of her strokes, Lizzy had probably had much less exposure to the outside world than most children her age. She was fascinated with everything—she had evidently never encountered a water fountain before, and they ended up spending fifteen minutes at a copier making copies of everything in Owen's pockets and, of course, their hands and faces. Armed with their sheaf of copies, Owen eventually got her to the room where the EEG machine was.

The test he really wanted to run was an fMRI, or functional magnetic resonance imaging test. He speculated that Lizzy might display significant activation of the right parahippocampal gyrus, but he had no access to such equipment. He wasn't sure what an EEG might show, but since it was available to him, and would not only be non-intrusive but also potentially fun and interesting for Lizzy, he thought he'd give it a try.

With Lizzy's help, he prepped his scalp for the test, cleaning the areas where the electrodes would be attached with a mildly abrasive gel, then applying a paste that held the electrodes in place. Once he was hooked up, he asked Lizzy to tell him a story, and she regaled him with a surprisingly long and involved tale of a caterpillar named Ziggy.

Not surprisingly, the setup was not ideal and the resulting readings would not have been useful for actual medical or scientific use, but the process achieved the desired result: Lizzy was even more enchanted by the EEG machine than she had been by the copier.

Once they got Owen detached from the machine, they went through the cleaning and pasting process for Lizzy, who complained only mildly about the annoyance of having her scalp scrubbed. Once she was hooked up, giggling when Owen gave her a mirror to see the effect, he opened up a video on his laptop and handed it to Lizzy.

It was an animation that a colleague had created to test the ability of children much younger than Lizzy to make an assessment of moral behavior. It involved two rudimentary puppets and a pile of Hershey's Kisses, with one of the puppets stealing the other's Kisses when the other wasn't looking. Owen watched the EEG readout, and could see no change from Lizzy's baseline reading.

When the video had finished, he asked Lizzy, "What did you think about that?"

She shrugged. "It's for *little* kids, right?"

Owen sighed. He had known the video was a bit young for her, but he had hoped it would elicit some response that might confirm their theory about her ability.

"Yes, you're right. You're a little too old for that," he said. "How about this one?"

The second video was a scene from *A Christmas Story* involving Scut Farkus bullying Ralphie. The EEG registered something faintly, but no more than might be explained by normal brain activity.

When the video had played, Lizzy turned to him. "That redheaded kid isn't very nice."

"No, he's not."

Owen was contemplating the third video he had reluctantly downloaded to his laptop—this one the scene from *My Dog Skip* where Willie hits Skip—when Lizzy asked, "Are we going to have to watch more videos of people being mean?" and he lost his motivation.

He patted her on the back. "No, Pumpkin, we're not." After a brief search, he found a video of a pack of golden retriever puppies galloping around a picket-fenced yard after their mother and played that for her, eliciting a peal of delighted laughter from Lizzy and a corresponding response from the EEG. He showed her the readout, and then helped her get the paste scrubbed out of her hair.

On the drive home, Owen silently scolded himself. It would have benefited Lizzy more in the long run if he had been able to be a little more the scientist, a little less the godfather, but the idea of showing a little girl things especially meant to upset her had been too distasteful. Maybe there was another way to test the Ballards' theory about her abilities.

As they approached Paoli, Lizzy roused Owen from his ruminations. "I'm hungry."

Owen glanced at his watch and realized that it was mid-afternoon and he had never gotten Lizzy lunch, an oversight that was unusual for him, to say the least. "Sure, Pumpkin. Want to stop at the diner again?"

"Okay," said Lizzy, sounding a bit grumpy.

As he had hoped, the waitress from breakfast was still there, and he asked the hostess to seat them at one of her tables. They looked over the menus propped between the napkin dispenser and ketchup bottle until she appeared at their table.

"Hey, did you like breakfast so much you came back for more?" she asked.

"Absolutely," he said. "Right, Pumpkin?" he asked Lizzy, who nodded. Owen consulted the menu. "I'll have a chocolate milkshake and a burger with fries." He turned to Lizzy. "You can have some of my milkshake if you want."

"Okay," she said without enthusiasm.

"What would you like to eat? Do you want to share my burger and fries, or do you want something else?"

"No scrapple," she said with a scowl.

"No, no scrapple," he agreed. He turned to the waitress. "We'll share."

"No problem," she said, and disappeared toward the kitchen.

Lizzy swung her legs and looked around the almost-empty diner, but without the excitement she had shown that morning. In a few minutes, the waitress delivered a chocolate milkshake divided into two glasses.

When she had left, Owen asked Lizzy, "So what did you think about our experiment today? Did you have a good time?"

"Yes," said Lizzy politely, then added. "I'm tired."

"I would think so, you've had a big day. We'll have our

snack and then get you home and you can have a nap."

"Okay," said Lizzy, poking her straw into her half of the milkshake.

"So, Lizzy," said Owen, as casually as possible, "do you remember a boy named Dylan at school?"

Lizzy scrunched up her face. "Yes."

"What was he like?"

"I didn't like him."

"Why not?"

"He was mean."

"What did he do that was mean?"

"He colored in my book."

Owen raised his eyebrows questioningly.

"We were having coloring and he was sitting beside me and he colored in my book." She used the milkshake straw to demonstrate frantic scribbling, spraying the table and Owen with droplets of milkshake. Owen wished he had thought to ask her about Dylan when he had the EEG cap on her.

"How did you feel about that?"

"He was being bad."

"Yes, but how did you *feel* about what he did?"

"Mad," she said sulkily, poking her straw back into her milkshake.

"And what did you do about that?" he asked.

"I squeezed him."

Owen felt his heart jump. "You did what?"

"I squeezed his head," she said, just as the waitress appeared with Owen's burger and fries, with a sharing plate for Lizzy.

Owen collected his thoughts as he portioned out half the burger and half the fries onto Lizzy's plate. She picked at it disinterestedly.

After a minute, he said, "What do you mean, you squeezed his head?"

Lizzy shrugged. "To make him stop." Then she put the french fry she had been holding down on the plate, gripped her head at the temples, and said in a chillingly adult voice, "I feel like my head's being squeezed in a vise."

Owen stared at her, wide-eyed. "What?"

She noticed his stare and suddenly looked uncertain. "That's what Mom says sometimes."

"Do you squeeze your mom?" It slipped out of Owen's mouth before he could stop it.

Lizzy stared back at him, now round-eyed herself, then tears began to fill her eyes. "No."

Owen reached over and rubbed her arm. "No, of course not, I don't know why I said that."

"No!" said Lizzy louder, as the tears spilled down her cheeks.

Expecting at any moment for a shard of pain to slice through his head, Owen fumbled his wallet out of his pocket and dropped two twenties on the table. "I'm sorry, Pumpkin, I didn't mean to upset you. Let's get you home."

Lizzy's crying was becoming more hysterical, and Owen was ashamed at his relief that her upset seemed more inwardly than outwardly directed. *Dear God*, he thought, *please don't let her be able to "squeeze" her own brain.*

The waitress appeared at the table. "Everyone okay?"

Owen scooped Lizzy up. "Just got to get her home. I left the money on the table."

The waitress picked up the bills. "I'll get you your change."

"No need," said Owen. "Thanks for your help."

"No problem," said the waitress. She looked sympathetically toward Lizzy, who had locked her arms around Owen's big neck and buried her face in his shoulder. Her crying was getting louder. "Good luck."

Owen hurried out of the diner and to the SUV. As he got Lizzy buckled in, her crying began to abate, but her look of confused consternation remained.

He talked nonsensically and, he hoped, soothingly to her as they drove the few miles to the Ballards' house. He found himself driving extra carefully, as if he were transporting a load of nitroglycerin. By the time they got there, her crying had tapered off, and she was gazing miserably out the window.

Patrick and Charlotte must have been watching for the SUV because, as he pulled up to the curb, Patrick emerged from the house and came down the walk. Charlotte waited in the doorway, leaning on her cane.

"How did the big day at Uncle Owen's work go?" Patrick asked cheerfully, then saw Lizzy's tear-streaked face as Owen lifted her out of the car and onto his hip.

"It's been quite a day, hasn't it, Pumpkin?" asked Owen.

Lizzy nodded, fiddling intently with a button on Owen's shirt.

Patrick looked in alarm from Lizzy to Owen.

"Want to go to your dad?" Owen asked Lizzy.

She nodded again and Owen transferred her from his hip to Patrick's.

"I think a nap would be in order—what do you think?" said Owen.

Lizzy nodded again, eyes still down.

Owen followed Patrick up the walk to where Charlotte stood at the door, her hand at her throat. Lizzy didn't look at her as Patrick carried her inside.

"I'll get her tucked in for a nap," said Patrick, and carried Lizzy upstairs.

Charlotte turned to Owen. "What in the world happened?"

"I think we got the answer to our question, but not the one we were hoping for," he said tiredly.

CHAPTER FOURTEEN

It took them several weeks to make the necessary arrangements for the move to the Poconos. Charlotte obviously couldn't manage by herself, and they couldn't give up Patrick's salary. After much discussion and calculations of added cost, they agreed to approach Ruby about staying in the Poconos with Charlotte and Lizzy during the week, and were delighted when she accepted. Patrick would drive up to relieve her on Friday nights and then Ruby would take over again on Sunday nights.

To afford even Ruby's surprisingly modest salary requirements, they needed to reduce their other expenses, so they sold the house in Paoli and moved to the less expensive Thorndale. Patrick could still take the train to and from Philadelphia, but on his way home he now continued on past the heart of the Main Line to the far western suburbs of the city.

The lower mortgage came not only with a less fashionable address, but also with a smaller house on a smaller lot. As Charlotte watched Patrick and a couple of his college buddies (although not Owen) carry furniture and boxes from the U-Haul truck into the house, she realized that they had unintentionally cemented the decision for her and Lizzy to live in the Poconos. The Thorndale neighborhood was one where every window overlooked a neighbor's window, and where everyone knew everyone else's business. It was not a neighborhood where it would be possible to keep a little girl sequestered in her house without causing gossip and raising suspicions.

To their family and friends, they explained the new arrangement with the excuse that Charlotte, with her increasing disability, benefited from the peace and quiet of the family cabin. Those who heard that story were either gullible enough or polite enough not to question it.

Charlotte and Patrick discussed at length how best to ease a six-year-old girl through such a transition. They debated the pros and cons of inflicting two moves on Lizzy—Paoli to Thorndale, then Thorndale to the Poconos—versus one move from Paoli to the Poconos, and decided on the first. There would no doubt be times when Charlotte and Lizzy would be staying in Thorndale, and Charlotte thought it was important for Lizzy to feel that it also was her home.

By the time they sat down with her to discuss the moves, they had worked themselves into a high state of anxiety, not only because of their concern about the impact the discussion might have on Lizzy, but also because of their concern about the impact Lizzy's reaction might have on them. But the result was anticlimactic. She hadn't been to school, or even out of the house much, since Owen's investigative visit to Mary Ann Totnam, and she mainly seemed happy for a change.

"Do you remember Grammy and Grampy's cabin?" asked Patrick.

Lizzy nodded.

"How would you like to go there for a visit?"

Lizzy perked up. "Okay!"

"We're going to go on a long vacation at the cabin. You and Mommy will stay there, and I'll come visit you on the weekends. How does that sound?"

"Okay," said Lizzy, sounding a little less enthusiastic. "You could stay too."

"I have to go to work at my job during the week."

"Miss DiMano will be there with us," said Charlotte. "She'll be taking care of the house so you and I can spend all our time together."

"The week will zip by with you and Mom doing fun

things at the cabin," said Patrick, "and then when I show up, the three of us can do fun things."

"How about school?" asked Lizzy.

"Mom's going to be your teacher while you're at the cabin," said Patrick.

Lizzy seemed not entirely convinced.

"I'll bring pizza when I come," added Patrick.

Lizzy thought this over. "Okay," she said finally. "Can I bring my Legos?"

Patrick hugged her. "Yes, sweetie, you can bring as many Legos as you want."

Patrick drove them up to the cabin on a rainy autumn Saturday, Ruby scheduled to arrive in her own car on Sunday night.

The family called the place in the Poconos "the cabin," but it was in fact much less romantic than that, its knotty pine paneling its only nod to rusticity. There were three bedrooms, an eat-in kitchen featuring harvest gold appliances, a living room furnished with the couch and recliners that had come with the house, two dated but functional bathrooms, and a large deck.

The location, however, *was* rustic, several miles from the nearest small town, with a long driveway winding through pine trees up a hill to the house, its brown siding camouflaging it against the backdrop of woods.

Charlotte and Patrick were astounded at Lizzy's adaptability through what for them felt like tremendous upheaval. For a week or two after she and Charlotte moved to the Poconos, Lizzy would complain about, and sometimes cry about, Patrick not being there. Soon, though, she fell into a pattern of mentioning him very little until the end of the week approached, and then seemed to appreciate her time with him without being traumatized when he left again on Sunday.

After they settled into their new circumstances, there followed a period of time that Charlotte remembered with a similar, though more complicated, fondness as she had felt for their first year with Lizzy. She began creating a more structured homeschooling program for Lizzy, requesting books that Patrick would bring up from the Exton library one weekend and return the next. Although never an outdoorsy person herself, Charlotte took Lizzy on nature walks on the cabin's several-acre lot, and they would consult Patrick's mother's books about the local flora, trying to identify the plants or flowers they encountered.

Their first Halloween in the Poconos, when Lizzy started agitating for trick-or-treating, Charlotte was able to mount a convincing argument that there were no houses nearby to visit, but Lizzy was insistent about getting a costume. Charlotte asked Ruby to drive them to the Goodwill, and Lizzy was enchanted. She found a pink tutu and decided she would be a fairy. Evidently rhinestones were a primary fairy accessory, and they found several large brooches in a one-dollar basket, as well as a long string of lustrous pink beads. Lizzy picked out a dark green top and made Charlotte promise to ask Patrick to buy her matching tights and bring them when he came that weekend. Finally, Lizzy added a small Christmas wreath to their cart.

"It's a little early for Christmas decorating, isn't it?" asked Charlotte. "Maybe we should get through one holiday at a time."

"It's a surprise," said Lizzy.

When Patrick arrived that Friday night with the tights, Lizzy rushed into her bedroom to change into her costume, calling out periodic cautions of "No peeking!" Then she stepped into the living room where Patrick and Charlotte were waiting on the couch.

Patrick laughed delightedly. "Look at you—the Fairy Queen!"

Lizzy had taken the small red balls off the Christmas wreath and hung them from the bottom of the tutu. She wore the pink beads not around her neck, but draped diagonally from one shoulder to the opposite hip, like the strap for a quiver of arrows. She had fastened the rhinestone pins here and there on her top, where they sparkled against the dark background. But most inspired, she wore the wreath on her head like a crown, white ribbon that they had found in Patrick's mother's sewing basket streaming off the back like a veil.

"Baby, you look ... beautiful," said Charlotte, squeezing Patrick's fingers, which she held in her right hand, torn between the desire to laugh with him and to cry.

Lizzy giggled and pirouetted.

Subsequent trips to the Goodwill provided costumes for Thanksgiving (a pilgrim), Christmas (an elf), and the spring solstice (a daffodil).

Patrick and Charlotte splurged on moving the piano from Thorndale to the Poconos, and Charlotte began showing Lizzy how to pick out "Twinkle, Twinkle Little Star." This discipline seemed to benefit both of them. For a time, Charlotte's condition improved a bit—she stumbled less frequently and she regained some of the use of her left hand.

Periodically, when cabin fever struck Charlotte or Lizzy with a vengeance, Charlotte would ask Ruby to drive them to the store to pick up some item or just to look around. Much to Charlotte's relief, Lizzy seemed happy to look at toys without necessarily wanting to own them—except for Legos. She was obsessed, and always trotted off to the toy section to check out what new kits might be available. Eventually Charlotte got a couple of plastic totes to hold her supply, and designated a section of the living room as the permanent Lego assembly area.

About Lizzy's attitude toward Ruby, Charlotte was simultaneously amused, relieved, and embarrassed. Lizzy treated Ruby the same way a celebrity might treat the server in a fancy restaurant—satisfied when the service was performed correctly but generally ignoring her presence. Ruby never appeared to take any offense at Lizzy's attitude, so Charlotte decided to leave well enough alone. It served their goal of minimizing Lizzy's interactions with Ruby.

Owen would occasionally visit on the weekends when Patrick was there, making the round-trip drive in one day. He said that sleeping in the room Ruby used felt intrusive, and sleeping on the sofa in the living room was out of the question. During the first year, he would sometimes bring with him the latest drug that he hoped would calm Lizzy enough that she could live a more social life without posing a danger to those with whom she interacted, but they made her listless and teary.

Finally Charlotte put her foot down. "I am not going to turn my little girl into a zombie one hundred percent of the time when she only has the problem one percent of the time!"

Patrick bit back the retort that it took only one "problem" for Lizzy to inflict permanent damage on someone else, as Charlotte's condition demonstrated.

When the isolation of the cabin, the absence of her friends in Paoli, or her inability to reliably cross a room without fearing a fall began to overwhelm her, Charlotte focused on her one goal: to get Lizzy safely to an age at which those who loved her could help her deal with and control her ability, and at which she could start living a normal girl's life in the world.

And Charlotte had already faced the fact that, despite temporary improvements in her condition, she would likely not be around to see the results of her efforts.

CHAPTER FIFTEEN

Ruby DiMano's alarm clock, a Westclox wind-up, jangled on her bedside table at its regular time: five-thirty. She slapped it off with an internal groan and pushed herself upright. Every Saturday and Sunday she asked herself why she set the alarm clock—these were her days off and she could have slept in, but sleeping in was not a practice with which Ruby was comfortable.

She pulled on the housecoat that was draped across the mahogany footboard of the bed and pushed her feet into fuzzy pink slippers that she had just gotten herself at the Kmart the weekend before. She went downstairs to the kitchen, filled her macchinetta with Illy, and put it on the stove to heat, then toasted a slice of bread from the Italian loaf she had bought at the market on her way home the night before. She ate her breakfast at the Formica table by the window, gazing out on the view of the alley and the backs of the houses on the next street, pretending to plan out her weekend.

There was, in fact, not much to plan—every weekend was largely the same. In the morning she would stop at the market to pick up food for Saturday night dinner at the home of her sister and brother-in-law, Opal and Tony Celucci. Saturday afternoon she would run whatever errands needed running: dropping off shoes to be re-heeled, picking up toiletries at the drugstore. If Opal had managed to schedule a Saturday appointment with one of the few of Tony's many doctors who were available on the weekends, Ruby might help Opal wrestle Tony into Ruby's Kia Rio—a process which often left Tony embarrassed, Opal in tears, and Ruby's thin mouth pressed even thinner than usual. For weekday appointments, with Ruby in the Poconos and their son Angelo usually at work, Tony and Opal were reduced to suffering through the whole humiliating process with an unsympathetic cabbie. If there were no doctor's appointments that weekend, then on Saturday afternoons Ruby and Opal would go to confession. Saturday night was dinner at the Celuccis' house, with Angelo sometimes joining them. Then, on Sunday morning, church.

Among all these activities would be cleaning and maintaining the Overbrook house that she had inherited from her parents. It was too big for one person, but she had no interest in taking boarders who would have the unsupervised run of the place while she was away during the week. Maybe it was time to think about selling—although she was sure the very thought sent her mother spinning in her grave.

Then Sunday evening, the house spick and span for its upcoming week of vacancy, Ruby would climb into the Kia for the drive back to the Ballards' house in the Poconos.

In an unusually small Italian family, Angelo Celucci had been the first-born—and then the only-born when Tony had broken his back in a fall at his job as a roofer. With their finances stretched to breaking to cover the medical bills, and the construction company legally absolved of responsibility since they had proven that Tony had had a beer with his lunch that day, the Celuccis decided that one child was all they could afford.

With Tony largely homebound and Opal spending most of her time caring for him, Ruby had taken Angelo under her wing. She thought back to the outings they used to take: to the zoo, to Chuck E. Cheese, once to Lancaster County to ride the Strasburg Railroad. She also thought back to one outing she had been especially proud to have thought of: to Philadelphia Park to watch the horse races. She had thought to encourage Angelo's budding interest in animals—there weren't many animals in their neighborhood, other than some feral cats—

and instead had wakened a burning passion for gambling.

She remembered the first time Angelo had missed dinner in favor of going to the races and, most terrible, the dinners he had missed because he was laid up with some injury inflicted by those bastards who worked for Anton Rossi—a man Angelo, for some reason, seemed to look up to.

And now he had found another man to look up to: Gerard Bonnay. Shortly after Ruby had started working for the Ballards—and, by extension, for Bonnay—he had put Angelo on the payroll. Bonnay told her that having a steady job might keep Angelo away from the bookies, but Ruby speculated that it was just a way of tightening his grip on her cooperation. Angelo described the position as an assistant. Ruby described it, to herself, as a gofer.

She had tried to warn Angelo away from Bonnay in a way she hoped would not come back to haunt her should Angelo choose to share his aunt's comments with his boss, but it made no difference. Angelo had seen the fancy house in Pocopson and the expensive cars, and had decided that Gerard Bonnay could do no wrong.

And he had no idea of the deal Ruby had made with Bonnay—in Ruby's opinion, a deal with the devil—to pay off that thirty-five-thousand-dollar gambling debt.

Late Sunday afternoon, Ruby folded the last article of clothing she needed for the coming week into her suitcase and snapped it shut. She lugged it downstairs and put it by the front door, then went to the phone in the kitchen and dialed a number. Gerard Bonnay answered after a few rings.

"Yes?"

"It's Ruby DiMano."

"Good afternoon, Miss DiMano. How are you doing?"

"I'm fine."

"Anything to report?"

"Mrs. Ballard is still doing the yoga and meditation with Lizzy."

"How does Lizzy seem to be taking to it?"

"Well, she's flexible, I can say that much for her."

He laughed. "Anything else?"

"Nothing much." She hesitated. "This week Mrs. Ballard started telling Lizzy to 'run away and hit your pillow' if she started to get mad. She said it once when I was there—I had moved some of Lizzy's toys so I could clean the floor and she started to get upset and said I had messed up the picnic, or something like that, and then her mother came in and said, 'Remember what I said, Lizzy: when you get mad, run away and hit your pillow.' I heard her say that to Lizzy a few times this week."

"And what did Lizzy do?"

"Well … she ran away and hit her pillow."

"And how did you feel?"

"Feel? I suppose it's as good a way as any to keep a child from misbehaving."

"No, I mean how did you feel physically?"

Ruby hesitated. "The same way I always feel."

There was a pause, then he cleared his throat. "It must be difficult having to take that long drive up to the Poconos twice a week, and then spending your weekends helping out your sister and brother-in-law. You say you feel the same as always, but how is that? Tired? Ever head-achy? You're dealing with a lot."

Having Gerard Bonnay ask after her health was such an unexpected turn in the conversation that Ruby was taken aback.

"It's not so much," she answered after a few beats.

"You feel fine?" Bonnay asked.

"Yes. Fine." There was no reply, so she added woodenly, "Thank you for asking."

"You'll let me know if the job starts becoming too much, if your health starts suffering, yes?"

Ruby was flummoxed. "I'll let you know," she said finally.

"Very good," said Bonnay. "Next week, same time?"

"Yes. Same time," said Ruby, and disconnected.

She sat gazing out the window into the alley, where the Sargento boys were squabbling over a basketball. Their father opened the back door, yelled, "Hush up, you two!" and banged the door closed as he retreated back onto the house. The boys trotted down the alley with the ball, no doubt moving their argument to the next block, out of earshot of their father.

Ruby turned and walked slowly to the front door, hauled the suitcase out onto the porch, and locked the door behind her. She headed for her car, steeling herself for the long drive ahead.

CHAPTER SIXTEEN

The next year, spring came to the Poconos late, but with a vengeance. The waterfalls in the area were rushing with snow melt, and peonies and daffodils were pushing up around the doorstep of the cabin. The beautiful weather brought to Charlotte's mind the garden she had put in at the Paoli house during Lizzy's first year—seven years ago now—and suddenly the longing to do some gardening hit her almost like a physical need. Patrick's mother was a gardener and Charlotte knew that the rickety shed in back of the cabin held an old bag of fertilizer and planting tools. She asked Ruby to drive her and Lizzy to a local market where she had seen plants for sale, and they picked up some bleeding hearts and sweet woodruff.

When they got back to the cabin, Charlotte made her slow way to the shed, Lizzy bouncing around her.

"I can do the digging," Lizzy said, then hummed a snatch of song.

"That would be great, sweetie," said Charlotte. She had been feeling a little better lately—in fact, had left her cane in the house—but she definitely wasn't up to turning over garden beds.

Lizzy turned the dial on the combination lock and wrestled the shed door open, then began poking around among the miscellany that had accumulated there.

"Don't touch anything, Lizzy," Charlotte said.

"Okay," said Lizzy. Pointing, she asked, "What's that?"

Charlotte looked. "That's Grampy's lawn mower."

"That's not a lawn mower," said Lizzy.

"It's an old-fashioned lawn mower. It doesn't have an engine, you just push it and the blades spin around and cut the grass."

"Let's see," said Lizzy.

Charlotte sighed and crossed the shed to the mower. She gave it a tug, expecting rust to have rooted it in place, but it rolled with ease, the blades making a whistling clank as they spun.

"Let me!" said Lizzy, trying to inch Charlotte aside.

Charlotte considered, then said, "Lizzy, this is a grown-up machine, so you have to act like a grown-up if you're going to use it."

"Okay," said Lizzy seriously.

Charlotte pointed at the handle. "This is the handle. This is the *only* place you can touch the mower. Do you understand?"

Lizzy nodded.

"Those things that spin when you move it are knives. They're what cuts the grass."

"Okay."

"So the handle is the only safe place to touch it," said Charlotte.

Lizzy nodded.

"Okay, go ahead and take hold of the handle."

Lizzy, who had backed away a little during this exchange, approached the mower again—with some trepidation, Charlotte was satisfied to note. Lizzy put a hand on each side of the handle.

"Now pull it—very slowly—out of the shed."

Lizzy leaned back a little and the mower rolled after her obediently.

"Watch behind you, you need to pull it down this little ramp."

Lizzy inched backwards down the ramp, pulling the mower.

"Good job, Lizzy," said Charlotte.

When the mower was on the grass, Lizzy said, "Now I'll

mow."

"Okay, just a little bit. And what do you have to remember about using the mower?"

"Only touch the handle," said Lizzy.

"That's right," said Charlotte.

Lizzy pushed the mower in a straightish line across the lawn, "like Dad," then wrestled it through a turn and came back to Charlotte. The high school boy who came by to plow during the winter and to mow in the summer was due in just a few days, so the grass was thick, but the mower must have been serviced recently because Lizzy could push it with relative ease.

"That's good, Lizzy," said Charlotte.

"I can do more," said Lizzy, surveying the yard.

"All right, one more."

"I could do a circle."

"All right, then we'll do some planting."

"Okay," said Lizzy, but Charlotte suspected that now that she had realized the possibilities for creative mowing, they might be at this for quite some time. She leaned against the side of the shed, suddenly tired. Perhaps the gardening would have to be postponed in favor of a nap, not likely to be popular with Lizzy once she was cranked up from the mowing adventure.

Lizzy mowed an oval around the perimeter of the lawn, then began an S-shaped path across the middle of the oval. She was moving at a pretty good clip, then suddenly stopped, looking down at her feet.

Then she let out a scream—not a childish shriek, but an adult scream that drained the blood from Charlotte's face in an instant.

Charlotte stumbled toward Lizzy. Her left foot caught in the grass and she fell, but not before she saw the blood on Lizzy's feet. Dear God, she had been looking right at her, how could she have run over her foot?

Charlotte was struggling to get to her feet when Ruby shot

out the back door, a dish towel gripped in her hand. Lizzy was still screaming, backing away from the mower, her eyes still fixed on where she had been standing. Ruby reached her and fell to her knees next to her, her eyes shooting from Lizzy's feet to the ground next to the mower. Her face tightened and she stood with surprising grace, sweeping Lizzy up in her arms. She carried her toward where Charlotte had fallen back on the grass.

"There, there, Miss, let's go to your mamma," she said. Lizzy's arms were locked around Ruby's neck and her face was buried in her shoulder. Ruby reached Charlotte and managed to kneel so that Lizzy's feet were on the ground. "Here we are, Miss, here's your mamma."

Ruby's scrawny shoulder did little to muffle Lizzy's screams. Charlotte tried to pry her arms from Ruby's neck.

"Oh my God, what happened? Is it her foot?"

"No, ma'am, I don't believe she's hurt. She hit a nest of baby rabbits."

"Oh, baby," Charlotte groaned. "Lizzy," she said loudly, "Lizzy, you need to let go of Miss DiMano."

Ruby dropped her arms from Lizzy's waist and tugged gently on her arms. "Miss, your mamma wants you."

A minute passed, then two, and Lizzy's screams gradually subsided into vast, hiccuping sobs. Eventually her arms loosened enough that Ruby could transfer her to Charlotte. Ruby stayed kneeling in the grass.

"Baby, baby," crooned Charlotte, stroking Lizzy's back.

Lizzy raised her head, her face smeared with tears and snot.

"Bunnies, Mommy. Baby bunnies!" And she hitched in her breath for what Charlotte feared would be a fresh round of hysteria.

"I know, sweetie, I know."

"That was just bad, bad luck, that rabbit building her nest in the middle of the yard like that," said Ruby. You would think they would build them off in the woods, where they could hide."

"Yes!" wailed Lizzy.

"But they hide them so good, you can't tell where you're going to come across one. Pretty near invisible."

Lizzy wiped her nose with her arm. "'Yes," she agreed.

"Yes, Miss, nobody could see a thing like that in this long grass."

Lizzy nodded her head and started to turn toward the mower and the nest.

Ruby shifted on her knees so she was between Lizzy and the nest. "Best not look, Miss. Looking won't help."

Lizzy looked to Charlotte for guidance.

"I agree with Miss DiMano, Lizzy, best not to look."

Lizzy took a long time to make up her mind, but eventually she nodded.

"Okay," she said sadly.

Ruby climbed to her feet, not quite so agilely this time. "Tell you what, Miss. You and me will go into the house the roundabout way, and I'm going to get you a cup of tea—tea's good for a fright. Then I'll come back out and help your mamma up."

Lizzy looked like she might be having second thoughts about looking at the nest, but Ruby pressed Lizzy's head to her own side, still blocking her view.

"You okay, Mrs. Ballard?" Ruby asked.

"Yes, I'm fine. I'm sure I can make it to the house myself if you can just keep an eye on Lizzy for a few minutes."

"Yes, ma'am," said Ruby, and started around the perimeter of the yard with Lizzy, eventually disappearing around the front of the house. In a moment, Charlotte could see some movement in the kitchen, then the blinds on the kitchen window went down.

Charlotte tried getting to her feet, but her left leg was numb. The most direct path to the back door would take her right past the nest. If she had to crawl, she didn't fancy having to crawl past that. She got herself arranged so that she would look relatively comfortable if Ruby looked out the window to check on her. In a few minutes, Ruby appeared at the back door with Charlotte's cane. She crossed the lawn and stopped by the nest, looking down for a few moments, then continued on to Charlotte.

She hooked her hands under Charlotte's arm. "Ready?"

Charlotte nodded.

"Up you go," said Ruby, and hoisted Charlotte to her feet. She put the cane in Charlotte's right hand and hooked Charlotte's left arm over her own shoulder. "Shortest way or roundabout?" she asked.

Charlotte looked toward the nest. "How bad is it?"

"Not pretty. I think she got two. There might be another couple in there, but I don't know if the mother will come back for them now."

Charlotte felt tears come to her eyes. "Poor little things."

"Yes, ma'am."

Charlotte realized Ruby was waiting to be told which route to take. "Shortest, I suppose," she said.

They started across the lawn, Ruby steering her a little to the right so that she would be between Charlotte and the nest. Like daughter, like mother, thought Charlotte, and gave a hiccupy little laugh. Ruby either didn't hear or chose to ignore it.

They got to the house and stepped into the cool dimness of the kitchen.

"I put her in the living room," said Ruby.

Ruby helped Charlotte into the living room where Lizzy sat, red-eyed but subdued, on the couch. In her hand was a mug with a tea bag string hanging over the side. "Hot tap water," Ruby whispered to Charlotte.

"I'm okay from here," said Charlotte. She undraped her arm from Ruby's shoulder and, leaning heavily on the cane, joined Lizzy on the couch. "How are you doing, baby?" she said, stroking Lizzy's hair.

"Okay," said Lizzy. "This tastes bad," she whispered

loudly to Charlotte.

"That was a quickie, Miss," said Ruby, taking the mug from her. "I'm going to make you and your mamma some proper tea now." She disappeared back into the kitchen.

Charlotte waited to see if Lizzy wanted to talk about it. After a minute, Lizzy said, "Can we take the bunnies to a doctor?"

"I'm not sure what the best thing to do is," said Charlotte. "Let me think about that for a minute." She would do anything to be able-bodied again, not to have to rely on Ruby for so much.

Soon they heard the kettle whistle, and a minute later Ruby came in, carrying a tray with two cups. She poured out a cup for Charlotte and put it on the table in front of her. There had been an unfortunate incident some weeks before when she had handed a cup of coffee to Charlotte and Charlotte had dropped it in her own lap. Ruby poured a few tablespoons of tea into the other cup and filled it the rest of the way with milk. She added a teaspoon of sugar and put that down in front of Lizzy.

"What do you say, Lizzy?" Charlotte murmured.

"Thank you, Miss DiMano," said Lizzy.

"You're welcome, Miss," said Ruby.

"Can we take the bunnies to the doctor?" asked Lizzy again.

Charlotte and Ruby exchanged looks. Ruby cleared her throat. "Two of them died, Miss, and taking them to a doctor wouldn't help." Lizzy's lower lip began to tremble again. Ruby continued, "I think two of them are okay. I'll move them to the woods where they'll be safe, and we'll have a funeral for the other ones."

Lizzy thought about this, Charlotte finding herself holding her breath. Finally Lizzy said, "Okay. Do we need a shoebox?"

"Yes, Miss, if you can find me a shoebox, I'll use that to move the live ones, and then we can use it for the funeral for the others."

Lizzy jumped to her feet. "Mom, can I have a shoebox from your closet?"

"Yes, baby," said Charlotte, and watched Lizzy run down the hall to the bedroom.

Charlotte turned to Ruby. "Thank you," she said.

"Yes, ma'am," said Ruby, and turned to go back to the kitchen.

"Ruby!" Charlotte exclaimed, suddenly frightened.

Ruby turned back to the room. "Yes, ma'am?"

"Do you have a headache? Feeling dizzy? Any changes in your vision?"

Ruby knit her brow. "Are you feeling all right, Mrs. Ballard?"

"Yes, I'm feeling fine. I'm wondering how you're feeling."

"I'm feeling fine, ma'am," said Ruby, and disappeared into the kitchen.

❖

After Ruby had moved the survivors to the woods and gingerly transferred the bodies of the victims to the shoebox, she found a shovel and a trowel in the shed, and she and Lizzy spent almost an hour digging the grave.

"Has to be deep enough that animals don't dig it up," said Ruby.

When they had put the shoebox in the hole and patted the dirt back over the grave, Lizzy stood back and surveyed their work. "It needs something."

"A marker?" asked Ruby.

"Yeah."

"We'll put our minds to that and see what we can come up with. In the meantime, you can stick that trowel in the ground so we can find it again."

Lizzy pushed the trowel in at the head of the grave.

"Now let's go in so I can get dinner started."

"Okay," said Lizzy, and she slipped her hand into Ruby's

as they crossed the lawn.

CHAPTER SEVENTEEN

That night, after Charlotte had tucked Lizzy in, she sat down on the edge of her bed. She had been rehearsing this all day.

"That was a very scary thing that happened today, wasn't it?" she asked.

Lizzy nodded, suddenly serious.

"Sometimes people do things that are completely an accident and something bad can happen even though the person didn't ever mean for anyone to get hurt."

Lizzy nodded again, her eyes tearing up.

"You never meant to hurt those rabbits, did you?" asked Charlotte.

"No!" said Lizzy, shocked.

"No, you didn't—it was totally an accident." She almost added, "It could have happened to anyone," but bit back the thought. That was not the message she needed to convey.

"But when someone has something very powerful—like a lawn mower—then they have to be extra, extra careful to make sure that no one gets hurt."

Lizzy nodded slowly.

"You know you have a special power, don't you, Lizzy."

Lizzy shook her head unconvincingly.

"Yes, you have a very special power, but also a very dangerous power."

Lizzy stared at her, eyes wide.

"You can do things to people with your mind."

Very slowly, Lizzy nodded once.

"Your mind is like that lawn mower—very sharp and very

dangerous if it isn't kept safe."

Again the nod.

"Lizzy, I need you to promise me that you won't use this power you have to hurt people. Do you remember all the conversations we've had about what to do if someone makes you mad?"

"Run away and hit a pillow."

"That's right. If anyone ever makes you mad, you need to run away from them. You can't let them upset you. Do you understand that?"

"Yes."

"I want you to say it back to me, Lizzy."

"Don't let anyone make me mad. And if they do, run away."

Charlotte leaned forward and hugged her. "That's right, sweetheart. That's the most important lesson of all. It's the lesson you need to remember all your life. Will you do that for me?"

"Yes, Mom," said Lizzy, and to Charlotte her voice sounded very grown up.

CHAPTER EIGHTEEN

Sunday mornings were usually Charlotte's favorite time at the cabin. She would cook a big breakfast—sometimes with Patrick's help, if she couldn't manage by herself—and she and Patrick and Lizzy would sit in the living room and watch cartoons or play Chinese checkers, Lizzy's new obsession.

That weekend, though, Lizzy had a cold and was grumpy and out of sorts. Charlotte herself was feeling bad, a pulsing throb behind her eye that even lying in her bedroom with the blinds drawn couldn't dull. She had thought that eating something might help and got in the mood for pancakes, but when she went to the refrigerator she found they were out of eggs.

Fine, she'd make oatmeal.

Patrick was drawn to the kitchen by the banging of pots and pans. He found Charlotte sitting awkwardly on the floor trying to get a pot out of the back of one of the cupboards.

"What are you doing?" he asked.

"I'm trying to get a pot for the damn oatmeal," said Charlotte. Charlotte never swore.

"Here, let me," said Patrick, and knelt beside her.

"I've got to at least be able to get a pot out of the cupboard on my own," said Charlotte, and then burst into tears.

"Oh, Lottie," he said. "Let's get you up."

He lifted her off the floor and set her down on one of the kitchen chairs. He sat in the chair beside her and took her hand.

"I wanted pancakes," she said, and then laughed sadly. "I sound like Lizzy."

"Then pancakes you shall have," he said.

"We don't have any eggs." She took a tissue out of her pocket and wiped her nose.

"I'll run out and get some," he said, then brightened. "And a newspaper! I haven't read an actual newspaper in forever."

She smiled wanly. "Thanks, sweetheart."

Patrick went upstairs to get his car keys, then popped his head into the kitchen on his way out the door. "You okay?"

"Yes."

"All right." He turned to go, then turned back. "Want me to bring Lizzy with me?"

"No, she's got a cold, I don't want her spreading it around," said Charlotte.

"Okay, I won't be long," he said. She heard the front door close and then his light tread on the front steps. It reminded her of college, when she would go to cheer him on in a game of pick-up basketball, admiring how graceful he was, how handsome he was. The car started up and she heard the sound of its engine as it receded down the road.

She sat at the kitchen table, looking out the big picture window onto the back yard. They had had many happy times there: Patrick grilling hotdogs, the table set with a plastic gingham tablecloth and blue and white plates; a nervous weekend when they had hosted Patrick's parents when they were visiting from Santa Fe, and his mother had taught Lizzy how to play marbles; the first time they saw a hummingbird visit the feeder that Patrick had brought up with him one weekend. But as she looked out at the cold, wet morning, the only scene that replayed itself with any vividness in her mind was the scene of Lizzy running over the rabbits' nest. Charlotte closed her eyes and pinched the bridge of her nose. It sometimes helped, but not today.

But sitting still was better than moving around, and she had actually started to doze off when she heard Lizzy's voice.

"Mom?"

She opened her eyes. Lizzy stood in the doorway in her

pajamas, flannel decorated with images of sock monkeys, holding her laptop. Patrick and Charlotte had gotten it for her for Christmas to help with her homeschooling. Her face was flushed and damp, wisps of hair stuck to her forehead.

"Oh baby, you don't look so good," said Charlotte. "Come here and let me feel your forehead."

Lizzy made her draggy way over to Charlotte and stood sullenly while Charlotte felt her forehead.

"How do you feel?" Charlotte asked.

"Okay," said Lizzy dully. Lizzy was the only child Charlotte had ever encountered who never admitted to feeling bad.

"Well, it feels like you have a fever," she said. "Maybe you should get back into bed."

"I don't want to," said Lizzy. Now she was sounding a little more typical. Charlotte sighed.

"Okay, fine. You're dad's going to be back soon with supplies and we'll have pancakes."

"Okay," said Lizzy. She put the laptop down on the table facing Charlotte. "Look what I found."

It was an animal adoption website, and Lizzy had pulled up the profile for a baby beagle.

Charlotte sighed. "Baby, we've talked about this before. We can't get a dog."

"Why not?" asked Lizzy, clearly not interested in the reason.

"Because you're not quite big enough to take care of a dog yet, and I can't help you, and we can't ask Miss DiMano to help with that."

"I am so big enough."

Charlotte was in no mood to have this conversation now. "No, Lizzy. We'll talk about it again when you're a little older."

"I never get to do anything normal!" Lizzy burst out.

The pain behind Charlotte's eye intensified fractionally. "Lizzy, I need to go lie down. I think you should go lie down, too, until Dad gets back."

"I can't have friends, I can't go to school, I can't do anything normal. If I had a dog, I could at least have someone to play with, but I can't even have a dog. It's not fair!"

The pain notched up another level and suddenly Charlotte realized that it wasn't just an intensification of her existing headache. This was turning into something new. The blood drained from her face.

"Lizzy, run away and hit your pillow," she said in a quavering voice.

"No!" yelled Lizzy. "I'm tired of running away and hitting my pillow!"

"Do it, Lizzy," said Charlotte through gritted teeth. "Do it now!" Then the pain spiked like a dagger being driven through her skull and she screamed.

Lizzy backed away, her face now as pale as Charlotte's. "No … no! Mom, I'm running away—I'm running away!"

CHAPTER NINETEEN

Lizzy turned and shot down the hall to her bedroom and slammed the door behind her. She ran to the bed and thumped her fist into the pillow, but now the anger was gone, replaced by an all-consuming terror. She ran back to the door and opened it a crack with a trembling hand. From the kitchen she heard the sound of groaning, and then a thump, like the time her mother had dropped a bag of flour on the floor and it had split, sending a white cloud across the room. It had struck them both as funny, and they had giggled as they cleaned up the mess.

She ran back to the kitchen to see her mother lying on the floor. Lizzy skidded to her side.

"Mom? Mommy?"

She patted her hand—her good hand—and Charlotte let out a low groan, but there was no other response.

Lizzy ran to the wall where an old princess phone hung, its curling cord looped and twisted. She pressed out her father's cell phone number, the buttons blurry in her tear-distorted vision.

"Hello?" he answered cheerfully.

"Daddy, Mom is …" She looked to where Charlotte lay motionless on the floor. "She's hurt." Lizzy swallowed. "I hurt her, Dad."

"Can I talk to her?" he asked, his voice tight.

Lizzy tried to go back to her mother but the tangled cord was too short. She let go of the phone and it banged off the wall. Lizzy leaned over her mother and shook her shoulder gently.

"Mom, Dad wants to talk to you."

There was no response.

Lizzy backed away from her and retrieved the dangling phone.

"She can't—" She choked on her tears. "She can't talk right now, Dad."

"I'm coming home right now, Lizzy, I'll be there as soon as I can. I'm going to call 911 and the ambulance will come and help your mom."

"Okay," she said, her voice trembling.

"Hold on, sweetie, I need to turn the car around." Lizzy heard a sound like the crunch of gravel and the muffled blare of a car horn, then her father was back. "I'm going to have to hang up for a minute to make the call, but if you need to talk to me before I get there, you just call me back, okay?"

"Okay."

"Sweetie, I want you to make sure the front door is unlocked so the ambulance people can get in. If they get there before I do, I want you to go to your room and lock the door, okay?"

"Okay."

"And don't come out until I get there, understand?"

"Yes, Dad."

"I'll be there as soon as I can."

"Daddy?"

"Yes?"

"I'm sorry."

CHAPTER TWENTY

The ambulance did arrive before Patrick, and the EMTs found the front door standing open and, just as they had been told, a woman unconscious in the kitchen. The caller had told the dispatcher that his daughter was autistic and would be greatly disturbed by having to interact with the emergency responders, and that she would stay in her room until he got there.

In fact, Patrick was afraid that something they might do to Charlotte—intubate her if she wasn't breathing, apply an electric shock to get her heart pumping if it had stopped—would make Lizzy angry with them, and his conscience couldn't afford any more casualties.

When he got to the cabin, one of the EMTs was working on Charlotte and another, despite Patrick's caution, was knocking lightly on Lizzy's bedroom door. When Patrick had taken the place of the EMT at Lizzy's door and the EMTs had gotten Charlotte onto the gurney and strapped in, they hustled her out to the ambulance, confirming that Patrick knew the way to the hospital.

He followed them a few minutes later, with Lizzy in the back seat—she refused to sit in front with him. When they got to the hospital, he didn't know what to do with her, still afraid of what effect her reaction to the situation might have on the people she would encounter there. He left her in the car with the promise that he would be back as soon as he had news about her mother.

The next hour was a nightmare of running from the emergency room to the parking lot and back, giving ridiculously optimistic updates on Charlotte's condition to the motionless, pajama-clad form huddled under a blanket in the back seat. Eventually, seeing no other option, he led Lizzy into the hospital. At a loss as to what else to do with her, he turned her over to one of the nurses, who asked her if she'd like to go to a room where there were toys to play with and books to read. She led Lizzy down the hall, Lizzy's hand resting limply in hers, Lizzy's swollen eyes on the floor.

It was late that night when the doctor told Patrick that there was no possibility of Charlotte recovering from the massive brain hemorrhage that had struck her. Charlotte's sister Marilyn had arrived by that time, and there was no debate about what needed to be done—Charlotte had been quite explicit.

"Would you like your daughter to be with her when we remove the life support?" asked the doctor. "Or would you like one of the nurses to wait with her in another room?"

It was another of those impossible logistical questions that seemed to comprise life with Lizzy. He kept his tear-filled eyes on Charlotte's gray face. "I don't know …"

Marilyn touched his shoulder. "I'll go sit with her, Pat."

"No, we can't let you do that—" he began.

"Patrick, she's not going to get mad at me. She's not going to get mad at anybody but herself."

Patrick nodded, and Marilyn slipped out the door.

CHAPTER TWENTY-ONE

After Charlotte's funeral, Patrick moved Lizzy into the Thorndale house, but it was ill-suited to keeping her off the radar. Patrick used the autism story again on his neighbors, but it was only a matter of time until someone who understood the actual symptoms of autism saw through that. Patrick asked the real estate agent, who had found the house in Thorndale when they needed to downgrade from their Paoli home, to look still further out along the rail line, for a place with a bit more privacy.

The agent found a house in Parkesburg: a nondescript two-story built around 1900. It was right on the road—not what Patrick had visualized when he thought of privacy—but it did include five acres of pasture and scraggly woods stretching out behind the house. As he wandered around the lot he realized that, on a busy road with no sidewalks, and with the surrounding houses having similar-sized lots, a chance encounter with a neighbor was unlikely. In fact, in all the years they lived there, Patrick never became friendly with—in fact, barely met—his neighbors. And in his rare and brief interactions with them, the topic of the girl, later a teenager, who lived at his house never arose.

When he realized the necessity of moving even further out from Philadelphia, Patrick assumed that Ruby wouldn't want to extend her train commute to the hour it took to get between Philadelphia and Parkesburg—the commute he would now be making to Penn. Much to his surprise and relief, she agreed to continue working for them. Patrick gave her a small raise—all he could afford—to help cover the added travel expense.

Ruby would now be home with Lizzy by herself, and Patrick considered what instructions he should give to both of them about how they should and shouldn't interact with each other. But Lizzy seemed loath to interact with anyone—even Patrick himself—and eventually he decided that he could rely on her self-isolation to keep Ruby safe. It was scarcely necessary to remind her what the consequences of an unpleasant interaction might be.

With his longer commute, Patrick was generally out of the house by seven in the morning and not home again until seven in the evening. He no longer had time to exercise, and he compensated by eating less, the result being that rather than gaining weight, he became gaunt.

He stopped seeing his old friends, claiming, quite truthfully, that he was too tired during the week and needed to spend time with Lizzy on the weekends. Even his monthly dinners with Owen at the Sleeping Owl had been suspended, although he was seeing Owen more now than ever.

Owen drove out to Parkesburg almost every weekend, not only to visit with Patrick, but also to provide some companionship for Lizzy. While Ruby was off on the weekends, Patrick and Owen would devise outings for Lizzy that they thought had little chance of stressing her or putting others in danger, the three of them comprising an unlikely looking group.

On those weekends, they picked their own strawberries at Highland Orchard, went on a wagon ride at Landis Valley, took Lizzy for carefully chaperoned trips to the outlets in Lancaster to replace the clothes she outgrew—whatever seemed unlikely to trigger an angry outburst. Years passed, and Patrick and Owen never witnessed Lizzy getting upset with another person, never sensed any harm coming to the people they encountered. If an interaction ever became even the least bit unpleasant, Lizzy would withdraw physically, or she would draw a deep breath and seem to withdraw mentally.

Patrick did his best to homeschool Lizzy, but he

recognized that her education was weirdly uneven, influenced by Patrick's own areas of interest. During the years they lived in Parkesburg, she became well versed in science, especially biology; read extensively about the Civil War, World War I, and World War II, but almost no other historical era; learned Spanish via online courses; and became fairly knowledgeable about software development practices.

Patrick floundered when it came to any discussion of literature, but he researched what children her age were reading and gave her the corresponding assignments. He soon found that she not only read the assigned books but ventured further afield on her own. Not only *The Adventures of Tom Sawyer*, but also *Innocents Abroad*. Not only *The Three Musketeers*—after which she went through a period of referring to Patrick as Athos, herself as Aramis, and Owen as Porthos—but also *The Black Tulip*. She loved science fiction and fantasy.

She taught herself to play chess and, after unsuccessful attempts to enlist Patrick and Ruby as opponents, played against her computer. She continued her practice of yoga and meditation.

Since the Parkesburg house wasn't walking distance from the train station, Patrick and Ruby worked out an arrangement to handle the transportation to and from the station. He drove his car to the station in the mornings, and she drove it back to his house when she arrived on a slightly later train. They did the reverse in the evenings. This also had the advantage of giving Ruby a vehicle to use during the day. After a few weeks at the Parkesburg house, when a delay in Patrick's train meant that they had been at the station at the same time, Ruby made a suggestion.

"If you'd pay for the supplies, I could do a little fixing up at the house for you," she said. "A little paint would help, and there are a couple of leaky faucets I could fix for you."

Patrick thought about the house to which he had brought his daughter, thought about the dinginess he had noticed when he first saw it but that had since become invisible to him when he got home exhausted from a day at work. It couldn't be a cheerful environment for Lizzy.

"Sure, that would be great, thanks," he said gratefully.

"You could give me a list of things you want done, what colors you want rooms painted," she said.

"Use your best judgement about the repairs," he said. "Lizzy can pick out the paint colors." He did some quick math in his head. "Let's say two hundred dollars a month for the materials, how does that sound?"

"That sounds fine."

The first week, Patrick arrived home to find the kitchen faucet no longer leaking and the entry hall a bright cherry red.

CHAPTER TWENTY-TWO

The year after Ruby began spending the weekdays in the Poconos with Charlotte and Lizzy Ballard, she had finally sold her row house in Overbrook and rented an apartment a few streets away. She had expected some resistance to the sale from Opal, but Opal's excitement over her share of the windfall trumped any reservations she might have had. She and Tony used the money to re-shingle the roof, upgrade the downstairs bathroom, and update the kitchen appliances.

Ruby had also sold off what seemed like most of the contents of the house, but there were some things she couldn't bear to part with, and there was no room for them in the Celucci's house, so her tiny apartment was crammed with dark, heavy furniture and bric-a-brac. In fact, the apartment felt more like a storage area, albeit an excruciatingly clean and tidy one, than like a home.

When the alarm clock went off that Saturday morning, she pulled on the housecoat that was draped across the foot of the sofa she now used as a bed and pushed her feet into balding mauve slippers. She passed from the room that doubled as a sitting room and bedroom to the kitchen, with a stop in the bathroom that, with the apartment not having a hallway, separated the other two rooms. If she had ever considered inviting a guest to her home, the idea of trapping them in the kitchen or sitting room were she to need to use the bathroom would have put the kibosh on that idea.

Normally her schedule was not much different than it had been before her move, although her Saturday afternoons were freer than they had been in the past, since she had stopped going to confession. Sunday morning would be church—she couldn't very well stop that without precipitating an awkward and ongoing argument with her sister. And Sunday afternoon meant her regular phone call to Gerard Bonnay, the weekly event that caused the knot in her stomach that started to form on Saturday. Was, in fact, forming even as she sipped her morning coffee that morning.

However, this weekend was special. It was Tony's birthday, and this morning's grocery shopping would be for steak, potatoes, and fixings for salad, plus the ingredients for a chocolate cake. After that she would stop by the drug store to pick up a birthday card.

That evening they baked the potatoes, wrapped in aluminum foil, on the gas grill that Ruby had bought Opal and Tony the year before. Then Angelo grilled the steaks— medium rare for the ladies, rare for the men—while Opal chopped carrots and radishes for the salad. They sang "Happy Birthday" and Tony blew out the twenty-nine candles that tradition dictated would top the cake of any family member over thirty.

After the meal, Opal stood with a groan.

"I can't believe I ate my whole steak! I thought we'd have leftovers for lunch tomorrow." She surveyed the others' empty plates. "But I guess not."

She began gathering up the dessert plates, but Angelo sprang up. "I'll get that, Ma, you wait here, you've been running around all day."

"No more so than usual," she said. "Plus, I need to make the coffee."

"I'll take care of that in a minute," said Angelo.

Opal raised her eyebrows, but sat down without protest.

Angelo stacked the dessert plates with a clatter and disappeared into the kitchen, with a wink at Ruby.

"Clearing the table? Making the coffee?" said Tony. "What trouble do you suppose that boy has gotten into now?"

"No trouble, I'm sure," said Ruby, smiling brightly.

Opal looked at her suspiciously. "And what's up with you?"

"Nothing," said Ruby.

"You're never that happy," said Opal.

They chatted for a minute, then Opal cocked her ear toward the kitchen door. "I do believe he slipped out the back door."

A horn honked from the front of the house.

"Maybe that's him," said Ruby, standing. "Let's go see."

"I don't know what's going on around here," said Opal, shaking her head. She got up from the table and, releasing the brakes on Tony's wheelchair, pushed him out of the dining room and to the front door. Ruby walked ahead of them to open the door.

When they stepped through, Angelo was at the curb, standing at the passenger door of a white Dodge Caravan, a wide grin on his face.

"Angie, what in the world ..." said Opal.

"It's for Pa," said Angelo. "It's from Aunt Ruby!"

Opal and Tony turned to Ruby, both their mouths open. After a long moment, Tony said, "You bought us a van?"

Angelo slid open the back door of the van. "Pa, come down and check this out!"

Opal, her mouth still open, wheeled Tony down the ramp that Ruby had had built two years before to supplement the rickety ramp they had in back. Ruby followed.

"Check it out," Angelo repeated. "There's a lift in back and you just sit in this sling and it lifts you right in!"

"No kidding," said Tony, examining the mechanism, wide-eyed.

"Give it a try, Pa, we just need to get this sling under you."

Angelo and Ruby positioned themselves on either side of the wheelchair, then lifted Tony while Opal slid the sling under him. Angelo attached the lift mechanism to the sling.

"Want to do the controls, Ma?" he asked.

"Oh, I don't know," said Opal. "You do it this time and I'll watch."

Angelo moved a lever and the mechanism rose, lifting Tony out of the wheelchair. Tony laughed. "It's like being on an amusement park ride."

"A very slow amusement park ride," said Ruby, her cheeks flushed and an unaccustomed sparkle in her eyes.

Angelo stopped the lift. "Then you just swing in." He pushed the arm and Ruby lifted Tony's feet and Tony swung smoothly into the car, over the passenger seat. "Then down you go," said Angelo, and lowered Tony onto the seat, then detached the sling.

There was silence for a moment, then Angelo said, "Now you and Ma can start going places again! What do you think, Pa?"

"Well, it's just … it's …" Tony dug in his pocket for a handkerchief and wiped his eyes quickly and blew his nose. "It's too much," he said to Ruby.

"Nonsense," said Ruby, and leaned over and gave him a peck on the cheek.

"Who'll drive it?" asked Opal. "It's huge!"

"Aunt Ruby learned to drive it," said Angelo. "And I can drive it. And I'll bet we can teach you to drive it, Ma."

"Good heavens," she said, her hand at her throat.

"Let's go for a ride!" said Angelo.

They loaded the wheelchair into the back of the van and locked up the house, then Angelo got in the driver's seat and Ruby and Opal climbed into the seats in back.

"Where do you want to go, Pa?" asked Angelo.

"I don't know …" said Tony. "Honey, is there somewhere you want to go?"

"It's your first time out not to a doctor's appointment in forever," said Opal, "you should pick."

"We could drive south on 95 and go past the city, see the skyline," suggested Angelo.

"Yes, that sounds nice," said Tony.

They drove in silence except for Angelo's whistling. Opal gazed around the spacious interior of the van, while Tony's eyes eagerly took in everything outside. They came abreast of Center City just as the sun was setting, the sky an indigo blue behind the skyscrapers, the last rays bouncing off the Comcast Center, Liberty Place, and the pyramid atop the Mellon Center. They passed the sports complex and the Navy yard, and against the darkening sky they could see the sparkle of the lights of the planes lining up to land at the airport.

Finally Tony broke the silence. "That's far enough, let's go home."

"We've got a full tank of gas, Pa—this baby could go for hours without a fill-up."

"That's far enough, Angie," his father repeated. "That's enough for today."

"All right," said Angelo with good humor, and turned around at Feltonville.

When they got back to the Celuccis' house, it was full dark. Angelo walked his mother through reattaching the sling, then showed her how to operate the lift.

When Tony was back in his wheelchair, he reached out his hand to Ruby. "That is the nicest thing anyone has ever done for me, Ruby. It *is* too much. But I love it."

Ruby's sister hugged her. "You're like a fairy godmother. That family you work for out on the Main Line must sure pay you well."

Ruby patted Opal's back and looked over to where Angelo stood next to his father, beaming at her. He gave her a thumbs up.

Angelo wasn't the only reason that Ruby DiMano had sold her soul to the devil.

That Sunday evening she had put off the call to Gerard Bonnay longer than usual—he had to ask her to hold while he excused himself from dinner with guests.

"It's better if you call me at the regular time," he said.

"Yes, I got held up."

"So, anything new to report about the girl?"

"No."

"Nothing?" said Bonnay, sounding irritated.

Ruby cast about for something to tell him—something to earn her keep—and was suddenly overcome by a wave of self-loathing.

"She's a good girl. Smart. Reads a lot," she said. After a pause she added, "Has a liking for bright colors."

"What?"

"She enjoys bright colors."

Bonnay waited for more, then said impatiently, "That's it?"

"Yes," said Ruby tiredly. "That's it."

"All right." She heard Bonnay sigh. "Regular time next week, correct?"

"Yes, regular time," said Ruby, and hung up the phone.

CHAPTER TWENTY-THREE

For one of Owen's regular weekend visits at the beginning of December, about a month before Lizzy's seventeenth birthday, Owen, Patrick, and Lizzy chose the Brandywine River Museum as their destination. They admired the giant decorated tree in the museum's atrium and exclaimed over the model railroad, then Lizzy became fascinated with the gallery of N. C. Wyeth book illustrations. After half an hour, Patrick and Owen announced that they were going to the museum's cafe for coffee. When they got there, they discovered that beer was on offer, and they retired to a table near the curved, floor-to-ceiling windows overlooking the Brandywine River with bottles from a local brewery, and a giant chocolate chip cookie for Owen.

"I can't believe you're eating a cookie with beer," said Patrick.

"I can't believe you're not. It's good, especially with dark beer." Owen broke off a piece of the cookie and held it out to Patrick. "Want to try?"

Patrick shuddered and shook his head. "I'll take your word for it."

They sat in companionable silence, gazing out at the river slipping slowly by between narrow borders of ice at its banks, and at a group of small children laughing and yelling as they climbed on the bronze cow statue near its bank.

"We watched *Miracle on 34th Street* the other night," said Patrick eventually.

"That's a classic," said Owen.

"Yeah. Not sure what got into her head that she picked

that, but now she's obsessed with going to New York City and seeing the sights."

"Ah," said Owen. After a pause he added, "Does she know it's not quite like that in real life?"

"Well, she started doing a lot of research on travel sites, and now she wants to see it for herself—the Rockettes, the Rockefeller Center Christmas tree, window shopping on Fifth Avenue."

"Just window shopping?"

Patrick shrugged. "I think so. Thank God she's not one of these kids who sees something and has to have it. Sometimes she just likes to see it."

Owen popped a piece of cookie in his mouth and chased it with a swallow of beer. "So, what are you going to do?"

Patrick sat back with a sigh. "I don't know. At first I said 'no' just out of habit. New York City stresses *me* out, and I've had a lot more opportunity to build up a tolerance for that kind of thing than she has. But she's so excited about it, I can't imagine she'd be likely to get angry at someone."

Owen raised his eyebrows. "In New York City?"

Patrick smiled weakly. "I know. But I feel like if that kind of situation started to develop, I could hustle her out of it."

"Maybe," said Owen, noncommittal.

Patrick sat forward and dropped his voice. "It's been nine years since Charlotte died, and you know how traumatic that was for her. I haven't seen any indication that she has ever used her ability to harm anyone since then. Ruby's been around for twelve years now, and there is no evidence that Lizzy has ever," his voice dropped further, "'squeezed' Ruby. In all the outings we've taken her on, she's never lost her temper. She's continued doing the yoga and meditation that Charlotte thought would help her calm herself." He turned to look out the window at the laughing children. "She's almost an adult now, and I feel like she's had adult-level self-control for a long time now. Hell, she's a lot more self-controlled than I am. How long can I keep her under wraps? I have to let her experience life eventually, don't I?"

Owen pushed the cookie away. "Yes," he said after a long pause. "I suppose so. But New York City? Shouldn't you start with something a little tamer?"

Patrick waved in the direction of the museum. "We just now left her alone with a bunch of unsuspecting potential victims, didn't we? We've let her go off on her own when we've taken her other places. And I'll be with her the whole time. I can watch out for situations that might upset her, and I can get her out of them if it seems too stressful."

"Maybe not trapped in a seat at Radio City."

Patrick nodded back. "Yes, maybe not that. Maybe more just walking around and seeing the sights."

"I always wanted to see the ice skating rink at Rockefeller Center."

"You could come along," said Patrick.

"No, this should be something just for the two of you," replied Owen. "I think it would be good for both of you to get away."

"I think so too."

"Are you going to stay overnight?" asked Owen, taking another bite of cookie.

"God, no. I actually thought about that briefly, but then I checked the hotel rates—they're crazy."

"Yeah, I can imagine, especially around the holidays. Are you going to drive up?"

Patrick shook his head. "No, that *would* be too stressful, at least for me. I figure we'll take the train. I think she'd enjoy that." He took a swallow of beer, a smile sparking his normally tired eyes. "Hurry up and finish your cookie, I want to tell her the news."

CHAPTER TWENTY-FOUR

Patrick bought tickets on the Amtrak Keystone train from Parkesburg to New York's Penn Station via 30th Street Station in Philadelphia. The morning of their departure, Lizzy was such a bundle of nerves that she had to use the bathroom twice before they could leave for the station. Patrick was glad that she was excited, but it also pained him to see her in such a state. For any other sixteen-year-old, the trip would have been only a moderate blip in a life filled with the school and sports and social events that had never been part of Lizzy's life.

The day was sunny, and relatively warm for early December. They drove from their house through the farmland that surrounded Parkesburg, then into the town itself. The station was tucked into a neighborhood comprised of an odd mixture of a few small stone structures left over from Parkesburg's first settlers, formerly imposing residences now broken into apartments, and more recent but more tired-looking houses on tiny lots. The station itself was equally bedraggled. On the outbound side was what could have been a charming brick station, but it was closed up, only its overhang protecting the passengers from foul weather. On the inbound side was a decrepit shelter, its metal structure rusted, its concrete footings crumbling.

Patrick parked in his usual spot on the outbound side. Although they would be leaving from the opposite track, he preferred the better-lit parking lot in anticipation of their after-dark detraining that night. They crossed under the tracks at Culvert Street and picked their way across the broken concrete of the inbound platform to where the train would take on passengers.

"It's …" Lizzy began. She looked vaguely dismayed. "… not how I expected," she finished.

Patrick silently rebuked himself. He used Parkesburg for his work commute because it was close to home and the parking was free, but for this outing he should have chosen the relative opulence of Exton, or even Downingtown.

"They're not all like this," he said. "If we have time, we should get out at 30th Street. Now that's a gorgeous station."

She nodded and examined their fellow travelers: a young man with a snake tattoo curling out of the neck of his T-shirt and a woman with hair in blonde dreadlocks. They carried camping-sized backpacks and were consulting a paper map.

Patrick and Lizzy waited in silence for a few minutes, then Lizzy asked, "Is there a bathroom on the train?"

"Yup," said Patrick. "Not fancy, but not bad."

Lizzy fidgeted for a few seconds, then whispered. "My stomach's sort of upset. I don't think I can wait." She nodded toward a Porta Potty in the parking lot of the outbound track.

Patrick glanced at his watch. Ten minutes. He wanted to ask if she could wait, but he knew that if she could, she wouldn't have asked.

"Okay."

They made their way back down the platform, down the steps to Culvert Street, under the bridge, up the steps on the other side, and across the parking lot, Patrick sensing every second ticking by. Missing the train would not be a good way to start the trip. They got to the Porta Potty and Lizzy pulled the handle, but then they saw that there was a padlock on the door.

She tugged futilely at the door. "Why would someone put a lock on it?" she asked, sounding a bit panicked.

Patrick shook his head. "It's Amtrak, who knows." He looked at Lizzy. "I could move the car to the other side and park it so you could go behind it."

She looked like she was going to cry from embarrassment.

"No, I'll wait," she mumbled.

They started back to the other platform. As they did, Patrick saw the light of the approaching train. He hoped Lizzy didn't notice—she didn't need to be any more stressed than she already was—but by the time they got to Culvert Street the train was pulling up to the platform. They broke into a jog, then ran up the steps to the inbound platform and toward the one open door where the conductor stood. The traveling backpackers were evidently already on the train.

"Holdin' the train for you," the conductor called to them.

They got to the door a few seconds later. Patrick was a little exhilarated from the run, and he glanced over at Lizzy with a smile, but her face was tense and unhappy. Patrick realized that if you had to use the restroom, running for a train might not be a preferred activity.

"Thanks," he panted when they reached the conductor, his temporary high further dampened by his realization of what poor shape he was in.

"Amtrak to 30th Street and New York City," said the conductor. "Quiet car to the right. Watch your step."

Patrick stood aside to let Lizzy go up the steps. "Let's go to the quiet car," he said, thinking that quiet might help calm her nerves.

They turned right, and almost immediately came to the restroom.

"Can I use the bathroom while we're in the station?" she whispered to him, her relief evident.

"Sure. I'll find us seats."

There were only a few other people in the quiet car, and Patrick took an aisle seat near the front of the car, letting a somewhat calmer Lizzy take the window seat when she emerged from the restroom.

Lizzy took off her red quilted parka and put on the Bose headset that Patrick had gotten her as an early birthday present. It had been expensive, but it screened out more of the potential irritants of the outside world than earbuds did. She fiddled with her iPhone and was soon tapping her fingers as she looked out the window. Patrick glanced over at the phone: "Christmas Wrapping" by The Waitresses. He smiled.

At Ardmore, a few more people entered the quiet car, including a fortyish woman in a mink-collared coat and a handbag decorated with the Prada triangle, accompanied by a younger woman who was pulling a wheeled bag. Prada slid into the seat behind Lizzy while the younger woman hoisted the bag onto the overhead rack with a grunt. Patrick had seen Prada on the train before, during his weekday commutes. He thought she usually continued on past Philadelphia—to New York City, he guessed.

Lizzy had switched from listening to Christmas music to perusing the websites of the places they planned to visit, her headset resting on her lap.

The ringing of a cell phone filled the car. "Yes?" said Prada, then, after a pause, "I thought I told you not to do that."

Patrick glanced over at Lizzy who was looking out the window.

"That's exactly what I knew would happen," said the woman in a loud and exasperated voice.

The conductor's voice came over the speakers. "30th Street Station in five minutes. Next stop: 30th Street."

"Well, I can't fix it if you keep going off script," said Prada, her volume rising a notch. "He went off script again," she said at a marginally lower volume, evidently to her traveling companion. Patrick heard some indistinct murmur in response.

Lizzy glanced back toward Prada. Others in the car were also throwing irritated looks at the woman.

Patrick turned in his seat. "Ma'am," he whispered. "This is the quiet car. No cell phone conversations."

The woman dropped the phone slightly from her mouth and said to Patrick, "Just calm down. We're practically at the station." She raised the phone to her mouth again. "No, I wasn't talking to you. You've got to figure out a way to fix this, it's your ass on the line."

Patrick looked back at Lizzy. Her face had blanched and her hands gripped the arms of the seat.

"Come on, Lizzy, let's go. Get your things together, we can step out for a breather on the platform when we get to 30th Street." It was the closest equivalent to "run away and hit your pillow" that Patrick could come up with in the close confines of the train car.

Lizzy disconnected her phone from the headset, slipped her phone into her pocket, and began fumbling with the headset cord, trying to roll it so she could put it back into its carrying case.

"Oh, for God's sake," said Prada. "I'm in the quiet car and this guy is making a big deal about me being on the phone. Come on," she said, evidently to her traveling companion. "We'll go to the next car so this guy doesn't have an aneurism." There was shuffling as the younger woman stood up to let Prada out. Prada got out of her seat, slung her bag over her shoulder, and walked down the aisle toward the door, thumping Patrick's shoulder with the bag as she passed. Lizzy kept her eyes down, fumbling with increasing franticness with the headset cord.

Patrick put his hand on hers. "Don't worry about it, honey. She's leaving. We can stay here."

The woman stopped near the door of the car and looked back at Patrick. "Now look who's gotten all chatty in the quiet car."

Lizzy looked up at her and a flush began spreading from her neck into her cheeks.

Patrick took her hand. "Let's go to the other end of the car," he whispered.

The woman shook her head, "This certainly is a shitty start to what's promising to be a shitty day," she said, in a voice just loud enough for everyone in the car to hear. She winced slightly and pressed the hand not holding the phone to her temple. "I'll call you back," she said into the phone, and dropped it into her bag.

Patrick was standing in the aisle. Lizzy grabbed her coat and knapsack and scrambled out after him, but now their way was blocked by Prada's young traveling companion, who was trying to get the wheeled bag out from the overhead rack.

"If you could just let my daughter by," said Patrick, "then I'll help you with that."

"Oh, I don't think so," said Prada, starting back down the aisle toward them. "Sally, don't let him mess with the briefcase. Who are you, anyway?"

Patrick and Lizzy were trapped, Sally behind them and Prada in front.

"Okay, fine, I won't touch your briefcase." He turned back to Sally. "Just let us by," he pleaded.

The train jolted, sending Prada stumbling toward Lizzy. Lizzy brought her elbow up in an instinctive move to fend off the woman, catching her in the breast.

"Goddamn it," Prada swore. "Bitch! I can't believe—" The rest of her sentence was cut off in a choking cough. Her hands came up to her temples. "Oh my God," she groaned.

Patrick turned to his daughter. "Lizzy, stop it," he hissed.

Lizzy's eyes were huge, her face white. "I can't!"

"Stop it now!"

"Dad, I can't," she cried, her voice cracking.

"What do you mean?" asked Sally. "What can't you stop?" Her eyes, too, were wide.

"Oh my God," cried Prada again, her voice rising tremulously. "It hurts!" She staggered and dropped to her knees.

"Now arriving at 30th Street Station," came the conductor's voice over the speakers. "If you are leaving the train at 30th Street, please check to make sure you have all your belongings. 30th Street Station is next."

People near the stricken woman shrank back in their seats, while people at the back of the car stood, trying to see what was happening.

"Honey, we just have to get past her and then we'll be out," Patrick whispered to Lizzy. Then, in a louder voice, he declared to the crowd, "She's not doing anything to her. That woman obviously gave herself a heart attack!"

He heard the squeal of the brakes and a moment later the train left the brightness of the sunny Saturday morning for the darkness of the tunnels under the station. Prada tipped forward to the floor of the car, then pulled her knees up into a fetal position, a thread of sound emanating from between her clenched teeth. Patrick stepped over her prone form, pulling Lizzy after him toward the front of the car.

"What did you do to her?" Sally yelled after them, half-defiant, half-terrified.

"Don't be ridiculous," said Patrick, trying to keep his voice steady. "We didn't do anything to her."

The door to the car whooshed open and the conductor started in, then stopped as he took in the scene. "What's happening?" he asked loudly.

Someone in the back of the car yelled, "That woman is having a heart attack!"

"That's Lucia Hazlitt, and it's not a heart attack, it's her head!" cried Sally. "That girl is doing something to her!"

The car was almost at a stop, and Patrick managed to squeeze past the conductor and pull Lizzy along with him. "We'll go get a doctor," he said to the conductor.

"What? No, just step out onto the platform, I'll radio for help." The conductor looked down at the woman on the floor, who was no longer making any sound, then back at Patrick. "What's that young lady talking about?" he asked.

"I have no idea," said Patrick.

The train, with a final jerk, came to a stop.

Other people began to squeeze past Prada and the young woman, pushing Patrick and Lizzy from behind. The doors between the cars were open, and Patrick could see the people in the next car craning to get a look at what was happening. He heard someone say "… bomb?" and suddenly the passengers in the next car began pushing toward the door of their car.

The conductor pulled a radio from his belt. "We have a medical emergency on the Keystone, the quiet car. We just pulled into 30th Street. We need EMTs."

The train doors opened and passengers spilled out of the car onto the platform and surged toward the stairs to the concourse, carrying Patrick and Lizzy along with them. Being jostled in the middle of the scrum, Patrick heard the conductor's yell—"Hey, you there with the girl, come back!"—but, gripping Lizzy's hand tighter, he pulled her along, keeping his head down. As they reached the stairs, they saw two transit police starting down.

He and Lizzy scrambled up the stairs with the other passengers. When the crowd burst out of the stairway onto the concourse, they lost their forward momentum and came to an untidy stop next to the clacking TRAIN INFORMATION board.

Patrick pulled Lizzy into the center of the crowd, but then realized that people were glancing their way, whispering to their neighbors and gesturing with their heads, backing away almost imperceptibly. He bent toward Lizzy.

"Let's go, honey."

Lizzy nodded, her eyes wide and wild.

Still holding her hand, Patrick pulled Lizzy across the concourse, their steps echoing alarmingly in the cavernous space. They had almost reached the exit when he heard someone call, "They're over there!"

He glanced back and saw two more transit cops striding toward them.

He pushed through the doors, almost bumping into a middle-aged man and teenage girl standing just outside. There was a line of taxis at the curb and Patrick almost heaved a sigh of relief, but then saw the longer line of waiting taxi customers. He looked around frantically—what options did they have? He considered running away from the station, but realized they would never make it through the rank after rank of traffic that circled the station like boats in a concrete moat. Could they get to the edge of the huge building and slip out of sight? Surely the cops would be at the door before they could get there.

A taxi was the only option.

Patrick wrapped his arm around Lizzy's shoulders. "Stay with me, honey, okay?"

Lizzy nodded, her eyes still determinedly on the ground.

Patrick walked quickly toward the front of the line. "Can my daughter and I get a taxi? We need to get to the emergency room right away." *Please don't let anyone be unpleasant*, he thought—*for their sakes.*

A pair of twenty-something women turned from the open door of the first taxi. One of them looked Lizzy up and down skeptically. "What's wrong with her?"

"Jeez, give 'em a break," said a redheaded man who was next in line. "Look at her."

Patrick himself glanced over at Lizzy. With her ashen face and unsteady legs, she did look like she could be in need of emergency medical assistance.

"I've been waiting here for fifteen minutes," said a middle-aged man who was in line behind the redhead.

"Good heavens," said a tall man who was half of what Patrick assumed was a gay couple who was next in line. He detached himself from the line and headed toward the first taxi. "Everybody, we can either each wait an extra sixty seconds, or we make this young lady and her father wait an extra fifteen minutes." He was already shepherding the young women away from the taxi door. "That's very kind of you," he said to them cheerfully.

"Thanks so much," Patrick mumbled as he propelled Lizzy into the back seat and slid in after her. He risked a glance back. The transit cops had emerged from the station and were talking to the two people Patrick and Lizzy had almost bumped into at the doorway. Patrick realized why they had stopped. The man was white, tall, and about his age, while the teenager with him had long hair—although darker and curlier than Lizzy's—and, like Lizzy, was wearing a red jacket and jeans.

"Good luck!" called the tall man, as he closed the door behind them.

"Where to, Bud?" asked the cabbie, activating the meter.

"Penn U Hospital emergency room," he said. "As fast as possible."

"Is your girl hurt?" asked the cabbie, looking at Lizzy with concern.

"No," said Patrick, and squeezed Lizzy's hand. "It's her mother. We just found out she was taken there."

"No problem, Bud," said the cabbie, and pulled out at a brisk pace.

CHAPTER TWENTY-FIVE

Patrick had thought that sending the cabbie to the Penn U emergency room was a stroke of genius, since it explained both his own rushed demeanor and Lizzy's incipient hysteria bubbling just beneath the surface. But as they made the short trip to the ER, he realized he had sent them to the very place that the EMTs, likely with police in tow, would be bringing the woman from the train. The hospital was an acceptable destination for the cabbie, but they would need to find somewhere else to go once they arrived.

How could he have thought taking Lizzy into public was safe? She was a sensitive girl, and he should have seen that the years at home—protected by her parents and Owen and even Ruby—hadn't equipped her to deal with even the minor annoyances of everyday life. He had thought he couldn't keep her under wraps forever, but maybe that's exactly what he needed to do. He had a sudden, stomach-lurching vision of his and Lizzy's future: Lizzy in her forties and himself in his seventies, maybe tended to by an eighty-something Ruby—moving further and further down the Keystone rail line, forever seeking that out-of-the-way location where no one would question the old woman and her even older father who never left their house, never spoke with their neighbors.

The cabbie got them to the Penn University emergency room in less than five minutes. He pulled up in front of the ER doors and Patrick stuffed a twenty through the slot in the partition.

"Thanks," Patrick said as he jumped out of the car and pulled Lizzy out behind him.

"Good luck, buddy," called the cabbie after them.

They stepped into the ER waiting room. In one corner, a boy sat with his head tipped back, a woman holding a wad of paper towels to his nose. In another corner, a group of hungover-looking frat boys were joking with one of their group whose leg was propped up across the chairs next to him. In another, a baby squalled in its mother's arms.

"What happened to her, Dad?" asked Lizzy in a trembling voice.

"Not yet, honey, let's find somewhere we can regroup."

He glanced back out the ER doors. The cab had pulled away, but he could hear the approaching wail of a siren. He considered his options. They were only a few blocks from his office at Penn, but he had no desire to go somewhere he was known. They could go to a coffee shop—plenty of those to choose from near the university campus—but Lizzy's obvious distress would attract too much attention. It was warm for December, but too cold to find a bench to sit on while Lizzy pulled herself together.

Then he thought of the William Penn Hotel, which served well-heeled visitors to the campus and the Annenberg Center. They could get a room there and then decide what to do.

"Come on, sweetie, we're going to go somewhere we can sit down and rest. And think."

They walked the half mile from the hospital to the hotel. Patrick let go of Lizzy's hand, thinking that a man holding the hand of a teenage girl might not have looked odd in a hospital emergency room but would likely attract notice on the streets of West Philly. But he held her elbow, giving her what he hoped was a reassuring squeeze now and then. His hold also enabled him to steer her around obstacles since she was keeping her eyes determinedly on the ground immediately in front of her feet.

When they got to the hotel, he left Lizzy on one of the couches in the lobby while he checked in. At the desk, he thought briefly of paying with cash, but that seemed like an attention-getting oddity, so he used his credit card. He also thought that preserving what cash he had was wise since he had no idea what the coming hours would bring.

When he had gotten the key to a room on the fifth floor, he went to the lobby to retrieve Lizzy. She was huddled on the couch, her hands trapped under her thighs, her head still bent forward. He was surprised and somewhat impressed that she had thought to put a magazine in her lap, so that from a distance it appeared she was reading, but he was certain she was not seeing the brightly colored ad for a Caribbean cruise that lay open in front of her.

When they got to the room and the door closed behind them, Lizzy broke into jagged sobs.

"Daddy, what happened to her?"

He enclosed her in a hug. "I don't know, honey. We'll find out."

"I killed her!"

He rubbed her back. "We don't know what happened to her. And whatever did happen, it's not your fault."

"It was! They're going to come get me!"

"Shhh, honey, shhh. I'm going to make sure nothing happens to you."

When Lizzy's sobs began to trail off, Patrick eased her off his shoulder, holding her upper arms. He bent so he could look in her eyes. "Lizzy, I'm going to see what we can do next. I need to leave you here for just a little while. Okay?"

"Okay. Let me know what I need to do."

He smiled at her. "I need you to watch some TV and eat some snacks from the fridge. But don't open the door to anyone except me. And don't answer your phone unless it's me. Understand?"

She nodded disconsolately. "What are you going to do?" she asked.

He had just that moment decided himself. "I'm going to talk with Uncle Owen."

CHAPTER TWENTY-SIX

The Keystone train was readying for departure from 30th Street after the delay caused by the medical emergency. Two Amtrak cops—Wisnewski and Hersey, according to their badges—stood on the platform.

"You hear who it was?" Wiz asked Hersey.

"No, who?"

"Lucia Hazlitt."

"Who the hell is Lucia Hazlitt?"

"That lady lawyer who's defending Dollar Slash."

"Who the hell is Dollar Slash?"

"Man," sighed Wiz. "Don't you get out at all?"

A young man sporting a snake tattoo stepped out of the train and, seeing the cops, walked over to them.

"Hey, I think the girl who was sitting in the seat a couple of rows in front of us dropped this," he said, handing a headset to Wiz.

"Okay, thanks, we'll get it to lost-and-found," he said.

"I think it was the girl who knocked down that bitchy woman."

"Oh, yeah?" asked Wiz. "Good to know, we'll take care of it."

After the tattooed man returned to the train, Wiz showed the object to his partner. "Check it out—Bose. Expensive," he added for the older man's benefit.

Hersey took the headset from him and turned it in his hands. "Lizzy Ballard."

"What?"

Hersey pointed to a label on the inside of the headset.

"Says 'Lizzy Ballard,' and a phone number."

"They're looking for the girl who left the scene," said Wiz.

"I'd better show it to the boss," said Hersey.

CHAPTER TWENTY-SEVEN

Patrick took the elevator back down to the lobby and found a secluded couch from which he could make his call. He pressed the speed dial for Owen.

The phone rang a few times and he was considering what message he could leave on voicemail when Owen picked up.

"Hello?"

"Owen, it's Patrick. There's been a problem and I need some help." He gave Owen the barest details about where he and Lizzy were, and why.

"Jesus," breathed Owen. "I can be there in half an hour."

"That's great. I'll meet you in the lobby."

They ended the call and almost immediately Patrick's phone rang. Must be Owen calling back about something.

He almost hit the button to answer and then hesitated. If it was Owen, why didn't his name appear on the caller ID?

He let it ring to voicemail, and then picked up the message.

"Hello, this is Officer Hersey from the Amtrak Police Department, I'm calling for Lizzy Ballard. We found a very nice headset that I think belongs to her. Can you give us a call so we can get it back to her?" He left a number.

Damn it. Patrick remembered Lizzy fumbling with the headset cord, remembered pulling her from the seat to get her away from that bitch on the train. She must have dropped it then. Lizzy had wanted to put her own cell number on the headset in case she left it somewhere—she was a trusting soul—but he had insisted they use his number on the label. Thank God.

But the police had already found something that put Lizzy and him at the scene, and he doubted whether the cop's only interest was getting the headset back to its rightful owner.

He pressed the speed dial for Lizzy. She answered on the first ring.

"Dad?"

"Hey, Lizzy, how's it going?"

"I can't find my headset," she said, sounding panicky. "I think I dropped it on the train."

"I know. Someone found it and called me."

"It has my name on it!"

"I know, that's how they knew to call me—your name and my number, remember?"

"Oh, right. Dad, are they looking for us?"

"They're probably wanting to talk with anyone who was on that train car. I wouldn't worry about it, we'll get the headset back."

There was silence for a beat. "I don't really need the headset back. Can we go home?"

Patrick sighed. "I don't know yet, honey. Owen's coming to the hotel and we're going to talk it over. We'll come up when he gets here."

"Okay. Don't be too long."

"I won't. Love you."

"Love you too," she said, and hung up.

Owen showed up only a few minutes after the thirty minutes he had estimated. He spotted Patrick and crossed the lobby, his breathing rapid and his face flushed. When he got to the couch, he dropped into it with a grunt.

"So?" he asked, unwrapping a red scarf from his neck.

Patrick felt a little of his resolve melt away, as if the presence of his friend had relieved him of some of the weight now on his shoulders. He scrubbed his hands across his face, then looked around to make sure no one could hear them.

"Lizzy 'squeezed' someone on the train."

Owen sat forward as far as his large paunch would allow.

"Was it serious?"

"Yes, I think so. She was unconscious when we got off the train."

Owen sat back. "Jesus Mary and Joseph."

"And Lizzy dropped her headset on the train—I just got a voicemail from the cops saying they had it and wanted us to call."

Owen groaned.

Patrick glanced around the lobby again, and leaned closer to Owen.

"Owen, I can't imagine a court convicting a teenage girl of causing someone to have a stroke—other than the normal 'strokes' most teenagers give the adults around them—but even if the justice system can't pin blame, who knows who else will develop an interest in Lizzy if the rumor gets out. Charlotte—" He stopped, his throat closing over a sob. In a moment, he continued. "Charlotte was so intent on keeping Lizzy out of the hands of people who would only care about the 'squeeze,' it killed her." He rubbed his eyes. "Maybe it would have been better to have put Lizzy away somewhere safe. Where she couldn't hurt other people. If we had done that when we first knew, Charlotte would still be alive, and the woman on the train would be going about her bitchy life with no idea what she had avoided."

Owen laid a hand on Patrick's knee. "Pat, I'm afraid for what would happen to Lizzy if we let people know what she can do." He sighed. "We need to keep Lizzy safe from the rest of the world, and we need to do a better job of keeping the rest of the world safe from Lizzy. She is remarkably self-controlled for her age, and I think we can keep trying to help her control this ability. And if she can't control it, we need to isolate her more than we've been doing up until now."

"The woman on the train was being such a jerk—" started Patrick angrily.

"I'm sure she was, but life is full of people being jerks—we can't risk people being hurt, or even killed, if they piss

Lizzy off."

"I could take her back to the Poconos, I guess," said Patrick.

"But that doesn't solve the problem of the police being after you," said Owen.

Patrick ran his hands through his hair. "I don't know what to do about that."

"We'll go to Lansdowne," said Owen, "and decide what to do."

CHAPTER TWENTY-EIGHT

Fifteen minutes later, after a trip to the men's room to splash cold water on his face and his red-rimmed eyes, Patrick went upstairs to get Lizzy, while Owen went to retrieve his car. Lizzy's nerves were on a hair trigger; she nearly backslid into hysteria when she saw Patrick's condition, but hearing that they were going to Owen's house seemed to buck her up. Patrick left the key in the room and checked extra carefully to make sure nothing was left behind. He briefly thought of wiping fingerprints off the surfaces they were likely to have touched, but then he thought of the credit card he had used to check into the room and discarded the idea. They went downstairs and waited under the green awning at the entrance, listening to a Salvation Army Santa ringing his bell just down the street.

In a few minutes, Owen pulled up in his Toyota SUV. Patrick opened the back door for Lizzy and then climbed into the front seat.

"Hey, Uncle Owen," said Lizzy dully.

"Hey, Pumpkin," said Owen. "How are you doing?"

"Okay, I guess," she said, sounding none too convincing.

"Your dad and I thought it would be best if you two stayed at my house for now," said Owen.

"Okay."

Lizzy turned her gaze out the window and Owen and Patrick exchanged concerned glances.

Owen drove them to his house in Lansdowne and got them settled in—Patrick in the kitchen making coffee and Lizzy on the couch in the living room with her phone. Then he went upstairs to his office to see if anything had been reported in the local news about the incident. He powered on his wireless mouse, logged onto his computer, and did searches for various combinations of *philadelphia, amtrak, 30th street station, passenger,* and *medical emergency,* specifying entries within the last twenty-four hours, but found nothing. He switched the mouse off, pushed in the desk chair, and squared up the blotter with the edge of the desk.

He returned to the living room to find Patrick standing by the window with his coffee cup on the table beside him, and Lizzy still on the couch, both typing into their phones and no doubt doing searches very similar to Owen's.

"We need to know what happened, and it's likely that we won't find out for a while," said Owen. "Why don't we watch a movie or two to pass the time?"

Owen and Patrick decided on a binge viewing of *Lord of the Rings* and Lizzy agreed listlessly, although when Frodo and his compatriots were attacked by Orcs, it appeared that the story might actually be distracting her from the situation.

As they neared the climax of *The Fellowship of the Ring,* Patrick's phone buzzed. He glanced at the display and hit Ignore, casting a meaningful glance at Owen over Lizzy's head. After the second call, he turned the phone off.

Lizzy stared intently at the television, her arms crossed over her chest.

While Owen queued up *The Two Towers* and Lizzy put a bag of popcorn in the microwave, Patrick pulled out his phone and powered it up. After a moment, he swore under his breath.

"Damn it!"

Owen turned. "What?"

"The woman on the train. She died." He passed Owen his phone with a browser open to phillychron.com.

Philadelphia Chronicle
"Hazlitt Dead of Stroke"
By Lincoln Abbott

Lawyer-to-the-stars Lucia Hazlitt, 42, suffered an apparent stroke on the Amtrak Keystone train this morning as it arrived at 30th Street Station. Hazlitt was traveling from her home in Ardmore to New York City, where on Monday she was scheduled to attend the arraignment of rapper Dollar Slash on drug charges. She was taken to the emergency room at William Penn University Medical Center and died shortly thereafter.

No stranger to controversy, Hazlitt took Dollar Slash's case, which other attorneys had described as "hopeless," suggesting recently that she had evidence to present that would exonerate her client. "He's being persecuted because he's rich and black, the favorite target of the white aristocracy of the judicial system," she said earlier this week.

According to family members, Hazlitt did not have any conditions that would lead to a stroke. Sally Lieberman, an assistant to Hazlitt who was accompanying her to New York, said that Hazlitt was accosted by a young woman on the train, and that the young woman's traveling companion, a middle-aged man, had displayed unusual interest in the briefcase in which the material for Dollar Slash's case was being transported to New York. Hazlitt's family as well as her partners in her firm Wright Hazlitt Blaine are already demanding that authorities investigate her death as a possible criminal act.

Amtrak police are asking two of the passengers, identified as Patrick Ballard, 48, and his daughter, Elizabeth Ballard, 16, to contact them at the number at the end of this article to share any information they might have about the situation.

Cab driver Jake Thalheimer reported that he drove a man and young woman matching the Ballards' descriptions from 30th Street Station to the William Penn University emergency room this morning. It's possible that the Ballards are related to Hazlitt and were following the ambulance to the hospital, but the timeline of events is not yet clear.

The article included a photograph of Patrick and Lizzy, a still taken from the station's security cameras. Lizzy's face was partially hidden, turned back to the concourse as they passed through the station's foyer to the entrance, but Patrick's was clear, his expression grim.

"That was Lucia Hazlitt?" groaned Patrick. "Holy shit. I heard the woman on the train with her say a name, but I didn't hear what it was."

"Not good," said Owen.

Patrick fell back on the couch. "Damn it. They don't really think that we're related to Lucia Hazlitt, do they?"

"I doubt it. The police are probably just feeding the reporter information to make it seem safer for you to turn yourselves in to them. Not outright accusing you of anything."

"What's that?" asked Patrick, pointing to a video link in the article.

Owen clicked on the link. A video loaded showing a heavy man with a comb-over. Patrick recognized the doors of the Penn University emergency room in the background. A banner across the bottom of the screen read: *Lucia Hazlitt's Law Partner Charles Blaine.*

"The papers in that briefcase were vital to our defense of Mr. Slash. I have no doubt that the plan was to create a diversion to enable the briefcase to be stolen. A diversion that evidently included physically incapacitating Lucia. I want the police to speak with every person on that train car—and I *especially* want them to speak with the man and woman involved in the altercation."

"Altercation?" hissed Patrick. "What the hell is he talking about?"

Owen ran his fingers through his hair. "I don't know. Maybe just grandstanding. Whipping up some support for Hazlitt and her client."

"They're making it a witch hunt," said Patrick. "They're

making us look like criminals. And we can't stay here with you—that would make you an accessory, or whatever they call it."

"Well, let's not do anything hasty, I can't imagine waiting another hour or two is going to make much difference at this point." He glanced toward the kitchen. "Should we tell her when she comes back?"

But at that moment Lizzy appeared in the doorway with her phone in her hand, her eyes wide, her face white.

"Daddy," she began tremulously, and then burst into tears.

CHAPTER TWENTY-NINE

Gerard Bonnay was in his office, sipping a mid-afternoon espresso. He was looking for a Christmas present for Louise—he had the Tiffany website open and was scrolling through a selection of sapphire earrings. He knew she would say all the right things when she opened her gift on Christmas Eve, albeit in her own brisk way, but Gerard suspected that almost any gift—Tiffany earrings or a home manicure kit—would elicit the same response. Well, perhaps not a home manicure kit, he thought with a small smile, and took a sip of his coffee.

Louise Mortensen had joined Vivantem twenty-five years before, when Gerard was looking for a forward-thinking head of research for his nascent business. She was in her mid-thirties—a couple of years older than Gerard—and had already made a name for herself in the fertility research field. Gerard was not a physician, but he was familiar enough with the science to be impressed by her groundbreaking ideas, as well as her single-minded focus on her profession.

The multi-hour interview in Gerard's office continued that evening over drinks and dinner. A cocktail and half a bottle of wine later, Dr. Mortensen was speaking somewhat more openly and enthusiastically about her cutting-edge research, although Gerard could notice little other change in her behavior. After dinner, Gerard escorted her to the lobby of the hotel where she was staying—she had flown in from Atlanta for the interview—fully expecting to be invited upstairs to her room, but she gave him a firm handshake and walked resolutely, if a tiny bit unsteadily, to the elevators. He offered her the job the next day.

A year later Louise Mortensen was a full partner in Vivantem, and a year after that they were married. And during that time, she opened up a great deal more about her research.

She was fascinated by what science offered in the way of molding the next generation—and what better way to put that science to effect than via fertility treatments. Eventually she divulged to Gerard that, before coming to Vivantem, she had experimented with treatments intended to produce babies with exceptional hearing or unusual stamina or extraordinary mathematical abilities. However, by the time Gerard hired her, she had turned her attention to telepathy. She felt sure that, with the right combination of genetic background and chromosomal tinkering, she could produce a person who could read minds. What would be more illuminating than enlisting one of those children, once they had grown to adulthood, to delve into the thoughts of her colleagues and competitors? And weren't they all really competitors?

For Louise, the thrill was in the chase: for knowledge and precedence, if not for prestige, since no one but Gerard would ever know. But for Gerard, the thrill was in what could be done with such a power. How much faster could Vivantem expand if he knew what was in the minds of his own colleagues and competitors? What couldn't he and Louise do if they knew what the power brokers around them were thinking?

As he waited for the results to show themselves in the growing population of Vivantem babies, he contemplated where this unexpected boon could take him. At first, the arena he imagined was his business—expanding Vivantem to the West Coast, perhaps internationally—but then that began to seem like too limited a vision. Why not politics? Why not aspire to the highest and most powerful position of all?

Those dreams had to survive the disappointment of the early experiments, which didn't seem to produce any results— one child after the other, all seemingly completely unremarkable. Gerard and Louise followed their development via unwitting relatives, babysitters, and schoolmates, and never got word of anything noteworthy.

Then there was a period in which results presented themselves, but not quite in the way Louise had intended. There was the baby who entered the world with a look of wide-eyed terror and died a few months later, of what his pediatrician listed on the death certificate as takotsubo cardiomyopathy but what he described to Louise, as one medical professional to another, as "scared to death." Was it possible, Louise speculated with Gerard, that this baby had had the ability to read minds, and that the experience, for which nature had never prepared it, was too traumatic for its infant brain to process?

Then there was the Ballard girl, in whom what had been intended to be a telepathic ability had evidently manifested itself as the ability to cause strokes, if her mother's symptoms were any indication. Also not the desired effect, but interesting nonetheless.

He was just about to take his last sip of espresso when Louise strode into the room.

"Did you see the news?"

"What news?" he replied, the small cup halfway to his mouth.

"That girl, Elizabeth Ballard—she's in the news."

Louise came behind the desk and held up her iPad, open to phillychron.com. It showed an image, clearly a still taken from a security video camera, of Patrick and Lizzy Ballard.

He took the iPad from her and scanned the article accompanying the image. "What happened?"

"She killed a woman on a train."

"It says that?" asked Gerard, alarmed, scrolling quickly through the article.

"No, it doesn't *say* that, but it's clear from the article that that's what happened. She and her father left the scene of the incident—it happened at 30th Street—and now the authorities are looking for her."

Gerard looked up from the iPad. "We can't let the police find her. We can't let Vivantem babies suddenly start hitting the news."

"I agree, we need to get to her first. But Gerard, think about it," she said, sitting on the corner of his desk and leaning toward him urgently. "We have a potential weapon."

"What do you mean?"

"We know she has the ability to bring on a sudden, massive stroke—not just the small strokes she was causing in her mother."

"That's true," said Gerard slowly, "but it's likely that this was an accident. I can't imagine that she intentionally injured this woman on the train."

Louise waved dismissively. "It doesn't matter whether she did it on purpose or not—the point is, we have the perfect untraceable weapon."

"Sure," said Gerard. "If we can make her mad enough at whoever is causing us problems."

Louise pushed her hair back impatiently. "I realize there are challenges, but we can work that out later. We need to get her here and get her sedated to keep her safe."

"You mean keep us safe from her."

"Yes, of course. We can send George."

"What's he going to do, shoot her with a tranquilizer dart and cart her away from under her father's nose? No," said Gerard, shaking his head. "We need to approach this a little more subtly. We need to get her father to give her up willingly."

"How do you propose we do that?"

Gerard tapped the iPad lightly on the edge of his desk until Louise lifted it out of his hands. "I don't know. But if they are in trouble, they'll probably go to Owen McNally."

"Yes, that's a good point. Get in touch with McNally and offer to help." She stood. "I'm going to see what other news might be out there about the event. The woman was taken to Penn ER. I could go there and poke around, see if I can get more details, just express some professional curiosity." She headed toward the door, leaving Gerard gazing thoughtfully out the window at the wintry scene. She turned at the door. "But Gerard ..." He looked up. "The father has to go."

He gazed at her for a long moment, then nodded sadly.

CHAPTER THIRTY

Patrick and Lizzy were in the living room, and Owen could hear the murmur of Patrick's voice and Lizzy's hiccupping responses. He was standing in front of the medicine cabinet in his bathroom, wondering if one of the sleeping pills for which he had gotten prescriptions at various times in the past might be a help to her. He picked up a bottle and looked at the label—it had expired almost a decade before. Well, maybe an expired pill would be better than a full-strength one. He headed to his office with the bottle to research that when his phone rang.

He glanced at the display, almost expecting to see the Philadelphia Police Department, or maybe Amtrak PD, on the caller ID. Instead, he was surprised to see Gerard Bonnay's name. He debated so long whether or not to answer that the call went to voicemail, and a moment later the voicemail icon appeared. He retrieved the message.

"Hello, Owen, this is Gerard Bonnay. I just saw the Ballards on the news and was wondering if I could be of any assistance. I'm thinking it might be best for Miss Ballard to have some quiet time away from the authorities, and I might be able to help with that. You can ring me back at this number."

Owen tapped the phone on his hand for a few moments, then continued on to his office. He had a file that contained all the information sheets he had received with his prescriptions, and he found the sheet for the sleeping pills and scanned it. But the sheet was as old as the prescription—probably older— and perhaps not the latest information. He tapped the sheets square, slipped them back into their file folder, and turned on the mouse to search for more current information.

After ascertaining that the worst that could happen to Lizzy from taking one of the pills would be nothing, he returned to the living room with the bottle. Lizzy was blowing her nose, a pile of used tissues on the coffee table in front of her, and Patrick was rubbing her back. Owen came and sat beside Lizzy on the couch.

"Pumpkin, I think you need to rest. You've had a terrible shock. I have some pills that I took a while ago when I was having trouble sleeping, and I think you should take one."

"No, I don't want to sleep," she wailed, and Owen winced as he felt a tiny twinge behind his right eye.

"Lizzy!" said Patrick sharply.

Lizzy slapped her hands over her eyes in a move that would have been comical if her anguish hadn't been so clearly real. Owen could hear her groaning, "No, no, no, no," into her hands. The pain receded. He looked at Patrick over Lizzy's bent head and nodded. The tension in Patrick's face relaxed marginally.

"Lizzy, I think Owen's right," said Patrick. "You're overwrought and … nothing good can come of that."

Lizzy sniffled, blew her nose again, then said, "All right."

Owen went to the kitchen to get a glass of water. She took the pill and handed the glass back.

"Pumpkin, let's get you tucked in upstairs," he said.

The three of them went upstairs to the guest room, and Lizzy lay down on top of the covers. Owen got a plaid Pendleton blanket from the shelf in the closet and covered her with it. "Your dad and I will be right downstairs, just call if you need anything."

"Okay," she said, and turned to look out the window, which showed a view of black tree branches and a few power lines against a darkening sky.

Owen and Patrick stepped into the hallway and Patrick started to close the door, but Lizzy said, "No, leave it open!"

"Okay, sweetie." He pushed the door partway open, then he and Owen returned to the living room.

Patrick fell onto the couch. "God, what a disaster," he groaned softly.

Owen lowered himself into a wing chair.

"Pat, I got a call from Gerard Bonnay, the head of Vivantem. Do you remember him?"

"I remember Vivantem, of course. Gerard Bonnay … the name sounds familiar."

"You and Charlotte met with him when you were being considered for the fertility treatments."

"Oh, right. Why was he calling?"

"I get together with him for lunch every couple of months. When Charlotte started showing symptoms of her strokes, I mentioned it to him and asked him if there was anything about the fertility treatments that could have caused the strokes. He said there wasn't, and I agree—when she started having the strokes, I checked all the medications she had taken and none of them should have caused the symptoms she was having."

"Did you tell him about Lizzy?" asked Patrick, alarmed.

"No, but he called just now and said he had seen you on the news and said it was probably a good time for Lizzy to have 'some quiet time away from the authorities.' Maybe he suspects what's been happening. Maybe he's found a link between Charlotte's treatments and what Lizzy can do after all."

"How?"

"He didn't say. But Gerard Bonnay is a powerful man, he may have some pull with the police, might even be able to intercede on Lizzy's behalf. In any case, it can't hurt to have him on our side. And if we have to tell anyone about Lizzy's ability, he's probably the only person I'd trust with that information, because he has motivation to keep it quiet—any news about a Vivantem baby has the potential to impact Vivantem's reputation, whether or not there is actually a connection with the Vivantem treatments. Bonnay is a well-respected man in the business and medical communities, but he's also a man who understands the value of discretion. Vivantem's a quiet company, and I sense that's very much his decision. If there's anyone who can help us out *and* keep our secret, I think it's Gerard Bonnay."

"Hey," exclaimed Patrick, "does he know we're with you?"

"I don't think so, he didn't mention that. I think he called me because he figured if anyone knew where you were, it would be me."

Patrick stood and walked to the window. Clouds had rolled in and a few snowflakes fluttered down through the flat gray light of the late December afternoon. He said, "I keep expecting to see some cop cars come screeching up to your house, guys jumping out with guns drawn, telling us through a bullhorn to come out with our hands up." He ran his fingers through his hair. "I'm really sorry I got you involved in this, Owen."

"Pat, I'm your best friend. I'm Lizzy's godfather. I wouldn't have forgiven you if you hadn't called me when you needed help."

Patrick scuffed his toe over the carpet, then smiled slightly. "Like with the RA and the glitter freshman year."

Owen grinned. "Yeah. Sort of like that."

Patrick looked back out the window, and finally said, "Okay, let's give Bonnay a call."

CHAPTER THIRTY-ONE

An hour later, Owen opened the door to Gerard Bonnay. A light snow was falling, illuminated prettily in the streetlights that had just come on. Gerard was wearing a precisely tailored pea coat, an intricately patterned Irish fisherman sweater, jeans, and Wellingtons. He stomped the snow off his boots on the porch.

"Where's Lizzy?" he asked as he stepped into the house.

"She's upstairs sleeping," said Owen. "I gave her a sleeping pill."

"Probably wise."

"Her father's in the living room."

Owen relieved Gerard of his coat, hung it on a rack in the foyer, and ushered him into the living room.

"Gerard Bonnay, Patrick Ballard," he said.

Gerard and Patrick shook hands.

"Can I get you some coffee?" Owen asked Gerard.

"No, thank you."

Owen gestured them into chairs, then they gave Gerard a rundown of events. Owen described their earliest suspicions about Lizzy's ability, and the steps they had taken to confirm it.

When he was done, Gerard said, "I usually don't trust anecdotal evidence, but in this case it seems quite compelling."

"I'd love to find out it isn't true," said Patrick, "and that everything that has happened to the woman on the train, to Charlotte, to Charlotte's sister, were just bizarre coincidences. Not," he added raggedly, "that I hold out much hope of that."

"Well, there are certainly tests that we could run that might help shed some light on the situation, and might identify a way to allow Lizzy to control her ability."

"Yes, I'm afraid that until she can control it," said Owen, "she really can't live a normal life. She'll always need to be isolated."

Gerard nodded. "Certainly taking her to the police is the worst thing you could do right now. The moment someone did something she didn't like, it would be a bad situation, and each incident would trigger escalations which would lead to more incidents. And if they were able to subdue her, the authorities would no doubt want to study her."

Patrick stood and paced to the window. "That's exactly what her mother didn't want for her. To be a guinea pig."

"I quite agree," said Gerard. "I can imagine that she could learn to control this ability, but it would take time and patience—neither of which official powers are known to have in abundance."

"I could take her away," said Patrick. "But where?"

"I believe that a life on the run would be just as stressful to her—and just as dangerous to others—as turning her over to the police," said Gerard.

"But what choice do we have?" asked Patrick. "We can't stay with Owen, we can't go home, we can't hit the road—what option does that leave?"

"I live in Pocopson," said Gerard. "A large house on a large property. And a team of lawyers who would put up quite a fight should anyone express interest in searching it, which I can't imagine they would do in any case. My wife is a doctor, and she has access to equipment at Vivantem that we could use to run some diagnostic tests on Lizzy. I propose that we take Lizzy to my house until interest in the case of the woman on the train dies down."

Patrick raised his eyebrows. "Really?"

"Yes, really," replied Gerard.

Patrick glanced at Owen, then back at Gerard. "What

would *I* do?"

"I recommend that you go to the police and tell them exactly what anyone else on the train would verify—that you and your daughter had a minor altercation with the woman, that the woman had an attack of some sort, that you and your daughter left the train with the other passengers, and that you took her away from what was obviously an upsetting situation."

"And where should I tell them I took her?"

"My recommendation is that you don't tell them. Don't volunteer the information and, if asked, say something generic. If they press you, tell them you want a lawyer, and I will provide one who will ensure you will be out of the police station minutes after he arrives."

"Assuming they don't try to hold me there, and you don't need to send your lawyer, what would I do after talking to the police?"

"I'd recommend you go home. I think it's unlikely the police would follow you, but in case they did, it would be better if you didn't lead them right to your daughter. Is your car here?"

"No, it's at the Parkesburg train station."

Gerard turned to Owen. "Is there a train that goes from near here to 30th Street Station?"

"Yes, there's a station right nearby. Walking distance."

"Good." Gerard turned back to Patrick. "You can take the train into Philly from here." Gerard pulled his phone out and tapped for a moment. "It appears there's an Amtrak police station at 30th Street, but I suspect it might not be staffed at all hours. If for some reason the Philadelphia PD gets involved, you might save yourself an additional trip by just going to them to begin with. There's a station on Market Street, near the Penn campus."

"Hey, Bucky Fernwalter works there," exclaimed Owen.

"Who's Bucky Fernwalter?" asked Gerard.

"Guy we went to Penn with," said Patrick. "Became a

detective and got assigned to that station."

"Ah, that's good," said Gerard. "Yes, I would recommend you go directly there—knowing someone there can't hurt. After you've spoken with him, or with whoever's there if he's not on duty, you can just take the train back to Parkesburg and spend the night at home. In the morning, if you can confirm that no one is following you—which, as I said, I think would be highly unlikely—you can come to Pocopson."

Patrick squeezed his hands together, his eyes on the floor, then said, "It's very generous of you to offer to help us, but why do you want to put yourself in this situation?"

"Lizzy is a Vivantem child, and that will always count with me," said Gerard. "But I can't deny that I myself am interested in understanding what caused her ability—and, in fact, confirming whether she has any special ability at all. There is absolutely nothing in the treatments that we gave your wife that has any history of causing such effects—and in fact, although I'm not a doctor myself, I find it difficult to imagine how a fertility treatment for a woman could have any such effect on her child. And, of course, we didn't give any drugs to Lizzy as part of the treatment. But I would like to prove to myself, beyond the shadow of a doubt, that there is no connection between your wife's treatments and your daughter's abilities."

"Mr. Bonnay—" began Patrick.

"Please, Gerard."

"Gerard, I'd like to talk with Owen in private for a minute, if you don't mind."

"Not at all," said Gerard, standing.

Owen levered himself out of his chair. "Gerard, why don't you stay here. Patrick and I will just step into the kitchen."

"Certainly," said Gerard, resuming his seat.

Owen led Patrick into the kitchen and pushed the swinging door shut.

Patrick raked his fingers through his hair. "What do you think? I'm so freaked I can't think straight."

"I think Bonnay's house is the best option."

"I know we're in a tough spot, but just to send her away with this guy—I don't even know him ..."

"What if I go with her?"

Patrick thought for a moment, then nodded. "Yes, that's good. That would make me feel better, and would make her feel better too, I'm sure. Do you think Bonnay will agree to that?"

"I don't know why he wouldn't," said Owen. "Only one way to find out, though."

Patrick nodded again, and pulled himself a little straighter. He led the way back to the living room and sat down.

"Gerard," he said, "we're going to take you up on your offer, as long as Owen can go along with Lizzy. She's pretty traumatized, and I think she needs a familiar face with her."

Gerard hesitated for a moment, then nodded. "As you wish. Any additional connection between Pocopson and Lizzy and her friends and family makes it slightly more likely that someone might trace her to that location, but I believe the chances are small and, as you say, having someone there whom she knows will make it less stressful for her."

"That's great," said Patrick. "I really appreciate your help, Gerard." He turned toward Owen. "We'll have to tell Ruby something."

"Ruby?" asked Gerard.

"She's the housekeeper you recommended to me for the Ballards," said Owen.

"Ah, yes," said Gerard. "Does she live in?"

"No, she just comes out to Parkesburg on weekdays," said Patrick. "She's off on the weekends."

"Then we have a little time before we need to decide what to tell her, if anything," said Gerard. "Perhaps everything will be back to normal by Monday."

"Let's hope so," said Owen.

"Excellent," said Gerard, standing. Patrick and Owen followed suit. "Will Lizzy still be out from the sleeping pill?"

"I think we can wake her up," said Owen. "She just might be a little groggy."

"Very good. Would you like to drive your own car, or drive with me and Lizzy?"

"I'll follow you, and take Lizzy in the car with me."

"Yes, of course," said Gerard.

The three of them trooped upstairs. They woke Lizzy and introduced Gerard to her. Patrick sat down next to her on the bed. "I'm going to go to Philadelphia to talk to the police. I just need to let them know that we were on the train and then hustled out of there because we were upset by the woman's attack. And that's all we know."

"Won't they want to talk to me too?" asked Lizzy blearily.

"I don't think so. And if they do, Gerard will take care of that."

She nodded uncertainly.

She was a little unsteady on her feet from the sleeping pill. Patrick held her arm as they went downstairs, and helped her on with her coat. When they reached the car, Lizzy turned to Patrick.

"Dad, you'll be coming soon, right?"

"That's right, sweetheart, I'll catch up with you guys soon." He folded her in a hug. "Don't you worry, Gerard and Owen and I are going to take care of everything. It's going to be sort of unsettled for the next few days, but I want you to remember that we are all looking out for you and we're not going to let anything bad happen to you." He held her out at arm's length. "Okay?"

She nodded. "Okay, Dad."

He gave her another quick hug. "That's my girl. I'll see you very soon. I love you, sweetheart."

"Love you too, Dad."

Gerard's and Owen's cars pulled away, and Patrick stood by the street, waving until they were out of sight.

CHAPTER THIRTY-TWO

Bucky Fernwalter wasn't at the Market Street station that night—in fact, Patrick learned, he had moved to Los Angeles the year before—but a reasonably polite desk sergeant put Patrick in a reasonably comfortable interview room with a cup of truly awful coffee and went to find someone Patrick could talk to.

After a time, the door opened and a man entered—tall, a bit soft around the middle, like a high school cornerback who'd let his exercise routine lapse in the last decade or two. He leaned across the table and extended his hand.

"Hello, Mr. Ballard, I'm Detective Joe Booth. Thank you for coming in."

Patrick half rose from his seat and shook the detective's hand.

Booth pulled out the chair opposite Patrick and sat down. "I understand that you have some information about the woman who had the medical emergency at 30th Street this morning."

"I don't know that I'd call it information. The news showed a picture of me and my daughter and said the police wanted to speak with me."

"That would be the Amtrak PD."

"Yes, I know. I looked it up and saw that there's an station at 30th Street, but I didn't know if there would be anyone there at this time of night. Plus, I thought Bucky Fernwalter still worked here. I guess I figured if I was going to be talking with the police, it would be nice to have a familiar face there." He gave a weak smile.

"Sure," said Booth, "I can understand that. Actually, I talked with Amtrak PD—they're a bit light-staffed at night, and since you're already here they asked if I could take your statement." He took a small notepad out of his shirt pocket and flipped it open. He glanced up at Patrick, who nodded.

So you and your daughter were on the train?" Booth asked.

"Yes."

"What's your daughter's name?"

"Lizzy. Elizabeth Ballard."

"Where is your daughter now?"

"Staying with friends."

Booth waited for more. His eyes were steady on Patrick, but not unkind. Likely a useful approach. Patrick steeled himself against saying more.

Finally Booth said, "Can you tell me what happened on the train at 30th Street?"

"My daughter and I were in the quiet car, and there was a woman who was talking very loudly on her phone."

"And who was that?"

"I didn't know who it was at the time. I saw on the news that it was Lucia Hazlitt."

Booth jotted a note. "Okay. Go on."

"I asked her to be quiet, and she gave me a rude response. My daughter is very sensitive about those kinds of things, so I thought it would be best if I took her to another part of the car, away from the woman, but the woman kept saying rude things to me. Then she seemed to have some kind of attack—she was grabbing her head. We were just coming into 30th Street and my daughter was getting more upset. I thought it would be best to get her off the train as soon as possible, so when the train stopped, we got off with the other passengers. I was afraid my daughter was going to have an anxiety attack, so I got a cab and we took it to the Penn University Hospital emergency room. By the time we got there, she seemed calmer, so we left."

"The cabbie who picked you up said you told him that you were going to see your wife at the hospital."

"I thought that it would be less stressful for my daughter to hear that than to hear me tell someone we were going to the ER because of her."

"I would think that it would be pretty stressful for a young woman to hear her mother was in the hospital."

"Well, she knew it wasn't true. Her mother passed away some time ago."

Booth raised his eyebrows slightly.

Patrick shrugged. "I know it doesn't make much sense, but I was pretty frazzled myself. The experience on the train had been upsetting for both of us. I felt as if having me tell the cabbie that my daughter was having an anxiety attack would be embarrassing for her."

Booth jotted briefly on the notepad.

"Ms. Hazlitt's assistant, the woman she was traveling with, said you seemed very interested in the briefcase that she put in the overhead rack."

"I offered to help her get it down, she was having trouble with it."

"The assistant seems to think that your daughter was somehow responsible for what happened to Ms. Hazlitt."

"Yes, I heard her say something to that effect."

After a pause, Booth asked, "What do you think would make her say that?"

"I have no idea."

"She said that your daughter may have actually shoved Ms. Hazlitt."

"What?" said Patrick, stunned. "No, that never happened."

After a beat, Booth said, "Ms. Hazlitt died."

"Yes, I heard that on the news."

"Of a massive brain hemorrhage."

Patrick nodded, looking somber.

Booth regarded him wordlessly for nearly half a minute, then sighed. "We may need to speak with your daughter."

"I don't think she can add anything to what I just told you."

"Still ..." said Booth. "Do you live locally, Mr. Ballard?"

"I live in Parkesburg."

Booth tore a page out of the notepad and slid it and a pen across the table. "If you can write down your address and phone number, we may need to be in touch with you again."

Patrick jotted down the information and slid the paper back to Booth.

"Is this your cell number?" Booth asked.

"Yes."

Booth stood up and Patrick followed suit.

"We appreciate you coming in, Mr. Ballard," he said. "I'll pass the info on to Amtrak PD."

Patrick nodded and they shook hands. Booth showed him out to the lobby, then headed back into the bowels of the building.

Patrick stepped outside into a cutting December wind, now chilly in the winter coat he had left on in the police station to hide the spreading sweat stains under his arms.

CHAPTER THIRTY-THREE

Lizzy had revived a bit by the time they got to Pocopson, and although she was still suffering under the pall of her role in the events on the train, Owen sensed a flicker of excitement at the adventure of the surreptitious trip.

They followed Baltimore Pike, then Route 1 west, the lights of shopping centers and neighborhoods giving way to the darkness of countryside. They passed through Chadds Ford and then turned north.

They had been following a seemingly endless stone wall, glimpses of it captured in the headlights when the road curved, and then the turn signal of Gerard's Range Rover flashed and Owen followed it between two stone pillars topped with ornate metal lamps, a decorative metal gate swinging open as Gerard pulled up to it. They followed a carefully plowed drive for a time, and then passed between another set of pillars decorated with stone lions.

They came out at a circle in front of the house, in the center of which was an enormous stone planter sporting a pine tree decorated with tiny white lights. Lights illuminated the entryway of a stone mansion, its wings disappearing into the darkness in either direction.

"Jeez, it's huge," said Lizzy, gaping at the house.

"At least you should be comfortable here," said Owen, gaping a bit himself.

Gerard had pulled his car a little ahead of the entrance, allowing Owen to pull up directly in front of the stairs that led to the front door. Gerard got out of his car and hurried back to them through the snow, the flakes now falling more thickly.

"You can leave your car here while we get settled," he said.

He led them into a marble-floored foyer, a huge crystal chandelier hanging from the ceiling, a curving staircase leading to a balcony.

"This way," he said, beckoning them up the stairs.

They passed through the upstairs hall and into a bedroom with cheerful yellow walls and bleached hardwood floors.

"You can sleep in here," he said to Lizzy.

"I'm not tired anymore," she said.

"Well, you can wait in here until your father arrives," he said. "There's also a sitting room just down the hall that has some books and magazines, would you prefer that?"

"Yes please."

Gerard led them down the hallway, to a feminine-looking room done in shades of gray and plum.

"Are you hungry?" asked Gerard.

"Not really," said Lizzy.

"I'm just going to talk with Owen for a few minutes, then we'll be back."

"Okay." Lizzy crossed the room to the bookshelves and began scanning the titles.

Gerard led Owen back downstairs, to a room that looked like it has been plucked from a nineteenth-century English gentleman's club.

"Please have a seat," said Gerard. "Would you like a drink?"

Owen shrugged out of his coat and lowered himself into one of the leather wing chairs next to the fireplace. "I think I'll pass for now, thanks." He pulled out his cell phone to check for calls or messages. "Do you have any idea when we might be hearing from Patrick? I haven't a clue how long he might spend with the police."

"I can't imagine it will be that long," said Gerard, settling into the other wing chair. "The accusation made against Lizzy sounds so ludicrous, there isn't much the police can do with it.

If it didn't involve Lucia Hazlitt, we wouldn't even be going through this rigmarole. They probably just want to make sure they've interviewed all the witnesses to the incident so that her law firm can't accuse them of mishandling the case. There's no love lost between Ms. Hazlitt and law enforcement."

Owen muffled a yawn.

"You must be exhausted," said Gerard. "There's another guest room near Lizzy's …"

"Thanks, I don't want to turn it into a slumber party," said Owen with a somewhat sheepish smile, "but maybe I will go up to that sitting room where we left her. I don't like leaving her alone right now."

"Of course," said Gerard. "I think I'll stay here and do a little research. Please let me know as soon as you hear from Patrick and we can decide on next steps."

Owen hoisted himself up. "Thanks again for your help. We would have been up a creek if you hadn't stepped in."

Lizzy pulled a book out of the shelves and got settled into the couch with it. The couch was enormously puffy, with some sort of velvet covering and lots of extra pillows to customize the perfect reading space. She kicked her shoes off and put her feet up.

She read a few paragraphs and found that she was, in fact, feeling a little sleepy, so she lay back on the pillows and looked around the room. The couch faced a gas fireplace, over which hung a large flat-screen TV. She looked around for a remote and found one on the table next to the couch. She clicked one of the buttons and, with a tiny whoosh, flames danced up in the fireplace. She hurriedly clicked it off. There wasn't another remote on the table. She climbed out of the couch and went to the TV and pressed what looked like a power button, but nothing happened. She peeked into the drawers in the tables at either end of the couch, but no remote. Shrugging, she circled the rest of the room until she came to a desk, on top of which were a blotter, what looked like an ivory block holding a pair of scissors and a letter opener, and a small brass clock.

A fine sheen of dust lay on the desk, noticeable only because in one corner was a rectangular dust-free area. Lizzy guessed that a computer usually stood there.

With another shrug she returned to the couch and picked up the book, but in a few minutes set it aside. When Owen stepped into the room, she was asleep in a cocoon of pillows.

CHAPTER THIRTY-FOUR

Patrick zipped up his coat and stuffed his hands into the pockets. It was still snowing, and an inch or so now covered the cars parked on the street. He removed his phone from his pocket and was calling up the Amtrak schedule from 30th Street to Parkesburg, wondering if he could still get home at this time of night, when he jumped at a voice at his side.

"Mr. Ballard?"

A dark-haired man of about his age stood next to him, a little shorter than Patrick, a little broader, a shirt and tie visible under his winter coat. His breath smelled of mint.

"Who are you?" asked Patrick.

"I'm Mr. Bonnay's assistant. Your daughter was getting agitated and he thought it would be best for you to come out to Pocopson to be with her."

Patrick glanced back at the door to the police station. "Isn't he afraid someone might follow me there?"

The man smiled. "I'll make sure that doesn't happen. If someone does follow us—and I think that's unlikely—I can just drive you to your house for now and we'll get you to Pocopson later."

Patrick looked back again, the brightly lit station now looking more appealing than it had when he had arrived an hour ago.

"All right."

The man nodded down the street. "The car's right down here," he said, and beckoned Patrick to follow him.

He was a few steps ahead of Patrick when he glanced into an alleyway as he passed and then did a double take. "Ma'am?

Are you okay?" He turned back to Patrick. "Wait here for a sec, there's a woman in there," he said, and disappeared into the darkness.

Patrick stepped up to the entrance to the alley, searching the dark for the man and the woman. "What's wrong?" he asked, and recognized a second too late what it was.

From the even darker shadows of the building, the man's hand shot out and grabbed Patrick's arm and jerked him into the alley. Patrick drew a breath to yell, but the sound was cut short by something slamming into his stomach. He sagged to the ground, grabbing at the man's arm, trying to bring him down too, but his hand no longer had any strength.

He landed on his back, staring upward. From between the black voids of the buildings on either side of the alley, the lights from the street sparkled across his vision. Far away, he could see a slice of sky. Then the man moved over him, and the sky disappeared.

He felt fingers of blood creep down his sides, and he understood that the man had shot him. He opened his mouth to gulp in air, but he choked on warm liquid in his throat.

He was rolled onto his stomach. His cheek rested on frozen concrete, and something cold pressed against the back of his neck. Then the world exploded, and he didn't feel anything more.

CHAPTER THIRTY-FIVE

At midnight, Owen rang Patrick's number but the call went to voicemail.

"Hey, it's me," he said. "We're wondering what's up. Give me a call."

He was in the sitting room alone, Lizzy having relocated to the bedroom. He had gotten a book from the shelves and was trying to read it, but without much success. He got off the couch after a bit of a struggle—the puffy ones were the worst—and went downstairs to the study. Gerard was seated at the desk.

"I tried calling Patrick," said Owen. "No answer."

Gerard glanced at his watch. "It does seem strange. He should be out of there by now. Any chance he went home and forgot to call you?"

"Seems unlikely. I could call the station, ask them if he's still there."

"What are you going to tell them when you call?"

"I'll tell them that a friend was visiting me, saw on the news that the police were looking for him, and went downtown to talk with them."

"What if they ask about Lizzy?"

"I'll say she's staying with a friend."

"What if they want to know where she is?"

"You said we wouldn't have to tell them that."

Gerard nodded. "True. If they ask that, or want any details beyond what you just told me, you could just tell them you'll be down in the morning, and I'll send a lawyer with you."

Gerard looked up the number of the Market Street police

station and gave it to Owen. Owen was on the phone for a few minutes, then disconnected, looking worried.

"They said he was there but left a while ago."

Gerard knit his eyebrows. "Very strange."

Owen reached for the coat he had draped across the couch. "I'm going to go down there to see what's going on."

"What would you do?" asked Gerard. "They would have told you if they were holding him, and I doubt he's just hanging around on the street outside the station."

Owen tossed his coat back down and ran his fingers through his hair. "What do you suggest?"

"You could drive to Parkesburg and see if his car is still at the train station there. At least that would let us know if he got that far."

Owen sighed. "I guess so."

He shrugged into his coat and headed out into the snow.

CHAPTER THIRTY-SIX

The old man took the padlock off the metal gate in front of the store and rolled up the gate, then unlocked the door. He noticed with satisfaction that Marco had swept the floor before leaving last night—the boy was coming along. He got coffee started—two large pots of Bustelo, one small pot of decaf—and set the pastries he had picked up at the bakery in the display case. He went to the trash can to throw out the cardboard box the pastries had come in and saw that it was still full.

"Ese muchacho," he muttered. He pulled the bag out and took it to the back door, then set it aside to get the shovel to clear the back steps and a path to the dumpster. He moved slowly—he had a terror of falling on ice and breaking a leg. At least the snow had let up for his drive into the store this morning. After shoveling a path, he shuffled back to the store, using the shovel as a walking stick, retrieved the bag of garbage, and then shuffled even more slowly back to the dumpster.

He had heaved the bag in and was turning back to the store, wishing he had brought the shovel out with him—was he going to need a cane soon?—when he noticed a snow-covered lump sticking out from behind the dumpster. Were his neighbors dumping their trash behind his store again? Probably the lady with the flower shop—he thought he had taken care of that. If she was going to do that, why not at least put the bags in the dumpster?

He prodded the lump with his foot and it shifted slightly, but not like you'd expect a bag of garbage to shift. He used his foot to brush away some of the snow, revealing dark wool.

His heart set up a painful hammering, and, supporting himself on the dumpster, he eased himself around the corner so he could see the rest of the lump. It was longer than a bag of garbage should have been. The old man flashed back to a white tablecloth that his mother had spread over the body of a man struck by a car and killed in front of their home in San Juan. And just like the tablecloth in San Juan, the snow covering the lump was stained red.

CHAPTER THIRTY-SEVEN

Detective Joe Booth sat across the desk from his boss, Margaret Fraker. Her crimson fingernails, filed to points that would make formidable weapons should the need arise, gripped a plastic stirrer, with which she was vigorously stirring Sweet N Low into her coffee. Some coffee splashed onto the stained blotter on her desk.

"He got shot a block from the station? Holy Christ," she muttered. She tossed the stirrer under her desk—probably in the direction of a trash can—but it skittered out the other side and slid to a stop next to Joe's shoe. She took a swallow from the Styrofoam cup. Joe had never seen her eat or drink anything other than the sludge that stewed all day in the coffeepot in the break room.

The body in the alley had been stripped of personal items—wedding ring, watch, wallet, phone—and it wasn't until the desk sergeant saw one of the crime scene photos that he recognized the victim as the man Joe Booth had questioned the night before.

"This is the guy who was harassing Lucia Hazlitt?" asked Fraker.

"I don't think he was harassing her—there some suggestion from Ms. Hazlitt's assistant that he was trying to get a hold of the briefcase that had her papers on the Dollar Slash case in it, but I think it's just as likely he was just trying to help her with it."

"You're a trusting soul, Booth," she said. "And the assistant said his daughter attacked Hazlitt?"

"From what other passengers have said, Ms. Hazlitt

stumbled into the girl."

"Jesus Christ," said Fraker. "Don't these people have anything better to do than to come up with conspiracy theories?" She scrolled through a report on her computer. "Did he say anything useful when you interviewed him?"

"No, just said that Hazlitt had been harassing him and his daughter and then had the attack."

She looked sharply at him. "He knew it was Hazlitt?"

"He said not until he heard it on the news."

She pushed the computer mouse away. "Why were *you* even talking to him? Shouldn't this be Amtrak PD?"

"Yeah, but the guy came here and they didn't have anyone to come interview him."

"I don't even know why anyone needed to interview him. Some woman gets bitchy on the train and then collapses—doesn't sound like police business to me," said Fraker. "Amtrak PD makes this guy come all the way into the city, then doesn't even have the time to talk to him, and then he gets killed on his way out the door. *Our* door." She glared at Joe, but from long experience Joe sensed she was more irritated at the situation than at him. "Who's his next of kin?"

"We don't know where the daughter is, and he said his wife is dead. We found out he works at Penn, in the IT department. We have a uniform over there now seeing what he can find out."

"Jesus. Well, don't let the press find out his name until we get in touch with someone. I don't want some relative—like his daughter, for God's sake—finding out about it on the news."

CHAPTER THIRTY-EIGHT

Owen got to the Parkesburg train station around one in the morning and found Patrick's car in the otherwise deserted parking lot. Since he was nearby, he drove by the Ballards' house, but it was dark and quiet. He let himself in with a key Patrick had given him years before. There was no one home, and no sign that Owen could discern of anything amiss.

He returned to Pocopson and after a brief strategy session with Gerard over coffee, Owen agreed to wait until morning, when he would go to the police station accompanied by one of Gerard's lawyers to see if he could get more information about Patrick's visit. Then Owen went upstairs and fell into a fitful sleep on the sitting-room couch.

He was woken at about eight in the morning by Lizzy tapping his shoulder.

"Uncle Owen?"

He sat up stiffly and rubbed his face. "Hey, Pumpkin."

"Did you talk to Dad yet?"

"No, he didn't call, I expect he'll call this morning."

"Should I try calling him?"

"Not yet, let's talk with Gerard first. If we can't raise your dad pretty soon, I'm going down to the police station with one of Gerard's lawyers to see what we can find out."

"Did they put him in jail?" asked Lizzy, aghast.

"They say no, but maybe they know where he might have gone after he left."

"Okay. Gerard stopped up and said he has breakfast downstairs."

"Okay." He struggled to his feet, helped by a tug from

Lizzy. "Man, I wish I had thought to bring a toothbrush."

"There are a couple of new ones still wrapped in plastic in the bathroom next to the guest bedroom," said Lizzy. "Also some deodorant and stuff in the medicine cabinet."

"Ah, good, I'll do that and meet you downstairs."

"Okay," said Lizzy. She left the room and a moment later he heard her running lightly down the steps. The night's sleep seemed to have done her good.

Owen found the toothbrushes in a glass on the bathroom vanity, and toothpaste in one of the drawers. He gave his underarms a surreptitious sniff and decided he would forego the borrowed deodorant. While he brushed he typed one-handed into his phone on phillychron.com. He froze in mid-brush.

A body was found this morning behind a convenience store just off the campus of William Penn University. Police are investigating the possibility that the deceased may have been the victim of a mugging, since he had no wallet, phone, or jewelry. The alley in which the body was found is less than a block from the Market Street police station where, it is reported, the victim had been interviewed last night. The name of the victim is being withheld pending notification of his family.

Owen stared at the screen as a thread of toothpaste foam dripped down his chin. Then he spit, wiped his face, and sat down on the toilet seat, his heart pounding.

It was theoretically possible that the body wasn't Patrick's, but he knew in his heart it was a vain hope. Could Patrick really have been the victim of a mugging? That too seemed unlikely, although not impossible. Could someone have followed Patrick and Lizzy from the train station to the hospital to the hotel, then to his own house, and then followed Patrick back to Philadelphia? He was hardly experienced in such matters, but it seemed unlikely someone could have done so unnoticed. And why would someone be following Patrick anyway?

His thoughts turned to Gerard Bonnay. He had accepted Gerard's explanation of why the man was interested in helping Lizzy because there seemed to be no alternative to handing Lizzy over to the authorities. Now he wished he had thought more carefully before involving another person. But it was Gerard who had called him. He wiped a hand across his forehead, which was slick with cold beads of sweat.

He would get Lizzy away from here, then find out for sure if the body was Patrick's.

Then he heard Gerard's voice coming from the hallway. "Owen?"

He started like a child caught with contraband and pushed himself to his feet.

"In here," he called. "Cleaning up a bit." He slipped his phone into his pocket and stepped into the bedroom.

Gerard stood in the doorway to the hall. "I have news. Not good, I'm afraid."

"Yes?" asked Owen, his voice sounding tremulous to his own ears.

Gerard stepped into the bedroom and closed the door. "There's a news story about a mugging victim, found in an alley downtown." He paused, his face tight. "Near the police station where Patrick went."

"Is it Patrick?" asked Owen woodenly.

"I don't know, but it's certainly a possibility."

"Does Lizzy know?" Owen asked, his voice regaining some animation.

"I don't think so. We were talking about other things at breakfast, and when I saw the news story on my phone, I gave her a book to look at. Hopefully that will keep her off the internet for a few minutes."

"What are we going to do?" Owen wanted to find out where Gerard would take the conversation.

Gerard sighed. "I am hoping it's not Patrick, but I think

we need to proceed under the assumption that it is. I think we need to give Lizzy a sedative in anticipation of the possibility that we will need to give her some bad news."

"Of course it will be bad news if it is Patrick, but shouldn't we wait to see how she reacts? She might not need a sedative."

"Do you want to be the one to give her bad news without some way to control her reaction?" asked Gerard.

After a moment, Owen said, "Damn," in a voice filled with sorrow. "No. I suppose not. How do you propose we get a sedative to give her?"

"We have sedatives at Vivantem, I'll have someone bring some over." Gerard turned to go, his hand on the doorknob, but stopped at the sound of Owen's voice.

"Gerard, how many people know Lizzy's here?"

"Just the two of us. And Patrick."

"Do you have help here at the house?"

"I have a housekeeper. She doesn't know who Lizzy is, and she doesn't speak a word of English."

"Aren't you married?"

"I am, but my wife is away at the moment."

"Aren't you going to need to explain to her why you have a teenage girl staying in your guest room?"

Gerard laughed shortly. "Yes, I'm sure I'll have to tell her, but I think we have other things to worry about now."

"How about the person who will be delivering the sedative?"

Gerard paused, then dropped his hand from the doorknob and turned fully toward Owen.

"Owen, I didn't need to get involved. I felt that removing Lizzy from the situation—a situation of her own making, I might add—was preferable to the alternative. And I think the alternative would have been that the police would have brought her in for questioning, she would have become upset, people around her would have started suffering life-changing and possibly life-ending strokes, and then she would have been hustled off to some secret government compound to be tested. Do you disagree with that assessment?"

"No," said Owen miserably.

"Then I suggest that we move quickly to address this latest dilemma, and then regroup and determine a long-term strategy."

Owen nodded reluctantly.

"There's a media room, I think that would be the best way to keep Lizzy occupied until the sedative shows up."

Owen resisted telling Gerard that movie-watching had been the ploy he and Patrick had used last time it had been necessary to keep bad news from Lizzy.

"While you keep her occupied," continued Gerard, "I'll see if I can get any information about the mugging victim."

When they got to the dining room, Lizzy had abandoned the book Gerard had given her—a collection of Jamie Wyeth paintings—and was looking at her phone. She looked up, a worried expression on her face.

"What police station was Dad going to?"

"He went to one near 30th Street Station but when he was done he went home, Owen just got a message from him," said Gerard.

"You did?" asked Lizzy, looking at Owen.

Owen nodded.

"What took him so long to call?"

There was a long silence, and Owen realized Gerard was waiting for him to answer.

"He was at the police station for a while, then he had to wait for a train to get to Parkesburg. It was late, so he decided to get a little sleep at home before he comes out here."

"How late do the trains run?" asked Lizzy, reaching for her phone.

"He caught the last one," said Owen.

"He'll be here soon," said Gerard, "but there's something he needs to take care of first."

"What's that?" asked Lizzy.

"He didn't say, but he did say he'd be here soon. Didn't he, Owen?" said Gerard, a barely perceptible edge in his voice.

"Yes. Soon," said Owen.

"So in the meantime, I thought you two might enjoy my movie room," said Gerard.

Lizzy sighed. "Okay," she said, pushing back from the table.

Owen surveyed the almost-empty bowl of scrambled eggs and plates of bacon and toast on the table, but for once his appetite had deserted him.

"Follow me," said Gerard.

He led them down a flight of stairs to a movie room furnished with reclining leather theater seats and a huge projection screen.

"What would you like to see? We can stream whatever you want."

"We didn't finish *The Return of the King*, want to watch that?" asked Owen.

"Sure," said Lizzy, playing with the recliner adjustments on her chair.

"I have some work I need to do," said Gerard, "so I'll leave you to it." He showed them how to work the projection system, then slipped out of the room.

Lizzy checked her phone. "The reception isn't very good. What if Dad calls while we're down here?"

Owen pulled his phone out. It was barely picking up a signal. "I've got good reception," he said, a little too heartily.

"Okay," said Lizzy. "If Dad shows up while we're watching, we can re-start the movie."

Owen coughed abruptly into his fist to cover what might otherwise have turned into a sob.

About an hour later, Gerard appeared in the movie room with a tray on which he carried three glasses, three bottles of ginger beer, and a bowl of popcorn. He caught Owen's eye and nodded slightly, his face solemn. Owen dropped his eyes, and examined a hangnail intently.

When he looked up, Gerard was at a side table, popping the caps off the three bottles and pouring each into a glass. He handed glasses to Lizzy and Owen and took one for himself and got settled into one of the chairs.

With Gerard sipping periodically from his glass and ostensibly absorbed in the movie, Owen took a sniff of his drink. He couldn't perceive anything amiss, but he put it aside untouched.

After a few minutes, Gerard said, "Lizzy?"

There was a long pause, and then Lizzy said, "Yes?" Her voice was faint and unfocused.

"How are you feeling?" asked Gerard, pausing the movie.

After another pause, the response came. "Okay."

Gerard and Owen got out of their seats and went to Lizzy. She had slumped sideways in the large seat so that her head was resting on the arm, her body curled in the seat. She stared at the paused image on the screen, but without any sense that she was seeing it.

"Do you feel okay, Pumpkin?" asked Owen.

"Yeah, okay," came the slow reply. "But kind of weird."

"We have something we need to tell you," said Gerard.

"We'll be back in just a minute," said Owen and, grasping Gerard's arm, propelled him toward the door.

Once in the hallway outside the room, Owen turned to Gerard.

"Are you absolutely sure it's Patrick?"

"Yes, I have some inside sources of information. The police at the Market Street station confirmed that it was the same person who had come in to talk about the incident on the train, and they had confirmed his identity as Patrick Ballard at that time. He was shot in the stomach and in the neck."

"Jesus," said Owen, leaning against the wall.

"Yes," said Gerard.

They stood in the hallway, silent, until Owen pushed

himself upright.

"Let me do this myself."

Gerard hesitated, then said, "Very well."

Owen pushed the door open and entered the still-darkened room, an image of Frodo and Samwise Gamgee still frozen on the screen.

Lizzy had sat up, but didn't look any more alert than she had earlier. Owen sat down in the chair next to her.

"Pumpkin, I have some bad news."

She looked at him blearily. "Uncle Owen, I feel funny."

"I know. We had to give you a sedative."

"Why?" Even through the fog of the drug, a specter of panic flickered.

"Pumpkin, your dad is dead. He got mugged in Philadelphia, and he died."

Lizzy stared at him. It wasn't clear to Owen whether or not she was seeing him.

"Sweetheart, can you understand what I'm saying?"

Then Lizzy dropped her face into her hands and the only motion was the shaking of her shoulders. Then, very faintly, Owen heard a sounds like a very weak keening, that finally resolved itself into words.

"I knew it ... I knew it ... I knew it ... I knew it ..."

Owen knelt on the floor in front of Lizzy's chair and folded her in his arms. "I am so, so sorry," he said, rocking her. He felt the tiniest twinge of pain behind his eye, then it was gone.

CHAPTER THIRTY-NINE

Ruby stood in her tiny apartment, folding and packing the clothes she would need for the coming week. She had postponed the weekly phone call as long as she could, although there was really no need for her to fret about it—she didn't have anything to report, other than the fact that Patrick was proceeding with his plan to take Lizzy to New York City. They would be back at home by now, anyway.

She picked up her phone and keyed in the number she knew by heart.

Gerard answered. "Yes?"

"It's me," she said.

"Did you hear?"

"Hear what?"

"About Patrick. And Lizzy."

Ruby stiffened. "What about them?"

"They were on their way to New York City on the train, and a woman on the train had an attack of some sort. For some reason, the police wanted to talk with Patrick about it. He went to the police station in Philadelphia Saturday night and …" Ruby heard him draw a deep breath. "He got mugged afterwards. He's dead."

Ruby lowered herself onto the edge of the daybed. After a long moment, she said, "Dead?"

"Yes."

"Where's Lizzy?"

"She's at my house. With me and my wife. And Owen McNally. She's being well cared for."

"Why is she at your house?"

Gerard sighed. "It seemed like the best place for her. I really need to get back—"

"Why is she at your house?" Ruby asked again.

"I think you know from your time with the Ballards that being out in public is very stressful for Lizzy. And certainly that stress level rises exponentially if that public place is a police station. Dr. McNally and Mr. Ballard thought, quite rightly, that with my connections, I could avoid some of that stress for her."

"Wait, I thought you said Mr. Ballard was dead?"

"He approved bringing her to my home before he went to the police station. He was fully in agreement with the plan." There was a long silence, and finally Gerard said, "Miss DiMano? Are you still there?"

"What are you going to do with her?"

"Dr. McNally and I are discussing that. He is her guardian now that her parents are gone."

"But—"

"I've greatly appreciated all your help, Miss DiMano. And I hope you have appreciated the benefits you have enjoyed as a result of our arrangement. But I believe Lizzy won't be needing your services any longer. If that changes, I'll certainly let you know. I'll send the balance of this year's salary and your bonus to you immediately."

There was another long silence. Gerard took a breath to end the call when Ruby responded.

"Well, it's certainly your choice, Mr. Bonnay."

"It's actually Dr. McNally's choice, but I have to say I concur with it. Also, Miss DiMano," he continued after a pause, "I don't think I need to remind you about our conversation so many years ago about the conditions of your employment. And about the results of a lapse in your discretion, which, I must say, has been admirable. The results that your nephew would suffer."

"I remember."

"Very good. Best of luck to you, Miss DiMano," said

Gerard, and the call ended.

She sat on the daybed for a long time, listening to the faint sounds of a Christmas carol coming from her neighbor's radio. Eventually she stood and began unpacking her suitcase, tucking the clothes into the drawers of the enormous walnut dresser that partially blocked her front door.

CHAPTER FORTY

Mitchell Pieda put aside the copy of the *Philadelphia Chronicle*, took a sip of his hot tea, and mulled over the article he had just read.

"Foul Play in Hazlitt Death?"
By Lincoln Abbott
The mystery has deepened around a man and young woman who left the scene of an Amtrak Police Department investigation Saturday morning when celebrity lawyer Lucia Hazlitt suffered an apparent stroke on the Amtrak Keystone train just as it pulled into 30th Street Station. Amtrak Police published a still from the station's security camera, asking the pair to contact authorities to answer some questions.

The man in question, Patrick Ballard, 48, reported to the Market Street station of the Philadelphia Police Department last night. Ballard's body was found this morning, less than a block from the station. Police report that there were no personal items such as a wallet, watch, or wedding ring on the victim, suggesting that he may have been the victim of a mugging. Philadelphia PD reports that Mr. Ballard's daughter, the young woman in the security camera image, did not accompany Mr. Ballard to the station. Her whereabouts are unknown.

Mitchell had been following the story since the previous day, when an internet search alert had notified him of the appearance of an article containing the words *news apparent stroke philadelphia*, although not the word *telepathy*, the other term in his alert. He pushed up the starched cuff of his shirt to glance at his watch—a Victorinox he had gotten last year—then tugged it back into place. 30th Street was just a short ride away on the Market-Frankford Line, and he could get there and back before his lunch hour was over. He flagged down the waitress and asked for his kale salad to be boxed up to go.

He felt awkward carrying the brown paper bag onto the subway, but he wasn't in a position to pay fourteen dollars for a salad and not eat it. At least no one could fault him for his appearance otherwise: perfectly cut dark blue suit, crisp light blue shirt, dark blue tie with a subtle red pattern. He was especially proud of the shoes: he had gotten them the week before—almost five hundred dollars—and he polished them carefully each night before slipping in cedar shoe trees. It would have taken a careful look for anyone to realize that Mitchell Pieda was barely out of college.

He hated the subway, frequented by riders wearing drooping pants and sequined shirts, a sea of synthetic fabric stretched over flabby bodies. Their minds were a jumble of lowbrow, low-income images—or, even more alarming, no images at all. He sometimes thought of getting an inexpensive car to avoid having to subject himself to the subway, but not only would dealing with a car in the city be inconvenient, it would mean tapping into the account in which he was saving for an Audi A3. He hadn't been able to buy his suit at Boyds by blowing a bunch of money on cheap, temporary clothing, and he wasn't going to drive off a lot in his own car until he could drive off in an A3.

He got off the subway at 30th Street, then walked the few blocks to the Market Street police station.

"Pardon me," he said to the desk sergeant. He got the double take he was used to getting when someone realized he was much younger than they had at first thought. "I read a news story about the man and the young lady on the security camera at 30th Street, the ones you're looking for in relation to the woman who had the stroke on the train on Saturday."

"Yes?" said the man.

"She looks like the sister of a friend of mine—Jim Frank, I think his sister's name was Cindy." He raised his eyebrows expectantly—eager to be helpful—and opened his mind to the man before him.

He picked up a wisp of thought. *Eliz—*

"Do you think it might be her?" he asked, leaning toward the man slightly. Sometimes proximity helped.

"No, we identified them—she's not your buddy's sister. But thanks for checking in."

"Not Cindy Frank?" He hated to sound stupid, but he needed to get the man to think of the real name again.

"Nope. But thanks." The man was turning away, and Mitchell could sense the name passing through his mind again, but this time he missed it completely, overridden by the man's annoyance over ... what, a delayed lunch break?

"Man, I thought for sure it was Cindy," he muttered, loud enough for the man to hear him.

This time the man might as well have said the name out loud, so clear was it to Mitchell.

Elizabeth Ballard.

"Trust me, buddy, it wasn't Cindy Frank," said the officer, his annoyance transferring from his postponed lunch to Mitchell.

"Ah, okay," said Mitchell. "Thank you, officer."

And he turned and walked briskly out of the station and back to 30th Street.

CHAPTER FORTY-ONE

Mitchell Pieda had been able to read people's thoughts for as long as he could remember.

The only person whose thoughts he could reliably read as a child had been his father, Robert. It certainly wasn't due to proximity—Robert had been a banker who left for the office before his son woke up in the mornings, and often didn't return home until shortly before Mitchell went to bed. And then, when Robert was convicted of wire fraud when Mitchell was nine, Mitchell had only seen him when he and his mother would visit Allenwood once a month. That is, until a guard found his father in his cell one morning, dead of a heart attack.

But Mitchell remembered clearly the images that would spring from his father's mind, especially during those prison visits—visions of the custom-tailored suits of fine wool he had worn in his former life, the precise stitching on the leather seats of the BMW that had been sold to pay the legal bills. The images were gorgeous and compelling, and Mitchell sensed the yearning that drove them. His father thought about these things the way a rancher transported to the big city might think about the great plains, or the way an artist trapped in a corporate cubicle might think about his paint brushes.

Mitchell's ability had expanded during his teen years, as if he had gone into the physical and emotional maelstrom of adolescence and had emerged on the other side with a clearer sense not only of his own thoughts, but also the thoughts of the people around him.

When he read other people's thoughts, they were sometimes auditory, the way he had heard the cop think

Elizabeth Ballard. More frequently they were visual. They were usually blurry, but sometimes startlingly clear, especially when the person was cooperating. He enjoyed having a classmate pick a card from a deck and concentrate on it, and Mitchell would guess what the card was—although he wasn't guessing at all, it was as if he were looking through the other person's eyes, and could have reached out his hand and touched that card. His classmates spent a good deal of time trying to figure out how he was stacking the deck to be able to get it right every time.

When Mitchell's mother found out about the card tricks, she told him to stop. She had played those sorts of games when she was young, she told him—quoting the serial number of a dollar bill as another person stared at it, surprising people by replying to a comment they had made only in their heads—and no good came of it.

Mitchell's mother was diagnosed with cancer when he was fifteen. In the last weeks of her illness, Mitchell found excuses to be anywhere but where she was—first at home, then in the hospital, then in hospice. His mother sent her sister out to find Mitchell, to ask him to come to her, but he stayed away. He knew that if he sat by her bedside, he would face not only the trauma that every child goes through watching a parent sicken toward death, but the additional horror of being able to see her thoughts as it happened.

There were the times when her mind was filled with jagged purple panic at the inexorable advance of her illness. There were the times when she imagined the cancer eating through her body, like a legion of wriggling worms working their insidious way through her veins. And worst, the times he saw the various ways she thought of killing herself before the cancer preempted her in that ultimate choice.

After she died—of the cancer, evidently she had never been able to quite make up her mind about suicide—he went to live with his aunt. Most of his parents' assets that hadn't already been sold off to cover his father's legal expenses were sold off then, but Mitchell came into possession of several boxes of his mother's personal items, among them her diaries. And in them, he found a possible explanation for his abilities.

Antonia Pieda had worked as a lab assistant at the Vivantem fertility clinic, and when she had trouble getting pregnant, she filled out the questionnaire that Vivantem provided to prospective clients. The questionnaire, she recalled in a later diary entry, actually asked about apparent telepathic abilities. After she filled it out, Gerard Bonnay offered to provide fertility treatments at a vastly reduced cost.

There had been a number of follow-up questionnaires in the years after Mitchell's birth—especially when he began talking—but over the years the questionnaires became less frequent and finally stopped altogether. Shortly after that, Antonia was fired over a misunderstanding about the documentation of results of an experiment with which she was assisting Dr. Mortensen. His mother believed the "misunderstanding" was an excuse to get rid of her. She believed, she wrote, there was something strange going on at Vivantem, and she speculated that, although Mitchell's ability to read thoughts might be rooted in a hereditary gift, it might have been magnified by the treatments she had received at the clinic.

And the ability to read minds wasn't the only skill that Mitchell Pieda had. He could not only access other people's minds, like reaching out a hand to touch the object of their thoughts, but could also close that metaphysical hand around their minds and tighten his grip. And if he concentrated hard enough, he could feel the infinitesimal rupturing of the physical matter of the brain.

He experimented with this ability: on a high school teacher who spoke condescendingly to him about a chemistry experiment gone embarrassingly wrong. On the prettiest girl in school, who not only said no when he asked her to the prom, but, worse, giggled when she said it. On the salesman who had asked him to leave when he had stopped by the dealership to look at the Audi. The person would wince, maybe touch their hand to their head, and his anger would dissipate. That would be that. In all cases but one.

After graduation, Mitchell got a job at a company that developed information systems for medical practices. He was hired as a sales assistant and, he was told, if things worked out, it could eventually lead to a promotion to a sales rep position. The early days had gone well—his colleagues in the sales department were smart and sophisticated, the office space was sleek and modern, and the product was reasonably interesting. The rep he was to be paired with was on vacation when he started, so he spent his first week accompanying one of the other reps on her sales calls and helping her with her presentations. By the end of the first week, he was pleased with his situation.

Then his supervising rep returned to work.

At first, it looked like the perfect match. Brett Ludlow was Mitchell Pieda, but ten years older—perfectly tailored clothes, smooth manners, and a self-confidence that Mitchell knew he himself would grow into. Brett was a chameleon with the doctors to whom he peddled his wares—the backslapping buddy of the young male doctors, respectful and deferential with the older ones, and chivalrous but a tiny bit flirty with the female doctors of all ages.

During Mitchell's third week, he helped Brett with a presentation for one of the largest and most prestigious physicians' groups in the Philadelphia area. Millions of dollars in revenue for the company and a hundred thousand dollars in commissions were on the line. The day of the presentation, Brett was pumped—helped, Mitchell suspected, by a line of coke. A few minutes into the presentation, most of the audience was falling under Brett's spell, but an older woman, identified by the company as one of the key decision makers, wasn't laughing at his jokes, wasn't smiling at his quips.

Mitchell could track her reactions to the presentation like watching a stock ticker. When Brett was reviewing the facts—

the case studies, the reference site input, the statistics of time and money saved—her interest rose. When Brett diverted to almost-but-not-quite inappropriate anecdotes, her interest waned and her annoyance spiked.

During a break, Mitchell spirited Brett away from a conversation with one of the younger and better-looking female doctors.

"It's going great," said Brett, straightening his tie.

"I don't think Dr. Montague likes it," said Mitchell.

"What do you mean? It's going great."

"Dr. Montague gets irritated when you tell the stories—she wants more facts."

"What are you talking about?"

"If you stick with the facts, you'll win her over."

"Sorry, Mitch, but how long have you been doing this? A couple of weeks? I guess I can read an audience, and I'm telling you, this audience is loving it."

The presentation continued, and at the end, there were happy handshakes and smiles all around—except for Dr. Montague, whose handshake was peremptory and whose smile was strained.

Back at the office, Mitchell got to listen and re-listen to Brett's recap of the presentation, one that portrayed a more glowing result with each retelling.

When Brett got called into the CEO's office at the end of the next day, he went in swelling with confidence.

He came out ten minutes later, his face red and his fists clenched.

"Pieda. Conference room," he hissed as he passed Mitchell's desk.

Mitchell followed Brett to the conference room. Brett closed the door.

"What the fuck did you say to Weichert?"

"What?"

"Weichert—what did you say to him about the presentation?"

"I didn't say anything to him about the presentation."

"The hell you didn't. You go on about how some bitch in the audience doesn't like my jokes, and then I get called into the principal's office the next day and get told the exact same thing. Now they're putting someone else on the account."

"I didn't say anything."

"'I didn't say anything,'" Brett whined back at him.

Mitchell felt his face grow hot. "Did you ever think maybe Dr. Montague complained about you?"

Brett snapped his hands up and smacked them into Mitchell's chest. Mitchell staggered backwards into a whiteboard, wiping a shoulder-high swathe of the board clean with the back of his jacket.

"Don't talk back to me, you piece of shit," spat Brett. "I've been working this deal for a year, and I don't care what Montague said—I wouldn't have been taken off the account if Weichert hadn't heard someone making up stories about the presentation. And *you* are pretty much the only candidate for that, *Mitchell*."

Mitchell jerked his jacket straight. "It wasn't me."

Brett sneered. "Why don't you take the poker out of your ass and act like one of the team. No one here liked you before, and for sure no one is going to like it when they find out we have a rat in our midst."

Brett banged the door of the conference room open and strode out, leaving Mitchell dizzy with shock and rage.

Brett was right—the attitude toward Mitchell cooled considerably after that. People who had said hello to him the week before passed him without acknowledgement. A lunch outing to celebrate a big sale by another rep occurred without an invitation appearing in his inbox. When he asked the CEO, Weichert, about the possibility of working with another sales rep, Weichert told him that these assignments were long-term, and he couldn't be swapping assistants around just because one had a bone to pick with his supervising rep.

Mitchell turned his power on Brett.

It seemed to work only when Mitchell was near him, when Mitchell could see him, but that wasn't a problem—Mitchell's sales-assistant desk was separated only by a glass wall from Brett's office, and with Brett off his main account, he was spending a lot of time at his desk.

On the first day, Brett complained of a headache and left work an hour early.

On the second day, he only lasted until noon.

On the third day, he emerged from his office after a morning meeting, with the white of his right eye a brilliant red.

On the fourth day, he stumbled climbing the steps into the office and broke his wrist.

When he got back to the office on the fifth day, unable to type, he had to enlist Mitchell's help filling out his reports and responding to his email.

Over the weekend, he fell in his home and was discovered the next day by his cleaning lady. The doctors diagnosed him with a stroke, and in the days that followed, Brett's colleagues commented on how thoughtful it was that Mitchell Pieda was spending so much time at the hospital with Brett.

A week later, Brett Ludlow was dead.

After his mother died, and after reading her diaries, Mitchell became a student of Vivantem. He found out where Gerard Bonnay and the research staff golfed, and became a caddy at the club. During one game, caddying for two Vivantem doctors, one of them mentioned Vivantem and Mitchell feigned surprise. His revelation that he was a Vivantem baby was greeted with much congratulatory, and self-congratulatory, back-slapping. He scanned their thoughts, but perceived nothing suggesting anything underhanded.

Then, about a year ago, he managed to run into Gerard Bonnay and his wife at a fundraiser. The wife's mind was a blank to Mitchell, but the jumble of images that flickered through Bonnay's mind when Mitchell introduced himself as

Antonia Pieda's son convinced him his theory was correct. In Gerard Bonnay, Mitchell had discovered the source of his skills.

Mitchell was certain that Vivantem and Gerard Bonnay were responsible for his ability. And if Gerard Bonnay had made him the way he was, then Gerard Bonnay was the one who could help him make sure he made the most of those skills. Because Mitchell wanted all those things he had seen in his father's mind for himself. And he was never going to allow the Brett Ludlows of the world to call him a "piece of shit" again.

CHAPTER FORTY-TWO

There was a knock on the door of Gerard's study and Louise entered, as she usually did, without waiting for an answer. Gerard looked up from his iPad, and the Vivantem financial report with which he had been trying to occupy himself.

"Where's McNally?" she asked without preamble, crossing to his desk, a padded yellow envelope in her hands.

"I finally talked him into going home for a shower and change of clothes ... and, I hope, a good night's sleep in his own bed."

"Can you keep him away?"

He sighed and put the iPad aside. "I don't know. I suspect he will be back. We need some sort of long-term plan for dealing with him."

"I leave the long-term plan for McNally to you, but I do have a short-term plan for keeping track of Miss Ballard."

She drew out of the envelope what looked like a bulky hypodermic needle and a tiny plastic bag.

"What is it?" he asked.

"A tracker and an implanting device. We can put a tracker on Ballard so we know where she is if we end up not being able to keep her here."

"Owen McNally isn't likely to approve of that."

"He doesn't need to know. Even Ballard doesn't need to know."

"How do you propose doing that?" asked Gerard, an edge of irritation creeping into his voice.

Louise picked up the device. "We implant the tracker

between her shoulder blades. That's where it would be put in a dog—this is usually used on pets—because it's a place that's difficult for a dog to get to. Even on a person, it's difficult to reach between the shoulder blades. And if we put some topical anesthetic on the site, she won't even feel it. It doesn't require an incision, you just shoot the tracker under the skin. After a short time, she wouldn't even be able to see it if she happens to be looking at her back in a mirror."

Gerard took the device from her and turned it over in his hands. "Where in the world did you get this?"

"From Evelyn, next door. She uses it on her hunting dogs."

"Don't you think she'll find it unusual that you are interested in a dog tracking chip?"

"Well, it's not used just for dogs—"

"Still—"

"It can be used for cats, too."

Gerard raised his eyebrows. "You didn't."

"I picked up a cat this morning at the shelter."

"A kitten?"

"God, no. It's actually quite attractive. It's in the kitchen with Angelo."

Gerard shook his head. He took the plastic bag, which contained a tiny capsule-shaped object. "How do you track it once it's implanted?"

Louise pulled her phone out of her pocket. "An app for every purpose." She showed him the screen, which showed an aerial view of the Pocopson house, with a pulsing blue dot over the house—in fact, over the very room where they stood. "The sooner we do it the better." She glanced at her watch. "We should give her another dose now. In half an hour she should be completely out. We can do it then."

"What if McNally comes back later on?"

"It doesn't matter, there won't be anything for him to see."

Gerard looked uncomfortable. "Do you need help to do it?"

"I just need someone to roll her over if she's on her back. I can get George to help me."

"Yes, do that," said Gerard.

Louise cocked an eye at her husband. "You're not getting squeamish, are you?" she asked.

Gerard put his hands in his pocket. "This subterfuge—sedating her, practically holding her hostage … it will make it more difficult to use her to help us later on."

Louise put the tracker and implanting device back in the envelope. "Perhaps. But we don't need her to be a willing subject to learn a great deal from her scientifically. She's an early effort." She turned to Gerard. "If what you want is a mind reader, then I'm sure anything we learn from her will help us toward that goal."

"Yes, I'm sure that's true." He resumed his seat and picked up the iPad. "Let me know when you and George are done with her, I'll be curious to see that tracker at work."

CHAPTER FORTY-THREE

Owen had finally left Pocopson early on Monday, haggard from sleeplessness, grief, and his indecision about what to do about Lizzy. He fell into bed, not even bothering to take off the clothes he had been wearing since Saturday, when he had rushed to Philadelphia in response to Patrick's call from the William Penn Hotel.

He awoke in the late afternoon just as the heavy December darkness was falling, both more alert and more panicked than he had been when he dropped off.

He tried calling Lizzy's number, but there was no answer. He called Gerard, who told him that Lizzy was still sedated. He paced around his house, straightening pictures that were already level, making cups of tea that then sat untouched, the milk forming a scummy skin on top. What could he do? He had always been able to count on careful research to help him determine logical next steps in the academic world, but when he sat down at his computer his fingers hovered uncertainly over the keyboard, and then fell uselessly into his lap. What search did you do in such a circumstance? *kidnapping*? *how to get a fake ID*? *witness protection*?

He wavered between a desire to believe the timing of Patrick's death had been a terrible coincidence and a certain knowledge that it could not have been. He became more and more certain that turning Lizzy over to Gerard Bonnay had resulted in Patrick's death, and put Lizzy in exactly the position that Charlotte had feared. And if Lizzy needed to be rescued, what resources did he, Owen McNally, academic and homebody, have to marshal? He took a disconsolate sip of day-old tea.

He jumped at the ringing of his phone, and looked with hope and trepidation at the caller ID. Then, for the first time in days, a small smile tugged at his lips. He did have a resource he could call on after all.

CHAPTER FORTY-FOUR

Mitchell walked into the Vivantem headquarters the next day. The receptionist was wearing a dark blue dress and a delicate silver necklace, and the effect blended nicely with the elegant surroundings. Mitchell approved.

The woman tucked one loose strand of hair behind her ear. "May I help you?"

"I'd like to speak with Gerard Bonnay. My name is Mitchell Pieda."

"Do you have an appointment?" she asked, glancing at the monitor on her desk.

"No, I would be glad to wait. I think that if you tell him I'm friends with Elizabeth Ballard, he'll want to see me."

The receptionist looked skeptical. "I'll call his assistant and let her know. Elizabeth Ballard?"

"That's right."

She waved toward the waiting area. "Please have a seat."

Mitchell sat down, carefully folding his overcoat over his legs. In a few minutes, another woman, this one slightly older but no less sleek, approached him.

"Mr. Pieda?"

"Yes."

"I'm Mr. Bonnay's assistant. He isn't in the office today, but he asked if you could meet him near his home in Chester County."

"Yes, I could do that," said Mitchell.

"Do you know where Longwood Gardens is?"

"Yes, generally."

"Mr. Bonnay asked if you could meet him in the café

there. Not the restaurant, the café."

"Certainly."

"Eleven o'clock?"

Mitchell glanced at his watch. He would need to take the train to his aunt's house and borrow her car. He did a quick calculation. "Yes, I should be able to do that."

"Very good. Do you know what Mr. Bonnay looks like?"

"Yes."

"Just so Mr. Bonnay knows who to be on the lookout for, may I take a picture of you to send him?" she asked, holding up a smartphone.

"No problem," said Mitchell. He stood, smoothed his tie, and squared his shoulders.

She took a picture. "Thank you."

"Thanks for your help," he said and, nodding to the receptionist as he left, passed through the doors to the lobby.

Gerard Bonnay's organization was a class act. He looked forward to being a part of it.

Mitchell paid his admission to the gardens—if Gerard Bonnay normally held business meetings here, the admission fee probably eliminated some of the less serious pursuers of his attention—and then scanned the map he had received with his ticket. He walked briskly through the visitor center and then up the walk toward where the map showed the café to be located. It had taken him a little longer than he had expected to get the train to his aunt's house, and it was already shortly after eleven o'clock.

Even if he had not known what Gerard Bonnay looked like, and even if the café had not been almost empty, it would have been easy to pick the man out. He sat at a table near the window with a cup of coffee, exuding that air of easy authority that men of means, men of power, always did. Mitchell's father had had that air, before he went to jail.

Gerard saw Mitchell and nodded an acknowledgement. Mitchell crossed the room to the table and extended a hand.

"Mr. Bonnay, very nice to see you again."

Gerard rose from the table and shook his hand. "I recall us meeting, but I'm afraid you're going to need to help me out on the details."

"It was the breast cancer awareness fundraiser that Vivantem sponsored last year," said Mitchell.

"Ah, yes—and if I recall correctly, you are a Vivantem baby." He gestured Mitchell to a chair.

Mitchell removed his overcoat and draped it carefully over one of the other chairs, then sat.

"Yes, that's right."

"But that's not why you wanted to meet," said Gerard.

"No. Well, not entirely. I think we have a mutual acquaintance."

"Yes?"

"Elizabeth Ballard. The young woman in the news. She was on the train with the woman who had a stroke."

Gerard shrugged noncommittally.

"She's a Vivantem baby, too, isn't she?"

"I wouldn't know," said Gerard.

Mitchell drew from his suit coat pocket a deck of cards. It was new, still wrapped in cellophane. He put the pack on the table in front of Gerard. "Would you humor me, Mr. Bonnay? Would you open the pack and take out a card, but don't show it to me."

Gerard smiled coolly. "You had me come out to Longwood on my day off to play card tricks?"

"You came because I told you I was friends with Elizabeth Ballard, so I think you know who she is."

Gerard's smile faded slightly.

"Please, Mr. Bonnay," said Mitchell, nodding toward the deck. "What's the harm?"

Gerard sighed and picked up the deck. He removed the cellophane, opened the box, and shook the cards out.

"They're probably in order, so please shuffle them first so you know I'm not guessing based on the location of the card you pick."

Gerard cocked an eyebrow at him, then shuffled the cards. After a few shuffles he looked up at Mitchell. "Enough?"

"Yes, that's fine."

Gerard leaned back in his chair and held the deck under the edge of the table and pulled out a card. He placed the remainder of the deck face-down on the table.

"All right."

"Now please look at the card, and concentrate on what it is."

Gerard looked at the card he held under the table edge. A few seconds went by. "I don't think—"

"Eight of hearts," said Mitchell.

Gerard looked up, surprised. "Yes."

"Pick another one."

Gerard picked up the deck again, held it out of sight under the edge of the table, and pulled out another card. He glanced at it and was putting the rest of the deck back on the table when Mitchell said, "Two of spades." This time it had been easy, because Gerard had wanted him to know what the card was.

Gerard put the deck back on the table and sat back. "Very impressive."

"But not all that surprising, right?"

"I don't know what you mean."

"That's what Vivantem wanted, wasn't it? Telepathy."

Gerard looked at him, expressionless, but Mitchell could sense a bubble of excitement behind the calm exterior.

"Telepathy and something else. Something that lets a person affect another person's brain. Like giving them a stroke. Like what Elizabeth Ballard did to the woman on the train."

The bubble receded slightly, replaced by the sudden red of alarm. He had proceeded too quickly. But he was committed now.

"Mr. Bonnay, I think you made me the way I am. And if

I'm right, then I thank you for it. I think I can do great things with the talents I have, but I can do greater things faster if I'm working with a man like you. I have goals, I know you have goals, and I think we can both reach our goals faster if we work together."

Gerard Bonnay looked at him for a long time, and the images became fuzzier—Gerard drawing a curtain down in front of his brain, whether he was aware of it or not. Finally Gerard picked up the cards, tapped them carefully together, and slipped them back into the box. "Let's walk in the conservatory," he said. "I'd like to hear more about this theory of yours."

CHAPTER FORTY-FIVE

That evening, in front of a fire in the library, Gerard described his encounter with Mitchell Pieda to Louise.

"Antonia Pieda's son?" asked Louise. "I remember her vaguely. We followed up for a while after her son was born but it seemed as if the treatments hadn't worked." She took a sip of wine. "If the skills didn't fully manifest themselves in Mitchell Pieda until later in life, or if the parents were intentionally misrepresenting their children's abilities, perhaps we should be revisiting the other subjects." Then she added sourly, "Pieda doesn't come with his own version of Owen McNally—that's a plus. Why can't that man just haul himself into his office at Penn and stay buried in his precious academic manuals?"

"You underestimate Owen McNally at your risk, dear. No," he amended, "at *our* risk. He may be inelegant and physically … unwieldy?" Louise gave a slight smile. "But he's intelligent and, I daresay, resourceful if he needs to be."

Louise's smile faded. "'Resourceful' is something we don't need him to be. I wish we could just have George take care of him as well."

Gerard shook his head. "It would be too much of a coincidence—"

Louise waved her hand at him. "I know, I know." She sighed. "It's becoming clear Ballard is not going to be as willingly cooperative as Pieda, but she still might prove useful." She swirled her wine. "Have you ever read about fighting dogs? They're killing machines, but not toward the people who control them. It's a matter of directing the force at the right target, and staying out of the way if things get out of control."

"But how do we do that?" asked Gerard. "A fighting dog is no good if it's drugged, and we don't dare take her off the sedatives in case she realizes what's going on and strikes out."

Louise sighed irritably. "I'm still considering options. But we have to find out if she still has the ability. Pieda grew into his, perhaps Ballard is growing out of hers."

"But what about the woman on the train?"

"It does seem likely Ballard caused that, but we need to be sure. The housekeeper hasn't reported anything noteworthy since the mother died, and even the mother's death could be attributable to an entirely different cause."

"So how can we tell if she still has the power?"

Louise tapped her fingernail on her wine glass. "We need a test subject."

Gerard narrowed his eyes. "A test subject? Not a plum assignment."

"No." Louise swirled the wine in her glass contemplatively. "We need someone expendable."

Gerard raised his eyebrows. "Expendable?"

"Yes." Louise took a delicate sip of wine. "I understand that Angelo has been having trouble with his bookie again."

"Yes, I heard—" Gerard stopped, then pulled his lips back in a slow smile. "Yes, I heard that as well. And it's becoming quite a nuisance."

Louise smiled back. "I think perhaps we can take care of that nuisance once and for all. And we can find out whether or not Elizabeth Ballard is also expendable."

CHAPTER FORTY-SIX

Angelo walked up the concrete walk to the house—a row house like all the houses on the block, but, as an end unit, a little larger, with worn green, white, and red trim. Just in case a passerby happened to think the occupant was a year-round Christmas fan, a large Italian flag, illuminated in the darkness of the December evening by the porch light, hung next to the front door, its corner caught on the edge of the aluminum awning of one of the front windows.

Angelo twitched the flag off the awning and knocked on the door. His hands were shoved in the pockets of his coat and his head ducked into his upturned collar, and not only against the bitter cold. He wasn't enthusiastic about anyone in this neighborhood remembering Angelo Celucci standing at Anton Rossi's door tonight, if Gerard Bonnay's plans panned out.

In a moment, he heard the rattle of a chain being unfastened and locks unbolted, then the door swung open.

Rossi had dressed up for the occasion, but the effect was probably not what he was aiming for—the shoulders of the double-breasted suit were a little too wide, the shirt no longer quite white, the tiny crossed flags on the gold tie-pin more appropriate for a VFW dance.

"Hey ya, Mr. Rossi," said Angelo. "You're looking great!"

Rossi raised an eyebrow at him, then pulled a coat—a long wool trench he had probably inherited from his father— off a coat rack by the door. He shrugged into it, then pulled a pair of gorgeous leather gloves from the pocket.

"I don't know why I can't just meet your boss at a

restaurant," he grumbled.

"He's Gerard Bonnay, he has to be careful who he's seen with," said Angelo.

Rossi raised his eyebrows and flexed his fingers to set the gloves in place. "Does he?"

Angelo shuffled his feet. "You know what I mean. He has dinner with folks like the mayor, and you've gotten yourself into trouble with the cops now and then."

"Yeah," Rossi replied with a cold stare. "Well, let's go."

Angelo started down the porch steps ahead of Rossi. A Cadillac ATS—a rental—idled at the curb in the lighted circle of a streetlight, and a boy of about eight was peering in the window.

"Hey, you get away from that," called Angelo, ducking his head deeper into the collar of his coat and deepening his voice.

The boy turned and looked sulkily up at him. "Just lookin'."

"Well, I don't want you just lookin'," said Angelo. "You back off."

Angelo saw the boy's eyes widen and almost congratulated himself on the effect he had had, when he heard the door close and Rossi's voice behind him.

"Get away from here, you little bastard," said Rossi in a voice hardly raised above a conversational tone.

The boy turned and walked quickly down the sidewalk, casting nervous glances over his shoulder as he went.

Angelo opened the back door. "Here you go, Mr. Rossi."

"What do you think, we're going to a funeral?" said Rossi. "I'll sit in front."

Angelo nodded. "Sure thing."

They wended their way through the South Philly streets and past the sports complex, then onto 95. They drove in silence until Angelo turned west toward Pocopson.

"So tell me again why Gerard Bonnay, who has lunch with the mayor, wants to see me," said Rossi.

"He didn't tell me, Mr. Rossi. He just said he wanted to

talk with you about business."

"What business is he in, anyway?"

"Something medical. Infertility treatments, like that."

"Not exactly my specialty."

"No," said Angelo. After a moment he added, "Maybe he wants to branch out."

Rossi snorted. After a minute, he continued, "You know, Angie, you and me have some business to settle up."

"I know, Mr. Rossi. I think we might be able to take care of it tonight."

Rossi turned to him. "You don't say. Did you just strike it rich?"

Angelo laughed nervously. "Wouldn't say I struck it rich."

Rossi turned back to face the road. "Better have struck it middling rich if you plan to take care of that debt tonight."

They entered the countryside of Chester County, the roads largely deserted, headlights picking up trees and the fence rows of horse farms. Suddenly a large tawny form was at the side of the road—a deer, turning its glowing eyes toward the car.

Angelo jerked the wheel to the left.

"Goddammit!" swore Rossi.

The deer turned and bounded into the woods.

Angelo drew in an unsteady breath and glanced over at Rossi's unbuckled seatbelt. "Better buckle up, Mr. Rossi, just in case one of those things jumps the other way."

"Better keep your eyes on the road and make sure that doesn't happen," growled Rossi. "Goddamned vermin."

A few minutes later, they turned off the road onto the long drive leading to Gerard Bonnay's house. When they pulled up at the door, Angelo hurried around to the passenger side to open the door, but Rossi was already climbing out of the car, looking around him appraisingly. Angelo led him to the front door and stood aside to let him enter, then stepped in front to lead him down the hall to the library.

"Right down here," he said, beckoning Rossi to follow

him.

The room was dimly lit by the light of one lamp and a fire crackling in the fireplace.

"I'll go get Mr. Bonnay. You want anything? Something to drink?"

"No," said Rossi, pulling off his gloves and putting them in the pocket of his coat.

Angelo stepped forward. "I can take your coat for you, Mr. Rossi."

"I'll just put it here," said Rossi, draping the coat over the back of one of the chairs.

"Sure, no problem. Okay, I'll be back in a minute with Mr. Bonnay."

Angelo trotted lopsidedly down the hall and knocked on the door of Gerard's study.

"Come in."

He opened the door—Gerard was sitting at his desk, a book in his hand.

"He's in the library, Mr. Bonnay."

"Very good, Angelo. I'll let you know when we're ready for Miss Ballard."

Angelo nodded and headed toward the back of the house to wait in the kitchen for the plan to unfold.

"Mr. Rossi, thank you very much for coming, I'm Gerard Bonnay," he said, crossing the room and extending his hand.

"No problem," said Rossi, shaking his hand. "I'm just curious about the reason."

"Of course, please forgive the cloak and dagger. May I get you a drink? Whiskey?"

"Sure. Neat."

Gerard went to a bar tucked discreetly into a corner of the library and poured whiskey into two pear-shaped glasses. He handed one to Rossi and waved toward a pair of wing chairs in front of a fireplace.

"Please, have a seat."

They settled into the chairs, Gerard taking a sip of the whiskey, Rossi taking a more hefty swallow.

"So, Mr. Rossi ... may I call you Anton?"

"Sure, why not, Gerard."

"Anton, as I said, I appreciate you coming out to see me."

"I'm a little curious about why you would want to talk to me."

Gerard chuckled. "Yes, I can imagine." He sipped his whiskey again. "I have recently become interested in the gambling habits of Philadelphians," he said. "I have been approached as a potential investor by an organization looking to open a casino in the area, and I wondered whether Philadelphia is really ready to support another casino. Then I thought that I have a connection to that world through Angelo."

"Yeah?" said Rossi.

"Yes. I understand Angelo is quite a committed gambler."

"Yeah, he's a regular." Rossi took another gulp of whiskey.

"Are there many like him in the area?"

"Sure, there are always guys who want to take a gamble on something—sports, horses, cards."

"Slots?"

"Sure."

Gerard settled back in his chair. "I like the idea of investing in something that's a human imperative—something you don't have to talk people into, something that has an inborn attraction."

"Well, gambling's certainly that." Rossi finished off his whiskey and raised his glass to Gerard.

Gerard crossed to the bar and came back with the bottle. He poured a generous amount into Rossi's glass, then topped off his own, although it was barely touched.

"So gambling has been a profitable business for you?" Gerard asked, resuming his seat.

Rossi drank from his refreshed glass and relaxed back into

the chair. "It's been good for me."

Gerard swirled his whiskey in his glass. "Gambling has its own draw. But combined with other 'human imperatives,' it seems like a winning bet."

Rossi drew his eyebrows together. "What do you mean by that?"

"Anyone can offer gambling. But offering gambling along with other ... attractions ... I think that would sweeten the pot. So to speak."

Rossi narrowed his eyes. "What do you mean, Gerard?"

"Gambling seems like a man's game. And a man might want a ... let's say, an accompaniment to his gambling activities."

"I suppose so."

"I propose catering to those men who are looking for an opportunity for a wager, and would appreciate a beautiful woman by their side while they lay down their bet." He raised his eyebrows questioningly at Rossi.

"I suppose so," he repeated.

Gerard sat forward. "Would you like to see what I have in mind?"

Rossi hesitated for a beat. "Sure."

"Let me show you," said Gerard, and reached into his pocket.

Rossi's eyes narrowed and his body stiffened.

"I just need to send a text to Angelo," said Gerard easily.

Rossi nodded almost imperceptibly.

Gerard pulled his phone out of his pocket and tapped in a text. In a moment, Angelo appeared at the door.

"Angelo, could you bring Lizzy to the room?"

"Sure thing, boss," said Angelo, and pulled the door closed behind him.

"Your big idea is to offer hookers?" asked Rossi, taking another gulp of his whiskey.

"That is exactly the issue," said Gerard. "People think in terms of 'hookers' when they think of gambling. But I'm interested in catering to a more sophisticated, more discerning type of gentleman. Ones who would value beauty and intelligence. And innocence." He glanced meaningfully at Rossi. "And who would be willing to pay a premium for it."

"You're offering virgins-for-hire?"

"We would not guarantee virginity—that business seems like one that would be challenged on the supply side—but certainly the young women involved wouldn't give an impression of tawdriness or looseness."

Rossi swirled his drink. "Not a bad idea. But not really up my alley."

"No, I would expect you to provide expertise only on the gambling side of the business. But I would be curious to get your input on the type of young lady I have in mind."

Rossi shrugged. "Sure."

"In fact, if you will wait here for a moment, I think I can give you an example of the experience." Gerard rose. "Please make yourself at home. I'll be back shortly." And with a little bow, he left the room.

Rossi raised his eyebrows, then a small smile played at his lips. A trip out to this Chester County pile might prove to be worth it after all. And Angelo claimed he'd have his money tonight. Yes, it might be a very good night after all. He took another drink of whiskey.

CHAPTER FORTY-SEVEN

Lizzy was awoken by a sound, although by the time she came fully awake she could no longer identify what it had been. She was curled in a large armchair in the guest bedroom at Gerard's house, her arm across the book she had been trying to read, its paper cover bent. She wished she had a watch—she hadn't seen hers since coming here. In fact, there wasn't anything in the room that showed the time, but the windows were dark. She pulled herself up and smoothed the book cover, then glanced around the room, trying to guess the source of the sound.

She realized that she was feeling more alert than she had in days, although that wasn't saying much. She had been at Gerard's house for a while—four or five days, she thought—and most of that had been a hazy blur. She had understood when Gerard explained to her that she needed to be sedated for his safety and the safety of the other people in his household. She had seen two other people—someone named Angelo, who seemed like an assistant of some sort and who walked with a limp, and, briefly, Gerard's wife, Louise. After all, the reason she was hiding at their house was because she had killed a woman with her mind.

But in the last day or two, she had tried to pull herself out of the routine she had fallen into: meals usually brought to her in her room by Angelo, books that she nodded over, movies that she never saw the end of because she fell asleep ... and then it was bedtime. When the fog began to lift a bit, she would wonder what was happening about her father and where Owen was. Gerard explained that Owen was busy arranging the funeral and taking care of legal and administrative matters associated with her father's death.

She wanted to be away from Gerard's house. It was a beautiful home, and they were taking great care of her, but she wanted to be out, to be helping Uncle Owen with the arrangements. She tried to think through the complications and come up with solutions, but the complications and the solutions kept muddling in her mind and soon she would drift off into a reverie or a nap. And then Angelo would show up with a beautifully appointed meal tray, always with a tiny crystal dish with a pill in it, and she would remember that she was indebted to Gerard for keeping her away from the police, and she would take the pill and drift off yet again.

But she realized that her last tray, whenever that had been, hadn't included the crystal dish. Coming awake was a simple act, not the maddening fight through cottony layers of confusion that she had experienced in the last few days.

She looked around the room and couldn't see anything that might have been the source of whatever the sounds had been. Maybe it was a dream.

She was considering whether she could take a walk around the house without attracting any unwanted attention—perhaps they had just forgotten the pill, and would give her another if they saw her up and about)—when she heard the sound again. It was a tentative knock on the door. She put the book aside, crossed to the door, and opened it. Angelo stood outside.

"Mr. Bonnay asks if you can come to the library," he said, addressing a spot somewhere behind her. She had noticed that about Angelo—never quite looking her in the face, never meeting her eyes.

"Why?"

"He didn't say, just asked me to come get you." Lizzy started to step out of the room, but Angelo continued. "He has a guest for dinner, so he thought you might want to dress up a little."

Lizzy felt a flush of excitement—an emotion that she hadn't felt much in the past few sedated days.

"Is it Uncle Owen?"

Angelo shrugged. "I wouldn't know about that."

"But I don't have any clothes to dress up in."

"He says check in the closet."

Lizzy crossed to the closet, which she hadn't opened since her first groggy investigation of the room, and saw, hanging on a padded hanger, a black dress. She took the hanger down and held it out. The dress was of a silky material, with long sleeves, a V-neck, and a skirt that Lizzy guessed would end just above her knees. Around the top of the hanger hung a necklace of small red beads—perhaps coral.

"There should be shoes in there too."

Lizzy glanced back in the closet and saw on the floor a pair of dressy black sandals.

She looked up at Angelo. "I'm supposed to get dressed up for Uncle Owen?"

"I never said it was Owen," said Angelo, then gave her a little wink. "I'll wait out in the hall for you to change, then take you downstairs." He shut the door.

"I guess I could get downstairs on my own," muttered Lizzy, but she was excited by the secrecy, and by the drama of having an outfit provided for the occasion.

She took the clothes into the bathroom, shed the jeans, turtleneck, sweater, and sneakers that were among the supply of clothes that Gerard had provided, and slipped into the dress.

Whoever had picked it out had known just what size to get, and had understood just what style would flatter her tall, slender figure. She turned in front of the mirror to examine herself from different angles, and was pleased with what she saw. She looked in the drawers of the vanity for a hand mirror so she could look at the back of the dress, but couldn't find one.

She fastened the necklace around her throat, and, on a whim, pulled her perennial ponytail out of its elastic band and let her long, straight hair fall around her shoulders. Finally, she slipped on the sandals. The heels weren't high in comparison to what she had seen some other girls wear, but she had never worn heels before. She took a few experimental, teetering steps. It was going to be a disaster. She took them off and carried them with her to the door.

Angelo was standing in the hallway, leaning against the wall, but jumped to attention when she appeared. "Hey, you look nice," he said, with undisguised surprise.

"Gee, thanks," said Lizzy, who started down the hall past him, toward the stairway.

"Hey," he said, trotting after her in his uneven gait, "aren't you going to put on your shoes?"

"I will when I get there," she said.

She skipped down the stairway, her spirits lifting at the thought of seeing Uncle Owen—and of seeing him in this oddly alert state. Maybe they had decided she didn't need to be sedated any more. She certainly hoped so.

She started in the direction she thought led to the dining room, where she had eaten breakfast one morning, but Angelo called after her.

"This way," he said, and led her down a different hallway. When they got to one of the doors, he whispered, "The shoes!" with some urgency.

She laughed and slipped them on. "Better?"

Angelo smiled nervously. "Yup. You go on in, I'll let Mr. Bonnay know you're here."

Lizzy smiled back at him, opened the door, and stepped past the threshold.

The room was dark, lit by only one light and a crackling fire, but she could see the top of a man's head over the back of one of the wing chairs by the fireplace. "Uncle—" she said, but as the man stood, the words died on her lips. He could hardly have been less like Uncle Owen—a pinched, rat-like face, hard black eyes, and a scrawny build that the wide shoulders of his suit jacket served to accentuate rather than disguise.

He stepped out from behind the chair, and Lizzy heard the door close behind her.

"I'm supposed to be your uncle, am I?" he asked with an oily smile.

"Who are you?" she asked.

The man swirled his drink and looked at her appraisingly, his eyes running down her dress to her sandals and back up.

"Not bad," he said.

"Who are you?" she said, louder.

"A friend of Mr. Bonnay's."

Lizzy looked around the room. "Where is he?"

"He stepped out for a minute. Maybe for a few minutes," said the man. "Why don't you come over here and keep me company until he gets back?"

"That's okay, I'll stay over here," she said.

"I don't think that's the game plan, sweetheart," he said, and took a step toward her.

She took a step back. Her heel turned and she staggered, catching herself on a table.

The man laughed. "Don't play up the 'sweet and innocent' thing too much, honey. You might hurt yourself." He put his drink down and took another step toward her.

Lizzy's ankle throbbed. She reached down and slipped the sandals off. "I'm going to wait in my room. Gerard can let me know when he's back." She turned back to the door and grasped the doorknob.

Locked.

She looked back over her shoulder at the rat-like man making his slow way across the room toward her, then turned back to the door. "Angelo!" she shouted. "The door's locked—let me out!"

She looked over her shoulder again, and the man was now just a few steps away. "Come on, sweetheart—I don't know what they told you to do, but you don't have to play the reluctant virgin with me." He took another step and clamped his hand onto her arm.

"Get away from me!" yelled Lizzy.

The man winced, and his grip on her arm tightened. "Goddamn," he muttered. He shook his head, then turned his lips up in a wolfish smile. "But I'm not going to let a little headache stand in the way of us getting to know each other better." He grasped her other arm and pulled her toward him.

He smelled of wet wool and too-heavy cologne, with the faint hint of unwashed flesh. She saw a tiny speck of food caught in the day-old stubble on his chin.

"Stop it!" she cried, twisting in his grasp. "Stop!"

His eyes squinted shut and his grasp on her arms loosened for a moment. She tried to twist away, but then his fingers clamped onto her arms even harder, although his eyes were still squeezed shut. "Goddammit—what the hell?"

She pressed her back to the door and screamed, "Angelo! Gerard! Open the door! It's happening again!"

His eyes flew open. "It's happening again?" he said hoarsely. "What the hell are you talking about?"

She was crying. "I don't mean to do it, just leave me alone!"

"Are you doing this to me, you little bitch?" He staggered as another spasm of pain crossed his face. "Jesus Christ!" he groaned.

"I mean it! Leave me alone and it will stop!"

He threw himself forward and his hands locked around her throat. "I'll make *you* stop, little girl," he grated out, and his fingers tightened on her neck.

Lizzy strained to push him away. He might look scrawny, but it was like pushing against the door to which her back was pressed. She kicked out, but her bare toes met boots under his pants. She tried to reach his eyes with her fingers, but at that moment he reared his head back and cracked her in the nose with his forehead. She screamed, and felt the warm fingers of blood creep down her face.

He snatched his hands off her neck, snagging the necklace

with fingers curled into claws. Red beads flew off her neck and mixed with the spatters of blood on the carpet. He gripped the sides of his head at his temples. "Stop it! Stop it!" he repeated, his voice almost a shriek. He staggered back and into the table, sending the lamp crashing to the floor in a shower of sparks and plunging the room into near darkness, only the fire casting flickering shadows on the wall.

He fell to the floor, but then dragged himself up onto his hands and knees and began crawling in a circle, the cries of "Stop it!" becoming weaker and weaker.

Lizzy slid to the floor, her hands at her throat. "Help me!" she croaked.

When the man's cries finally stopped, she became aware, over her own hitching gasps of tears, of pounding on the door.

"Lizzy!" It was Gerard. "Open the door!"

"It's locked!" she cried.

"It's locked on your side," he called. "Unlock it on your side!"

She dragged herself to her feet and fumbled at the door. Her efforts were tipping toward hysteria when, almost by accident, she hit the button and the door swung open. Gerard and Angelo stood in the hall, their faces pale, with Louise behind them, her mouth a tight line. "You must have locked yourself in," said Gerard unsteadily.

Lizzy staggered and he caught her. "Who is he?"

"A man here on business, I was trying to send him away. I didn't realize you would go in the library."

Lizzy turned toward Angelo, who took a quick step back. "That's where he told me to go!" she rasped.

Angelo held up his hands. "I'm sorry, I thought that's where you were supposed to go!"

"I told him to take Lizzy to the library," said Louise. "I didn't realize there was someone in there."

"I put him in there because I thought Lizzy was going to go to the dining room," said Gerard, running his fingers through his hair. "Never mind that now." Gerard took a pressed white handkerchief out of his pocket and handed it to Lizzy. "Your nose …"

She took the handkerchief and dabbed at the bridge of her nose. It came away with a streak of blood.

"Is it broken?" Lizzy asked in an unsteady voice.

"Let's get you upstairs and Louise can check that out. Angelo and I will check on that man." He took Lizzy's shoulders and turned her toward the stairs. "Are you okay to walk upstairs on your own?"

Lizzy nodded, but then stumbled when she took a step. Louise stepped up and took her other arm.

"I'm okay," said Lizzy tremulously, shaking Louise's hand off. "Is Uncle Owen here?"

"Owen? No, Lizzy, he's not here. Louise and I just thought you might like a nice dinner downstairs as a change of pace."

Lizzy stopped at the foot of the stairs. "I want Uncle Owen," she cried, the tears coming harder now, mixing with the blood leaking from the cut on her nose.

"I'll try to get him for you, Lizzy," said Gerard, "but for now let's get you away from here."

Gerard and Louise led her up the stairs, Angelo watching them from the hallway. When they got to her room, Gerard stepped aside and Louise took his place at Lizzy's side and led her to the bed. She knelt in front of Lizzy and moved the girl's hand and bloodstained handkerchief away from her nose, then probed Lizzy's face gently with her thumbs.

"Broken?" asked Lizzy thickly.

"No, it's not broken, and the cut's not bad. We just need to clean it and put a little bandage on it. I'm going to get the first aid kit and I'll be right back."

Louise was back in a moment with a glass of cloudy liquid. "Lizzy, I'm going to give you something that will help calm you. Can you drink this up for me?"

"No, I don't want to be drugged anymore," cried Lizzy miserably, her fingers twisted in her lap, her back hunched.

Gerard stepped over to the bed. "Lizzy, it's for you, but it's for us, too. For our protection. Do you understand?"

Lizzy was silent for long seconds. Gerard and Louise exchanged a glance over her head. Finally, Lizzy nodded and reached for the glass without looking up. Louise put it in her hand and she and Gerard watched as Lizzy slowly drained it.

"Good girl," said Louise, taking the glass from her. "Now let's get that nose taken care of." She cleaned and bandaged the cut, then eased Lizzy back onto the pillows and helped swing her legs up onto the bed. She pulled a comforter up from the foot of the bed and spread it over her. "You rest, and Gerard and I will take care of everything." Lizzy turned her face toward the wall, her shoulders shuddering with the last of her tears, but in a minute the hitch of her breath was already smoothing. Louise and Gerard crossed the room and closed the door quietly behind them.

CHAPTER FORTY-EIGHT

Angelo drove toward Anton Rossi's neighborhood, his hands clammy on the wheel of the Caddy, his heart thumping at each red light that delayed his errand. The black vinyl bag with Rossi's body in it was in the back seat of his car, covered with a green and white Philadelphia Eagles stadium blanket.

It had happened just like Mr. Bonnay had said. Angelo had spent years living in fear of Anton Rossi, of feeling that jolt, like a punch in the gut, when he saw one of his thugs coming. Of knowing that, in the neighborhood they shared, a call for help would result in a quick glance out the window, then the shades would be drawn and the TV volume turned up, and the next time he ran into those neighbors, they wouldn't meet his eyes.

And now that skinny girl had done Anton Rossi in. And however she had done it, based on what Angelo had heard standing in the hallway with Mr. Bonnay and Dr. Mortensen, it hadn't been an easy end. If Angelo could just get rid of the body, his problems would be solved. He would make good on his perennial promise to Zia Ruby to stop the gambling. Or at least find a more understanding bookie.

He got to the neighborhood and did a reconnaissance pass, regretting the few unbroken streetlights that illuminated the bundle in the back seat. He was grateful to see that, although it wasn't late, the plummeting temperature and a nasty wind whistling over the Delaware had left the streets largely deserted.

He pulled into the alley that ran behind Rossi's house. This was Rossi's usual shortcut to his favorite bar two streets away, a shortcut that only Anton Rossi had felt comfortable taking after dark. Angelo had been walking or driving that alley all his life, and knew that the couple of seemingly intact security cameras were fakes.

He pulled over, partially hidden from one end of the alley by a battered dumpster and from the other by a rusted-out Buick that had been parked in the same place for months. Switching the dome light off, he stepped out of the car and opened the back door. He zipped open the bag, eased Rossi's feet out, and gave a tremendous pull. He hadn't counted on the slipperiness of the bag's interior, and Anton Rossi shot out of the back seat and tumbled onto the cracked pavement. Angelo staggered backwards, pinwheeling his arms, his bad leg threatening to give way, and was only saved from a fall by fetching up smartly against the dumpster on the opposite side of the alley.

"Merda!" he sputtered under his breath, rubbing his head where it had caught the edge of the dumpster.

He glanced nervously up and down the alley, then limped to the car, taking a quick glance to make sure Rossi's head was clear of the tires. There was a brief screech of rubber on pavement as he hit the gas, then he managed to slow the car to a sedate pace as he rolled to the end of the alley.

As Angelo pulled onto the street, at the other end of the alley George Millard stepped out of the shadows and began walking briskly down the sidewalk. As he walked, he pulled his phone out of his pocket and speed dialed a number. "Yeah, he did it. It wasn't pretty, but it's done." After a moment he said, "Yes, sir," and slipped the phone back into his pocket. "Amateurs," he muttered, and popped a mint into his mouth.

CHAPTER FORTY-NINE

Owen and Andy McNally sat in the living room of Owen's house in Lansdowne, watching football on a large television usually hidden behind a screen covered with handprinted wallpaper in a William Morris design.

"Oh my God," groaned Owen. "Not again."

"You're going to owe me big time, bro," crowed Andy, who had lost the pre-game coin toss that determined which brother would be rooting for the Eagles' opponent—in this case the Detroit Lions—in the McNally brothers' traditional buck-a-sack bet.

"I can't watch, it's too painful." Owen clicked the volume down a few notches with the remote. "Hey, there's something I need to talk with you about."

"This isn't just an excuse to spare yourself the trauma of watching your life savings trickling away dollar by dollar, is it?"

"Nope."

Andy sat back. "Shoot."

"Do you remember Lizzy Ballard? Patrick and Charlotte Ballard's daughter?"

"Sure. I mean, I never met her, but I remember you talking about her. How's she doing?" Andy asked sympathetically. Andy hadn't seen the news coverage of Lucia Hazlitt's death, and Owen had told him only that Patrick Ballard had been killed by a mugger.

"Well, not so great, as you can imagine."

"Poor kid," said Andy, "losing both her parents so young. How old is she, anyway?"

"Sixteen. Almost seventeen."

Andy shook his head. "That's tough. Who's taking care of her?"

"Well, Lizzy ended up being—" Owen hesitated. "—taken in by someone. Gerard Bonnay. Have you heard of him?"

Andy scratched his chin. "Sounds sort of familiar."

"He heads up Vivantem."

"Ah, yes. Why did she end up with him?"

"Actually, she's staying with Bonnay and his wife. It's complicated, but I need to get her away from them."

"What do you mean?"

"They have her at their enormous house in Pocopson and they don't want to let her go. They're not even letting me talk to her."

"Why not?"

"I'd rather not say."

"It's not ..." Andy paused, "... *kinky*, is it?"

Owen waved his hand. "No, nothing like that."

Andy cocked a skeptical eyebrow at Owen.

"Lizzy's a Vivantem baby, and they want to study her. Experiment on her."

"Why?"

"Jeez, Andy," Owen burst out, "can you just trust me when I tell you they're not having orgies with her but I still need to get her away from them?"

Andy waved his hand in a conciliatory gesture. "Okay, okay, calm down, don't give yourself a heart attack." After a pause he asked, "So what's your plan?"

"I can't just sneak her out of the house. There are too many people around, and locked gates at the entrance. I need to get her out with their cooperation."

"Like *The Sting*."

"Exactly."

"And you're going to be Paul Newman in this scenario?"

"Yup."

"And who, dare I ask, is Robert Redford?"

Owen gave a wan smile. "I'm looking at him."

Andy took another sip of beer. "Of course you are," he sighed.

CHAPTER FIFTY

Gerard slipped his phone into his pocket. "He did it." They sat in the dining room, having cleaned up the broken lamp and gathered the scattered necklace beads in the library.

"Without a hitch?" Louise asked.

"Evidently without any *serious* hitches."

"Good lord, Gerard, you need to get rid of him, he's incompetent. We should have had George take care of it," she said.

"Anton Rossi wouldn't have come to the house with anyone he didn't know," countered Gerard, "and if we had to have Angelo bring him here, it made sense to have Angelo take him away. One less person involved." He took a breath. "Lizzy Ballard may be a fighting dog in the making, but Angelo Celucci is a faithful hound. Not too smart, but he'd never turn against us."

Louise sighed. "I suppose so. But we need to surround ourselves with higher caliber people."

They sat in silence for a minute, Gerard sipping a scotch and Louise a glass of port, then Gerard said, "Well, she's clearly a force to be reckoned with."

"Yes," replied Louise. "But she's too unpredictable. Not only can't we control her, she can't even control herself." She took another sip. "Plus, she's too traumatized by her effect. We need someone whose weapon is a scalpel, not a sledgehammer, and who isn't put off by the sight of blood. Figuratively speaking." She leaned forward. "From what you told me, Mitchell Pieda could be that person—he may not have the brute force that Lizzy does, but I think he could learn to use his powers with more finesse."

"So, where does that leave us?" asked Gerard.

"Mitchell has the ability we were aiming for to begin with—telepathy—and his ability to cause strokes, although much less than Ballard's, is icing on the cake. Imagine what we can accomplish with his help. Imagine being in a meeting with our competitors and knowing what they're planning. Imagine being in a meeting with government officials and knowing what regulations they're thinking of imposing. And," she said, reaching out and touching his hand, "if we can further develop Mitchell's ability to cause strokes, imagine being able to eliminate the intractable ones with no suspicion."

Gerard shook his head slowly. "It means taking him on as a partner, not just an employee. It means letting him be part of calling the shots."

Louise sat back and smiled. "I'm enough of a mind reader to know that Mitchell realizes we can create opportunities for him that he could never create for himself. If we treat him fairly, I believe he will open opportunities for us that would be far more difficult for us to create for ourselves."

They were silent for a moment, sipping their drinks.

"Rock, paper, scissors," said Gerard musingly.

"What?"

"Didn't you ever play rock, paper, scissors when you were little?" asked Gerard. "Rock crushes scissors, scissors cut paper, paper covers rock."

"What in the world are you talking about?"

"Lizzy Ballard's power is the rock, Mitchell's is more like scissors."

Louise raised an eyebrow. "We have to make sure that in our game, scissors beats rock." She leaned forward. "Lizzy Ballard is a liability. Her goals aren't our goals. Her scruples are the scruples of a girl who has never had to face the real world, who's lived a sheltered existence, protected by her parents. Plus," she added, "we can't keep a teenage girl hostage and under sedation forever."

Gerard nodded slowly.

"Gerard, don't become emotionally attached. She's an experiment that didn't work out."

He sighed. "Yes. I know." They sat in silence for a moment, Louise waiting for more from him. Finally he said, "I wonder what paper is?'

Louise threw back the last few drops of her port and put the glass down on the table beside her. "Paper covers rock? Then that's George. We need to get rid of her, Gerard. And that's not a job I'm going to entrust to Angelo."

CHAPTER FIFTY-ONE

Owen pulled his SUV up to the metal gates at the beginning of the drive to Gerard Bonnay's home and pushed the Talk button on the intercom. In a moment, a voice with a distinct South Philly accent answered.

"Help you?"

"Hello, this is Owen McNally. I need to speak with Gerard Bonnay."

"Do you have an appointment?" asked the voice uncertainly.

"No, but it's very important I speak with him." Owen's pulse thudded in his ears.

"Hold on a minute," said the voice.

At least three minutes went by before the voice was back. "All right. Pull up to the front door." The gates swung open.

Gerard was standing on the front step when Owen pulled up, and stepped up to the driver's door. Owen buzzed his window down.

"How are you doing, Owen?" asked Gerard, his breath puffing white in the chill December air.

"Well, you know …" said Owen. After a pause, he said, "Not used to having things so topsy turvy."

Gerard nodded. "Yes, I can sympathize."

"I'm here to see Lizzy," said Owen.

"It's not a good idea," said Gerard. "She's still traumatized by what's happened."

"Still sedated?"

"Well, yes," said Gerard. "For the protection of the people who are caring for her, but for her own benefit as well."

Owen took a deep breath, hoping his voice wouldn't tremble. "Gerard, it's been a week. She's my goddaughter. I need to see her."

Gerard regarded him, and Owen managed to meet his gaze. Finally, Gerard said, "Very well. Come with me."

Gerard led him into the house. They were met in the front hall by a man who, based on his accent, had been the voice on the intercom. The man took Owen's coat, then Owen followed Gerard to the second floor.

Gerard knocked on the bedroom door and then eased it open and looked in. He turned back to Owen. "I think she's asleep."

"I can wait with her until she wakes up," said Owen, and pushed past Gerard and into the room.

The light was dim, some sort of new age-y music playing softly. Lizzy lay on the bed, propped up on a stack of pillows, on top of the puffy comforter but under a light blanket. She wore a long-sleeved white T-shirt and, where she had kicked the blanket away from one foot, socks but no shoes. Owen approached the bed. Her lips were parted slightly, her face relaxed. There was a small cut on her nose, and a yellowish tinge around her eyes.

"What happened to her face?" asked Owen, his voice raised in alarm.

"She got dizzy and fell a couple of days ago."

"Why didn't you call me?"

"It wasn't an emergency. We adjusted the dosage of the sedative so she wouldn't be so woozy."

"She looks pretty woozy to me," said Owen.

Gerard said tightly, "Based on what you told me, this young lady killed someone using only the power of her mind. You will forgive me if I take precautions to ensure it doesn't happen to a member of my household."

Owen turned to Gerard. "Please don't think I don't appreciate everything you're doing for her—I do. I just feel like I need to be more involved in her care. I'm her godfather.

With both her parents gone, I'm the closest thing to family she has."

Gerard sighed. "Yes, of course."

"I'd like to take her home with me. The news coverage of Lucia Hazlitt's death has died down and, as far as I know, the police's interest in it died down with it. There really is no reason for anyone to think that the death of the woman on the train was anything other than a medical anomaly, and since you've been able to keep Lizzy out of the fray since that happened, it seems like I could take her to Lansdowne now, or maybe somewhere further away."

Gerard shook his head. "I appreciate your interest in her well-being, but the fact is she did kill a woman—I think we all agree that the evidence supports that theory. I can't in good conscience let her back out into an unsuspecting world without a better plan of action in place."

"And do you have a plan of action in mind?"

"Not entirely. But I believe it would be irresponsible to expose her to the general public. She will always need a controlled environment to ensure she doesn't harm anyone else."

"And you're going to provide that controlled environment?"

"Yes. I think my wife and I are uniquely qualified to do just that."

"And to understand her ability."

"Yes, certainly."

"Perhaps to experiment on her."

Gerard held up his hands. "Don't paint me as a Mengele, Dr. McNally."

Owen puffed out a breath. "No, I certainly didn't mean that. It's just that it doesn't sound like much of a life for a young lady, locked away from the rest of the world."

Gerard smiled tiredly. "I believe my wife and I can ensure that her life is a pleasant one."

Owen looked around the elegantly appointed room, out

the window at a sweep of snow-covered lawn and a graceful curve of carefully pruned holly hedge. "Yes, I'm sure you could." He sighed. "I'd like to talk some more, I'd like to be part of the plan. But first I'd like to spend a little time with her." He crossed to an antique vanity and pulled out the delicate bench. He put it down next to the bed and eased himself gingerly down onto it.

Gerard stood next to the bed, looking, for once, uncomfortable.

"You don't need to stay," said Owen.

After a brief pause, Gerard said, "Certainly. I'll be downstairs. Please let Angelo know if you need anything. Just call for him from the front hall, and he'll hear you."

Owen imagined Gerard Bonnay instructing his South Philly associate to watch the stairs, to make sure that Owen McNally didn't leave with the girl. "Thank you," he said.

After another brief pause, Gerard stepped out of the room and eased the door shut behind him. There was a minute during which Owen sensed Gerard was still just outside, but then he heard, barely audible on the thick carpet of the hallway, steps receding toward the stairway.

"Lizzy?" he whispered. He took her hand and patted it lightly. There was no response.

"Lizzy," he said, a little louder, patting her hand a little harder. Still no response.

"Lizzy!" he hissed as loud as he dared, and reached out to pat her cheek.

She stirred slightly.

He kept patting and in a moment her eyes opened, vague, then slowly focused on him.

"Uncle Owen?"

He squeezed her hand. "Yes, sweetie, it's me." He felt tears spring to his eyes. "It's me, Pumpkin."

She tried to sit up, but fell back on the pillows. "Are we home?" she asked, disoriented.

"No, we're at Gerard Bonnay's house."

She looked around, at first confused, and then settled into recognition. "Oh. Right." Her head fell back onto the pillow. "Are you going to take me home?"

"I'm going to take you away from here, Pumpkin," he said. "But Gerard doesn't want you to go. We're going to need to trick him."

"Trick him?" said Lizzy, slipping back into a listless uncertainty.

"Yes."

She seemed about to nod off again, and he reached out and patted her cheek once more, perhaps a little harder than he had intended because she jumped. The fogginess left her eyes for a moment.

"Ow!" she said.

"Sorry, Pumpkin," said Owen, "but I need you to be alert."

"I'm alert," she grumbled.

Owen glanced toward the door, straining to hear any pad of muffled steps in the hallway. Hearing nothing, he dug in the pocket of his jeans and pulled out a small bottle.

"Pumpkin, I think the only way to get you out of here is to convince them that you're sick."

"Okay."

"If you take this, it will make it seem like you're sick. It won't do you any harm, but it will be ..." He hesitated. "... sort of unpleasant."

"Uh, okay," she said uncertainly.

"I'm sorry, sweetie. I wish I could think of another way."

She struggled up in the bed, pushing herself into a semi-sitting position. "I want to go home, Uncle Owen. I don't mind if it makes me sick for a little while."

Owen felt himself tear up again. "That's my girl." There was a water pitcher and glass on the bedside table, and he filled the glass. He opened the bottle and handed it to her. "Okay, drink this down. Don't sip it, drink it all at once."

Lizzy threw back the tablespoon or so of liquid in the

bottle, then contorted her face. "What is that? It's horrible."

"Don't worry. Drink this water."

She grabbed the glass and gulped it down. "It doesn't help," she gasped.

He took the glass from her and put it back on the table. "I know, it's gross. But it won't last long." He glanced at his watch. "I need to go downstairs for a minute, but I'll be back, and then we'll be out of here, okay?"

Lizzy was working her tongue around her mouth as if she were trying to scrape the taste off it. "What are you trying to do, kill me?"

Owen flushed, knowing it was going to get worse before it got better. He patted her hand.

"I'll be back, Pumpkin."

He got his phone out of his pocket and placed it on the floor next to her bed, then crossed to the hallway. He glanced back as he closed the door and saw her lean back on the pillow, and was suddenly afraid she might fall asleep again—maybe so deeply that she wouldn't wake up when the drug's effects began to kick in. His heart was an escalating drumbeat in his ears. What the hell was he doing?

He hurried back to the bed.

"Pumpkin, roll over on your side, okay?"

"Why?"

"It's just better that way, okay?"

She shrugged, her mouth still working, and rolled over.

"I'll be back soon," he said.

He went downstairs and, when he got to the foyer, called, "Hello?"

Gerard and Angelo appeared at the same time.

"All in order?" asked Gerard.

"Yes, thank you," said Owen. "I think I'm ready to discuss that plan now."

Gerard nodded to Angelo, who retreated toward the back of the house, then he led Owen to the library. He gestured Owen into a chair while he remained standing by the fireplace, his elbow propped nonchalantly on the mantel.

"So, you propose to keep her here?" asked Owen.

Gerard sighed. "I must admit that this is not a situation for which my experience has prepared me but, yes, it's the best plan I can come up with."

"I feel terrible that you've been pulled into this," said Owen.

Gerard waved his hand. "Don't be silly. I'm the one who contacted you."

"But you can't keep her here forever," said Owen. Then, interjecting what he aimed to be a note of hopefulness into his voice, added, "Can you?"

Gerard shrugged. "Well, perhaps not forever, but certainly we can keep her here for the time being. Provided," he added, "we can continue keeping her under a certain amount of sedation."

Owen nodded gravely. "Yes, I can understand that."

"She's in no distress," said Gerard. "I feel certain that soon we will come up with an approach that will balance the safety of the people around her and her own emotional and developmental well-being. Hopefully we will soon be able to wean her off the sedatives."

Gerard bent to adjust the logs in the fire with a brass poker, and Owen seized the opportunity to glance at his watch. He needed a few more minutes.

Gerard continued, "I believe that you, my wife, and I will be able to come up with a viable plan for Miss Ballard."

Owen cleared his throat loudly, then followed that up with a volley of coughs.

"Are you all right?" asked Gerard.

Owen gestured to his throat. "Could I have a glass of water?" he croaked.

"Certainly," said Gerard. He went to a small bar in the corner of the room and retrieved a bottle of water, which he handed to Owen.

"Sorry," Owen croaked, waving his hands feebly.

"No problem," said Gerard, but Owen could tell that the urbanity was wearing a little thin in the face of an obese man hacking away in his library.

When Owen had allowed the attack to subside, Gerard said, "Perhaps we should sleep on this, consider our options. We could get together again tomorrow."

"Tomorrow?" asked Owen. "Let me check my calendar." He reached into his pocket, then began patting his clothing in some confusion. "I wonder if I left my phone in Lizzy's room? I better check."

Gerard sighed. "Very well."

Owen stood, taking another surreptitious glance at his watch, and followed Gerard out of the library and up the stairs, passing Angelo who was again in the entrance hall.

When they got to the bedroom, Gerard opened the door and stepped in.

"My God," he said, as Owen stepped into the room after him.

CHAPTER FIFTY-TWO

Lizzy was on her hands and knees on the floor, swaying over a puddle of vomit. As they stood there, she groaned and vomited again.

"What's wrong with her?" exclaimed Owen, having decided that the best defense was a good offense.

Gerard looked at him with exactly the look of surprise that Owen had hoped for. "What?"

"What are you giving her?" asked Owen.

"What am *I* giving her?" exclaimed Gerard. "You were just with her!"

"Well, she wasn't like that when I left her," said Owen. "Call 911!"

"She's just throwing up—" began Gerard.

"That's not just a case of having eaten something a little off," said Owen. "Look at her!"

Lizzy's face was gray, and as they watched she clutched her stomach with one hand, her other arm trembling with the effort of holding herself up.

"Uncle Owen," Lizzy gasped out. "You ..."

Owen stared at her, waiting in a panic for what she would say next.

"... you need to get me to the hospital." She swayed, threatening to topple into the mess she had left on the carpet.

Good girl, thought Owen. He turned to Gerard. "She's right—driving her to the hospital is better than waiting for an ambulance to get here," he said, his voice rising in panic.

"I can't be seen with her," retorted Gerard.

"Fine," said Owen. "You stay here and I'll take her. But

for God's sake, we have to do it now!"

"All right," said Gerard, running his fingers through his hair. "You take her. I'll send Angelo with you. He can drive."

"Fine," Owen muttered.

"Angelo!" Gerard yelled. A moment later Angelo appeared in the doorway.

"Yes, boss?" he said, gaping at Lizzy as she attempted to drag herself toward the bathroom and then vomited again.

"Miss Ballard is sick. Drive her and Dr. McNally to the hospital."

"In the car?" asked Angelo, his eyes wide.

"Yes," Gerard snapped. "Take the old car."

"Chester County?" asked Angelo.

"No, Mercy," said Owen. Gerard started to say something, but Owen interrupted him. "I know people there, I can get her in fast, avoid the red tape."

"It's probably closer anyway," said Angelo.

Gerard thought for a moment. "Fine. Mercy." He turned to Owen. "Keep an eye on her, Dr. McNally—I'll be right back." He gestured to Angelo and the two of them disappeared out the door.

Owen knelt by Lizzy, his hand on her back.

"Pumpkin?"

"What did you—" she began, and then was wracked with another heaving attack. She fell to her side and curled into a ball. "My stomach ..."

Owen pulled the blanket off the bed and covered her with it, but she kicked at it feebly. "I don't want that," she groaned, her voice weak.

Owen was stroking her hair, tears in his eyes—it wasn't supposed to be this bad—when Gerard returned.

"Angelo's bringing the car around to the front." He looked down at Lizzy. "Can she walk?"

"I doubt it," said Owen. He bent down. "Lizzy, can you stand up?"

Another cramp must have seized her, because she groaned

again but her eyes stayed shut.

Owen turned to Gerard. "Help me get her up, then I can carry her."

Gerard took a small step back. "She's …"

Just then they heard uneven steps running down the hall toward the room and Angelo appeared in the door.

"Angelo, help Dr. McNally with the girl," said Gerard.

Lizzy let out a cry when they heaved her to her feet, then Owen lifted her with a grunt. As he stepped past the bed, he managed to kick his phone where it lay on the ground.

"Oh, there's your phone," said Gerard, and hurried over to pick it up.

"Ah, right, thanks," wheezed Owen. "I forgot about that."

Owen dearly wished he could have found a way of avoiding the trip down the stairs, which introduced yet another element of anxiety into the proceedings—what if, after all this work, the drama ended with him falling down the stairs and crushing Lizzy?

Angelo had pulled the car right up to the bottom of the front steps, for which Owen was immensely grateful. Lizzy was a slender girl, but their combined weight was over four hundred pounds, and his breath was coming in gasps by the time they reached the car.

They got her settled into the back seat as best they could in her semi-conscious state.

Gerard handed Owen the phone he had picked up from the bedroom floor.

"Thanks," said Owen. He got into the passenger seat as Angelo slipped into the driver's seat.

Gerard stepped up to Owen's door before Owen had a chance to close it. He leaned toward Owen, one hand on top of the car, one hand on the open door. "Come back with her when you're done, we have some unfinished business to discuss."

There was a look in Gerard's eye that Owen didn't recall having seen before. Gerard had recovered from the initial shock of Lizzy's condition, and now his face was composed, but tight with what Owen guessed was anger at this unanticipated turn of events—and, no doubt, a suspicion that Owen had had something to do with Lizzy's condition.

"Yes, I'll be back," said Owen. He and Gerard locked eyes for a moment. Then Gerard stepped back and swung the door shut.

"Buckle up," Angelo said cheerfully.

Owen doubted whether Angelo cared what happened to Lizzy, but he couldn't fault the man's speed in getting her to the hospital. He drove fast but smoothly, passing slower cars on the narrow two-lane country roads, and pushing the speed up once they got to the highway.

Owen pulled out his phone.

"What are you doing?" asked Angelo.

"Calling the hospital, letting them know we're coming."

"You know the number to the emergency room?"

Owen tapped on his phone. "I'm looking it up." After a moment he put the phone to his ear. "Hello, this is Dr. Owen McNally. I'm on my way to the emergency room with a sixteen-year-old female who is vomiting and appears to be having severe stomach cramps. Can you have someone meet us when we get there?" After a pause, he said, "Thank you," and dropped the phone back into his pocket.

"Must be nice to have friends in high places," said Angelo.

"More than you know," answered Owen.

When the car screeched up to the doors of the ER, a nurse with a wheelchair was waiting for them. Next to the nurse was a man in a white doctor's coat and scrubs—he was tall and thin, with a fair complexion, light blue eyes, and a luxuriant reddish mustache.

The nurse and doctor loaded Lizzy from the back seat into the wheelchair. She looked, if possible, worse than she had in Gerard Bonnay's guest bedroom—her eyes squinted shut in pain, her face slick with sweat. They wheeled her through a sparsely populated waiting room and Owen started through the swinging doors to the main treatment area when he felt a hand on his arm.

"I think it's best if you wait here with me, Dr. McNally," said Angelo.

The doctor turned back to them and then, at a shake of the head from Owen, continued back to the treatment area.

"You wait here," said Angelo. "I'm going to move the car."

"Okay, fine," said Owen shortly.

Angelo hustled out the doors, a hitch in his gait.

Owen went to the waiting room, which was furnished with completely inadequate chairs, and lowered himself carefully onto one of them. He fidgeted until Angelo reappeared, taking the seat next to him. Angelo pulled a phone out of his pocket and tapped it to life. Owen picked up a magazine from the table next to him and pretended to read, but he was curious as to whether Angelo was going to tap out a text update to Gerard.

Instead, Angelo opened a GPS-like application, with the familiar blue dot in the center. Owen recognized the streets surrounding Mercy on the screen. Angelo zoomed in, expanding the hospital building to fill the screen, and Owen noticed that the dot that he had assumed represented Angelo's phone was actually located slightly closer to the center of the building than where they were sitting. In fact, it was located exactly where he assumed Lizzy had been taken.

He stood, and when Angelo appeared to be about to tell him to sit down again, he said, "I was supposed to have a meeting, I just need to let them know I'm running late."

Angelo looked uncertain, then nodded.

Owen moved a few steps away and pulled out his own phone and tapped out a text.

check her for a tracking device

CHAPTER FIFTY-THREE

The nurse rolled the wheelchair into one of the ER rooms. The doctor followed and pulled the curtain closed, then they got Lizzy transferred to the stretcher.

"I can get her triaged," said the nurse.

"That's all right, it's slow, I don't have anything else to do," the doctor replied.

"I haven't seen you around here before this week, Doctor," said the nurse as she strapped a blood pressure cuff on the patient's arm. "Are you new to Mercy?"

"Yes, usually I'm at Bryn Mawr but I'm doing a little moonlighting here." He pulled up Lizzy's eyelids and shone a light in her eyes, which elicited a soft groan. He laid the back of his hand against her forehead.

"Give me four milligrams of Zofran and five milligrams of Versed."

She raised her eyebrows. "What's wrong with her?"

"Ipecac. It's a new thing the kids are doing."

"Ipecac? Why in the world would anyone drink ipecac?"

The doctor shrugged. "Who knows with kids." He raised his eyebrows as the nurse. "The Zofran? And Versed?"

"But a sedative after vomiting?"

"I think she's all vomited out."

"Still—"

"Nurse ..." said the doctor, drawing his eyebrows together sternly.

Glaring back at him, she stalked out of the room, returning in a minute with two syringes. Just as he gave the second injection, there was the buzz heralding the arrival of a text.

Despite a look of disapproval from the nurse, the doctor pulled out his phone. He glanced at it and then slipped it back into his pocket.

"I'd like to talk to the girl's parent or guardian," he said. "Can you bring him back? It should be the fat one."

The nurse nodded her head. "Certainly, Doctor," she said coolly.

"But don't let the other one back here," the doctor called after her as she slipped around the curtain.

She was back in a minute, Owen behind her, looking almost as pale as Lizzy.

"Thank you," said the doctor. "That's all for now." He pulled the curtain closed behind the nurse and turned to Owen.

"What do you mean, there's a tracking device on her?" he asked in a whisper.

Owen hurried over to Lizzy, whose condition had already improved—her face still sweat-slicked but more relaxed, her hand unclenched where it lay on her stomach. "I don't know. The guy who drove us here has what looked like a GPS tracking app on his phone, and it looks like it's centered on her."

"She didn't come in with a handbag, right?" asked Andy.

"No. Maybe in a pocket?" Owen jumped as the curtain rattled on its rod as someone passed by on the other side.

Andy began patting Lizzy's pockets. "What am I looking for?"

"I have no idea. They wouldn't have given her a cell phone. Maybe it's something sewn into her clothes."

"What, like in a seam or something?"

"I don't know!" said Owen, running his fingers through his hair. "Maybe that nurse could come back and help …"

"I thought this was supposed to be all hush-hush," whispered Andy. "What are we supposed to tell her she's looking for?"

"Well, let's check her back pockets," said Owen. "Maybe she does have a phone. Lots of kids carry their phones in their back pockets, and at least we will have eliminated that possibility."

"Okay," replied Andy. "You stand over there and make sure she doesn't fall off the stretcher. I'll turn her on her side."

Owen positioned himself on the side of the stretcher opposite Andy, and Andy rolled Lizzy onto her side. She groaned softly.

"She's looking better," said Owen.

"Yeah. How much did you give her?"

"I gave her what you told me to give her!"

"Well, I think you overestimated her weight. I gave her Zofran, and with the Versed she'll be out for a while," said Andy. "Nothing in the pockets." He began to lower her back down onto the table, then stopped. "Wait a minute."

"What?"

Andy peered at Lizzy's back for a moment. "Let's roll her all the way over."

The two of them maneuvered Lizzy onto her stomach.

"What is it?" asked Owen.

Andy pointed to a small dark stain between her shoulder blades. "Looks like a bloodstain." He worked Lizzy's shirt—a long-sleeved white T-shirt—up her back. "Look at this." He pointed to her back.

Owen bent over to look more closely. "What is that?"

"Maybe that's your tracking device."

The nurse was consulting with the woman at the reception desk when the Italian man who had come in with overweight gentleman and the sick teenager hurried over.

"How's she doing?" he asked. A sheen of sweat had broken out on his forehead.

"I can check for you," she said, and began to turn away.

"Is Dr. McNally still with her?"

"Yes, I'm sure he is."

"When will he be coming out?"

"I'm sure he'll be out when he has something to report."

"Wouldn't the doctor be giving the report?"

The nurse sighed. "Yes, as soon as he's done with the examination, he'll be out to let you know what he's found." She disappeared in the direction of the treatment area.

Angelo watched her go in some confusion, then shrugged. Maybe the ER was busier than it looked, and they needed Dr. McNally to pitch in.

Andy washed his hands, then probed delicately at Lizzy's back. There was a red, raised area running over and parallel to her spine, less than an inch long and no more than half an inch wide. At the top of the raised area was what looked like a small cut, from which the smudge of blood had come. Andy pulled a lamp over the stretcher and shone it on Lizzy's back.

"I think it's an implant. And it's been done fairly recently."

"An implant? Could it be used to track her? Jesus, we have to get it out!"

Andy probed the area a bit more. "Shouldn't be hard, it's not very deep."

"How long will it take?"

"Not long."

At that moment the nurse swished back the curtain and stepped into the room, then stopped when she saw Lizzy on the table, face-down, with the back of her shirt hiked up. Owen and Andy gave her the same look they had doubtless given their parents when interrupted in the middle of some non-approved activity decades before.

"Doctor …?" said the nurse uncertainly.

"We discovered what appears to be a malignant mole," said Andy. "As long as she's out, I figured I'd remove it."

"That's … highly irregular," said the nurse, her brows knit.

"No time like the present!" said Owen brightly.

The nurse glanced at her watch. Half an hour until her shift ended. She didn't care if it was only mid-afternoon, she was going to have a glass of wine when she got home. She shook her head. "Well, I came back because the other gentleman is looking for an update on the patient."

"Please tell him that we're waiting for the medicine we gave her to take effect," said Andy, "and that she can probably go home later today."

"I'm sure he'll ask how much later ..." said the nurse.

Andy glanced at Owen. "Oh, in an hour or so, I'd say."

She nodded. "All right, I'll let him know." She turned to go.

"Oh, nurse," said Owen, "please don't tell him about the mole—we don't want to alarm him unnecessarily."

"Fine," she said and, with another uncertain glance at Lizzy, pulled the curtain shut behind her.

Andy washed his hands, got a scalpel and Adson forceps out of a cabinet, placed a small metal tray on a rolling table, then washed his hands again and pulled on latex gloves.

"You're not going to be woozy about this, are you?" he asked Owen.

"No," said Owen, looking distinctly woozy.

"How you got through medical school as squeamish as you are is beyond me," said Andy. "If you feel lightheaded, sit down. God knows I don't want to try to hoist you onto a stretcher if you faint."

Andy disinfected the area, then used the scalpel to make a small incision, blotting away a trickle of blood. Owen sat down on a stool in the corner of the room. Andy used the forceps to lift out a tiny object, which he dropped with a ping into the metal tray. He cleaned the area, then covered the incision with a butterfly closure.

"Okay, that should do it," said Andy.

"You know, assuming that really is a tracking device," said Owen, "it could actually work to our advantage."

Andy glanced over. "You mean, they'll think she's still here even when you move her?"

"Exactly. We can keep the tracking device here for thirty

or forty minutes, and that will give us a nice long head start." He looked down at Lizzy, now unconscious and breathing evenly. "Can she leave now?"

"Yup."

"Do you have the sling?" asked Owen.

"Yeah, it's in my locker, one sec," said Andy, and disappeared around the curtain. He was back in a moment with a canvas contraption that they draped over the seat of the wheelchair. Then they rolled Lizzy over onto her back and lifted her into the wheelchair. They stepped back and examined her.

"How do we keep her from slumping over like that?" asked Owen.

"Pillows?" asked Andy.

"Okay."

Andy started out of the room and Owen whispered after him, "And a blanket. It will cover up the sling."

"Yeah," said Andy. "Plus, it's December and she's not wearing a coat."

"Good point," said Owen.

Andy reappeared a minute later with two pillows and a blanket. They wedged a pillow on either side of Lizzy and tucked the blanket around her.

"Okay, I've got it from here," said Owen.

"I'll walk with you, in case someone tries to stop you."

They pulled open the curtain and wheeled Lizzy out of the room. They turned right, away from the waiting room, and wheeled her down the hall and through another set of swinging doors.

As they passed through the doors, the nurse came around the corner carrying a tablet computer. She stopped when she saw the empty room. She put aside the tablet and crossed to the rolling table and peered into the metal tray, expecting to see the excised mole and surrounding tissue. Instead, she saw a small oval object, not much bigger than a small pharmaceutical capsule, covered with a smear of blood. She put on a pair of gloves and picked up the tray. The object rolled around, making a faint metallic noise against the tray. Sighing heavily—that post-shift glass of wine couldn't come soon enough—she stepped out of the room and turned right, toward where the Pathology lab was housed in the back of the building, carrying the tray and its mysterious contents.

CHAPTER FIFTY-FOUR

Angelo had gotten bored with watching the motionless blue dot on the GPS app, and was now dividing his time between the phone and a copy of *Main Line Today* he had found in the waiting room, wondering periodically what help Dr. McNally was providing for Mercy's emergency room doctors. He had positioned his cell phone in the chair next to him so he could glance over periodically from the magazine. This time, when he glanced over, the dot was on the move.

He shot to his feet, the magazine tumbling to the floor, and hurried to the desk.

"What's going on with Lizzy Ballard?" he asked the receptionist.

She glanced at a computer screen. "We don't have a record of a Lizzy Ballard—"

"We just brought her in—" he glanced at his watch "—not half an hour ago. Me and Dr. McNally."

The receptionist knit her brow. "Dr. McNally? He's been on since …"—she glanced again at the computer screen and clicked her mouse a few times—"… since noon."

A dim glow of understanding flickered in Angelo's head. "Big fat guy?"

"Uh, no, tall and skinny," said the receptionist, confused.

"Damn!" swore Angelo.

He glanced again at the tracker, where the blue dot was moving toward the back of the hospital. He ran out of the ER toward the parking lot, his run having deteriorated to a hobble by the time he reached the car. He backed out of the space with a squeal and hit the gas. If they thought they were going to sneak that girl out the back entrance, they had another think coming.

Owen and Andy navigated a number of turns, the areas becoming less and less patient-care-oriented, until finally they came to the hallway leading to the hospital's loading dock.

"Okay, I really can take it from here," said Owen. "Thanks, bro, I owe you one."

"I can go the rest of the way with you," said Andy.

"No, I have someone meeting me in back, and I'd just as soon you didn't see who it was," said Owen.

"Ah, very mysterious, I feel like I'm in a John le Carré novel," said Andy. "Okay, I'll go back and act surprised that my patient has disappeared." He started to turn away, but Owen put a hand on his arm.

"Andy, thanks. I know this is going to cause you problems."

Andy shrugged. "She's a patient, not a prisoner. I'll just tell them that you decided to leave and I couldn't stop you. That you used your weight advantage to overpower me."

"Okay, hopefully you won't have any problems with the hospital. But watch out just the same."

Andy cocked his eyebrow at Owen. "You really think these guys might be dangerous?"

"I hope not, but I'm going to disappear for a few days just in case."

Andy examined him appraisingly, then nodded. "Well, if you think the girl was in danger, it's worth taking a risk for, right?"

"That's what I think," replied Owen.

Andy grinned. "I always knew that under that layer of protective fat lay the heart of an avenging superhero." He clapped Owen on the shoulder and strode back in the direction of the ER.

When Owen emerged onto the loading dock, he surprised two workers who were taking an illicit smoke break. They quickly stubbed out their cigarettes and hurried back into the building.

A white van with a magnetic sign on the driver's door reading *Kintsfather Construction* idled near the dock, and as Owen pushed the wheelchair down a loading ramp, the side door slid open. The driver, wearing a Phillies baseball cap, appeared from around the back of the van and helped maneuver Lizzy into the passenger seat using the van's lift mechanism. Owen was pleased at the unexpected advantage they had gained by finding and removing the tracking device—he had expected this part to be a scramble, but now they had extra time.

He tucked the blanket around Lizzy and used one of the pillows to make a cushion between her head and the passenger side window. He lifted the wheelchair into the back of the van, then slid the door shut and gave it a slap. The van pulled away.

It was just turning right onto the service road that ran behind the hospital when Angelo's car squealed around the corner. Owen stepped back onto the shadows of the loading dock, his heart thumping. Through the darkened windshield of the car, he saw Angelo do a double take at the receding van, then continue into the loading dock area.

He had a bad moment when Angelo spun the car in a tight circle and headed away from the dock, but the car turned left toward the public entrance rather than following the van. Owen heaved a bushel-sized sigh of relief.

He walked quickly across the pavement to a rental SUV, which was hidden from view behind an out-of-service ambulance. He squeezed himself behind the wheel and drove away.

Andy got back to the ER, pulled the curtain closed, and began clearing away the instruments and cotton swabs. He then turned his attention to the wheeled cart where he had put the small metal tray and the implant, and felt his heart jump when he saw that the tray was gone. Just then he heard footsteps and the swish of the curtain being pulled back.

The nurse stood in the opening. "Doctor, what happened to the patient? It turns out she was never formally admitted."

"Really? Well, that's inconvenient. She and the fat guy must have walked out when I left for a minute. What happened to the tray that was here?"

"I took it to Pathology." The nurse shook her head. "It's all very irregular, Dr. McNally."

Andy sighed. It was going to be a long afternoon.

CHAPTER FIFTY-FIVE

Angelo had circled the hospital and seen no sign of Lizzy or Dr. McNally, but that blue dot was still hovering within the hospital walls—maybe he wasn't too late. He circled the building again, more slowly this time, and determined that the loading dock was the closest entrance to the location of the dot. He pulled the car to the edge of the loading dock area, and put a call in to Gerard Bonnay.

"Yes?" Gerard answered.

"Dr. McNally and the girl aren't in the ER anymore, but according to the tracker, she's still in the hospital. Looks like she's near the back of the hospital, where the loading dock is."

"Maybe they're waiting for someone to come pick her up," said Gerard. "See if you can get in there and take a look around. Here's what you can tell them …"

A minute later, Angelo climbed awkwardly from the car and limped to the open loading dock doors. He stepped inside and had only gone a few steps when he heard someone call, "May I help you?"

He turned. A man in a gray security guard uniform was walking toward him.

"Main entrance is around front," the guard continued.

"Hey, I'm sorry to bother you," said Angelo, "but a friend of mine lost his cell phone in the hospital. It has a tracking app on it." He held out his phone and pointed at the screen. "It's that blue dot."

"Where's your friend?" asked the guard.

"He's visiting a sick relative. I told him I'd look for his phone."

The guard looked at the screen. "That looks like the Pathology department, if it's on the first floor." He looked back at Angelo. "Your friend was in Pathology? It's not a place where visitors normally go."

"He thinks he might have put it down on one of the carts or trolleys and someone moved it without realizing it was there."

"Well," said the guard, "if you go to the information desk in the main lobby and explain to them what happened, they could send someone back there to look for it."

"Maybe I could just take a quick look, save them the trouble," said Angelo conspiratorially.

"No, I'm afraid not, sir." The guard gestured toward the loading dock door. "Now I'm going to have to ask you to leave this area—this is for employees only."

"Sure, no problem. Thanks for your help."

"No problem, sir," said the guard, and followed Angelo to the door. As Angelo crossed the parking area, he heard the dock door rumble down and the guard's voice calling back into the building. "Who left this door open?"

Angelo climbed back into his car and called Gerard. "I couldn't get in through the loading dock, but the guard said it looked like the tracker was in the Pathology area."

"Pathology? What would she be doing in Pathology?"

"I don't know, boss."

"No, of course not," muttered Gerard, then exclaimed, "Pathology? Damn it, they must have found the tracker and removed it!"

"Oh, I forgot to tell you," said Angelo sheepishly. "I think there's another McNally who works in the hospital."

"What?"

"Yeah, they kept talking about 'Dr. McNally' and I thought they were talking about *our* Dr. McNally, but I think there's another Dr. McNally who works in the ER. He's the one who treated Lizzy."

"Christ," muttered Gerard. "Did McNally bring in

reinforcements?"

Angelo decided it was best not to respond.

"I'm coming down there," said Gerard. "I'll talk to this new Dr. McNally you've stumbled across. You keep an eye on the tracker. Stay by whatever entrance is closest to the signal."

"You got it, boss," said Angelo disconsolately. "Sorry I screwed up."

"I think we all screwed up on this one," Gerard muttered, and banged down the phone.

CHAPTER FIFTY-SIX

Gerard strode into the empty ER waiting room and went to the reception desk, where a nurse was talking with the receptionist.

The receptionist looked up. "May I help you?"

"I'm looking for a Dr. McNally. I believe he treated a friend's daughter, Elizabeth Ballard."

"Do you know the patient? They left without ever registering," said the nurse with obvious disapproval. "With a hospital wheelchair. I'll get Dr. McNally for you. I'm sure he can explain everything," she added peevishly.

Gerard paced in the waiting area and in a moment a man emerged from the swinging doors. He was tall, fair-skinned, and redheaded—only an idiot like Angelo Celucci wouldn't have recognized him as a thinner and better-looking relative of Owen McNally. He approached Gerard.

"May I help you?"

"You're Dr. McNally?"

"That's right."

"Am I right in assuming you are Owen McNally's brother?"

"That's right."

"I'm Gerard Bonnay, and I understand that Elizabeth Ballard was brought in here for treatment."

"I'm afraid I can't discuss any information about people we may or may not have treated."

"All right," said Gerard. "I'm going to proceed on the assumption that your brother brought Miss Ballard in here and that you treated her."

"Knock yourself out," said Andy.

Gerard glared at him. "And I further assume that you not only treated her for her vomiting and stomach cramps, but also performed an additional procedure on her."

"Much as I'd love to chat with you, Mr. Bonnay, I'm in the midst of being chewed out by the admitting clerk. I think she'll go easier on me if I don't leave her alone and fuming for too long."

"I believe you and your brother are taking steps that will make an unfortunate situation far, far worse, both for Miss Ballard and for those unfortunate enough to cross her path."

"Do you? Interesting," said Andy, sounding not at all interested.

Gerard took a step toward Andy. "Do you know what Miss Ballard is capable of?" he said in a low, angry voice.

"Do tell," said Andy. "No, on second thought, don't tell. I have to get back to being chewed out by a nice-looking young woman, which I have to say is more appealing than standing here getting chewed out by you, Mr. Bonnay." He turned and strolled across the waiting room. At the swinging doors, he turned back to Gerard. "I think I can win her over," he called back cheerfully. "Wish me luck!" And he disappeared through the doors.

Gerard drew himself up, nodded stiffly to the receptionist, who had been watching with curiosity from behind the desk, and walked outside. He pulled out his phone as he walked to his car and rang Louise, whom he had briefed after Angelo and Owen left for the hospital.

"I don't think she's in the building," Gerard told her. "They must have found the tracker and removed it. According to the app, the tracker's in the hospital, but I'm fairly certain she and Owen are both long gone. Plus, it turns out that the doctor who treated her is Owen's brother."

"I wouldn't have thought Owen McNally had it in him to arrange such an operation," said Louise.

"I always warned you not to underestimate him," Gerard

shot back. "Just because he's big and slow doesn't mean he's not smart and resourceful."

"Evidently," she replied tightly. "What about the brother? Maybe he knows where they are. We could get George to find out what he knows. Or," she added, "Mitchell. It could be a test—"

"No," Gerard interrupted her. "Do you really want to do another 'test,' like the one we did on Rossi? It's no good blundering around like a bull in a china shop—and a blind bull, at that. It's just going to attract attention at the time we need it the least. The other Dr. McNally doesn't strike me as a man who could be easily pressured. But more importantly, I suspect that Owen wouldn't have told him more than was absolutely necessary get his little ruse in the ER to work. To protect his brother *and* Lizzy."

By this time, he had reached his car—a Boxster that rarely saw the outside of the garage in winter. He opened the door and fell heavily into the driver's seat. "I think our best bet is to lay low and keep our eyes and ears open. They're not professionals at this. They're going to slip up and give away her location. Once we know where she is, we can decide what to do."

"What about Owen?"

Gerard laughed shortly. "It will be a little harder to hide away Owen McNally than Lizzy Ballard. Plus, although he may be smart and resourceful, he doesn't seem very adventuresome. He strikes me as a bit of a homebody. Maybe we can have George stake out his house." After a pause, he added, "Or maybe do a little reconnaissance there to see if he can find out some information about where Owen planned to take her."

"If Owen McNally gave her something that made her as sick as you described," said Louise, "then when she finds out he was responsible, maybe she'll get mad enough at him that she'll use her power on him and save us the trouble."

Gerard slowly shook his head. "No, I don't think so.

That's the paper. Lizzy only hurt her mother because she was too young to understand what she was doing. That's why no one else close to her—her father, Owen McNally, Ruby DiMano—ever suffered any ill effects. She loves them. Love is the paper. Paper covers rock."

CHAPTER FIFTY-SEVEN

Ruby's drive had taken her out of the Philadelphia metro area and into Lancaster Amish country. When she had bought the van, Angelo had given her some driving lessons and she had eventually gotten used to the large vehicle. She was finally comfortable driving Tony and Opal, who would never think of driving the van herself, to doctor's appointments and, increasingly, on outings like the occasional day trip to the Shore.

But it was the obstacles of the city she was used to, not the hazards of the countryside. When she encountered one of the Amish buggies plying the roads—the horse's breath puffing out in great clouds, serious-faced children looking out the back window—she inched past, much to the annoyance of the cars behind her. She periodically pulled to the side of the road to let the accumulated traffic pass, flexing the cramps out of her fingers.

About an hour after leaving the hospital with Lizzy, Ruby pulled the white van off Route 340 in Smoketown, into a drive marked with a sign for Smoketown Cottages. She pulled into the parking space in front of one of the small buildings, the one furthest from the road.

Lizzy was still unconscious in the front seat. Ruby got the wheelchair from the back of the van, hooked up the lift to the sling that was still under the girl, and lowered her into the wheelchair.

With a nervous glance around—no one was visible, and the windows of the other cabins were dark—she wheeled Lizzy to the door of the cottage, unlocked it, and maneuvered her into the room. She moved the wheelchair next to the bed, put on the brakes, turned down the covers, then set about getting Lizzy into the bed.

Lizzy was slender, but she was about three inches taller than Ruby. Although Ruby was used to helping her brother in and out of the wheelchair, at least he was always conscious and able to help. With the unconscious Lizzy, it was like trying to move a rolled but untied rug single-handed.

When Lizzy was finally on the bed, Ruby used a washcloth from the bathroom to clean some specks of vomit from the unconscious girl's sleeves and pants. Concerned Lizzy might be alarmed to find her clothes in disarray, Ruby straightened them, then folded Lizzy's hands on her chest. She was about to pull up the covers, but then hesitated. Lizzy looked a little too much like someone laid out for a viewing. Ruby moved her hands to her stomach and pulled the sheet and blanket over her.

She went to the door, then returned to the bed and cracked open the cap of the bottle of water she had put on the bedside table at her earlier visit. She stepped out of the room, easing the door closed quietly, and began the nerve-wracking, buggy-infested trip back to Philadelphia.

CHAPTER FIFTY-EIGHT

Lizzy became aware of her surroundings gradually, as if a heavy velvet curtain was being lifted slowly above a dimmed stage. At first she registered an undercurrent of noise, a hum that turned eventually to a rattle, then a descending whine, like a dying Pac Man on the old video game her dad liked playing.

Next she became aware of a vague sense of filtered light. She couldn't tell whether her eyes were open or closed, and then confirmed they had been closed by dragging them open.

The view was off-white, with a blotch like a giant tick in the middle. She drew in a quick breath, which made her cough weakly, but as her eyes focused she realized that the object was a ceiling fan, the "legs" its dark brown paddles.

After some time she mustered the energy to turn her head. The large red numbers of a digital clock swam into view— 6:00 a.m. Next to the clock was a bottle of water.

She pushed the covers off and rolled on her side, setting the room spinning around her, and then carefully lowered her legs off the edge of the bed and pushed herself up.

She reached a trembling hand out to the water bottle, dully worried that she wouldn't have the strength to open it, but when she turned the cap she discovered it was already open. She hesitated for a moment, blearily suspicious, but then her thirst trumped her caution and she gulped down half the bottle, some of the water dripping down her chin.

She placed the bottle on the bedside table, her hand slightly more steady, and took stock of her surroundings. By the light filtering in around the edges of the roller shades on two large windows, she could see that she was sitting on one of two double beds covered with faded quilts. The furniture was standard, if old-fashioned, motel-room fare: a low dresser in wood veneer with a boxy television on top, a bedside table with an attached lamp, and a round table with two chairs. The walls, however, were decorated with what looked like hand-stitched samplers, the wood floor softened with a few rag rugs.

After taking stock of the room, she took stock of herself. She was wearing the same clothes she had been wearing at Gerard's house, and she could sense her own sour odor. Her stomach rolled, then settled back into a general queasiness. She located the door to the bathroom and, pushing herself upright, hobbled across the room.

She used the toilet, then went to the sink to wash her hands and rinse out her muggy-tasting mouth. She noticed a travel-size toothpaste and a plastic-wrapped toothbrush in a glass by the sink. She got the plastic off after a slow-motion wrestle.

As she brushed her teeth, she noticed that the vanity contained other items. In addition to a battered coffee maker, a basket of coffee packets and "condiments," and a few plastic-wrapped bars of soap, there was also a quart-sized Ziploc in which she could see deodorant and dental floss, a comb and brush. She took out the brush and gave her hair a few half-hearted swipes. There was also a box of hair color on the vanity. She picked it up—Preference by L'Oreal, Light Brown.

In one corner of the large bathroom was a microwave on top of a mini fridge. On top of the microwave were small stacks of paper plates, plastic cups, and paper napkins; a cup containing plastic utensils; plastic salt and pepper shakers; some packets of sugar; a sampler box of Twinings tea; four bananas; and a box of Raisin Bran.

The mini fridge contained a quart of low-fat milk, a quart of orange juice, a loaf of bread, a tiny container of mayonnaise, a package of Oscar Mayer bologna, a package of pre-sliced cheese, two apples, and two oranges. She poured some orange juice into one of the plastic cups and drank it greedily.

She returned to the bedroom and noticed an envelope on the table. On it was her name, in Uncle Owen's handwriting. She sat down and pulled a sheet out of the envelope.

Pumpkin, I hope that I will have time to explain to you what I'm going to do to get you away from Gerard Bonnay, and why, but I suspect I may not be able to. I think that Gerard had something to do with your dad's death, and maybe even with your own special ability, via the Vivantem treatments. I was afraid that he wasn't going to let you go, and making you sick so I'd have an excuse to take you to the hospital was the only way I could think to get you away from him.

There's a phone in the purse (password = PMKN). There's a number in the contact list under "Pizza" — that's me :) — but please only use it in an emergency. Is all this cloak-and-dagger stuff necessary? Who knows, but I figure better safe than sorry. I'll be in touch as soon as I can.

I hope this will be an okay place for you to stay while we decide what to do next. The room is paid up through the end of the month, although I don't think you will be here more than a couple of days. There's an iPad with some books loaded on it in the dresser. There won't be maid service, so you don't need to worry about anyone coming into your room. I told the manager that you would only need to have the towels changed once a week, so if you are still there on Monday morning, you can just leave them outside the door.

I think you can walk to most of the places you would need to go (see list below). There's some cash in the purse—it will probably seem like a lot of money, but it may have to last for a little while, so don't go on a shopping spree yet! If you haven't found it already, there's some food in the fridge and clothes in the dresser.

Lay low, and stay in Smoketown.

Lots of love.
Uncle Owen

Below was a list that included a couple of restaurants, something called Sheetz, a Target, and a coin-op laundry. It also listed a hair salon along with the note, *Do you mind getting your hair cut in a different style?*

She put the note aside and went to the dresser. On top sat a faux leather purse with multiple pockets on the outside. In it she found a phone, a plastic-wrapped pack of tissues, a ChapStick, a small comb, a pair of sunglasses, and a wallet containing a sizable number of twenty dollar bills. She counted a thousand dollars.

In the top drawer she found four pairs of white cotton underpants, two white bras, four pairs of cotton socks (two black and two blue), and a flannel nightgown. In the next drawer were a pair of black pants, a pair of jeans, four turtleneck shirts (black, white, gray, and blue), and two wool sweaters (one gray and one blue). On the floor next to the dresser was a pair of black leather shoes.

If Uncle Owen wanted her to fade into the background, he had certainly done a good job of outfitting her for it.

CHAPTER FIFTY-NINE

Owen called Lizzy at seven o'clock the next morning. As he waited for her to pick up, he looked out the window of his own hiding place—a chain hotel near the airport.

"Uncle Owen?"

"Yes, Pumpkin, it's me. How are you feeling?"

"I'm okay. I felt a little queasy when I woke up, but I feel better now."

"I'm so sorry about that, Pumpkin. It was ipecac—dramatic symptoms but nothing dangerous. I wish I had been able to explain what was going to happen beforehand."

"I do sort of remember you saying it would be unpleasant. What's going on, Uncle Owen?"

"I don't have much to add to what I put in the letter—did you find the letter?"

"Yes. You think Mr. Bonnay had something to do with ... dad dying?" she asked, her voice tightening. "It wasn't a mugging?"

"It could have been, but I don't think so. Maybe we'll never know for sure, but I figured better safe than sorry." Owen paused. "Bonnay had implanted a tracking device on you. Did you notice the bandage on your back? I didn't mention it in the note because I didn't know about it when I wrote it."

"What bandage?"

"Up between your shoulder blades. There was a tracking device and An— we took it out. We put a bandage on the area, but if it hasn't come off already on its own, you can probably take it off any time."

He heard some shuffling, as if she was moving around. After a few moments, she said, "I can just barely see something in the mirror. I totally missed it when I took my shower. Did you take it out?"

"Let's just say for the record that it was me."

"Ah, eet eez a see-cret," she said in a horrendous French accent.

He laughed. "Yup."

"But what about you? Isn't Gerard going to be angry with you?"

"Well, I'm hiding out, too."

"Where are you?"

"Eet eez a see-cret."

"Why didn't you stay in Smoketown with me?" A question, not an accusation.

The "stay" confused Owen for a moment, then he realized that Lizzy thought he had been the one to drive her to the motel. That was good—he had no plan to share with Lizzy the roles that Ruby and Andy had played in her escape. In his opinion, the less information she had, the better for her, and for them.

"Well, I asked—" He caught himself again. "I got the hair color for you, and I started to think about what I could do to disguise myself, then I looked in the mirror and thought, 'How do you disguise someone as big and ugly as I am?'"

Lizzy laughed, and his heart warmed at the sound. "You're not ugly, Uncle Owen." Then she added, "Although you are big."

He laughed too. "Anyhow, I figured it would be easier for you to stay off the radar if you weren't with me. Plus, I didn't have a lot of time to plan out much beyond getting you away from Bonnay, so I figure I'll spend a day or two here working on that. You don't mind spending that time in Smoketown?"

"I guess not. I haven't seen much of it yet. I was just getting ready to go out."

"It seems like there's everything you'd need right nearby,

and it seems like a safe area. Check it out. But remember, we're hiding out, so don't get seen in the same place too many times. Remember: lay low."

She sighed. "Okay." After a pause, she continued. "Nobody's going to miss *me*—" Owen felt a lump form in his throat, "—but what about you? Isn't someone going to miss you if you're hiding out too?"

"No, I don't think so. I left a message at work that I was taking a personal trip, and left a message with friends that I was taking a business trip, so that should hold them for a while."

There was a companionable silence, then Owen said, "Well, enjoy your little vacation in Amish country, because you'll be home in no time."

"But where's 'home' now?" she asked, and he heard her voice catch.

"With me, Pumpkin. How does that sound?"

She didn't answer for a moment, and he held his breath.

"That sounds good to me, Uncle Owen."

"It sounds good to me, too, Pumpkin."

CHAPTER SIXTY

She was on her own. She realized she had never been on her own before—she hadn't interacted much with the people around her, especially after her mother's death, and when she did, she was always monitored, always chaperoned. But here she was in a new place, with all sorts of possibilities, and no one to tell her not to pursue them. Strange as it seemed, part of her was actually enjoying the adventure.

She went to the window and pulled up the shade. She expected to see a view as innocuous as her new persona—parking lots and shopping centers, McDonald's and 7-11s—but instead she had a view across an open field with gray clouds hanging ominously on the horizon. Across the field was a row of low, shed-like buildings with no windows. Warehouses?

It took her a moment to realize the field was a small airport and the buildings hangars. This was confirmed a moment later when a small, high-wing plane went buzzing off the runway, which was hidden by a slight rise in the ground, and passed noisily over the motel.

She put on the blue turtleneck, the gray sweater, and jeans. The tops were a little too large and the pants a little too short, which, she thought, added to the general impression of … no impression at all.

She slipped on the coat she found on a hook next to the front door—nondescript black wool, with black leather gloves in one pocket and a rolled-up wool hat in the other—scooped up the purse, and went outside.

She found that what she had thought was a motel room

was actually a small, free-standing cottage, one of six. The cottages were tidy looking, with rockers on the front porches and flower boxes, now empty, under windows flanked by dark green shutters. They were anchored by a two-story brick building that, according to a sign in front, housed the office.

She walked to the back of the cottage and crossed a small lawn to the parking lot of the airstrip. She could see another plane coming in to land, and one at a set of fuel pumps near a low concrete-block building. There was a picnic table near the building, and despite the cold she walked over to it and sat down, pulling on the wool hat and turning the collar of her coat up. She watched some planes come and go—some with high wings, some with low, one with two sets of wings, and one that she thought was a Piper Cub. Then a couple with a little boy piled out of a car in the parking lot and headed toward the picnic table and she suddenly felt awkward and vulnerable. Plus, she was starting to shiver. She headed back to the cottage, nodding at the family as she passed, her face ducked behind her collar.

Back in the room, she bumped up the thermostat on the heater and made herself a bologna and cheese sandwich, which she ate with a glass of milk and an apple. She sat at the table by the window, looking up when a plane took off, and sampled the books that Owen had loaded on the iPad: *Sherlock Holmes: The Complete Collection* and a bunch of books by Jane Smiley. She got engrossed in *The Hound of the Baskervilles*, getting up just twice to make herself tea using the coffeemaker on the bathroom counter, and almost didn't notice as darkness fell and the airstrip grew silent. When she got hungry again, she made herself the same meal, watched TV for a little while, and then switched back to Sherlock Holmes.

She thought about calling Owen back, but what would they talk about? She suddenly realized that she hadn't told him about the man with whom it now seemed likely Gerard had intentionally locked her in the library. Any desire she had had for a phone call with Owen disappeared.

She did some yoga and meditation practice, but by nine o'clock she was so bored that going to bed seemed like the best option. She turned out the lights and climbed into bed, then got out and found an extra blanket in the dresser, which she added to the bedspread.

The room was eerily quiet—she hadn't seen any other cars in the parking lot, and she couldn't even hear the hum of cars on the road. Then a loud *clunk* made her body jump and her heart race, until the following hum reassured her it was just the heater turning on. It chugged away for a few minutes then whined down to silence, and soon she was dreaming of running through a black maze floored with yellow dots, pursued by colorful ghosts, to the accompaniment of sirens.

CHAPTER SIXTY-ONE

George Millard cruised slowly down the Lansdowne street, past Owen McNally's house. The lights had been going on and off since McNally had disappeared from the hospital the day before, but the one time Millard had happened by when a light came on, it wasn't followed by the shadowy movement of the person who might have turned it on—a sure sign of timers. If that wasn't enough, there were no tire tracks going into or out of the detached garage in the light snow that had fallen since McNally had disappeared.

Tonight the usually quiet street was enlivened by a party going on at the house next to McNally's. At one point, when Millard had pulled over across from McNally's house on one of his passes, he had seen the neighbor knock on McNally's door then, after a minute, shrug and return to the party.

Millard would have preferred uninterrupted surveillance from just down the street, but in this neighborhood a car occupied hour after hour by a lone man would have attracted attention. If the residents were inviting each other to their holiday parties, they were likely the type to call the cops about someone casing a neighbor's house.

Millard drove down the alley behind the house, and saw no sign of life from the back of the house either. He drove to the parking lot of a nearby Chinese restaurant, killed the engine, and pulled out his phone. He speed-dialed Gerard Bonnay.

"Still nothing," he said.

Bonnay sighed. "Can you get in the house?"

"Normally I could, but there's a party at the neighbor's

house tonight—it's too risky."

"Okay. We'll do it tomorrow night."

"You want him to know someone paid him a visit?"

Bonnay was silent for a minute. "No, keep it neat. We just want to see if he left anything that indicates where he took the girl. Start with the computer if you can access it—or his desk drawers. Or file cabinets," Bonnay added. "He seems like the kind of guy who still has file cabinets."

"No problem." Millard ended the call without waiting for Bonnay's response. *We'll* do it tomorrow night. Right, like Gerard Bonnay would ever soil his hands with the dirty work. But he was generally willing to let a professional operate without interference, and was willing to pay handsomely to have these types of problems taken care of. Millard had no complaints.

He made one more pass of McNally's house, called it a night, and headed for home.

CHAPTER SIXTY-TWO

The next morning, Lizzy had orange juice and Raisin Bran. By noon, boredom and an unwillingness to eat another bologna sandwich drove her out of the cottage.

She was walking down the driveway leading to the road, wondering which way she should turn when she got there, when she spotted a small shopping center separated from the motel driveway by a narrow lawn. The parking lot included an area "For Horses and Buggies Only," which was marked with the deposits of its last occupants.

The restaurant was called Glick's, and a hand-lettered sign on the door advertised its hours as "Daily 11-8 Closed Sundays." She pushed the door open to the jingle of a bell and found herself facing a counter with a cash register, a glass cabinet of desserts, and a "Hostess Will Seat You" sign. The only other customers were an elderly woman reading a book, and an overweight, middle-aged couple making their way morosely through pieces of pecan pie.

A young woman, probably in her mid-twenties, looked up from a magazine she had spread out on the counter. "Just one?"

"Yes, please."

She pulled a menu out of a wooden rack. "How about the table by the window?"

"Thanks."

The woman put the menu—a Xeroxed piece of paper—on the table and stood by while Lizzy shrugged out of her coat.

"Something to drink?"

"Just water, thanks."

Lizzy looked quickly over the menu and, when the woman showed up with her glass of water, said, "I'll have a BLT."

"White or whole wheat?"

"Whole wheat, please."

"Chips?"

"Yes, thanks."

"You got it," said the woman. She jotted on her order pad, then returned to the counter. She snapped the order slip into a rotating rack in the pass-through window to the kitchen and spun it to the kitchen side.

Lizzy took out her iPad and was reading when the woman returned to the table with her sandwich.

"BLT on wheat with chips. Anything else?"

"No, thanks."

"What're you reading?" She gestured to the iPad.

"Sherlock Holmes."

"Is it good?"

"Kind of old fashioned, but interesting."

"Never read that myself, although I saw the movie with Robert Downey Jr. and Jude Law. It was pretty good."

"Robert Downey Jr.?" asked Lizzy. "That doesn't seem right."

The woman shrugged. "Seemed okay to me, but maybe it wouldn't have if I had read the books. I usually go for romances myself." She nodded to a shelf in the back of the dining room. "We have a lending library. It doesn't help if you don't have an actual book, but if you do get a book, when you're done with it you can drop one off and pick up a new one. You from around here?"

"Just visiting," said Lizzy. She feared her face was turning red. She wasn't prepared to be providing a cover story already. Should she give her real name? According to the blue plastic name tag on her uniform, the waitress's name was Christine.

Christine nodded and then, not getting more, said, "Well, check out the library. If you like the books we have, it might be worth buying one real one to have something to swap in."

"Sure. Thanks," said Lizzy.

When Lizzy had finished her sandwich, Christine stopped by to take her plate.

"Left room for dessert?"

"No, I don't think so."

Christine pulled the check out of her apron pocket. "Just pay at the register when you're done, no hurry."

The restaurant seemed like a more cheerful place to pass the time than the cottage, so Lizzy returned to her book, reading until a busload of tourists showed up and she vacated the table, to the appreciative nod of the newly busy Christine.

For dinner, she went to the pizzeria on the other side of the motel. The pizzeria was staffed by half a dozen young men who joked and flirted with her. At first she was concerned. Would they remember her? Be able to identify her if someone ever came around with a photo? Eventually she realized, with a mixture of embarrassment and relief, that they flirted with every young woman—and some not so young—who came in unaccompanied by a boyfriend or husband. Their attention was so unfamiliar to her that she didn't know how to respond, beyond a shy smile and a duck of her head so that her long hair fell over her face. She took her slice and salad to go, and ate it at the table in her room, trying to distract herself with *A Study in Scarlet*.

CHAPTER SIXTY-THREE

That afternoon, Millard, decked out in an Eagles jacket and stocking cap, walked up to McNally's front door and knocked briskly. After waiting a minute, he cupped his hands around his eyes and peered into the sidelights that flanked the door—just someone trying to see if his buddy was home.

His "buddy" wasn't home, but he could see by the control pad blinking just inside the door that McNally's alarm system was set. It looked like a basic set-up—monitoring front and back entrances but not, as far as Millard could see, the windows. And a glance at the windows revealed that they were secured with nothing more sophisticated than a standard latch. Gotta love a trusting soul.

That night, his luck continued to hold. The neighbors' windows overlooking McNally's yard were dark, and a quick investigation revealed a low window behind a dense holly bush. Days might go by before a neighbor or passerby noticed the broken glass. Borrowing a trash can from behind the detached garage, he hoisted himself up and peered in—a laundry room. He smiled. Days might go by before even anyone in the house noticed the broken glass. If a place needed to be trashed, he didn't mind trashing it, but if a job was supposed to be quiet, no one could do quiet as good as he could.

He pulled off the Flyers sweatshirt he was wearing—ubiquitous and black, the perfect combination—and wrapped it around his hand. He was gauging the most opportune time to risk the noise of the breaking glass when he heard the wail of a cop car turning off the main road a few blocks away and approaching McNally's house.

An amateur would have run, but Millard knew they weren't coming for him. When the siren had reached its loudest pitch, he drew back his fist and knocked it through the glass. He was through the window before the sound of the siren had entirely faded away.

CHAPTER SIXTY-FOUR

By Lizzy's third day in Smoketown—Owen evidently still trying to formulate a plan—she was already a recognized patron at both Glick's and the pizzeria. In an attempt to comply with Owen's instructions to "lay low" and not let herself be noticed, she decided she should vary her dining routine a bit.

She decided to try the Happy Days Diner, just down the road, for lunch. That plan was cemented when she saw a large tour bus parked in the shopping center parking lot; Glick's was bound to be packed. Then she saw Christine's old Taurus in the employee parking area, and she almost detoured to the comfortable familiarity of Glick's, despite the inevitable crowd. Then, scolding herself for her lack of adventurousness, she continued on to the diner.

It was no doubt intended to look as if it had been built in the fifties, but was clearly counterfeit. Molded plastic panels replaced the stainless steel of a traditional diner, LEDs replaced neon. Inside, with a little more than a week to go before Christmas, every free inch of floor space was jammed with holiday kitsch: artificial trees sprouting metallic silver needles, illuminated snowmen next to plastic crèche scenes. The few patrons were talking loudly to be heard over a swing version of "Jingle Bells."

The sensory onslaught had almost convinced her to brave the crowd at Glick's, but then a harried-looking hostess in white cap and apron snatched up a menu and was leading her to a booth—one right across the aisle from one of the few other occupied tables in the restaurant.

"Do you know what you want?" asked the hostess as soon as Lizzy sat down. Lizzy realized she was likely the waitress on duty as well as the hostess since no other employees were visible in the dining room.

"I have to look at the menu," said Lizzy, startled.

"Okay. Just didn't want to make you wait if you already knew what you wanted," the hostess grumbled, and hurried back to the front counter, although no one was waiting to be seated.

Lizzy took a couple of deep breaths, counting backwards from ten with each breath as her mother had taught her to do, then opened the menu. It was huge—multiple laminated pages, with everything from steak to pancakes to shrimp cocktail. She glanced around at the other patrons, who all seemed to be eating burgers. She remembered her mother saying once to her father, when the three of them still sometimes went out to dinner, that you should only order seafood at places where they had a lot of turnover because then you could count on it being fresh. Lizzy had been pretty little at the time, and didn't have a chance to ask what "turnover" was before the conversation had moved on to other topics. She had seen a fish flop around on the bottom of a boat one time when her dad had taken her fishing at Mauch Chunk Lake. That fish had certainly turned itself over.

She smiled at the memory, and then swallowed back a sudden sob as she thought back to that fishing trip, and the photo from it that her mother had kept stuck to the refrigerator with a magnet until … well, until she died and the photo had been packed up for the move to Parkesburg. In the picture, Lizzy was proudly holding two fish she had caught, and was wearing a baseball cap of her dad's, the too-big hat sitting low so that she had to tilt her head back to see the camera.

She didn't notice that the hostess had returned to her booth, her pencil poised over her order pad.

"Decide what you want?"

"Oh, sorry, I haven't looked yet," said Lizzy, red creeping

up her neck and beginning to flush her face. She took another deep breath.

The hostess opened her mouth with a reply, but at that moment the father of the family group at the table across the aisle said, "Hey, could we get our check?"

"I'll be with you in one minute," said the hostess. "Just as soon as I get this girl's order."

She looked at Lizzy, her eyebrows raised expectantly, her mouth a thin line.

"I don't know yet," said Lizzy. "Maybe you could take care of them first." She felt her heart begin to pound, and she took several fast breaths until she realized she was risking hyperventilating.

"See," said the father, "she doesn't mind if you get us our check." He turned to Lizzy. "Right, honey?" He said "honey" in a way that made his wife, who was dealing with an imminent meltdown by a toddler strapped into a high chair, shoot him a dirty look.

The hostess turned toward the family's table, and Lizzy sensed it was not to rush off to get their check. She slid out of the booth.

"I don't see anything I want," she said. "Sorry."

She grabbed her purse and coat and headed for the door. When she got there, she risked a glance back and saw the hostess glaring after her. She just caught the hostess say, as she turned toward the family in the booth, "Doesn't see anything she wants" in a whiny imitation of Lizzy's voice, followed by the father's over-loud laugh.

As Lizzy turned back to the door, she caught a glimpse out of the corner of her eye of a rotating book rack next to the cash register. The sign on top read *A Roll in the Hay! Amish Romance - $4.99*. She glanced back into the restaurant. The hostess had disappeared, maybe into the kitchen. Lizzy stepped out into a small foyer, standing to one side so she was out of sight of the table and, she hoped, the hostess, and got a five and a one out of her purse. She slipped back in and hurried to the book rack, grabbing one at random. Just then the hostess appeared from the kitchen, striding toward the cash register and Lizzy.

Lizzy dropped the money on the counter and called, "This is for the book!" and scuttled toward the door.

"Hey, wait a minute," said the hostess, and broke into a trot.

"The money's right there on the counter," said Lizzy as she slipped out the door.

By then the hostess had gotten to the counter and seen the bills. She looked in confusion back at Lizzy. "It's only five twenty-nine with tax," she called after Lizzy.

"Keep the change!" Lizzy called back, and turned and ran across the parking lot and down 340 in the direction of Glick's.

The restaurant was filled with senior citizens. All the women seeming to be wearing Christmas-themed sweatshirts, and one of the men wore a reindeer antler hat. The noise level wasn't much less than it had been at the diner, but it was a happy buzz, friendly chatter punctuated by laughter. Lizzy saw Christine hustling from table to table, a water pitcher in one hand and a coffee carafe in the other. There was one table open, one that was in Christine's normal area—maybe her luck was turning. Lizzy waited, fidgeting, by the "Hostess Will Seat You" sign.

An older woman with gray hair pulled back in a severe bun hurried by, four full plates balanced on her arms. She called out to Lizzy, "That table over there okay, hon?"

"Sure," said Lizzy.

"Help yourself, someone will be right with you. There's a menu on the table."

Lizzy sat down and pulled out the book she had gotten. The cover showed a pretty young woman in an oddly form-fitting dress, a white cap having been apparently Photoshopped onto her head. In the background, in front of what Lizzy guessed was a stock picture of a tidy-looking barn, stood a handsome young man leaning on a pitchfork, his white shirt unbuttoned to his navel. She giggled.

She sensed someone standing next to her and looked up, still smiling, ready to show Christine the funny cover. But the woman standing by her table was the older woman, her pencil poised over her order pad.

"What would you like, hon?"

"Isn't this Christine's table?" Lizzy blurted out.

"She's working the register now," said the waitress.

Lizzy looked toward the front of the restaurant and saw Christine dealing with the line that had formed as the people from the bus began finishing up their meals and filing out. Much to her horror, Lizzy felt tears begin to well up.

"I'll have a piece of pumpkin pie and tea." She didn't want a whole lunch any more, and she also didn't feel like replaying the incident at the diner by getting up and leaving.

"Sure thing," said the waitress, looking at her with some concern before she hurried away.

Lizzy sat forward as if she was reading the ridiculous book, pulling her hair out of its ponytail to let it fall forward to hide her face. She thought she could get it under control, but her thoughts were a jumble—the inauthenticity of the Happy Days Diner, the too-loud music, the tacky decorations, the rude hostess, the creepy guy at the next booth, and, hardest of all, the treachery of the happy memory of eating dinner out with her parents and fishing with her dad, ruined by everything that had happened since then. She had hoped to put all that behind her for just a few minutes by laughing over a silly book with Christine who, pathetic as it sounded, was the only person other than Uncle Owen that she thought of as a friend. Her throat clamped shut and she brushed tears away behind the curtain of her hair.

When the waitress came back with the pie and tea, Lizzy said, "I'm sorry, I don't feel well. Can you box up the pie for me?"

"Sure, hon," said the waitress. She patted Lizzy's

shoulder, then disappeared with the plate. She was back in a minute with a Styrofoam take-away container and a Styrofoam cup. "I made the tea to go, too," she said. "It's going to be four-fifty. Want me to take your money up to the register for you? Save you having to stand in line."

"Yeah, that would be great, thanks," said Lizzy. She gave the waitress a five, and she was back in a minute with Lizzy's change. Lizzy realized she didn't have any singles, but she didn't want to have to ask for change. She dropped another five on the table. This was turning out to be an expensive lunch for just pie, a tea, and a crappy book, but she had eaten out with Uncle Owen enough that she would never leave a restaurant without tipping. Suddenly exhausted, she struggled into her coat. She headed for the door, intentionally turning away from the counter and Christine, who was ringing up the last of the departing bus crowd.

"Hey, it's the bookworm," Lizzy heard, and turned toward the counter where Christine stood.

Christine grinned at her, then noticed Lizzy's reddened eyes. "Are you okay?"

Lizzy nodded. "Yeah, I just suddenly didn't feel good. Probably just need some fresh air."

"Sure, probably. Hold on a sec." Christine counted out the customer's change. "Have a nice day!" she said to the customer with a quick but genuine smile.

Lizzy was standing near the door, but Christine beckoned her over to the counter. "You staying at the cottages? I've seen you head over that direction a couple of times."

Lizzy hesitated, then nodded.

"Well, at least you don't have far to go," said Christine. "Is it your stomach?"

Lizzy, regretting that she had used the illness excuse, nodded again.

"You know what's good for that," said Christine. "Flat ginger ale. Hold on." She disappeared into the kitchen and returned a minute later with a can of Canada Dry. "Let it sit open for a little while until it gets flat. It works better." She handed the can to Lizzy.

"Thanks," said Lizzy, fumbling for her purse.

Christine waved her hand. "Don't worry about it, I'll just add it to your tab next time you're in. Hope you feel better."

"Thanks," said Lizzy, and turned from the counter. Then she turned back. "Hey, I got a book." She held it up.

Christine looked at it and laughed. "Well, it's not what I would have recommended, but when you're done with that one, stop back and you can swap it for another one. I know which ones are the good ones."

The bell rang merrily as Lizzy pushed the door open and stepped into the blustery December day, a foolish smile on her face.

CHAPTER SIXTY-FIVE

George Millard wiped the last of the egg yolk off his plate with his last bite of toast just as the waitress stopped by his table with the coffee. He liked places that served breakfast all day.

"Top off?" she asked.

"Sure, thanks." He moved the cup to the edge of the table. "I may be around here for a couple of days on business. Construction. I'm looking for a place to stay." He nodded out the window toward Smoketown Cottages. "Know anything about that place?"

The waitress glanced out the window. "I've never stayed there myself, of course, but I hear it's nice. Probably cheaper than a chain hotel."

"Know if they do long-term stays?"

"I'm sure they'd let you stay as long as you want, as long as you're paying your bill," said the waitress.

Millard laughed. "I'll bet you're right—" He glanced at her name tag. "—Christine."

Millard had seen Lizzy leaving the restaurant a couple of hours before, and had called Bonnay.

"She's at a motel in Smoketown."

"Smoketown? Why in the world …"

"Low key. Out of the way."

"Any sign of Dr. McNally?"

"No. I figure he decided it was safer for her not to be with him, him being so noticeable. He must have holed up somewhere else. Want me to bring her back?"

There was silence for a few moments, then Bonnay said, "No, leave her there and keep an eye on her. This is actually not a bad development—she's taken herself out of circulation, and we don't need to worry about having a drugged teenager in the house. Of course, if you see anyone out there—Dr. McNally, the police—or if she tries to leave Smoketown, do what you need to do. She has incentive to keep the facts about herself private," he continued, "but we can't risk her having some crisis of conscience and taking her story to the *Chronicle*."

"So, what do I 'need to do' in that case?" asked Millard.

"She mustn't speak with anyone else under any circumstances," said Bonnay. "I expect you to ensure that doesn't happen. Are we in agreement?"

"Yes," said Millard, "we're in agreement."

Now Millard, pleasantly full from his meal, strolled over to the motel office, opening the door to the jingle of a bell. Seemed like every door in Amish country had a bell on it. In a moment, a man emerged from a back room.

"Help you?"

"Just checking to make sure you're open, I didn't see any cars in the parking lot."

The man shrugged. "Slow time of year—lots of shoppers, what with Christmas coming, but not a lot of overnight tourists. We're a lot busier in the summer and fall."

"But you are renting out rooms?"

"Oh, yeah—and it would be quiet. That's one advantage for you, being here in the slow season."

"No one else staying here?"

"Just one other cabin in use at the moment."

"Big family? I hope not—I like the idea of quiet."

"No, just one girl—" The manager checked himself. "Just one person staying in that cabin. And it's way over there." He nodded toward the cabin furthest from the office. "I could give you one over on this side, lots of quiet and privacy."

"Sounds good," said Millard, pulling out his wallet. "I'm not sure how long I'll be staying, let's just go day by day."

CHAPTER SIXTY-SIX

The next day, desperate for some diversion—and some different clothes—Lizzy headed over to the Target.

Although the day was cold and dreary, the mile-long walk was a pleasant change of routine. She passed tidy self-storage units, farms surrounded by white wooden fences, cupola-topped barns, and well-kept ranch-style homes on large lots. A small stream rushed with water from the recent snowmelt. A sidewalk followed the road for some time, but when that ended she walked on the road, stepping aside when one of the Amish buggies passed her.

Then suddenly she was at the intersection of a busier road—two lanes each way, with the Target anchoring a small shopping center that could provide for any needs she might have for coffee, cell phones, pet supplies, or a desire to See How Real Amish Families Live.

The store's automatic doors whooshed open and Lizzy pulled a clunky red shopping cart out of the row. Her mother had gotten into the habit of buying Lizzy's clothes—and her own, for that matter—online, and going to a store had always been a bit of a thrill.

Pre-Christmas sale stickers shouted from the shelves, hawking gift items and a diminishing supply of holiday decor. A jazzy Christmas carol played in the background. A mother, father, and little girl, all wearing Santa hats, passed her, the parents arguing good-naturedly.

"It's James Earl Jones."

"No, I'm telling you it's Boris Karloff. James Earl Jones is Darth Vader."

"I know *that*, but I think he's the Grinch too."

"'They're finding out now that no Christmas is coming!'" said the father, in a decent imitation of the Grinch. "'They're just waking up, I know just what they'll do ...'" Their voices trailed off as they disappeared down one of the aisles.

Lizzy smiled, but felt the prickle of tears in her eyes. It was a week before Christmas—she shouldn't be all by herself in some strange motel in some strange town that had horse parking at the restaurants. She should be—

She didn't know where she should be, but she knew it shouldn't be here.

She ducked into an aisle—tablecloths and placemats—and wiped her eyes with the back of her hand. She felt her throat tighten, but she knew that having a meltdown in the Target didn't exactly qualify as "laying low." She closed her eyes and slowed her breathing.

Uncle Owen had said it would only be a couple of days. By Christmas, he would have taken her away from here. In the meantime, she thought, brightening slightly, she'd buy herself a present. But the first priority was to replace the horrible clothes he had left her at the cottage.

She started for the Misses section, intent on getting pants that were long enough and any article of clothing in a primary color, but was distracted by the handbag section. Of all the horrible clothes, the handbag was the worst. Lizzy smiled at the thought of Uncle Owen standing befuddled in front of a display of handbags—or more likely just grabbing one without paying much attention.

Her shoulder felt hunched from trying to keep the bag on her shoulder during the walk from the cottage, so she decided a messenger bag would be better. She found one in an aqua nylon, with purple, orange, yellow, and white flowers printed on it.

With the messenger bag in the cart, she made her way to the clothing section. The store was already stocking spring clothes, and just looking at the colors cheered her up. She decided that wearing several layers of warm-weather clothes would be just as effective as one layer of winter clothes. She put a pair of jeans in the cart—she couldn't see needing anything other than jeans—and a variety of brightly colored cotton shells and cardigans. In the shoe department, she found a pair of dark purple hiking boots that looked like they'd be comfortable and waterproof. She anticipated she'd be getting around on foot while she was in Smoketown, and her leather shoes were soaked from the walk to the store. She looked at the coats—there was a pretty blue one—but the black coat she was wearing wasn't bad, just boring, so she compromised by getting a rainbow-colored scarf.

She got out her phone and added up what she had in the cart, then considered the total. Uncle Owen had told her the money would have to last for a while, but it wasn't as if she was going to go clothes shopping every day.

She went next to the home goods section and added a pair of scissors to the cart, then a flashlight—she had almost fallen the night before on her unlighted walk to the pizzeria.

She detoured to the beauty products section. After almost half an hour of agonized indecision, she added eyeliner, eye shadow, and mascara to the cart.

Her final stop was the toy section. She was tempted by the Lego Ferris Wheel kit, but it was expensive. More importantly, if she was going to be leaving Smoketown Cottages soon, it would be better to pick something more portable. She finally settled on the Volkswagen Camper Van. That and the books should keep her occupied until Uncle Owen came to get her.

CHAPTER SIXTY-SEVEN

Lizzy's hair was now L'Oreal Light Brown, and she was moving on to the second part of her transformation.

She glanced from the video on her iPad to her image in the mirror. She had her hair in a foot-long ponytail over her forehead, just like in the video. She had measured out the distance the video recommended for bangs and put in another rubber band. Taking a deep breath, she picked up the scissors and started to cut.

It was surprisingly hard to cut through hair. She could see that the scissors weren't going through the ponytail straight, but didn't know what to do to correct. Well, she was committed, not much she could do now.

After some sawing with the scissors, the ponytail fell away, leaving her looking like a unicorn with a spray of hair in place of a horn. She removed the other rubber band, shook her hair back, and examined the result.

Layers and bangs replaced what had been, for her whole life, long, straight hair. She remembered once hearing her mother tell her father that she didn't want to risk Lizzy being upset with a hairdresser due to an unsuccessful cut. But while before her hair had looked just like pretty much every other teenage girl's hair, now she had an actual hairstyle—even if it was a little lopsided.

She used the tiny wall-mounted blow dryer. When she was done, she posed in front of the mirror, experimenting with parts on the side or the middle, tucking the layers behind her ears or letting them fall free. She liked it.

She was seized with a desire to share her new look with

someone else. She glanced at her phone: three o'clock. Glick's was likely to be quiet, and Christine was usually there this time of day. If she wasn't, Lizzy would just get a cup of tea to go—the tea from Glick's was much nicer than the tea made from water heated in the coffee maker in the room. She put on her new jeans and boots, and topped it with a pink T-shirt and purple cotton cardigan.

The bell on the door of Glick's jingled as she went in, and she was both gratified and suddenly nervous to see Christine at the register, a magazine laid out on the counter as it had been the first time Lizzy had met her. Christine looked up with her standard customer welcome smile.

"Good afternoon, table for ..." her voice trailed off. "Hey, is that you?" she asked, then her face split in a grin. "Wow, that's quite a makeover."

Lizzy tugged at her hair and flushed. "I wanted a change."

"So I see," said Christine, still grinning.

"I cut it myself. I think it's a little crooked."

Christine flipped the magazine closed. "Turn around and let me see."

Lizzy did a slow turn.

"It just needs evened out a little bit."

"Yeah, I suppose so," said Lizzy.

"I trim my sister's hair, want me to have a go at it?"

"Uh, sure," said Lizzy, looking around the restaurant, which was deserted. "Here?"

"No, I'd probably get arrested cutting someone's hair here. Can we go to your place?"

Lizzy hesitated.

"It's okay if you don't want to, I'd understand," said Christine.

"No, no, it's fine," said Lizzy, then added, "I was just trying to remember if I'd straightened up this morning."

Christine rolled her eyes. "It's not going to make any difference to me, believe me." She went to the pass-through window to the kitchen. "Marge, is it okay if I go out for a couple of minutes? Maybe fifteen?"

"Sure," came a voice from the kitchen. "Just be back by four."

"No problem." Christine disappeared through the swinging doors to the kitchen and came back again in a moment, shrugging into her coat. "By the way, what's your name?"

"Oh, jeez, sorry. I'm … Elizabeth."

"Hey, Elizabeth, nice to meet you. I'm Christine."

As they walked to the cottage, Lizzy thought this was probably not what Uncle Owen had had in mind when he'd told her to "lay low." What if he showed up now and saw her with Christine? But let him be mad, she thought, with sudden vehemence—she was sixteen years old, almost seventeen, and she had never had a best friend, not since Rosalie back in Paoli, and she guessed why that friendship had been cut short. She hoped that Rosalie wasn't suffering the effects of some long-forgotten spat she had had with Lizzy.

"Got some company over here," said Christine, nodding toward the only car in the motel parking lot. "I think he was in the restaurant yesterday, said he was in construction."

When they got to the cottage, Lizzy opened the door and led Christine in. The advantage of not having much stuff was that it limited how messy the room could be. She hadn't made the bed that morning, but she had at least pulled the sheet and blanket up. The pillowcase she was using for dirty laundry was tucked into the closet alcove, ready for the trip to the laundromat that she had planned for that evening. She was relieved that the as-yet-unopened Lego set was still in the Target bag.

Christine shrugged out of her coat and put it on the bed. "I've never been in one of these cottages. Pretty nice."

Lizzy shrugged. "Yeah, it's okay."

"Do you get a lot of channels?" Christine nodded toward the television.

Not having any basis for determining what constituted a

lot, Lizzy shrugged again. "I guess so."

Christine looked expectantly at her, then sighed. "You've got scissors, I guess."

Lizzy went to the bathroom to get the scissors and Christine followed her. "We should do it in the tub, then it will be easy to clean up."

At Christine's direction, Lizzy sat on the edge of the tub facing out, Christine standing in the tub. Christine draped a towel over Lizzy's shoulders, then combed out her hair. "It's longer on the right side than the left side, I'd need to take about an inch off to make it even, okay?"

"Yeah, sounds good."

Christine combed and snipped for a few minutes.

"There, that's better."

She had Lizzy turn around so her feet were in the tub and gazed critically at her bangs.

"The right is a little longer than the left, but I'm afraid if I even them out, they'll be too short. If I make the left side a little shorter, it will look like it's on purpose."

"Okay."

Christine snipped at the bangs, then worked on the sides a bit, periodically pulling the hair on either side of Lizzy's face straight to match up the length. Then she stepped back, brushed a few strands of hair off Lizzy's shoulders, and said, "There you go."

"That's it?" asked Lizzy, surprised.

"Yeah, I told you it wasn't bad, just needed some evening up."

Lizzy stood up and went to the mirror. Christine was right, it looked more styled now, and even the crooked bangs looked good.

"You know, those clothes look really nice on you," said Christine.

"Really?" asked Lizzy, blushing.

"Yeah, really. One thing all my friends would tell you, if I didn't think it looked nice, I'd tell you. Brighter is better on you. Cheers you up."

"Thanks." Lizzy looked back at the mirror. "Thanks for everything."

Christine undraped the towel from Lizzy's shoulders. "No problem." She shook the towel into the bathtub. "Do you have paper towels or something we could use to wipe up the hair?"

"Oh, don't worry about that, I'll take care of it," said Lizzy. "I really appreciate it."

Christine folded the towel and hung it on the towel rack. "Sure. I better get back." She put her hands into her pockets. "Are you okay? In trouble or anything?"

"No," said Lizzy. Then, with Christine still looking at her, continued. "Not anymore, I mean. I was in a bad situation, but a friend of mine got me out of it. I'm waiting here until he figures out what to do with me."

Christine nodded. "Well, I'm glad you're out of the bad situation. But maybe you don't need to wait for your friend to figure things out. You've been here for a while now, and I can't imagine it's much fun. Maybe you could figure things out yourself." She grinned again. "You seem pretty ready to strike out on your own, if you ask me."

CHAPTER SIXTY-EIGHT

In the two weeks since Ruby had gotten the phone call from Gerard Bonnay letting her know her services were no longer required, she had been trying to settle into a new routine, and trying to find a new job. She was relieved to be getting away from Bonnay, but sorry—sorrier than she would have thought—to be getting away from the Ballards as part of the bargain. Well, getting away from the one living Ballard, the others being dead.

The market for housekeepers seemed to be on the downturn. It looked like anyone with money to spend on in-home help was spending it on an au pair—babysitter, in Ruby's parlance—or was opting for assisted living if the help they needed was for their parents or themselves rather than their children.

She had thought about giving up the apartment and moving in with Opal and Tony to save some money until she found a job, but their house was barely big enough for the two of them. Ruby would have had to sleep on the living room sofa, and when she factored in the cost of storing her furniture, it hardly made sense.

She had thought she would need to start having the *Chronicle* delivered rather than reading the copies Tony and Opal saved up and gave her on Saturdays, so that she could get the Help Wanted ads. Then she found that Help Wanted ads were moving, along with everything else, to the internet. That morning she had tired of scanning the ads on her very old, very slow computer, so she was taking a break by reading through the back issues of the *Chron*.

She was idly paging through the Friday edition when a name on the obituaries page caught her eye. She scanned the write-up, trying to muster some stirring of sorrow—after all, she had known the decedent for most of her life. Instead, she felt a general sense of relief. She put the paper aside, got her phone out of her purse, and speed dialed Angelo.

"Hey, Zia, what's up?" he asked in the usual enthusiastic way he greeted her phone calls. It made her think of the young, pre-gambling, pre-Anton Rossi Angelo.

"Angie, I saw Anton's obituary."

"Oh. Yeah." The enthusiasm was gone, his voice suddenly wooden. "How about that."

"The obit didn't say what he died from."

"No, I don't think it did."

"Angie," she said, exasperated, "do you know what he died from?"

"They found him in the alley between his house and Luigi's. Must have been heading over there for a drink."

"He just dropped dead in the alley?"

"How should I know, Zia?" he said, a hint of a whine entering his voice.

"Well, you knew him pretty well, Angie, and you know a lot of his … colleagues. I thought you might have heard something."

"I don't know anything." The whine had morphed into truculence, a tone that would have earned the little Angelo a quick swat on the fanny from his father several decades before.

"Well, keep an ear out, okay? I'm curious."

"Why do you care?"

"I'm curious, okay, Angie?"

"Okay, Zia, okay."

They were silent for a few moments, each irritated with the other, then moved on to a discussion of the logistics of a drive Tony wanted to take to Wildwood in the spring.

After Ruby hung up with Angelo, she went back to the

paper, but the question about what had happened to Anton Rossi continued to niggle at the back of her mind. Finally, she put the paper aside again and dialed her sister.

"Opal, it's me," she said when her sister answered the phone. "Did you hear about Anton Rossi?"

"Oh, yes, I forgot to mention that to you. Can't say I lost too much sleep over that, although I shouldn't speak ill of the dead." Ruby could picture Opal crossing herself.

"So, what happened to him? There wasn't anything in the obituary."

"Looks like he just fell over dead," said Opal. "I heard someone say he had a stroke."

Ruby closed her eyes at the news, which she had suspected since she saw the obit.

"Seems a little young for a stroke," she heard herself say.

"Yes, that's what I thought, too," said Opal, and she was off on a discussion of friends and relatives who had died from age-inappropriate ailments.

Ruby paid attention enough to say "Really?" and "Good Lord!" at all the right points, but her mind was ticking through the calculations of the likelihood that two youngish to middle-aged people she had known—Charlotte Ballard and Anton Rossi—had died of strokes. Plus that woman traveling on what was probably the same train Mr. Ballard and Lizzy had been on.

She thought of Gerard Bonnay hiring Angelo right after he had paid off Angelo's debt with Anton Rossi and placed Ruby in the Ballard household to spy on Lizzy and her mother. She thought of the Ballards' instructions to Lizzy to "not bother Miss DiMano," and of Mrs. Ballard and Gerard Bonnay asking her how she felt after encounters with Lizzy. She thought of Mrs. Ballard telling Lizzy to "run away and hit a pillow" when she got angry. She thought back to the yoga and meditation Mrs. Ballard had practiced with her daughter.

As soon as she reasonably could, Ruby extracted herself from the phone call with Opal and dialed Owen McNally's number.

CHAPTER SIXTY-NINE

That morning, Owen had had a quite satisfactory complimentary breakfast at the hotel—waffles one could make on an actual waffle iron. He spent his time in his room, ostensibly trying to decide what to do next, but in reality succumbing to the allure of the stack of academic journals he had brought with him. Every few hours, he would watch the news or scan the *Chron* website for any reference to Lucia Hazlitt or Gerard Bonnay or Vivantem. At first he listened nervously for his phone to ring and for Gerard's name to appear on the caller ID, but as time passed with no contact from Gerard, the tension subsided.

After a few days had passed with no discernible reaction from Gerard, Owen began to think his actions had been driven by paranoia. What had he been thinking—a middle-aged academic drugging a young woman and kidnapping her from a hospital emergency room? He began to contemplate with less pride and more embarrassment the steps he had taken to pull off the caper and cover his tracks: the separate hide-out locations, the payments with cash, the throwaway phone for Lizzy with, for heaven's sake, his number programmed under *Pizza*. Was it possible that if he had insisted more strenuously that he had to take Lizzy away, that Gerard would have acquiesced? Owen would never know, because he had been intimidated by Gerard's stature, by the trappings of that stature, and by the presence of that South Philly assistant, who had seemed more like an enforcer.

Owen was making another halfhearted search on the *Chron* website when his phone rang and Ruby DiMano's name appeared.

When he had been planning his "rescue" of Lizzy, he knew immediately that he would be enlisting the help of his brother. But every plan he came up with required the help of a third person—if he didn't want Lizzy to be seen with a person of his memorable appearance, someone else had to get her away from the hospital and deliver her to her hideout. He had considered and discarded various friends and colleagues for the role, and eventually his thoughts had turned to Ruby DiMano.

Considering how long she had worked for the Ballards, Owen barely knew her. His visits with Patrick and Lizzy were usually on the weekends, when Ruby was off, and the times he had visited during the week, she had always removed herself to some other part of the house.

On top of his lack of familiarity with her, the way she had entered the Ballards' lives—through the recommendation of Gerard Bonnay—gave him pause. But it was clear to Owen that Charlotte and Patrick had trusted her. And Gerard had fired her after Patrick died, so perhaps she would no longer feel any sense of loyalty to him, if she ever had. Eventually, when Owen had eliminated all other potential accomplices, he called Ruby, telling her the same story he had told Andy: that he feared for Lizzy's safety with Gerard Bonnay. She had agreed to help him.

But the agreement they had made was that Ruby would not contact Owen after she dropped Lizzy in Smoketown except in an emergency, so seeing her name on the caller ID gave Owen a start.

"Hello?" answered Owen.

"Dr. McNally, it's Ruby."

"Ruby, you can call me Owen. What's up?"

"I have some news."

"What news?"

"My nephew, the one who works for Mr. Bonnay, he got in with Bonnay because of his betting—Mr. Bonnay helped

it."

"Yes, I think that's probably the wisest course. Do you think ..." There was another silence, and this time Ruby didn't help him out. "Do you think that Lizzy might be in danger from this man's ..."

"Fellow crooks?" Ruby finished for him. "I don't know. But I'm thinking we should assume she may be." After a pause, Ruby asked, "Have you been in touch with Lizzy?"

"Yes. She didn't mention anything about this bookie ..."

"Anton Rossi," prompted Ruby. "Can you call her back? Ask her?"

"Yes," said Owen, "that's a good idea. I'll do that right now."

"Okay, let me know what she says," said Ruby, and ended the call.

Owen paced to the window of the hotel room. He looked across the parking lots of the other anonymous chain hotels and restaurants that had made this seem like such a good place to hide out, to the skyline of Philadelphia beyond. He thought he could just pick out the skyscraper that housed the Vivantem offices. How had he gotten himself into this? He had thought he was being clever, had thought of every angle, and now he was taking direction from a housekeeper. He shook his head ruefully.

CHAPTER SEVENTY

Owen had found the Rossi obituary on the *Chronicle* website. After reading it a few times, he sighed and dialed the number for Lizzy's phone—the number that would flash *Pizza* on caller ID.

"Hello?" she said. She sounded more cheerful than she had in days.

"Hey, Pumpkin, it's me."

"Hey, Uncle Owen."

"How's it going there?"

"Good. I got a Lego set at Target—the VW camper."

"That's great—I wish I had thought to get one for you."

She laughed. "Not something that you might automatically think of for a sixteen-year-old." There was a pause. "Although the box does say, '16 plus.'"

"Yeah, but sometimes doing that kind of thing from your childhood can be therapeutic."

There was a comfortable silence, and Owen thought he could hear the click of Lego blocks being snapped together.

"Hey, Pumpkin, have you ever heard of someone named Anton Rossi?"

"Anton Rossi? No, why?"

"I just read his obituary in the *Chron*. He lived in Philly—died last week. Of a stroke."

The clicking stopped. Finally Lizzy said in a voice laced with a combination of caution and dread, "So?"

"So ... he wasn't that old. Just seemed odd."

There was a long pause—this one not so comfortable—and then Lizzy said, "What did he look like? Was there a photo?"

There was a photo, but based on the clothes and hairstyle of the subject, Owen guessed it had been taken a decade or two ago.

"Thin face. Dark hair. Dark eyes." He waited, and when Lizzy didn't say anything, he said, "Does it sound like someone you know?"

"I don't know. That could be anybody." Her voice was wooden.

"Take a look at the obituary in the *Chron* online—there's a photo. Anton Rossi."

The click of the Legos stopped, and in a few moments Owen could hear her breathing become ragged.

"Do you recognize him?"

"No."

"Are you sure?"

"Yes, I'm sure. I don't recognize him." Her voice was stiff and distant—not the voice he associated with his goddaughter.

He sighed. "Okay, I just had to ask."

"Can I go now, Uncle Owen? I'm tired."

But she didn't sound tired. She sounded upset. She sounded angry.

"Sure, sweetie. I'll call again tomorrow."

"Okay. Bye." And she hung up before he could say goodbye back, something she had never done before.

CHAPTER SEVENTY-ONE

In the hours since Uncle Owen had called, Lizzy had been gazing out the window overlooking the airport. She had become quite an expert on planes frequenting the airport—she found you could get a lot of information about them if you searched on the numbers painted on their tails—but they were coming and going unnoticed today. The photo in the obituary Owen had directed her to was definitely the man in Gerard Bonnay's house. He must have died, and Gerard had had his body taken away and dumped somewhere.

That would be three. Three people she had killed. That she knew of. What about all those people she had encountered when she was little, before her parents understood what she could do? Before she herself understood the importance of not getting angry, of running away and hitting a pillow? How many of those people were dead, or living with damage she had unwittingly inflicted? And if Gerard Bonnay was locking her in a room with a horrible man, knowing what the outcome was likely to be, probably performing some kind of test of her ability, it seemed pretty clear that he was the cause of everything bad that had happened to her—the cause of her power, and the cause of her mother's death. And mostly likely her father's, as well.

She sat motionless in the chair, but her mind was roiling. She had to get back to Philadelphia, and then she could plan what do to about Gerard. But how could she do that? She didn't know how to drive, and the only person she knew in Smoketown was Christine. She didn't think it would be right to involve her in what looked increasingly like a deadly game.

She jumped at the jangle of the phone on the bedside table. She turned from the window and stared at the ringing phone, her heart thumping. After ten rings it stopped. Probably a wrong number. Or a telemarketer. She remembered her dad complaining about telemarketers. Too bad, she thought bitterly, that her force couldn't flow through telephone wires and over cell connections to deal with that annoyance.

She sighed and had turned back to the window when the phone rang again.

She got up from the chair and walked to the phone, her heart racing again. Was there an innocent explanation for the calls? It could be from the motel office, maybe with some question about the room, or the maid service. It wasn't the day she was supposed to put the sheets and towels out, was it?

The phone rang ten times and went silent again.

She was still standing by the bedside table looking down at the phone when it rang again.

She picked up the receiver with a shaking hand and pressed it to her ear. Silence. She was getting ready to hang up when she heard a long intake of breath.

"Lizzy? It's Ruby DiMano."

CHAPTER SEVENTY-TWO

Ruby sat in her Kia in the parking lot of the Sheetz. Cars pulled up to the gas pumps, and people left the store sipping from cups of coffee or tapping cigarettes out of just-acquired packs. She pressed the phone to her ear, listening for any sound. She could only hear a light breathing.

She had hoped Lizzy would say hello so she was sure who she was talking to, but she couldn't blame her for wanting the caller to make the first move. Finally, she took a deep breath and spoke.

"Lizzy? It's Ruby DiMano."

She paused, but heard nothing.

"Lizzy, don't hang up, I need to talk to you."

She waited a beat, still hoping for some final confirmation that this was, in fact, Lizzy, but she figured that once she had given her name, she was committed.

"Lizzy, I'm the one who brought you to Smoketown."

There was a long pause, then finally a small, confused voice. "Really?"

Ruby let out the breath she hadn't realized she had been holding. "Really. Dr. McNally arranged to get you out of the hospital, and I drove you to the cottage."

"He didn't tell me that," said Lizzy uncertainly. Then, with more conviction, she said, "Wait, I remember Mom telling me once that she and Dad hired you because someone at Vivantem had recommended you. I think you work for Gerard."

"I did. I don't anymore."

"No," said Lizzy with more conviction. "I think Gerard

sent you to find me."

"Lizzy, I obviously know where you are—I took you there myself. I called you on the motel phone to prove I know where you are. But I could call you on your cell, because I have that number too. If I were working for Gerard, you'd already be back with him."

"If you know where I am and you want to talk to me, why didn't you just come to me?"

"I'm right down the road, at the Sheetz."

"Why didn't you just come to where I'm staying?"

"Because I knew you had reason to be angry with me, and I wanted to explain what happened before we saw each other in person."

"Oh. Right." Lizzy's voice was faint.

"I'll tell you why I was working for Gerard, and I'll tell you why I'm not working for him anymore. Then I think we have some planning to do, and I'm hoping you'll be willing to do that in person."

There was silence, Ruby counting off the seconds by the beat of her heart. Then she heard Lizzy's voice.

"Okay, I'll listen. Then I'll decide."

Ruby finished telling her story, then waited through a full minute of silence. Lizzy was so quiet that in the background Ruby could hear the faint sounds of a small plane taking off, and then would see it a moment later as it passed over the Sheetz.

Finally, Lizzy spoke. "So Gerard blackmailed you into working for him?"

"Yes."

"Whatever happened to your nephew?"

"The bookie's goons broke his thumb. That was before Gerard got involved. Later on, when Gerard could have helped if he had wanted to, they broke his kneecap with a hammer."

"Holy cow," breathed Lizzy. She was silent for a moment, then said, "Did your nephew ever find out what you were doing for him?"

"No."

"So, is he okay now?"

Ruby's eyes dropped to her lap. "He walks with a limp."

"I'll bet, but—"

"With a limp, Lizzy. Does that sound like someone you know?"

Ruby heard a gasp. "Angelo?"

"Yes."

"But … why would he work for Gerard after what Gerard did to him?"

"But Gerard never did a thing to him, did he?" Ruby said bitterly. "Kept him out of trouble with Anton Rossi—most of the time, anyway—as a favor to his Aunt Ruby. And then gave him a job that made him feel like a big man." Ruby felt her throat tighten and drew in a deep breath. She hadn't cried in fifty years—not since Opal, in an uncharacteristic fit of spite, had burned Ruby's doll in the fireplace. She wasn't about to start now. "Lizzy, my family has done you and yours a disservice, and I am going to do everything I can to make it up to you, if you'll let me."

"But, what about your nephew? What if Gerard finds out you're helping me?"

"He's not a boy anymore. He made his bed, let him sleep in it."

"But what can you do? What can either of us do?"

"Will you meet with me? Maybe at that airport next to the motel? It would be easier to talk about in person."

"Aren't you scared of me?" asked Lizzy.

"Do I need to be?"

There was a long pause. Then Lizzy said, "No, you don't. I don't think you ever did."

CHAPTER SEVENTY-THREE

Ruby turned into the road leading to Smoketown Airport, passing a faded wooden sign advertising flying lessons and sightseeing flights. She saw a person, hunched against the cold, sitting on a picnic bench next to the airport building—definitely Lizzy.

She also saw a man crossing the snow-covered ground between the motel cabins and the airport. She slowed the car. The man's head was down, watching his footing, but he was headed right for Lizzy, whose back was to him.

Just then the roar of a small plane filled the air, and the man looked up as it took off over their heads. Ruby was thrown back a dozen years, to a drive with a man to deliver a suitcase of money to Anton Rossi—the money that Ruby had hoped would get Angelo out of trouble and put him on a better path. She turned the Kia into one of the parking spaces in front of the pizzeria, angling it so she could keep an eye on the man, and pulled out her phone. She pressed in a number with trembling hands. Would Lizzy pick up if she didn't recognize the number? She couldn't see Lizzy from where she was parked, but she could see the man continuing to make his way toward the picnic bench.

The call connected.

"Lizzy, it's Ruby. Don't look around, but there's a man walking toward you. He works for Gerard Bonnay. Go into the airport office. Stay on the phone with me."

Ruby heard movement, then the sound of a door shutting. The sounds of the airport she'd heard from the phone muted.

"Is there someone in the office?" asked Ruby.

"Yes."

"Do you have money with you?"

"Yes."

"How much?"

"Uh, pretty much."

If she didn't want to say how much she had, Ruby thought, it was probably enough.

"Get someone to fly you to—" Ruby racked her brain. "—the airport in Coatesville. But if that man comes into the office, don't let him know where you're going."

"He's standing outside," said Lizzy.

"Okay, go ahead and ask them about the flight, I'll stay on the line."

Lizzy must have dropped the phone away from her mouth, but Ruby could still hear the conversation.

"Hi. Can I hire someone to fly me to the airport in Coatesville?"

"Chester County? Just one way?" Ruby heard a slow voice ask. "No sightseeing?"

"No, just one way."

"Well, it's not usual …"

Ruby held her breath.

"… but I don't see why not. How about one fifty? That's the charge for the normal sightseeing flight, and Chester County wouldn't take much longer."

"Okay."

"Okay, then, let me just see if this gentleman outside needs anything—"

"He doesn't need anything," said Lizzy, and Ruby felt her pulse thumping in her throat. "Well, he's looking for me. He's … he's my boyfriend's dad. My boyfriend is pretty mad at me, and sent his dad after me. But I don't want to be with him anymore. I'm going to Coatesville to be with family—that's who I'm on the phone with, my aunt in Coatesville—but he can't know where I'm going. Don't let him know I told you."

There was a long pause. Ruby held her breath.

"Well ... I guess that's okay. We'll just say we're taking a little sightseeing flight and that we'll see him when we get back."

"That would be great. Thanks."

Ruby let out her breath.

The outdoor sounds filtered through the phone again, and Ruby heard the man's voice: "Just taking this young lady for a quick sightseeing flight, sir, and then I'll be right back."

Ruby heard Bonnay's goon say something she couldn't hear.

"Oh, no more than thirty minutes or so. There's coffee on in the office—help yourself."

A few minutes passed with occasional comments of "Right over here, miss," and "Just got her gassed up this morning," then Lizzy was back on the line.

"Okay, we're about to get in the plane. I'll see you in Coatesville."

"Good job, Lizzy."

"Thanks," Lizzy said, the hint of a smile in her voice.

CHAPTER SEVENTY-FOUR

The small plane that had departed with Lizzy Ballard buzzed back into Smoketown Airport about an hour after it had left. Even as it taxied back to its hangar next to the airport office, Millard could see that there was only one occupant. He swore under his breath.

The pilot—an old geezer wearing overalls, an enormous plaid coat, and a John Deere hat—pried himself out of the little plane and walked stiffly to the office.

"Now, then, what can I do for you today?" he asked when he got to Millard.

"The young lady enjoy her sightseeing tour?" asked Millard sourly.

"Oh, yes, I think she did. Would you be interested in one? It'd be two hundred dollars."

"I don't know, it looks like it's a one-way trip."

"One-way or round-trip, customer's choice," said the geezer.

"Where did the girl go?" Millard asked, knowing it was hopeless. "Maybe I'd like to take the same trip."

"Oh, I couldn't tell you that, sir."

Millard looked over at the plane. "How fast does that thing go?"

"Not fast, but she's a workhorse. Cessna 172. Makes about a hundred and twenty knots."

"Interesting. Well, I'll keep that sightseeing trip in mind. Thanks."

Millard trudged back to his car in the motel parking lot. On his phone he typed in a search for *convert 120 knots to mph* and got the result: about a hundred and forty. He got a map of Southeastern Pennsylvania out of the glove compartment and eyeballed it to estimate the area the old man could have covered in the plane in the hour he was gone. Then he drew from his pocket the aviation map he had lifted from the airport office—he had been pretty sure Ballard wouldn't be in the plane when it returned—and compared the maps.

Jesus, it seemed like there were dozens of airports she could have gotten to, even if he eliminated the big ones like Philly—you never saw little planes at those. He guessed she hadn't come to the airport intending to fly out—otherwise, why would she have been sitting on the picnic bench. No, she must have seen him coming—maybe he hadn't been as careful as usual in his surveillance —and decided on her escape method on the spur of the moment.

She would go somewhere familiar to her. The Poconos looked too far, but there was an airport near Parkesburg. He squinted at the map: Chester County.

It wasn't far from Pocopson. He could call Bonnay and tell him to send Celucci over there, but that idiot would likely make a mess of it—get the girl riled up, and no good would come of that—and Bonnay wouldn't want to go himself, having seen what she did to Rossi.

If she had gone there, it was possible he could catch her there, or nearby—if not, he would come back to Smoketown and search her room. And call Bonnay. It would be humiliating to have to tell Bonnay that Ballard had gotten away, but at least he could tell him that she had cut her hair. And if Bonnay complained—well, then he'd just suggest that he have Celucci take care of it. That should put things in perspective.

As he pulled out of the driveway of the motel, he popped a mint to take away the sour taste in his mouth.

CHAPTER SEVENTY-FIVE

Ruby stood in the glass-enclosed waiting area of Chester County Airport, listening to the crackle of radio transmissions. A big plane had come in—not airline big, but still big—and its passenger had been whisked away in a limo, but there had been little other activity in the time she had been waiting. Then she heard from the radio the voice she had heard over the phone.

"Chester County, Cessna left downwind for runway two-nine, Chester County."

She could see the small plane and followed its progress as it turned, the pilot announcing his position with radio calls about "base" and "final." It touched smoothly down and taxied to the terminal, where the pilot shut down the engine, the propeller spinning to a stop.

She could see Lizzy talking enthusiastically, the pilot nodding and smiling. He pointed to something on the dashboard, or whatever they called it in an airplane—evidently explaining the purpose of some instrument.

"Come on, Lizzy," Ruby muttered under her breath.

After what seemed an eternity, Lizzy climbed out of the plane and crossed the ramp to the terminal, turning once to wave at the pilot, who waved back. The engine on the little plane fired up, and it turned and trundled back toward the runway.

When Lizzy got to the terminal and saw Ruby, her smile faded a bit, replaced by worry.

Ruby took her arm and steered her toward the exit.

"Let's get away from here—I don't know how he could

know where you went, but let's not take any chances. I should have sent you to an airport further away, but this was the only one I could think of on the spur of the moment. How did I get here before you, anyway?"

"I asked him to fly me around a little," said Lizzy. "I've never been in a plane before."

When they reached the parking lot, Ruby unlocked the car and Lizzy fell into the passenger seat with that combination of grace and awkwardness that was the blessing and the curse of teenagers. A faint hint of her earlier smile had returned to her face.

"Have you ever been in a plane?" she asked Ruby.

"Once. Long time ago. A big one."

"It was really cool. I hope I get to do that again."

Ruby turned right onto Business 30, foregoing the bypass, which was the most likely route for Bonnay's henchman to take if he was headed this way.

"Where are we going?" asked Lizzy.

"We'll find an inexpensive motel room," said Ruby. "We'll figure out what to do next. I hadn't planned on finding out you had been followed to Smoketown." She drummed her fingers on the wheel. "I'm pretty sure no one followed me when I drove you out there. I wonder how they found you."

"Do you think they might have found out from Uncle Owen? Maybe they … forced him to tell them where I was." Lizzy's face had gone pale.

"Maybe. We'll figure out a way to check on him when we get settled. I'd just as soon not have Dr. McNally know you've left Smoketown just yet, until we decide what to do."

A minute passed in silence, then Lizzy said, "I'm worried about Uncle Owen, can we call to make sure he's okay?"

"If we call him now, he'll hear car noises in the background and know something's up," said Ruby. "Why don't you look up a place for us to go on your phone— somewhere cheap—and we'll call him as soon as we get there." To change the subject, she said, "Where did you get those clothes?"

"Target. You should have seen what Uncle Owen left for me in the motel room." She started to roll her eyes, then glanced over at Ruby, her cheeks reddening. "Uh, unless …"

Ruby waved her hand. "Shopping for teenage girls was never my strong suit."

Lizzy located a Courtyard hotel just a few miles from the airport. It was pricier than Ruby had wanted, but Lizzy was starting to get frantic about Dr. McNally and Ruby figured they could relocate after a night.

When they got to their room, Ruby said, "Okay, I'm going to call Dr. McNally now. Actually, he was supposed to call me back after he spoke with you, so I'll use that as an excuse. Don't say anything while I'm on the phone with him."

"No, I won't," said Lizzy, sounding offended.

Ruby dialed Owen's number and he answered immediately.

"Hello?"

"Dr. McNally, it's Ruby. Just calling to see how your call with Lizzy went."

"Please call me Owen. She claims she didn't know Anton Rossi, but I'm not sure that's the case."

Lizzy was sitting on the bed, twisting the scarf that still hung around her neck and staring at Ruby. Ruby gave her a thumbs-up.

"Well, as long as she stays in Smoketown, I guess that's okay," she said. "I could go out there and check on her—"

"No, I appreciate the offer, but I really think the less involvement you have, the better off you are," said Owen. "Now that we have Lizzy away from Gerard Bonnay, I'm thinking that it's time she and I moved a little further away from Philadelphia until things calm down. Somewhere where it doesn't matter if she's seen with someone as 'noticeable' as I am." He laughed weakly.

"No, I'm sure she's fine where she is," Ruby said quickly.

"That way if you *do* end up needing me, I'm right here."

"I appreciate that," said Owen, "but I think you've done more than enough already—I really can't thank you enough for your help."

Merda, thought Ruby. This was not the turn she had planned for events to take.

"Well, don't do anything rash," she said. "Good luck."

"Yes, you too. And thank you again."

They ended the call, and Ruby sat down on the other bed and sighed.

"So Uncle Owen is all right?" asked Lizzy.

"Yes, he's fine. But now he wants to take you away from here. Away from the Philly area."

"But what about Gerard?"

"I suspect he's hoping he can stay away until things settle down. I don't know if he's had a chance to think beyond that." She looked at Lizzy. "His main goal is keeping you safe. I don't think he's spent a lot of time figuring out what to do about Mr. Bonnay."

"But if Gerard is really as bad as you—as *we*—think he is, then what are we going to do? Just be on the run all our lives?" She jumped up and walked to the window. "He has people working for him. Angelo—"

Ruby snorted. "I wouldn't be too concerned about him."

"—the man who found me in Smoketown."

Ruby said nothing.

Lizzy turned from the window. "We could report them to the police."

Ruby sighed. "We could. Don't think I haven't thought about that. But what would we tell them? 'We think Gerard Bonnay and Vivantem made this little girl who could make people's brains bleed'? That would be more likely to get us in trouble than them, and we need to make sure you don't get in a stressful situation that could turn out badly for innocent bystanders."

Lizzy's back stiffened and she turned back to the window.

Ruby regretted she had put it so baldly, expecting to feel that twinge she had seen Charlotte Ballard experience when she made little Lizzy angry, but there was nothing.

A minute ticked by in silence. Finally, Ruby said, "You need to get away from here with Dr. McNally. Or you need to take the fight to Gerard Bonnay."

Lizzy looked back from the window. There was a hard look in her eye, one that Ruby had never seen there before. One that she had never seen before in any sixteen-year-old's eye. "How can I do that? How can I take the fight to him?"

"Lizzy, the man's so scared of you, he had to drug you to feel safe around you."

"Do you think we could win the fight?" asked Lizzy.

"Yes," said Ruby. "I think we could."

CHAPTER SEVENTY-SIX

The next day, they decided on their plan.

Ruby DiMano's earlier perusal of the *Chron*'s online Help Wanted ads had unearthed another job opportunity—a temp position on the cleaning staff of the building which housed the Vivantem offices.

"According to Angelo," said Ruby, "Gerard is usually in the office late on weekdays. I'll take the job, then I'll sneak you into the building after hours."

"It's too complicated," said Lizzy. "By the time you checked if Gerard was in his office and then snuck me in, he might be gone. I think I should be the one to take the job."

"Your hair may be shorter and darker, but it's not much of a disguise," said Ruby. "Someone will recognize you."

"I can do better than this," said Lizzy. She asked Ruby to drive her to the Goodwill, and made her wait in the car while she did her shopping. She also requested a stop at a CVS.

When they got back to the motel room—a Motel 6 near the airport—Lizzy disappeared into the bathroom. She emerged an hour later.

"Good heavens," said Ruby.

Lizzy's hair was a dark purple, almost black, and she wore glasses with heavy black frames. She was at least two sizes larger, her legs straining the seams of a pair of stretch jeans, her stomach pressing against the buttons of her shirt.

"Pretty good disguise, right?"

"Your hair is purple."

"It's Aubergine," said Lizzy.

"And you got fatter," said Ruby.

"I'm wearing a sweatshirt and sweatpants under my clothes."

Ruby tried to scowl, but she could feel a smile tugging at her lips. Lizzy smiled tentatively back. Finally Ruby succumbed to the smile and shook her head. "Well, I wouldn't recognize you myself. Okay, if you're that set on it, you take the cleaning job."

So, two days after leaving Smoketown, Lizzy found herself emptying wastebaskets in the cube farm of an insurance company contact center three floors below Vivantem's.

Her shift ran from five in the evening to midnight. When Lizzy started her shift, Ruby would take up position in a coffee shop across the street from the Vivantem building. Gerard did work late—until eight or nine o'clock, when a car would pick him up at the front of the building. Ruby and Lizzy didn't have much of a plan besides keeping an eye out for an opportunity for Lizzy to get to the Vivantem offices and find Gerard alone.

Lizzy's phone buzzed and she pulled it out of her pocket and looked at the text: *Haven't seen him leave yet.*

She glanced at the time: seven o'clock.

She took the radio off her belt and pushed the talk button. "Davey, it's Beth. I've got to take a break. A smoke break," she amended. Davey seemed like the kind of guy who would understand the compelling need for a smoke break.

The radio crackled. "Okay, Pocahontas," said Davey, her supervisor. "Don't bother punching out, just make it up at the end of the night."

"Okay." She turned the radio off and typed a text to Ruby: *going upstairs now.*

Bringing a spray bottle of window cleaner and a rag with her, she took the service stairway up to the Vivantem offices.

She emerged into the elevator lobby and crossed it soundlessly. The first night on the job she had worn sneakers, but they squeaked on the marble floors, so she had gotten a pair of suede moccasins—hence Davey's nickname for her.

The first night she had found the door to the offices locked. Tonight, though, it swung open.

She stepped through the door and listened for a moment, but didn't hear anything. She sprayed some window cleaner onto the glass wall and began polishing it, still listening for any indication that there was anyone in the offices. Maybe Gerard had left by another entrance than the one Ruby was watching.

After a minute, she stepped away from the glass wall and into the reception area.

She made her way silently across the lobby and stopped at the hallway that led to the offices. Light spilled from two open doors, one about halfway down the hall on the right, and one toward the end of the hall on the left. She polished the glass wall of a conference room, her ears straining to pick up any sound. She thought she heard what might be the faint click of fingers on a computer keyboard.

She moved down the hallway, taking swipes at the brushed metal handles of closed office doors when an expanse of glass wasn't available. Her heart pounded and her throat tightened so that she could barely swallow the saliva that flooded her mouth.

She came to the first door and looked in—it was a break room, the corner of a vending machine visible from the hallway. She stepped in, thinking that a moment out of the exposed expanse of the hallway would give her a chance to collect herself.

She gasped as a man looked up from the table at the other end of the room. His suit jacket was draped across the back of the chair. Under his arm was a gun in a shoulder holster. It was Angelo.

He examined her disinterestedly, his eyes scanning from her chunky glasses to her sweatpants-padded legs. "You're not the regular cleaning girl."

"No," said Lizzy, in a speedily acquired Southern accent.

"She's out sick."

"There's some water leaking on the floor that needs mopped up. I'll show you." Angelo stood and began crossing the break room toward Lizzy.

"No. I only do windows," Lizzy drawled in a panic.

"I don't really care who does it," said Angelo. "Just that it gets done. You can tell your boss to send someone who can take care of it. I'll just show you where it is."

He was now just a few feet from Lizzy, whose wide eyes were frozen on his face, but Angelo barely glanced at her as he passed. "This way." He stepped out of the break room and turned right, toward the other lighted doorway.

"I only do windows," she repeated to his retreating back. Her mind was swirling. What would he do if he turned around and saw her retreating down the hallway? Would he come after her, angry that she hadn't followed him? And he had a gun—her ability would be no defense against that.

He turned back to her. "I heard you the first time. I just need to show you what the problem is so you can tell your boss." He started to push open a door next to the employee lounge.

"What's going on, Angelo?" came a voice from a room down the hall. Gerard Bonnay's voice.

"I'm just trying to explain to the cleaning girl about the leak in the men's room, boss," said Angelo.

"I can't go in the men's room!" Lizzy blurted. "I'll tell my boss you need to talk with him."

She turned and started toward the lobby, trying not to break into a run. Then she heard Gerard's voice again, but this time unmuffled by intervening walls. She could tell he was standing in the hallway.

"Miss, I think my assistant is just trying to explain to you what the problem is."

"There isn't anyone in there," Angelo called after her.

Lizzy turned the corner of the hallway and trotted toward the doors to the lobby. She thought she heard footsteps—an uneven gait—approaching. She hauled the door open and broke into a run toward the service stairway. The footsteps behind her sped up. Just before the door to the stairway closed behind her, she caught the faint sound of Gerard Bonnay's voice.

"Let her go, Angelo. You're scaring her."

CHAPTER SEVENTY-SEVEN

Lizzy got to her assigned floor, slipped into the women's room, and turned on her radio.

"Davey, it's Beth."

"Yo, what's up?"

"I don't feel good. I've got to go home."

"Jesus, Ballard, it's only your second night—"

"I threw up," she interrupted.

"Aw, Christ," he muttered. "What the hell. Do I need to send someone up there to clean it up?"

"No, I took care of it."

"Well, if you're feeling good enough to clean that up, you should be able to finish your shift. It's just emptying wastebaskets, for God's sake."

Lizzy felt her face flushing. It was one of the signals her mother had taught her to watch for, her prompt to run away and hit a pillow. But she knew that Davey was safe wherever he was—probably clicking through porn sites in his basement office, as he had been when she arrived for her first shift. Her effect depended on physical proximity—like a thrown rock, its power diminished with distance. She took a deep breath.

"I still don't feel good. I might throw up again."

Davey sighed dramatically. "Okay, fine, I'll get Lou to finish your floor. Don't forget to clock out. And Pocahontas—"

"Yes?" said Lizzy.

"Tomorrow night let's try to get through an entire shift without bailing, okay?"

"Sure, Davey. Sorry."

Lizzy switched off the radio, got her cart stowed in the cleaner's closet, returned the radio to its charging station, clocked out, and headed for the service entrance by the back stairs. She could hear her phone buzzing periodically in her pocket.

When she got outside, she circled to the front of the building. Across the street she could see Ruby, whose eyes were hidden behind gigantic sunglasses, seated at the window of the coffee shop. She was tapping her phone, and in a moment Lizzy's phone buzzed again. She thought she would suggest to Ruby that wearing sunglasses at night was probably not a good undercover practice.

She entered the largely empty coffee shop and Ruby looked up, starting when she saw Lizzy. The plan had been for her to pick Lizzy up after her shift a few blocks away.

Lizzy fell into the seat across from Ruby.

"What happened?" asked Ruby.

"Angelo was there."

"Angelo? What was he doing there?"

"Just hanging out. He had a gun."

"He had a gun?" said Ruby, just as a skinny young man with acne approached the table.

He gave Ruby a dubious look and then turned to Lizzy. "Get you something?" he asked, a pencil poised above his order pad.

"Uh, no, I don't think so," she said. "Maybe we should go," she whispered to Ruby.

"Yes, I agree," said Ruby. She opened her purse and took out a twenty, which she handed to the young man. "Thanks."

He nodded, pocketed the money, and wandered away.

Ruby stood and shrugged on her coat. "Let's go," she said, and led Lizzy out of the restaurant.

Lizzy was several inches taller than Ruby, but she had to hustle to keep up. Ruby led her to a parking lot several blocks away, the lots nearer the Vivantem building being more expensive. Ruby handed over more cash to the parking lot attendant, then navigated streets still crowded with late rush hour traffic to 95 South, exiting a few miles later onto Wanamaker Avenue and pulling into the parking lot of the Motel 6.

Lizzy hurried behind Ruby as she marched up the stairs to their second-floor room. Ruby unlocked the door, then relocked it behind them. She took off her coat, put her purse on the bedside table, and lowered herself stiffly onto one of the beds.

"Angelo. With a gun," she said dully.

Lizzy sat opposite her on the other bed. "Yeah."

Ruby sighed. "I thought he was just being a gofer for Bonnay. What can Bonnay be thinking, giving him a gun?"

"Maybe he's Gerard's bodyguard."

Ruby laughed mirthlessly. "He's not levelheaded enough to be a bodyguard." She shook her head. "We need to rethink our plan. I won't have you dealing with a man with a gun."

"Do you think he's with Gerard all the time?"

Ruby shrugged. "I don't know. I thought that whoever was driving Gerard to work did something else during the day and just came back to pick him up, but it seems like he has someone with him all the time. Whoever is driving him that day must park the car somewhere and then go into the building from the back."

Lizzy nodded. "It seems like someone who runs an honest company wouldn't feel like he needs a bodyguard all the time."

"Yeah."

"If Angelo's there, I can't …" Lizzy's voice trailed off, and she looked at her hands.

"I know. We'll figure out how to get him out of the way." Ruby examined Lizzy for a moment, then leaned forward and put her hand on top of Lizzy's. "Are you okay?"

Lizzy nodded.

"Having second thoughts?"

Lizzy shrugged.

"Because if you're having second thoughts, we can change our plans. I don't want you to do anything unless you think it's the right thing to do."

"But then what's going to happen to you?"

"Me? Don't worry about me."

"What about Uncle Owen?"

Ruby patted her hand. "I think Dr. McNally would say the same thing."

"But if I don't do something about it, I'll spend my whole life looking over my shoulder and being afraid someone's going to catch up with me and lock me away. Do experiments on me. Make me hurt people."

"Yes, that's true," said Ruby.

"And I'll know the person who killed my dad is still out there."

Ruby nodded.

"And the person who made me so I killed my mom ..." Her voice broke.

"Lizzy, I agree—what he did, he needs to pay. And you need to live a life where you're not always worried about what Gerard Bonnay might do."

Lizzy took a deep breath and wiped her nose with the back of her hand. "Excuse me, I need a Kleenex," she said, and disappeared into the bathroom.

She was back in a minute, her eyes red but dry, her mouth set. "I'm going to do it. I'm going to take care of Gerard Bonnay so he can't hurt anyone ever again."

CHAPTER SEVENTY-EIGHT

Owen was trying to be honest with himself about the best plan for Lizzy. Despite his reluctance to leave her alone, he had believed it was safer for her to be somewhere other than where he was. And in his first calls to her in Smoketown, she had sounded fine—cheerful, even.

The call four days earlier, though, had veered hard away from cheerful when he mentioned Anton Rossi. Something related to the bookie had changed her mood. And perhaps had changed her outlook; if Lizzy had been responsible for Rossi's death, he would be her third victim, and that would be a heavy weight for a young woman to bear. Owen had spoken to her several times since then, but the conversations were stilted and she ended them after only a minute or two.

He needed a new plan—hell, he needed a first plan. How long could he leave a teenager on her own in an unfamiliar place—a teenager who had had an unusually limited exposure to the outside world? And as if all that weren't bad enough, it was now Christmas Eve day. How had the holiday snuck up on him like that? He had never intended for Lizzy to still be stranded in Smoketown for Christmas.

He needed to take her away from here—maybe far away. He had a friend from medical school who lived in Baja and whom he had been promising to visit for some time. Maybe now was the time. Let Gerard Bonnay try to find them there.

He would stop by his house to pick up his passport, then stop by the Ballards' house in Parkesburg to get Lizzy's—he knew Patrick had gotten her a passport a few years before when she had gotten a yen to go to Nova Scotia, although that trip had never panned out. Patrick had gotten his own passport out to laugh with Owen over the incredibly unflattering photo, and Owen recalled it was in an unlocked fireproof box in Patrick's desk. It seemed likely Lizzy's would be there too. If it wasn't, he'd just pick a destination in the US. Maybe she'd enjoy Yellowstone.

He packed up, checked out, and, half an hour later, was coasting slowly down the street in front of his house. The landscaping company he used had kept the drive and sidewalk clear of snow, timers were turning the lights on and off, and he had stopped the paper delivery so there was no tell-tale accumulation of copies of the *Chron* on the porch. Everything looked compellingly normal.

He drove around the block and then down the alley to the detached garage behind the house. He hit the remote that raised the garage door, and peered in from his car. In the dimness of the weak December afternoon light, the dark interior looked ominous, boxes and patio furniture offering convenient hiding places from which someone might spring. He hit the remote again, closing the door, and parked the car on the gravel next to the garage.

He crossed his small backyard and unlocked the door, then hesitated. After a moment, he took his phone out of his pocket and hit one of the speed dials.

"Yo, bro, what's up?" answered Andy. "Any new news?"

Owen had been updating him periodically since Lizzy's rescue.

"Well, I decided to stop by the house. I need to pick up some things."

"Really? You think that's a good idea? What things do you need that you can't just buy at the store?"

"I need my passport. I think I'm going to take Lizzy away for a little while."

"Ah, a fugitive on the run."

"That's me—a veritable Harrison Ford. Listen, everything looks okay, but I'm just about to go inside and I thought I'd have you on the phone while I do."

"It's not like I can do much if someone jumps out from behind the shower curtain," said Andy.

"No, but I'm going to be clear I'm on the phone with someone who can call the police if necessary."

"Okay," said Andy skeptically.

Owen unlocked the back door and leaned into the kitchen. "I'm coming in, and I'm on the phone with someone who will call the police if necessary," he said loudly. He was glad the cold weather was keeping his neighbors inside. "I'm at the back door. If you need to leave, you can leave by the front door and no one will see you."

"Smooth," said his brother.

"Shut up," Owen muttered.

He counted to sixty twice, straining his ears, then made a cautious tour of the house, peering into closets and under beds, narrating his progress to Andy as he went. Except for the scattering of mail on the floor of the foyer, and the fact that the house was unusually cold, normalcy reigned inside as well. When he got back to the kitchen, he said, "Well, it looks like I'm the only one here. Thanks for hanging on the phone."

"Sure thing. Make sure you set the alarm."

"Will do."

"Take care of yourself."

"You too."

Owen disconnected, then locked the door and set the alarm. He gathered up the mail and brought it to the kitchen.

He realized that if he was going to be traveling to Mexico, he would need different clothes. There was obviously no one in the house—no reason not to enjoy a cup of tea while he packed. He put the kettle on and, while it heated, he went up to his study to get his passport.

He sat down at his desk, accidentally nudging the wireless mouse as he did so, and the screen sprang to life. Out of habit, he picked up the mouse to turn it on, then realized that it was already on—that's why the screen had come on. He always turned the mouse off when he was done at the computer. He put it down slowly, rolled back from the desk, and examined it.

Everything was right where he had left it. Wasn't it? The blotter was perhaps a bit off-kilter, but maybe he had moved it when he sat down. Maybe he was just being paranoid.

He slid open the drawer with the file folders and reached for the one labeled Passport. Then he froze. A detail that would have been meaningless to anyone else: the edge of a paper sticking untidily from the top of one of the folders. He pulled it out—it was labeled just "P," for Pumpkin. He flipped it open to reveal the one piece of paper it contained: the handwritten receipt on a Smoketown Cottages notepad sheet for his payment for Lizzy's room.

Alarms started clanging in his head just as the rising scream of the tea kettle reached his ears.

CHAPTER SEVENTY-NINE

Five minutes later, Owen was parked outside a McDonald's, his heart still beating hard, sweat sticking his shirt to his back despite the December cold. He pulled his phone from his pocket with shaking hands and speed dialed Lizzy's number.

He was afraid the call was going to go to voicemail, when she answered.

"Hi, Uncle Owen."

"Don't answer the phone that way," he snapped. "What if someone else was calling you from my phone?"

There was a stunned silence on the line, and he took a deep breath. "I'm sorry, Pumpkin. Are you all right?"

"Sure," she said hesitantly.

"I was just at my house," he said. "Someone searched it."

"Really? Did they tear it apart?" She sounded like someone trying out a new language.

He sighed. "No, they didn't tear it apart. In fact, it was so neat that if I wasn't such a neatnik myself, I might not have noticed. But I think they found a folder where I had a receipt from Smoketown Cottages. If they did, then they know where you are." He paused, expecting a comment from Lizzy. When she remained silent, he continued. "Have you seen anything suspicious? Anyone hanging around the motel?"

"No."

"I think we should move you somewhere else. Plus, I don't want you to be alone for Christmas—that's why I went to my house, to get my passport. We can go anywhere you want. How about Christmas in Baja, Mexico? I'm going to come out there and get you."

"I don't think you need to do that," said Lizzy.

"Probably not, but let's not take any chances."

"No, Uncle Owen, don't come out."

A frightening suspicion began to sneak into Owen's head. "Lizzy, where are you?"

"I'm at the cottage."

"In your room?"

"Sure. Yes."

"Is there a lot of airplane traffic today?"

"Yup."

"Open the window so I can hear it." There was a long pause and Owen gripped the phone. "Lizzy, tell me where you are."

"Uncle Owen, I'm fine."

"But you're not at the cottage, are you?"

No answer. In fact, the line went so quiet that he looked at his phone to make sure the connection was still open. She must have muted her phone.

"Lizzy, please. Someone broke into my house and went through my things." He closed his eyes. "We're dealing with people who are willing to kill to get what they want—I think that's what happened to your dad. They needed to kill him so that they could keep you."

The faint buzz of background noise returned to the line.

"I made a friend in Smoketown. I'm going to spend Christmas with her."

"Lizzy," Owen said, pleading, "I'm so scared something's going to happen to you. I think we need to go somewhere far away for a while."

"Don't worry, Uncle Owen, I'll be okay. Merry Christmas."

And the connection went dead.

CHAPTER EIGHTY

Even though he didn't expect to find her in Smoketown, Owen had nowhere else to start, so he decided he'd go there anyway. Maybe he could get some information from the motel manager.

He was able to make good time on the Route 30 bypass, pushing the SUV up to eighty. He expected as he crested every hill and rounded every turn to see a police car parked behind a bush, then to see the flashing lights in his rearview mirror. Or, even worse, to see a car—probably dark-colored, with tinted windows—matching his speed, matching him lane change for lane change. Fortunately, he saw neither.

When the bypass ended, he was forced by traffic to what felt like a crawl on Business 30. He peered at the occupants of the oncoming vehicles in the vain hope of seeing Lizzy in one of them.

When he finally pulled up to Lizzy's cottage, it seemed apparent even from the car that the room was uninhabited. The curtains on the windows overlooking the front walk were drawn, there were no footsteps in the light dusting of snow that had fallen the night before. He knocked on the door and, after waiting a minute, circled the cabin. The curtains were drawn at the other windows as well. He knocked on one of them and called out, "Lizzy!" in a low voice. Nothing.

He crossed the parking lot to the office in the old farmhouse, and opened the door to the jingle of a bell. In a moment, the manager emerged from the back room.

"Hey, how are you doing?" the man asked.

"Pretty good, thanks. Listen, I was supposed to meet up

with my niece today." He had decided this was an easier and less Mafia-esque explanation of his relationship to Lizzy than *I'm her godfather*. "I stopped by the room, but she's not there. Probably got the time mixed up, you know how kids are. Have you seen her today?"

"No, I haven't seen her for a couple of days," said the manager. "That's a pretty big mix-up." He gave a snorting laugh at his joke then, at Owen's glare, shrugged. "You might want to check at Glick's, she went there pretty often. That's the restaurant right next door," he added, with a nod of his head.

"Okay, thanks," said Owen, turning away.

"I sent your brother over there," said the manager.

Owen turned back. "My brother?"

"Well, he also told me the girl was his niece, so I guess he's your brother, right?"

Owen asked, although he knew what the answer would be, "Tall guy, reddish hair—looks like me but thinner and better looking?"

The manager laughed. "No, average height, dark hair." He knit his brow. "Hey, he's not related to the girl? Hope there's nothing fishy going on ..."

"No, that's her uncle on her mother's side," said Owen. "When was he here?"

"Three, four days ago."

Owen groaned internally. Had Lizzy really been gone from Smoketown for that long?

"Well, thanks for the information," he said, turning back to the door.

"Hey," said the man. "You think she'll be coming back?" he asked hopefully. "I can give you a great discount for a monthly rental."

"No, thanks," said Owen over his shoulder. "I think it's time we moved on."

CHAPTER EIGHTY-ONE

Owen made his way across the motel parking lot and lawn to the small shopping center the owner had indicated. "Average height and dark hair" could conceivably describe Gerard Bonnay—although Owen would have put him on the taller side of average—but it seemed unlikely Gerard would be following Lizzy himself. He no doubt had people on his payroll to take care of those things for him. The same people, thought Owen with a lurch in his stomach, who had taken care of Patrick, and of Anton Rossi.

The dinner crowd was just starting to arrive. A dark-haired woman in her mid-twenties looked up from where she was wiping down one of the tables near the door.

"Table for one?" she asked.

"No, thank you," he said. "I'm actually looking for someone and I understand she came here frequently. Sixteen, tall and slender, long blonde hair." He remembered the hair color that Ruby had purchased. "Actually, more like light brown. Have you seen anyone like that?"

"Long and light brown?" said the woman, knitting her brow. "No, I can't say there's anyone with long light brown hair that's been coming in frequently."

"But long hair? Sixteen?"

"Nope," said the woman, whose name tag, he noticed, read *Christine*. "No one with long hair. Why are you asking?"

"I'm her uncle," said Owen, hoping this would be sufficient explanation for the waitress. Owen realized he should have come prepared with a story. In fact, he should have provided Lizzy with a story so their stories could be consistent; he had never thought to instruct her beyond suggesting that she keep to herself.

The waitress nodded noncommittally.

"We're having the house redecorated," he said.

"I thought you were her uncle."

"Her parents are dead." Owen said it automatically, as a way of explaining why a teenage girl would be living with her uncle, but he surprised himself with the thought of Patrick's death, and he felt tears spring to his eyes. He pulled a handkerchief from his pocket and mopped them quickly.

"Uh, sorry to hear that," said the waitress uncertainly, obviously unsure as to whether this sudden display of emotion was sincere or an over-dramatic attempt to win her sympathy.

Owen waved the handkerchief and then stuffed it back in his pocket. "Anyway," he said, "she was staying here while the house was being redecorated, but it's done now and I came to pick her up and bring her home." He vowed to provide no additional details that might trip him up in any further discussion with this skeptical young woman.

The waitress examined him for several moments, while Owen attempted to look as honest and likable as possible, then shook her head. "Can't help you. Hope you find her, I'm sure she'd like to see the house after all this time."

"After all what time?" asked Owen.

The waitress shrugged. "It takes a long time to redecorate a house, right? She's probably looking forward to settling down after having everything all verhoodled."

Damn, damn, damn, thought Owen to himself as he hurried back to his car by the motel office. He hadn't even been able to figure out how to broach the topic of whether Lizzy's other "uncle" had stopped by the restaurant. The waitress obviously knew something about Lizzy, but how to get her to tell him? He wasn't exactly the strong-arm type. He thought briefly about waiting for her to get off work and following her, but he wasn't exactly the stalker type, either.

But even if he had been, he suspected that the waitress wouldn't lead him to Lizzy. He doubted Lizzy was still in Lancaster County at all. He suspected she was stalking Gerard Bonnay.

He had told Lizzy that Gerard was likely responsible for her father's death. He had written in his note to her, left in the Smoketown cottage to find when she woke up after the trauma of the ipecac dosing, that Bonnay was likely also responsible for her ability, and so, by extension, for her mother's death. For a lifetime of limitations and isolation. And then he had left her all alone, during the most family-centric time of the year, to ponder that revelation. She was a kind-hearted young woman, but she was also a young woman with a strong sense of right and wrong … and how long would she have had to ponder before she decided not to wait around any longer for her slow-moving and, in this case, slow-thinking uncle, and take matters into her own hands?

She might go to Gerard's home—but would she even know where that was? It had been dark the first time she had gone there, and she had been violently ill when she'd left—he doubted she would be able to find it herself. That brought him up short.

How was she getting around? She didn't know how to drive.

Maybe … maybe the man whom the motel manager had described had been someone whose help she had enlisted. Maybe she hadn't been "laying low," as he had asked her to do.

Then a more likely scenario struck him. He pulled out his phone and dialed Ruby DiMano's number.

Ruby looked at the caller ID on her ringing phone: Dr. McNally. She was stooped over the Kia's right rear tire, having dropped Lizzy at the Vivantem building half an hour before. The low hiss of air coming out of the tire was barely audible over the ringtone and the roar of traffic on 95. When the Kia's wheel had settled to its rim, and the phone was quiet, Ruby removed the bobby pin from the valve, got out her phone, and pressed the speed dial for Angelo.

CHAPTER EIGHTY-TWO

It was Christmas Eve, and Angelo sat in the employee lounge at Vivantem, scanning online betting sites on his phone. His preferred sport was horse racing, but he was willing to place a wager on any sport: football, basketball, soccer. Once, he had placed a bet on the Iditarod. Right now all his bets were online. The experience with Rossi had at least temporarily achieved what years of nagging by his family, broken thumbs, and a broken kneecap had not done—scared him off betting with a bookie.

He was speculating about who he would bet on for the upcoming Flyers game when his phone rang, the caller ID showing *Aunt Ruby*.

He thumbed Accept. "Hey, Zia, what's up?"

"Angie, I got a flat tire and I can't get the lug nuts loose. Can you come give me a hand?" He heard the low roar of traffic in the background.

Angelo glanced toward the door of the lounge. "I don't know, Zia, I'm on the job. Mr. Bonnay's working late and I'm supposed to stay here with him. Can't you call Triple A?"

"I don't have Triple A. And I don't like the idea of some man I don't know coming. Can't you get away? Where are you, Mr. Bonnay's office? That's in Center City, right? I'm not far away, just in Essington. It wouldn't take you long."

Angelo sighed. Old ladies were always paranoid. Plus he was wearing his best suit. But it *was* Zia Ruby; he had to admit he owed her more than a quick trip to loosen a lug nut. He could always take his jacket off and do a quick tire change for her.

"Okay, let me ask. I'll call you right back, okay?"

"Okay."

He ended the call and crossed the hall to Gerard Bonnay's office. The door was open and the light low, Bonnay's face illuminated by the light from the computer screen. Angelo knocked lightly on the doorframe.

"Hey, Mr. Bonnay, I had a favor to ask."

Gerard looked up. "Yes?"

"My aunt got a flat tire. She's in Essington and needs a hand. Is it okay if I run over there quick and help her out? Shouldn't take me more than about half an hour, forty-five minutes tops."

Gerard glanced at his watch. "Okay. But try not to let it take any more than that."

"Thanks, Mr. B." Angelo started down the hall and then turned back. "Hey, Mr. B., I'm likely going to need to take my jacket off to help my aunt, and I'd hate her to see I've got a gun. Can I leave it here until I get back?"

"Yes," said Gerard. "Put it over there." He waved to a small conference table near the door.

"Great." Angelo took off his jacket and unfastened the shoulder holster, put the gun and holster on one of the chairs, and pulled the jacket back on. "Be back in a jiff." He jogged lopsidedly back down the hall.

Gerard called after him, "Don't forget to lock the front door."

"Will do!" Angelo called back. He grabbed his coat from the employee lounge, keyed his phone and, when Ruby answered, said, "Okay, Zia, I'm on my way. Should be there in about ten, fifteen minutes."

In the elevator lobby, the chubby Southern girl was polishing the V on the Vivantem sign. As he was locking the door to the offices, she drawled, "Hey, could you do me a favor?"

Must be his day to be the knight in shining armor. "What's that?"

"I'm supposed to clean the windows in there but I left my passkey in my other uniform. My boss'll kill me if he knows. Can you let me in?"

He sighed. "Hold on." He unlocked the door and said, "Wait here a minute." He locked the door behind him, then walked down the hallway as quickly as his now-sore knee would let him.

"Angelo?" he heard Gerard call. He sounded a little nervous—but who could blame him? The guy was probably worried about one of Anton Rossi's buddies coming to pay him a visit. Angelo had those same worries these days.

"Yeah, it's me, Mr. B.," he called back. He reached the door of Gerard's office. Gerard was standing behind his desk, evidently stretching a kink out of his back. "Hey, the cleaning girl lost her key. That nervous one from the other night. Can I let her in?"

"Fine. Tell her she doesn't need to clean in here."

"Sure thing," said Angelo, and hurried back down the hall. His knee was starting to ache now. It didn't put him in much of a mood to go kneeling next to a car to change a tire.

The girl was standing on the other side of the glass wall, adjusting those chunky black glasses.

He unlocked the door and held it open for her. "Okay, you can come in, but don't clean in Mr. Bonnay's office. He doesn't want to be disturbed."

She nodded. "Okay. Thanks."

She passed into the reception area and crossed to the desk. She sprayed some cleaner on it and began polishing it with her rag.

"Don't you have different stuff for marble than for stainless?" he asked.

She continued polishing without turning around.

Angelo shrugged. Maybe she was feeble-minded. He turned toward the elevators, then turned back.

"Hey!" he called to her across the reception area.

"Yes?" she said, still polishing, still not turning around.

"Did you mention that leak in the men's room to your boss? It's still there."

"Oh. Sorry, I forgot," she said. "I'll tell him tonight."

"Okay. I don't want anybody to slip on a wet floor."

There was no response. He shook his head and closed and locked the door behind her. He snapped his fingers impatiently as he waited for the elevator, anxious to get the favor for Zia Ruby out of the way.

CHAPTER EIGHTY-THREE

Lizzy breathed a sigh of relief as Angelo stepped into the elevator. She didn't really bear him a grudge—she was willing to believe that Angelo was just a pawn in the game Gerard was playing. However, if he had recognized her, and then tried to hold her or turn her over to Gerard, she would have fought back in the only way she knew, and she wouldn't have had much control over the damage she caused. And if he had pulled his gun? Her ability wouldn't have been much help then.

She looked around the deserted reception area, lit only by a few security lights, toward the twinkle and electric glow of the city beyond the floor-to-ceiling windows. She listened for some sound, but couldn't hear anything other than the ambient buzz of a largely uninhabited office building.

She placed the bottle of cleaner and rag on the reception desk—she wanted to have her hands free for whatever might transpire—and passed through the reception area, her moccasins soundless on the marble floor. When she got to the hallway leading to the offices, she stopped again to listen. She thought she could hear the click of fingers on a keyboard.

She passed the employee lounge, and jumped as the light clicked off. She froze, waiting for someone to emerge, then realized that some motion-sensing timer had probably turned the light off. Just to be sure, she eased into the room, and jumped again as the light clicked back on. She waited, her heart pounding, expecting to hear Gerard Bonnay call out, "Angelo?" but the faint keyboard clicking continued uninterrupted.

She continued down the hall, past empty, glass-fronted offices and a conference room, toward the source of the sound—the last room on the hall, from whose door a rectangle of light spilled across the hallway. When she got to the doorway, she peeked around the corner.

She could see the desk, but it was unoccupied. She could see the computer, but there was no one using it.

She leaned slowly into the room. Was there a second desk, a second computer that Gerard could be using? But the room was empty, although that clicking continued.

She stepped into the room, turning her head to try to identify the source of the sound. It was coming from the ceiling, from some loose flap of metal in a heating duct, from some unbalanced fan recirculating air through the building. She was stalking a bit of HVAC annoyance.

The realization that Gerard Bonnay wasn't here brought on an almost dizzying wave of relief, a weakness as the muscles in her stomach unclenched. Suddenly she didn't want to see him, didn't want to play the role of judge and jury. It seemed clear that he had kept track of her through her whole life, but what evidence did she have that he had killed her dad, or had him killed? What evidence did she even have that Gerard was somehow responsible for what she was and what she had done to her mom? Maybe she was the way she was not because of any devious scheming by Gerard or Vivantem, but because of some completely accidental development, some random combination of genes or environment.

Gerard Bonnay had enlisted Ruby to keep an eye on her, but who was to say what his motivations were? He had been spying on her and her family, but what would their lives have been like if they hadn't had Ruby to help them? And even if Gerard had held Angelo's gambling over Ruby's head to get her to cooperate, even if he had let Angelo's bookie break his bones, that wasn't her problem.

But more important than all these considerations was the memory of those baby rabbits in the backyard of the cabin in the Poconos, and the promise she had made to her mother not to use her power to hurt people.

She needed to think about this more. She needed to get away from here.

She moved quickly to the door and had just stepped into the hallway, her shadow stretching distorted across the marble floor in the rectangle of light from the office, when she heard in the silence of the almost-deserted office a whoosh of water.

Gerard was in the men's room.

She froze, and a moment later heard an even fainter sound—water running in a sink, and then that stopped. How many seconds before he came out? She looked frantically around. There was a door to a stairway opposite Gerard's office door, but the large "Door is Alarmed" sign made it a less-than-ideal escape route. She didn't even have the cleaning supplies to use as a cover.

She had decided that a dash down the hallway was her best chance when the door of the men's room opened and Gerard emerged, drying his hands on a paper towel.

She dropped her eyes, letting her black-purple bangs fall over her face as his footsteps approached, and then slowed. He stopped a dozen feet away.

"Lizzy?" he said uncertainly.

She ventured a glance at him from under her bangs, her heart hammering. He didn't look like a killer, he looked like a perplexed business man, the paper towel crumpled in his hands. She didn't say anything.

"It is Lizzy, isn't it?" he said. Then he gave her a slight smile. "Although I have to say that's quite a disguise."

She raised her head a bit, then gave one brief nod.

"Where have you been? We've been worried about you."

She continued to watch him, to assess his reaction to her appearance. He didn't seem afraid—wouldn't he be afraid of her if he had done the things that Ruby accused him of having done? He just seemed surprised, but also … what was it? Almost relieved.

"Well, let's not stand in the hallway," he said. "Let's go into my office and talk." He took a step toward her, then stopped. "Is that okay? To go into my office?"

She gave another single nod, then stepped aside to let him pass by her to his office door. She was careful to stay out of his reach, even though she couldn't imagine what he could do to her that wouldn't have a worse result for him.

He walked past her into the office and, as she followed him in, he went to the conference table near the door and dropped the paper towel into a wastebasket next to the table.

"Can we sit and talk?" he asked, nodding toward the table.

"You can sit if you want," she said. She stepped to the opposite side of the room, near Gerard's desk and the floor-to-ceiling windows.

He shrugged. "Okay." He pulled out one of the chairs and sat down, then folded his hands. "We've been very worried about you," he repeated.

"Who's 'we'?"

"Me and Louise."

Lizzy examined him from across the room, her heart thumping. This was so different from what she had expected.

Gerard shifted in his chair, then rubbed his elbow. "Man, my arm is killing me. Tennis elbow the doctor says, even though it's been years since I've played any serious tennis." He pulled one of the other chairs over to him and draped his arm over the back of it. "That's better."

"So, what were you concerned about?" she ventured.

"Owen and your father asked us to help them take care of you. We felt a responsibility, and when you disappeared we didn't know what to do. Louise is going to be very relieved to find out that you're all right. I can call her up on videoconference. Is it all right if I do that?" Gerard shifted his arm to drape it a bit further over the back of the chair.

"No," said Lizzy, her heart suddenly tightening in her chest. "I only want to talk to you."

"Let's just check in with her and then, if you want, I can

turn it off." With the hand that wasn't draped over the chair, he pushed a button on the conference table and a monitor on the wall next to the table flickered to life.

"Stop it," said Lizzy, her voice tinged with fear. Gerard's wife? She had barely met the woman, why should she have to talk with her now?

A slight wince flickered on Gerard's face, then passed. "We'll just let her know you're all right and then you and I can talk."

He pushed another button, and there was Louise, life-sized, looking almost as if she were sitting at the table with Gerard. Behind her Lizzy could see a computer and the corner of what looked like a piece of lab equipment.

Louise glanced up at the monitor. "Will you be finished soon? It is Christmas Eve—" she started, then her eyes narrowed as she looked past Gerard and toward Lizzy. "Who is that?"

"That, my dear, is Lizzy Ballard in disguise," he said, with a light chuckle.

"Turn her off," said Lizzy, her voice rising a notch.

"My arm is really bothering me," said Gerard to Louise, gesturing with his chin toward where his arm was draped over the chair.

Louise's eyes followed the gesture to the chair, then she nodded. "Do it."

"Do what?" said Lizzy, beginning to sidle back around the room toward the door.

"Do it now, Gerard," said Louise.

Gerard Bonnay reached toward the seat of the chair next to him, and fumbled with something hidden by the conference table.

"What are you doing?" cried Lizzy just as Louise said, "Hurry!" and Gerard let out a low moan.

Then he stood, and he was pulling a gun from a holster and swinging it toward Lizzy.

"Shoot her!" hissed Louise.

"I can't, she's in front of the window," Gerard ground out, the hand not holding the gun going to his temple. "If I miss it will go through the glass." He stumbled away from the table, heading for a position that would put a large bookcase behind Lizzy.

Lizzy was torn between wanting to stay by the window, which evidently offered some protection against Gerard firing, and running for the door. Her mind was made up by the first shot, which tore through her bicep and punched a hole through a painting.

She screamed as a fiery pain shot up her arm. She ran for the door and was halfway across the room when her foot caught on the rug and she went sprawling. Behind the blaze of pain in her arm, she could hear Louise yelling from the monitor, "Gerard, finish it!"

She heard another shot and felt a streak of pain up her back. She tried to push herself to her feet, but her arm collapsed and she landed on the floor again.

Her anger toward Gerard Bonnay was replaced with a whirling confusion of pain and fear. Why was he still shooting? Why wasn't he down, like that horrible man in the library of Gerard's house?

She managed to push herself into a sitting position and turned to face Gerard.

He was approaching her from across the room, holding the gun in front of him with two hands.

"Gerard! Do it!" yelled Louise.

"I'm sorry, Lizzy," he said, and raised the gun.

Years of anger about the isolation her ability had forced on her and her family, years of frustration over all those milestones of a normal girl's life she had missed, years of guilt about what she had done to her mother through her power, days of guilt about what others had likely done to her father in pursuit of her power—they boiled up in her like a pot left too long over a flame. Boiled out of her and over Gerard.

Gerard screamed and staggered back, his scream echoed

by Louise's from the monitor. The gun went off again, the bullet flying far over Lizzy's head. Lizzy pushed herself to her feet and advanced on him, feeling the waves of hate roll off her, feeling the squeeze as the blood vessels in his brain burst under her attack. He tripped, fell, and the gun skittered out of his hand and across the floor.

"Stop it!" screamed Louise, but Lizzy ignored her as she stood over Gerard's writhing body.

"You are never, never going to hurt me again," she sobbed, and the metal bands of her mental fist gripped tight. Finally, Gerard Bonnay lay still.

She stood breathing heavily, looking down at him, then turned to face the monitor.

Louise stared out of it, her eyes wide, her face white, her hands gripped onto the edge of the table at which she sat.

Lizzy walked toward the conference room table, her arm singing with pain, the blood on her back sticking her shirt to her skin. When she got to the table, she felt lightheaded and grabbed one of the chairs to steady herself. Louise stared at her, unmoving.

Finally, when the dizziness had passed, Lizzy leaned toward the monitor. "You better stay where you are, because if you come here, I'll do the same to you." And she reached out and pushed the power button on the conference room table console. Gerard's wife flickered into black.

She looked down at her arm. Blood soaked the sleeve of her shirt from her bicep to the wrist, but she sensed the flow was slowing. She used her other hand to try to probe her back, but wherever the bullet had hit was too high for her to reach. She had to get away from here.

She looked around the room and noticed Gerard's coat hanging on the back of his desk chair. She crossed the room, cradling her arm, then pulled on the coat, tears springing to her eyes when she pulled the sleeve over her injured arm. With her added layers of clothing, she couldn't get it buttoned. The sleeves hung below her hands, but she couldn't afford to stay around looking for a better solution—how long would it be before someone arrived to investigate gunshots in the Vivantem offices?

She had another bout of dizziness on the way to the door but fought it off. If someone were to find her passed out on the floor of Gerard Bonnay's office, the consequences would be bad, and not only for her. She skirted Gerard's body and closed the door of the office behind her. She staggered down the hall, steadying herself with a hand to the wall, her fingers leaving a smear of blood. When she got to the reception area, she tried to pick up the cleaning supplies from the reception desk, but her injured arm was useless and she needed the other arm to hug it protectively to her side. She left the supplies behind.

In the lobby, she pushed the button, leaning on the wall and breathing hard as she waited for the elevator. But when the door opened with a *bing*, she hesitated. Where would she take it other than to the lobby, where a security guard sat at the building's reception desk? On any other floor she was likely to encounter a cleaning crew or a security guard doing rounds. She would be more likely to avoid encountering someone by using the service stairway.

She turned away from the elevator door, already closing, to the stairway next to the elevator bank, and began her agonized progress down the thirteen flights, stopping to rest when she got dizzy.

When she emerged from the building at the service entrance, she started down the street toward the rendezvous point she and Ruby had arranged, but after half a block she knew she wouldn't make it. And there were people on the street. She needed somewhere to hide, to lie down—she was afraid the next time the dizziness struck her, she might not be able to fight it. She had a nightmare vision of waking up in an emergency room staffed by people who didn't know that she needed to be sedated—of them doing something to her that hurt her, that made her angry. Of those people falling to the floor, clutching their heads, like Gerard, like that Rossi man. Like her mother. She let out a sob.

She and Ruby had thought they had eliminated the danger posed by a gun by luring Angelo away. The squeeze could kill a person, but bullets beat the squeeze. Wasn't there a nursery rhyme about that …?

cant get to mtg place, come get me

Ruby sent her response to Lizzy's text—*i'll be there as soon as i can are you ok?*—just as Angelo was lifting the spare tire onto the rim, having eventually loosened the lug nuts that Ruby had tightened to the best of her ability before he arrived.

"That's weird that I can't find the hole," he said for the third time.

"Hurry up," said Ruby, staring at her phone, willing a response to come.

"Keep your pants on, Zia, where've you got to be going in such a hurry?"

"Never you mind."

"Hey, I'm the one out here in my shirtsleeves in the middle of December—you don't think I have reason to hurry up?"

Ruby had patted down his suit jacket and coat, which he had laid out on the back seat of his car, while he was occupied with the tire. She couldn't feel a gun. Maybe it was smaller than she imagined. Maybe he had put it in the glove compartment or the trunk before he came here. Maybe—and at this thought her stomach dropped—he had left it in the Vivantem offices.

When he was done, still muttering about his inability to find the hole in the tire, he rolled his sleeves down, put on his suit jacket and coat, climbed in his car, and headed back to Center City.

Ruby waited until he was out of sight before pulling out of

the parking lot where she had disabled her car. It was full dark now, but she quickly spotted him on 95. He was driving in the same direction—in fact, to generally the same destination, she was sure—as she was. She hung back, her hands wringing the steering wheel, knowing that passsing him in her Rio would have been an anomaly even Angelo couldn't ignore.

She took the exit off 95 behind him, but got caught at an intersection that he had slipped through on the tail end of the yellow light. Although the wait ratcheted up her anxiety another notch, at least it put him out of sight.

When she got to the location Lizzy had given in her text, she drove slowly along the street, peering right and left for some sign of the girl, her eyes straining in the darkness that hung beyond the reach of the streetlights. After her second pass, she pulled to the curb and tapped out a text.

i'm here where are you?

Nothing. She waited a minute and tapped out another text.

are you there?

Nothing.

She parked the car in a space in front of a hydrant and walked up and down the block. Finding nothing, she walked the few blocks to the point where she and Lizzy had originally planned on meeting up, but still found nothing. She had begun her walk back to the address Lizzy had sent her, when she heard sirens. A moment later a police car sped past, then pulled up in front of the Vivantem building.

Angelo must have found whatever there was to be found there, she thought. She turned the collar of her coat up around her face and continued on.

She was walking past an alley a block from Vivantem when she heard footsteps behind her.

"Lady? Hey, lady!" came a hoarse whisper.

She quickened her pace. The last thing she needed was some homeless person asking for a handout.

"Hey, lady, are you lookin' for someone?"

She slowed and turned. The person following her was tall

and thin, of an indeterminate gender and race.

"Why?"

The person looked her up and down. Ruby decided it was a man. "*Are* you lookin' for someone?" he asked.

"Why do you want to know?"

The man made a dismissive snorting noise and turned back the way he had come.

"Okay, maybe I am," said Ruby.

"Yeah, I thought so," he said. "Well, you follow me, I'll show you where she *maybe* is."

Ruby glanced around, back toward the police car in front of the Vivantem building. An officer stood next to it, speaking into a radio. She turned and hurried after the man.

He disappeared into an alley, and when she came abreast of it she saw he was kneeling next to a shape on the ground.

"Passed out, I think," he said. "This who you're lookin' for?"

Ruby crossed herself, then hurried over to where the man knelt. He began to stand, and she flinched back.

"You go on and check her out," he said. "I'll wait over here. Let you know if anyone's comin'."

Ruby watched as he walked to the mouth of the alley, then, her heart hammering, she knelt down in his place. The light filtering in from the streetlights was dim, but there was no question—it was Lizzy.

Ruby smoothed the purple-black hair back from her face.

"It's me," she said, not wanting to say either of their names in front of the man. Getting no response, she leaned closer. "Lizzy, it's Ruby," she whispered.

The shape stirred. Ruby rested her hand on the arm of the coat Lizzy wore—not the one she had been wearing when Ruby had dropped her off—and Lizzy groaned. Ruby pulled her hand back and it came away with a sticky film. Blood.

"Think she's hurt," said the man.

Ruby tried to assess the extent of Lizzy's injuries, but the light was too dim. She turned to the man.

"Do you know what's wrong with her?"

"Don't know, just seen the blood on her coat. She was awake when she came in here, then passed out."

The wail of another siren approached, and the man pressed himself against the wall of the alley while Ruby bent over Lizzy's body. The car passed them, momentarily setting off a crazy dance of red and blue light in the alley.

"Something's going on down at the office building," said the man. "But it's none of my business."

Lizzy groaned again and stirred.

"But you best get her out of here," he continued. "Don't guess either one of you much wants to talk with the cops."

Ruby nodded, pulled out her phone, and dialed Owen McNally's number.

CHAPTER EIGHTY-FIVE

When Ruby reached Owen, he was headed back from Smoketown with only a vague notion as to his destination. She described Lizzy's condition, and their location.

"Does she need immediate medical attention?" asked Owen.

"I think the bleeding has stopped," she said. "She's unconscious, but her breathing is even. I tried taking her pulse—I'm not an expert, but it seems strong. I think if I can find something to keep her warm with, we'll be okay until you get here."

"I'm not far from Villanova," said Owen. "My brother lives there—he's the doctor who treated Lizzy at the Mercy ER. I'm going to pick him up, then we'll be there as soon as we can."

Ruby ended the call. She began to unbutton her coat to put over Lizzy, then jumped at a voice at her side.

"Hey, lady." It was the man who had led her to Lizzy. He held out a quilted blanket—the type movers would use to wrap furniture. "You can use this. It's warm."

She took the blanket from him. "Thank you." She tucked it around and under Lizzy.

While she waited, Ruby paced fretfully between Lizzy and the sidewalk, trying to keep an eye on goings-on down the street. Finally, she saw an SUV making its way slowly down the street. She stood at the alley entrance, trying not to pay it too much attention in case it wasn't Dr. McNally, but the vehicle pulled over in front of her. She glanced down the street just in time to see an ambulance pull away from the

Vivantem building, lights off and siren silenced. It was replaced by a white van with *Medical Examiner* on the side.

Andy jumped out with his medical bag. Owen lumbered after him. They both stopped when they saw the man hovering at the back of the alley.

"Who's that?" whispered Owen to Ruby.

"He's the person who led me to her, and gave her the blanket."

"Sounds like one of the good guys to me," said Andy, and hurried over to Lizzy, who was now conscious but disoriented. He knelt beside her.

"How is she?" Owen asked.

"We need to get her somewhere better lit," said Andy. He looked around. "And cleaner. No offense, buddy," he said to the alley's resident. Andy turned to Owen and Ruby. "You guys get the back door open, tell me when it's clear, and I'll carry her."

Owen nodded and hustled back to the mouth of the alley, but Ruby beat him to the vehicle and opened the door. One car passed, then the street a block either way from the alley was empty again.

"Okay," Owen called softly.

Andy got his arms under Lizzy's back and knees and lifted her. She struggled a bit and gave a whimper.

"It's okay, champ," said Andy soothingly. "We're taking you away from here."

As they got Lizzy loaded in the back of the SUV, Ruby saw a black sedan emerge from a side street between them and the Vivantem building and pull up behind the ME van. Angelo got out and hurried inside. Looked like her nephew had gotten through the events unscathed, she thought, with a combination of relief and resignation.

Owen appeared at her side. "Do you think we should give him some money?" he whispered to her.

"It can't hurt," she said.

He opened his wallet and fanned out some twenties. "Is

this enough?"

Ruby grabbed five of the bills and hurried back to the alley, where the man was folding the quilted blanket. "Thank you for your help."

"You're gonna take care of her, right?" said the man dubiously, peering toward the SUV.

"Yes, we'll take care of her." She held out the bills. "We'd appreciate it if you didn't tell anyone we were here."

The man's eyes grew big at the sight of the cash, and he took the money and stuffed it into his coat pocket. "You got it, lady," he said, and disappeared into the shadows at the back of the alley.

Andy got in back with Lizzy, with Owen and Ruby in front. Owen pulled out of the alley, turning in the opposite direction from the Vivantem building. Ruby looked back as they turned at the next corner, just in time to see Angelo exit the building at the side of a woman wrapped in a fur coat, who glanced toward the Medical Examiner van before walking stiffly to the sedan.

They drove in silence for a minute, then Owen asked, "How is she?"

"Looks like she's been shot," said Andy. "She's lost quite a bit of blood. She has an awful lot of layers on. We need to get her somewhere where I can take a better look at her."

"Not an emergency room, if we can help it," said Owen.

"No, I figured not," sighed Andy.

"What about your place?"

"It's okay with me, but if you don't want to take her to a hospital, I'm guessing you don't want all my neighbors seeing us carry a bleeding girl into my apartment."

"Good point," said Owen.

"Same problem with my place," said Ruby.

"But we should get her somewhere pretty quick," said Andy. "I can't get a good look at her in the car."

"Okay. We'll go to Lansdowne," said Owen.

"Your house?" asked Andy, surprised.

"I'm guessing the person who ordered the break-in is dead," said Owen, casting a look at Ruby.

After a moment, she said tightly, "Seems likely."

"And I'm guessing that as long as Lizzy's with us, any of his compatriots will be unlikely to bother us, at least for now."

Ruby was silent.

When they arrived at Owen's house, he pulled into the detached garage. He hoped that his guesses were correct, and that the person who had broken in wasn't lurking behind the barrel of lawn care implements or a long-unused croquet set.

Owen went to the house and switched off the lights that normally illuminated the back yard, then Andy carried Lizzy to the house and through to the living room.

Owen left Andy and Ruby to take care of Lizzy while he hurried back to the car to get the medical bag that Andy had brought with him. When Owen returned, Andy was easing the jacket off Lizzy's arm as Ruby covered as much of the couch as she could with a sheet she must have gotten from the linen closet. Lizzy was more alert, her face scrunched in pain, but doing her best to help Andy with his examination.

Owen knelt on the ground next to the couch. "How are you doing, Pumpkin?"

"Okay," she said, not meeting his eyes.

"This is my brother, Andy."

"Yeah, we met," she said.

"Is it okay that he's helping you? You're not going to … you know … get upset with him, are you?"

"You're such a ninny, Owen," said Andy as he began cutting away the sleeve of Lizzy's cleaning uniform and the sweatshirt underneath. Lizzy smiled slightly through her wince of discomfort. "I guess the layered look must be in again," he added.

Andy cleaned the wound with a basin of water and a washcloth that Ruby brought. "It's actually not as bad as it looks," he said eventually. He looked up at Lizzy. "You've lost some blood, and it's going to leave quite a scar, but nothing's broken."

"How about my back?" she asked.

"Your back? Well, you had an implant there—"

"No, I got shot there too."

"Let's see."

She turned on the couch and Andy contemplated the multiple layers. "Kiddo, is it okay if I just cut this off you? It'll be more comfortable for you."

Lizzy nodded.

Andy began cutting through the material and Ruby disappeared upstairs. She returned in a moment with one of Owen's flannel shirts, which she slipped, backwards, over Lizzy's arms.

After a quick examination, Andy said, "Just got grazed by that one." He whistled. "Man, an inch difference and we would be dealing with some serious shit."

Owen left Andy and Ruby to bandage Lizzy's wounds, and hurried around the house, closing curtains and checking the locks on doors and windows. When he got back, Ruby had bundled away the discarded clothing and Andy was fashioning a sling out of a sheet he had torn up.

"I found out how they got in," said Owen. "Broken window in the laundry room."

"You got any plywood?" asked Andy. "We can close it up once we get Lizzy settled."

Owen didn't have any plywood, but they did find some two-by-fours in the basement, and Andy hammered them over the window. It wouldn't keep the cold out, but at least it would prevent anyone from using that method of entry again. When they were done, Owen started back toward the living room, but Andy stopped him with a hand on his arm.

"Owen, did Lizzy kill someone?"

Owen hesitated a moment, then nodded. "Yes, I think so."

"Gerard Bonnay?"

"Yes."

Andy waited expectantly.

Finally, with a deep sigh, Owen said, "It's a long story. Let's check on Lizzy, then let's pour some Scotch and I'll fill you in."

CHAPTER EIGHTY-SIX

They spent that night—Christmas Eve—huddled in the dark house, as if they all felt that to turn on any light not absolutely essential to their activities would be to attract unwanted attention. Owen had poured Scotch for himself, Andy, and Ruby, while Lizzy nodded over a mug of hot chocolate. He was amused to find that Ruby matched him and Andy glass for glass.

By Christmas morning, they had made their plans. They set out early, although not as early as Owen might have wished, thanks to the Scotch. Andy had called Bryn Mawr Hospital and told them he needed to take time off to deal with a family emergency, and Ruby had called Opal and Tony and told them she was going out of town for a job interview. They piled into the SUV, Ruby and Lizzy in back, Andy riding shotgun. Owen's suitcase was in the trunk, and they would stop on the way to buy clothes for the rest of them.

Andy pulled out his phone and opened the GPS app. He tapped in their destination, then said cheerfully, "Twenty hours, twenty-six minutes—you better get a move on, bro!"

Owen rolled his eyes and pulled out into the alley.

Andy turned in the seat and grinned at Lizzy and Ruby. "Ready, ladies?"

Lizzy grinned weakly back, and even Ruby looked faintly excited.

Andy turned forward. "Key West, here we come!"

CHAPTER EIGHTY-SEVEN

They spent two weeks in the Keys. Key West itself proved to be too expensive, so they stayed on Sugarloaf Key, in a lodge that was a flashback to the seventies—for those of their group who had been alive in that decade. They visited the Bat Tower and marveled over the tiny Key deer on Big Pine. They watched, and sometimes heard, the tourists during their skydives from the paint-faded plane that took off from the asphalt-and-gravel runway of the Sugarloaf Shores Airport. Owen spent the entire two weeks dreading the possibility that Lizzy would ask to try skydiving herself. What might happen if she changed her mind, but the pilot or skydiving instructor good-naturedly insisted she jump?

Lizzy, much to Owen's relief, became obsessed instead with snorkeling, floating for hours at a time, a T-shirt protecting her back after a bad sunburn her first day. Owen spent most of his time searching for a shady area to sit and catch up on his academic journals. Andy borrowed the SUV a few times to check out the sunset antics at Mallory Square. And after a day or two at loose ends, Ruby discovered John McDonald and read all twenty-one Travis McGee novels.

Owen tracked the Philadelphia news, which reported that Gerard Bonnay had suffered a stroke, evidently brought on by the stress of confronting an intruder in the Vivantem offices, as suggested by the bullets embedded in the walls. The turnout at the memorial service was impressive, and one of the news cameras caught a grim-faced Louise glancing periodically, and nervously, into the crowd of mourners.

By the second week of January, Andy and Ruby were

ready to head back to Pennsylvania. Ruby was willing to wager that Louise would have no reason to link her to her husband's death, since based on Ruby's conversations with Angelo, it had not occurred to him to question the timing of his aunt's flat tire. She was anxious to get back to Opal and Tony. Andy had exhausted the options for entertainment in the Keys and was looking forward to getting back to work—and back to the Mercy ER nurse with whom he had been exchanging texts. But Owen wasn't yet willing to go home and put Lizzy into the sphere of influence of anyone at Vivantem.

In mid-January, they checked out of the lodge and drove to Miami, from where Andy and Ruby would be flying back to Philadelphia. Andy had sprung for Ruby's plane ticket, saying, "If you don't come with me on the plane, I'll feel like I have to do it by car again—and if I have to drive by all those South of the Border signs again, I'll go insane." Then Owen and Lizzy hit the road for Arizona.

The colleague who had had the house in Baja had sold it in favor of a place in Sedona, but he had cancelled his winter trip when his wife broke her hip, and he was glad to offer it to Owen and his "niece" for a nominal fee.

The house was near Coffee Pot Rock, in a residential neighborhood with street names like Maxwell House, Nescafe, and Farmer Brothers. Owen, grateful finally to be able to settle down, tried to recapture some normalcy by throwing himself into research and writing.

Lizzy threw herself into the new-age vibe of Sedona.

CHAPTER EIGHTY-EIGHT

Lizzy stepped out of the cool dimness of Namaste Yoga and Meditation into the blinding brightness of the Arizona spring afternoon. One of the other students in the yoga class hurried to hold the door for her. She had sensed his interest over the last few weeks and today he had evidently summoned the courage to talk to her, and she had summoned the courage to be talked to. He introduced himself as Eric. She introduced herself as Elizabeth.

"So, you're pretty new here, right?" he asked, as they stood in the parking lot.

"Yes. I'm just here for a little while."

"With your family?" he asked.

"My uncle."

"Where do you usually live?"

"Pennsylvania."

"I used to live in New York. Bet you were glad to get away from the winter there!"

She smiled. "Yeah. I'm kind of looking forward to going home. But I like it here, too."

He nodded toward the pendant that hung around her neck. "I see you got a fetish."

She fingered the pleasingly rounded shape. "Yeah."

"Do you know what it is?" he asked, clearly ready to enlighten her if she didn't.

"The Zuni bear. It changes passion into wisdom."

He weathered being thwarted in displaying his knowledge with good humor. "Yeah. Pretty cool."

"And it helps you forgive yourself for past mistakes." A

shadow crossed her face.

"Yeah," he said, a little uncertainly, then rallied. "Hey, you want to grab a cup of coffee? Or tea? I know a good place near here."

She had been holding her flowered messenger bag in front of her, and her grip on it tightened. "Maybe ..."

"Or I could just show you the place," he added hastily. "You could check it out, and if you like how it looks, we can grab a cup of coffee. If you don't, no worries."

She hesitated, then smiled tentatively. "Okay."

He grinned. "Great! It's right nearby. You could follow me there in your car."

"I don't have a car, I have a bike. But I can follow you."

"Are you sure?"

"Sure. It's not too far, right?"

"Yeah, less than a mile."

She was able to keep up with him on the short trip. When they got to the cafe, they ordered their drinks—coffee for Eric and herbal tea for Lizzy—and had an awkward moment when he asked to pick up the tab. She finally yielded to his argument that she was there at his invitation, and they settled at a table.

They chatted about the yoga class and what brought them to Sedona. Lizzy told Eric she was accompanying her uncle on one of his research trips. Eric had moved to Sedona to wait tables and hike after graduating from Utica College.

"Do you like hiking?" he asked. "There are lots of great trails around here. Some of them go to the vortexes."

"We're staying near Coffee Pot Rock, I've hiked around there a lot."

"Yeah, that's a nice hike. I could show you some other ones—Doe Mountain, Boynton Canyon. Have you done Cathedral Rock?"

"No."

"It's great—pretty steep, but just awesome views from the top. You seem like you're in good shape. We could go sometime."

She took a sip of tea to hide her nervousness, but then smiled. "Okay. I'd like that."

He smiled back. "That's great! How about Sunday?"

He got out his phone and was checking his calendar when Lizzy's phone buzzed. She glanced at where it lay on the table: *Alert - Louise Mortensen.*

She frowned.

"Everything okay?" asked Eric.

"Yeah," she said, distracted.

They were discussing the logistics of meeting up at Cathedral Rock when Lizzy's phone buzzed again.

Alert - Gerard Bonnay.

"Sorry," she said. "I need to check this."

"Sure. I'm going to grab another coffee. Want another tea?"

"No thanks," she said, already opening up the internet search alerts. She clicked the link, titled *PA AG Russell Brashear Collapses in Front of Courthouse.*

It took her to a video from one of the network television stations in Philadelphia. She turned up the sound slightly to hear the solemn-looking news anchor over the buzz of the cafe, and hunched over the phone.

"This is Tim Spencer with a breaking news story. It appears that Pennsylvania Attorney General Russell Brashear has had an attack of some sort. Let's go to reporter Cindy Haruguchi, who is outside the courthouse."

The reporter was standing on a city street, several lanes of cars inching by behind her.

"Thanks, Tim. I'm outside the federal courthouse, just steps away from Independence Mall, where about half an hour ago, Attorney General Russell Brashear collapsed during a press conference related to his investigation of the Vivantem fertility clinic. Let's go to the video. This might be disturbing for some viewers."

The crawling traffic was replaced as background by the beige stone of the courthouse. Brashear, a gaunt black man with jutting cheekbones and a military stance, stood behind a bristle of microphones. He spoke in a gravelly voice.

"Our investigation has uncovered some troubling facts, facts that suggest that the claims made by some of Vivantem's clients are not as outlandish as they might seem on the surface. There is evidence that Vivantem may have manipulated the treatments of the women who came to them for help, and that these treatments are now producing disturbing symptoms in the children born to those women. You may recall that Vivantem was founded by the late Gerard Bonnay, and is now run by his wife, Louise Mortensen. It is my office's intent—"

Brashear's statement was interrupted by a murmur from his small audience of reporters and curious passersby, and then one voice was discernible amid the buzz: "Hey, it's her!"

The camera swung away from Brashear to a couple walking toward the group: Louise Mortensen, mouth set, back ramrod straight, and a young man in impeccable suit and tie.

The same voice rose above the buzz again. "Who's he?"

Louise and her escort reached the group, and now the camera panned back to capture both them and Brashear in the frame.

"Dr. Mortensen—a little early for your hearing, aren't you?" asked Brashear, clearly irritated at the interruption.

"On the contrary, Attorney General, I believe it is you who are late." She nodded to the young man at her side and disappeared into the building. One of the reporters peeled away from the group and followed her, but most stayed with Brashear, eyeing the young man who had remained outside with the crowd.

"Very theatrical," said Brashear, "but theatrics won't distract my office from—"

He winced slightly and put a hand to his head.

"—won't distract my office from the investigation into claims that were ignored for too long by my predecessors. Claims that, although, as I have said, may seem outlandish at first glance—"

He winced again, this time clamping his eyes shut and dropping his head.

"... on first glance ..."

He stepped back from the microphones just as one of the men who had been standing behind him stepped up and took his arm. The microphones picked up his murmured question.

"Are you all right, sir?"

"Yes, yes, I just—"

Then Brashear sagged, the man grabbing him as he fell. The podium blocked everything but Brashear's legs, which kicked out once, twice. The microphones picked up his groan. "Jesus Christ!"

The camera lurched as the cameraman tried to change position to capture what was going on behind the podium. There was a scream, and then someone yelled, "Call an ambulance!"

The camera panned up again, showing the young man who had arrived at the courthouse with Louise Mortensen. He was standing behind the man who had caught Brashear when he dropped, and whose hands Brashear was gripping. The young man was staring intently at Brashear, his brow knit, his mouth a thin line. Then the camera was jostled again and the video ended, returning to the reporter and the crawling Market Street traffic.

"Obviously the Attorney General suffered an attack of some sort, although we're still waiting for a statement from Jefferson Hospital, where he was taken by ambulance. We'll be back as soon as more information is available. Back to you, Tim."

The view switched back to the anchor desk, Tim Spencer now joined by a woman in a suit, their faces somber.

"We just heard from a Jefferson spokesperson," said the anchor, "that Attorney General Russell Brashear died shortly after he arrived in the emergency room." He paused for a beat, then continued. "We are joined by Dr. Roberta Smedley of Mercy Hospital. Doctor, in the face of this very sad news, is there any perspective you can offer on what might have happened?"

"Of course this is all purely speculative, and will need to be confirmed by an autopsy, but it looked to me like the reaction of someone suffering a stroke." The screen was filled again with the video of the event. "If we stop the video *here*," said the doctor, and the video froze, "you can see him holding his head, as if he were suddenly struck by a severe headache …"

Eric returned to the table with a coffee and a tea. "I thought I'd bring one for you too—I don't want to be drinking alone—" but he stopped when Lizzy looked up from the phone. Her eyes were large, her face drained of blood.

"I'm sorry, I have to go," she said, her voice tight. She grabbed her bag and stood up.

"Are you okay? Did you get some bad news?"

"No. Yes. I'm sorry. Thank you for the tea." She headed for the door.

He followed her. "Are we still on for Sunday?" he asked. He jumped ahead of her to open the door, juggling the cups to free a hand.

"I'm sorry, I don't think so." She walked quickly to her bike. She unlocked it, hopped on, and pushed off.

"Hope to see you in class again next week," he called after her.

She waved without turning around.

She shot through the streets of Sedona and around the traffic circles. She felt the buzz of her phone in her pocket but didn't stop to pick up the call. She pedaled furiously up Coffee Pot Drive, and dumped the bike in the driveway next to the elderly SUV that Owen had bought to replace the one that, as far as they knew, still sat on Gerard Bonnay's property. She ran up the steps and burst through the door. Owen looked up from his cell phone, his face even whiter than usual, a partially eaten sandwich and glass of milk sitting unattended on the table next to his laptop.

"Did you hear?" he asked, his eyes wide.

"Yes," said Lizzy. "They made another one of me."

ACKNOWLEDGEMENTS

Many thanks to all the people who shared their expertise on various aspects of the story: Ken Fritz, Lisa Huis, Jeff Mateer, Marco Pozo, Kathy and Wade Rogers, Eileen Scott, and John Thalheimer.

Special thanks to Dr. David L. Fried, MD, FACP and Dr. Robert Mcandrew, DO, for their help with the medical aspects of the story.

Thanks to Mary Dalrymple for her multiple reads of the evolving book.

Thanks to editor Jen Blood for taking this craft on its shakedown cruise.

And, as always, thanks to my partner in crime, Wade Walton, not only for his tireless support and encouragement, but also for the book's title and back cover blurb.

Any deviations from strict accuracy—intentional or unintentional—are solely the responsibility of the author.

ABOUT THE AUTHOR

Matty Dalrymple is the author of the Ann Kinnear Suspense Novels, *The Sense of Death* and *The Sense of Reckoning*, and the Lizzy Ballard Thriller *Rock Paper Scissors*. Matty lives with her husband, Wade Walton, their dogs in Chester County, Pennsylvania, which is the setting for much of the action in *The Sense of Death* and *Rock Paper Scissors*. They enjoy vacationing on Mt. Desert Island, Maine, where *The Sense of Reckoning* takes place.

Matty is a member of Mystery Writers of America, Sisters in Crime, International Thriller Writers, and the Brandywine Valley Writers Group.

Learn more at mattydalrymple.com, and follow Matty on Facebook, Twitter, and Goodreads.

Review are the lifeblood of a book—if you enjoyed this Lizzy Ballard thriller, please consider posting a review on Amazon or Goodreads! For every review posted, Matty will donate $1 to the Animal Welfare Institute.

46117362R00211

Made in the USA
Middletown, DE
23 July 2017